PRAISE FOR THE NOVELS OF CHANDLER MCGREW

NIGHT TERROR:

"Plays on the primal fears that cause most adults to lose sleep . . . An author to watch, and read."
—*The Denver Post*

"Unsettling . . . an engaging read . . . Fans of Kay Hooper and Linda Howard will readily dig into this fantastic tale." —*Publishers Weekly*

"A spine-tingling blend of mystery, thriller, and a bit of the paranormal, where a surprise lurks around every corner." —*Old Book Barn Gazette*

"Suspense at its best." —*Book Review Cafe*

"In the small-town Maine that Stephen King has made famous, Chandler McGrew sets a new tale of terror."
—*Forbes Book Club*

"Chandler McGrew's *Night Terror* is a skillful tale, well-paced and intricately constructed—a good read."
—Chelsea Quinn Yarbro, author of *Blood Roses* and *Night Blooming*

"*Night Terror* sweeps the reader along at an unrelenting pace. Beyond being a chilling novel, it is a story of love—of a mother's love and devotion to her son and the bond between parent and child. It is also the story of a devoted couple facing the imminent death of one of them. This is a read-it-in-one-sitting book that will have you awake long past midnight, looking at the shadows outside your window." —*Romantic Times*

"Chandler McGrew has written a masterful work of psychological suspense. . . . *Night Terror* is a fascinating reading experience." —*I Love a Mystery Newsletter*

COLD HEART:

"The best opening 10 pages I've read this year . . . This suspense mystery reads like a good martini tastes: icy cold, with flecks of terror where the ice chips should be."
—*Contra Costa Times*

"This first-time author has crafted a tale that compels the reader to turn page after page. This book has incredible tension and suspense (I couldn't put it down), which keeps ratcheting up and up. . . . Get a copy soon."
—*Mystery News*

"An engrossing reading experience."
—*The Midwest Book Review*

"A fast-moving tale of suspense and bloody mayhem."
—*Sun Journal* (Lewiston, Me.)

"A very well-constructed, action-packed novel . . . a tense and satisfying read." —*I Love a Mystery Newsletter*

ALSO BY CHANDLER MCGREW

Cold Heart
Night Terror

Chandler McGrew

A DELL BOOK

THE DARKENING

THE DARKENING
A Dell Book / July 2004

Published by
Bantam Dell
A Division of Random House, Inc.
New York, New York

ISBN 0-553-58603-3

Manufactured in the United States of America
Published simultaneously in Canada

OPM 10 9 8 7 6 5 4 3 2 1

For my eldest daughter, Keni, who waited far too long for this

Thanks to Jes Pryor, my science wiz, even though I'm sure I broke the rules, anyway. And to Sempei and Sensei Petrovich, who patiently led me through four long years of sweat. Kyokushin is a painful and difficult style to learn and never mastered. Any martial arts mistakes or stretches of artistic license are completely my own. Also to Father Louis Dufour, always helpful, who has consistently borne my agnosticism with grace. Thanks to the two Irenes in my life, my steadfast wife and my stalwart agent, both of whom have supported me through thick and thin. To Abby Zidle, a patient woman of many talents, not least of which is turning lead to gold. And finally to my editor, Caitlin Alexander, who polishes until it gleams.

Our deepest fear is not that we are inadequate. Our deepest fear is that we are powerful beyond measure. It is our Light, not our Darkness, that most frightens us.

—Nelson Mandela

THE DARKENING

I do not care to see my soul,

There's never light upon it.

Last time I looked it was still whole,

But I wish I had not done it.

—"Night Land" by Cooder Reese
From *Dead Reckonings*

Lucy Devereau spent her days worming information out of people she didn't trust, searching for men and women she didn't like, on behalf of clients she rarely connected with. She was a private investigator specializing in tracking down birth parents for adopted children, and she worked diligently in their employ, often not clocking her hours or her miles. But a strange and indefinable void kept her from viewing her clients as anything other than two-dimensional, cardboard cutouts.

She existed in a constant state of tension, waiting for some unseen ax to fall, some magic bullet to burst through the wall of her foggy past and blow a giant hole in her head to match the one in her heart. From her earliest childhood she had sensed that something as deeply rooted within her psyche as her spine was rooted within her flesh had been stolen from her, but without knowing what it was, she had little real hope of ever getting it back.

A little after midnight the darkness outside her window—illumined only by the glow of one dim streetlamp lighting the tall hedges between her and her neighbor's house—mirrored her own gloom, and a cool night wind rustled under the eaves, stroking the old soffit boards softly, like raven feathers.

A copy of *The Universe in a Nutshell* lay open but untouched on her nightstand. Although Stephen Hawking usually left her gasping for air and with a severe headache she had managed to worm her way through *A Brief History of Time* and was now struggling diligently to comprehend the sequel. If anything could relax her mind it was contemplating how to fit an eleven-dimensional cosmos into a three-dimensional space.

But she could not bring herself to lift the book that night. Some morbid intuition forced her to lie docilely atop the covers in her cotton nightshirt, her short brown hair as disheveled as her thoughts, watching the cable news into the wee hours instead. The stories were all the same, Palestinian Muslims murdering Israeli Jews, Irish Catholics murdering Irish Protestants. Religious zealots killing and dying for a myth. Useless bloodshed, wasted lives.

When sleep finally took her she dreamed of an emaciated old man who chased her across a vast, empty plain screaming that he was a friend of God, that he would reveal to her the secrets at the end of the rainbow.

At two A.M., men broke down her front and back doors, the noise blasting through her dream like thunder, the sound of booted feet slapping hardwood floors echoing down the hall. She barely had time to reach for her robe before bright lights blinded her, and she was whipped around and forced facedown into the mattress so hard the wind blasted from her lungs. Powerful hands jerked her arms behind her, binding them with something thin that gouged painfully into her wrists. A balled sock was shoved into her mouth and secured with a strip of duct tape, so that her first scream was little more than a feeble moan. The lights went out as a cloth sack slipped over her head, tightening around her throat. Her mute assailants lifted her from the bed, dragged her through the front door and tossed her unceremoniously into a vehicle.

The engine roared to life, and she was pressed back into the seat, and in no time at all the car had made so many turns she was hopelessly lost. Just when she was certain she was going to die from asphyxiation, rough hands untied the bag and slipped it off. She blinked and sniffled. A giant of a man on the seat beside her regarded her with eagle eyes. He wore a coal black jumpsuit with a gunbelt and a large knife in a scabbard. His thick red moustache glowed like neon in the reflected headlights.

"You going to struggle anymore?" His voice sounded like boots crunching sand.

She shook her head.

"Gonna scream?"

Another shake of her head.

The man reached out and ripped the tape off her mouth, taking some skin with it. She spit the sock onto the floorboards, gagging.

"We on time?" said the man beside her, glancing at the driver.

The driver nodded.

"What do you want with me?" asked Lucy.

"The Boss wants to see you," said the man, frowning.

"Who? What is going on?"

The man shrugged.

She glanced quickly around, memorizing details as a way to control her fear. The car was new. From the interior it was apparently a Crown Vic. Black leather seats. Tan carpet. The night outside exhibited the sullen darkness of deep countryside. She could see the lights of town in the distance behind her, barely illuminating a small bowl of sky, but there were no road signs, and she had no idea where she was or in what direction they were traveling. Studying the well-armed kidnapper beside her and his taciturn partner in the front seat, she tried to convince herself that the whole thing was a case of mistaken identity. They were probably working for some drug dealer and had gotten the wrong address, although which of the middle-aged couples living around her might have rightly been this pair's target she couldn't imagine.

"My name is Lucy Devereau," she said. "I live at *Forty-two* Mayfield Lane—"

"We know all that."

"I'm not who you think I am. I'm a private detective."

"And I told you we know all that. You think we drove all the way to a shithole like Ruredaga, Alabama, to get the wrong address?"

"Then why—"

"I told you we're taking you to see the Boss," he said, smirking. "And you don't want to disappoint the Boss. Does she, Frank?"

The driver glanced over his shoulder, smiling like a wolf and shaking his head. "I can guarantee that, Ed," he said. His voice was just as raspy as the first man's. Lucy wondered if they were on some kind of drugs that affected their speech. The fact that they didn't mind using each other's names in front of her bothered her as well.

"Whoever the Boss is, I don't want to meet him," she said, using the window as a mirror to brush her short brown hair out of her eyes.

Ed frowned. "You don't have any choice, lady. Or at least you wouldn't *like* the other choices."

The road outside was a country lane, skirting rolling fields lit by bleak yellow moonlight. Other than the car they were in, there was no traffic. Even so, Ed kept glancing quickly to front and rear. Suddenly he reached across the seat, tapping the driver on the shoulder.

"Pull over," he said.

The car decelerated and stopped, and Lucy's breathing slowed with it. In the distance she could see the faint lights of a farmhouse. She leaned forward a millimeter and noticed a bright screen on the dash between the driver and passenger seats. Words scrolled along the bottom, but they seemed to be in some foreign script.

"We got company," said Ed, opening his door. He stepped outside, then leaned back into the car. "Get out."

She shook her head. Why get her *out* of the car now, in this deserted place? She'd already flunked lesson one of Lucy Devereau's Important Rules of Self-Defense: Never get into a car or go *any*place with men you don't know. She wasn't flunking lesson two: Never get *out* of said car on a deserted road.

"I mean now!"

The driver slipped out of the vehicle with a fluid grace surprising in a man the size of a two-legged rhinoceros. Her door jerked open, and she was dragged around the car onto the shoulder. She struggled, but her hands were still bound tightly behind her back, and the man's grip on her arms was as hard as steel manacles.

"Shove her under the car," said Ed, pulling a rifle out of the trunk.

Frank complied. Maybe they weren't going to kill her after all, but apparently no one cared if she was scraped or bruised. Pinned painfully close to the hot exhaust pipe, she twisted her head enough to stare back down the road, but no one seemed to be coming from that direction, and she hadn't noticed any oncoming headlights, either.

"I'll do anything you want," she gasped.

Both men laughed.

"What?" said Frank. "You think we want you? If we did we'd have had you already."

"No, you wouldn't," she whispered.

These men were hired muscle with plenty of experience. Whoever the Boss was, he had most certainly paid them well to bring her to him, so she was supposed to at least arrive untouched.

Only silence came from above. In the narrow slit between the back bumper and the road, headlights suddenly appeared like twin dawns. The trunk lid slammed shut, and Lucy heard what she thought was the rifle bolt clacking into place. She could see Ed's boots where he crouched beside the rear tire, and twisting her neck she spotted Frank's shoes ahead and on the other side of the car.

"Take them out," said Ed.

The headlights grew brighter. The rifle fired. Then a pistol opened up, but beneath the sound of gunfire Lucy noticed a distant rumble—another vehicle approaching fast from the other direction. Suddenly she heard the whine of ricochets bouncing off the asphalt. She hoped to God the other shooters were police. Of course, it didn't matter who they were if she got caught and killed in the cross fire. She began nudging her way out from under the car into the gravel on the shoulder.

Frank was by then prone in the ditch, firing at the second car that had stopped two hundred yards ahead. Ed had his back to her, blasting away in the other direction. She rolled as quietly as possible down the incline, coming to rest on her side in the bottom of the ditch, gasping for air, struggling ineffectually with the bindings on her wrists. As she glanced back toward the car she saw Ed turning in her direction.

"Fuck!" he shouted, waving at Frank and shouting for him to get her as she stumbled to her feet and staggered toward a barbed-wire fence.

Frank took two lumbering steps toward her and fell flat on his face, blood blossoming from his forehead and chest like bubbles in hot spaghetti sauce. She glanced quickly up and down the road, but there were no flashing lights, no bullhorns, and she had the sinking feeling that rather than a police assault, she had stumbled into the middle of a gangland shooting. The bullets whizzed closer around her, and she dropped to the ground again, pressing her body into the dry grass, trying to belly-crawl under the sagging lower strand of wire, as Ed cursed and crouched beside the car again.

A barb caught on her bindings, and the rusted metal sliced into her wrist. She cried out but kept shoving herself along with her bare feet until she was clear, struggling to her feet, then racing toward the dark shape of a copse of trees in the distance, running for her life, her heart pounding, lungs stretching to bursting, afraid to glance over her shoulder again lest Ed be there to drag her back to the car.

Behind her she heard someone shouting, but she had reached the trees before she realized that the voice calling her name didn't sound like gravel at all.

The night was even starker within the shelter of the woods, a world of dim, limb-slashed sky and even darker, looming shadows, dangerous paths filled with grasping brambles and treacherous footing. Lucy sprinted through the trees, certain that any second a bullet would find her, or that one of her mysterious abductors would leap at her out of the gloom, that each shaky footfall would be her last. But the ground was solid and reassuring beneath her feet, a reality that she clung to in a world that had changed in minutes from depressing and confusing to dangerous and deadly.

Because she kept herself in shape—running six miles or

more a day—she was winded but not exhausted when she made it through the woods and onto a starlit side road. Pebbles stabbed her feet as she frantically searched for hiding places in case headlights appeared behind her. When she reached a sandy drive leading to a dark farmhouse she raced up the steep slope, pounding on the doorbell with her elbow until an old man and woman opened the door only enough to peer out with sleepy eyes. The woman finally jerked the man out of her way and drew Lucy inside. Lucy insisted they turn off the porch light before calling the police. While the old man gave directions over the phone, she shivered with residual terror, peeking through the curtains in the living room.

"You poor thing," said the woman, squeezing Lucy's shoulders, reminding her of her mother. "I can only imagine how terrible an experience this has been for you."

"I'm all right, now," lied Lucy, still counting to ten with each breath.

"The Lord was surely watching over you tonight."

Lucy bit her lip. The old woman's faith was writ deep in the lines on her face, in the warmth of her soft green eyes. But if anyone had come to her rescue out on the road it wasn't the Lord but men with guns to match the goons' who'd taken her prisoner. More than likely they had their own agenda that had nothing to do with her. *Irony* and *burlesque* were the watchwords of Lucy's cosmos, not *fate* or *faith*.

When they finally came to get her the cops questioned her for hours. They, too, seemed to believe that she was either part of a drug ring or the whole thing had been a case of mistaken identity. They had no ideas when she told them what Ed and Frank had said about *the Boss*, other than to question her about her business, and after a while Lucy got the feeling that they were just dragging the interview out in order to convince her of their thoroughness. The detective in charge assured her that her case was top priority—as she could imagine it would be in a town the size of Ruredaga—that something was bound to turn up, and in the meantime she'd have police protection. But she had the distinct feeling that the cops still believed it was somehow her fault.

A uniformed officer gave her a ride home a little after noon, and she insisted that he search the house while she watched, even though he made it clear that they'd been all through the place as soon as she'd informed them it was a crime scene. Yellow tape still hung across the front porch. The cop pointed out the unmarked car parked down the street, and she breathed a little easier when she saw the steely-eyed man behind the wheel. His presence seemed to promise at least a few hours' respite for her to decide her next move.

As soon as the officer left, Lucy pulled down a small box from the shelf in her bedroom closet, placing it gently on the bed and removing the gleaming black Beretta. She shoved the clip into place and jacked a shell into the chamber, frowning at the pistol. She'd trained with the weapon enough to be proficient, because starting out in the business she'd thought PIs were *supposed* to own a gun. But she'd never felt comfortable with it, and because of her reluctance to keep the weapon near her, when she'd needed it the gun had been hidden beneath her extra sheets. That wasn't going to happen again. She placed it on the bed beside her pillow.

She had no intention of going in to the office, so after showering, she slipped on a pair of jeans and a T-shirt. Then she called a carpenter listed in the yellow pages, who said he could make it by to look at the damage later that afternoon. Lucy hoped to induce him to fix the doors when he arrived, but regardless she was going to spend the night in a hotel, under an assumed name, trying to *think* her way out of the mess she was in. What to do after that was not so cut and dried. Over the intervening hours she had found ample time to ponder the assault. Ed and Frank had known exactly who she was.

That left the unfortunate probability that they had abducted her *because* of what she was.

Only she had no idea what that might be.

Her mother had died of pancreatic cancer when Lucy was sixteen. Her father passed away just two months after watching her receive her high school diploma. But since early childhood Lucy had realized that her family was different from all the others around them. Other families didn't live in fear of questions like "Where are you from originally?" or "Don't I know you from somewhere?" Other children were not warned to refer all questions regarding family history to their parents. It was only after her father died that Lucy discovered his journal.

We got the little girl today, read Bill Devereau's familiar jagged script, dated July 1, twenty-eight years earlier. *She's beautiful and Emily and I have already fallen in love with her. Emily wants to name her Lucy, after her mother. The good Lord has been kind to us, and I thank him for his bountiful blessings.*

Lucy had sat there in her father's bedroom, shaken to the core, flipping page after page. Wondering how her life could have turned out the way it had. Wondering how a man who'd had to live the way her father had could have continued to *thank the good Lord for his bountiful blessings* all the rest of his life.

Most of the journal had to do with her dad's daily business dealings—he was a salesman who over the years had sold a little bit of everything, everywhere—and silly squabbles he'd had with Lucy's mother. It was the entry for April 2, the year after Lucy was born, that she couldn't understand.

***—the asterisks were her father's—*caught me on the street last night. I haven't seen him since the day we got Lucy. He's an odd one. Frightens the heck out of me, I have to admit. Made me promise again never to tell anyone about Lucy's past. As if I would. He brought me the papers just like he'd promised, though. I have no idea how he arranged it, and I'm not going to ask. Lucy now has a birth certificate that looks real as daylight, showing that she's Emily's and mine naturally.*

Fifty more pages of daily trivia and then one final meeting with ***.

*I think there's a good chance he's not all okay in the head. I haven't told Emily, but I fear that maybe he took Lucy from her rightful parents. I lose sleep at night over that thought, wondering if there is a mother or father somewhere crying in the night because of me. But what can we do about it now? Lord knows how the law would look at Emily and me. *** claims that Lucy is in terrible danger if she's found. I can't believe that, either. More than likely the only one she's in danger from is ***. But we love her more every day and God help us there's just no way either of us could give her up now. When we go we're leaving no forwarding address.*

Who was the mysterious man who had delivered her to Bill and Emily Devereau twenty-eight years ago, and why had he done so? Could the men who had tried to kidnap her possibly be connected to him? Lucy had spent the past ten years quietly trying to research her past and always ended up at a dead end. Could *** be *the Boss*? Her father had apparently wondered about the man's sanity, but what kind of lunatic had the power to hire killers like the ones who had broken into her home? The same kind who had the power to falsify hospital and state and even federal records, maybe? But then who were the men in the other cars? Had they been trying to help her, or did they have their own agenda?

She stared up and down the hall at the chairs she had propped against the broken doors, and the sight threatened to take her right back to that moment when the two thugs had burst into the house. Her heart pounded, and she forced herself to take a deep breath. She had to think, to reason. Panic wasn't going to help her now. Wearily, she dropped into her favorite lounging spot in the living room, a decrepit armchair she had rescued from an old lady up the street and covered with a fleece throw. She propped her feet on an ottoman that matched the chair in age, if not infirmity, and wiggled around to find a spot between the springs that still gave her good light from the window, and she closed her eyes to concentrate. There must be a logical explanation for all of this.

She was well on her way to a headache when the phone in the hallway rang, and she tossed off the blanket to go get it, assuming it was her secretary. Half the time Andrea didn't check the damned message machine at the office, so she probably didn't realize Lucy had called from the police station to tell her she was taking the day off. Lucy raised the receiver to her ear, leaning back against the wall.

A man's calm, self-assured voice chilled her. "That was very close last night."

She jerked the chair barring the front door aside and carried the cordless onto the front porch, waving at the undercover cop, pointing at the phone. "Who is this?"

This time there was tension in the voice. "The cops are no friends of yours, and the men who are after you won't make the same mistake twice. They may kill you this time."

She glanced up and down the street, backing into the house, still waving at the cop. The car started up, heading her way.

"I lost two good men on that road," said the voice. "Thank God you got away."

"You were in the other car?" she whispered.

"Just my men. You can rest assured that the people who took you are both dead, though."

"Who are you? What do you want?"

"Only to keep you safe."

She hurried back to the living room, using the drapes to shield herself from the street. "What's going on? Do you know the men who are after me?"

"Listen carefully. You can't stay where you are. There are too many of them, and I can't get any more of my men there in time."

"Tell me who you are."

"Don't write this down. Memorize it." He gave her a location and a time. "Don't stop to pack. Get out of there.

You must not allow them to take you again. They're only biding their time until it's dark. And they may not wait."

"I'm not going anywhere," she lied. What the hell was taking the cop so long?

"Can you remember what I told you?"

"I can remember. Now tell me who you are."

"You have to get to the location I gave you. If you don't make it we'll try to set up another meeting, but they're everywhere, and it's difficult."

The line went dead.

Lucy rested the phone on the lamp table, trying to make sense of the call. She glanced toward the door into the hall and was startled to see the detective from the car. He stepped into the living room, his hands behind his back like a soldier at ease. His cheap suit and black tie lent meaning to the term *plainclothes,* but something in his stance or his sharp black eyes chilled her. He had the look of a predator. The same look that Ed and Frank had given her, and his voice was low and rattly.

"Who was that on the phone?"

"It was garbled." she said, wondering who in the world was on her side, suddenly certain it wasn't this cop.

"Bullshit," said the detective, taking a step forward.

"No, really. He just hung up."

The cop shook his head, and she noticed how much his smile looked like Ed's. When he swung his hands in front of him, a short length of electrical cord dangled between them.

"What's that for?" she gasped. "What do you want?"

"I don't want anything. I'm just finishing a job that should have been done last night. Ed and Frank were two good men, but they're lucky they died out on the road."

"You're a cop," she whispered.

"Everybody's got to be something."

He edged toward her like a wrestler corralling his opponent, and she backed away, cursing herself for once again leaving the pistol where she couldn't get to it.

"Stay back!" she said. "Or I'll scream."

"Go ahead. Everyone in the neighborhood is at work."

She jerked sideways as though to break for the door, and he shifted his stance, but when she twisted in the other direction he was faster, taking another step closer. She backed away again until she was pressed tightly into the corner. He took his time making up the distance, snatching at her with the electrical cord, trying to loop it over her head. She gasped with each swipe, her muscles tensing.

"Why are you doing this?" she pleaded.

"You should have gone quietly last night. This morning the Boss said to bring you in dead or alive. Dead's easier."

He lunged, crushing her against the wall. Suddenly the phone cord was tightening around her throat, constricting not only her larynx but her carotid artery. She knew she had only seconds until she blacked out. She gouged at his eyes, and the cord loosened enough for her to suck in a breath. She tried to shove him away, but her fingers slipped across his shirt, up under his arm.

When she felt the hard, checkered handle of his pistol, she jerked the trigger. The gun fired into the floor, and the cop's eyes widened as he staggered back, releasing the cord. Carried along with him, she held on to the pistol.

"Bitch!" he shouted, slapping her head so hard her ears rang.

She twisted the gun in its holster, pulling the trigger again. This time the sound was deadened by flesh, and the cop stumbled, dragging her down on top of him. She squeezed the trigger again. The cop made a grunting sound, then was still. She rolled away from him, dry heaving, a thin trickle of spit dripping onto the carpet.

Blood oozed from a wound under the cop's arm and another on the inside of his right thigh, and he wasn't breathing. Lucy shook so hard she had to use the curtain to pull herself to her feet. She glanced outside, surprised that a large crowd wasn't running toward the house, but the cop was right, the neighborhood was deserted.

She tried the phone, but it was dead, and she stared at the receiver in disbelief. The display showed a full charge, and the detective couldn't have cut the line outside. She'd just hung up when he stepped into the living room. What the hell was going on?

She snatched her cell phone off the kitchen table, but as she was dialing 911 the man's voice sounded in her memory.

The cops are no friends of yours.

She pocketed the phone and slipped cautiously down the walk to the detective's sedan. She didn't know what she expected to find, but she *was a* private investigator and the son of a bitch had just tried to murder her. She ought to find *something.*

But the car was as nondescript as the detective's clothes. The registration in the glove compartment was in the name of a Patrick Flynn, telling her nothing. She did find an unused body bag in the trunk which sent chills up her spine.

The Boss said to bring you in dead or alive. Dead's easier.

She was about to slam the driver's door when the radio crackled.

"Pat, are you there? Pat? The Boss wants to know if you've got her."

The Boss? Was the guy on the phone right? Could she trust no one at all? The uniformed cop had said the plainclothesman would be there *until she didn't need him anymore.* At the time his words had sounded reassuring.

She staggered back up the front steps and into her bedroom, trying desperately to get her brain to work. She had half filled a suitcase when she noticed the cop's blood spattering her pants and shirt, and she hurriedly slipped into fresh clothes. She dug the little leather hip holster out of the box in her closet and hooked it to the back of her pants, shoving the pistol into it. She didn't know how long the detective's shift lasted, but she didn't intend to stick around to find out. The cop on the radio would be coming to check on Pat soon.

Dylan Barnes awakened dizzy and naked in the foyer of his home. Shaking off the sense of dislocation he experienced every time he took one of his unexpected nocturnal jaunts, he slipped stealthily into the living room. Ragged threads of moonlight danced in the air, and deathly silence surrounded him. And like every time before, as soon as he awoke he knew he was not alone.

He centered himself, concentrating on that space in his head where the air from both nostrils came together. He could feel every drop of perspiration on his body, smell his own fear in the air. Tuning his ears to the night, he discovered sounds in the silence. He could hear the remnant of a breeze tickling the eaves with wasted fingers, the faraway rumble of the furnace, the refrigerator humming a dirge in the kitchen. A mournful cry behind him stilled his breathing, but it was just a creak as the old house settled.

He was standing *zenkutsu dachi*—left leg extended in front of him, knee bent, right leg behind—as he performed a slow, controlled *gedan bari*. His left fist now protected his groin and left side, his right was chambered, tucked in close beneath his right underarm.

Dylan's fingers were long and delicate, but his knuckles were permanently swollen from years of practice on the hand boards, and the knife edge of his palm was a line of calluses, as were the balls and heels of both feet. At five-foot-eight, one-hundred-eighty pounds, Dylan Barnes was as close to being a perfect Kyokushin Karate machine as one was likely to find in the state of Maine, certainly in a town the size of Needland.

He flipped on the light and searched the room. There was no one behind the sofa or his recliner, no one hiding behind the drapes. He noticed for the thousandth time that the room needed a good cleaning, but so did the whole house. Magazines littered the floor, and he didn't want to look into the coffee cup on the bookshelf. Realizing he was spotlighted through the window, he flipped the light off again. In a moment his eyes readjusted to the feeble moonlight and the reflected glow of his bathroom night-light in the gloomy hallway.

After a cursory inspection of the rest of the house he was headed back to his bedroom when the hair on the back of his neck stood on end. A wisp of air foul and dank slithered between his bare legs. With a brief buzzing sound, like a short in the wiring, the bathroom light went out.

He spun, flowing automatically into *kumite dachi*—the fighting stance—his hands swirling in the fanlike stow block. He was blind, but his other senses were sharpened by adrenaline. He tried to place his opponent's position by the movement of air currents, listening so intently he thought he could hear cockroaches crawling in the walls.

He sniffed, catching a hint of the odor again, fetid and rank, with an almost metallic tinge to it. He had the sudden image in his head of decaying equipment, but what kind of machine could rot?

His pupils adjusted slowly once again to the moonlight. There were ominous shadows in the hallway, but he put a name to them one by one. The bookshelf along the right wall. The phone table opposite it. The open door to the attic.

Why was that door open?

The attic was nothing but bare joists and dusty, blown-in insulation. He had only been up there once in the eight years he and his late wife, Ronnie, had owned the house. There was a rusted sliding latch on the cheap panel door, and it was always locked. He slid slowly around the bookshelf, his hands ready to swing in any direction like swords. His center was tensed, but the rest of his body was relaxed, fluid.

Without warning, Ronnie's voice sounded in his head.

I'm sorry.

The thought was gone so fast he barely had time to realize it had happened. But its passing interrupted his internal rhythm, jarred his balance, and it took him a moment to recover.

As he crept toward the attic door he microscopically readjusted his stance with each step, and his hands with each movement. He knew he could drive his fist through the plaster beside him, crush the old wooden lath beneath, and quite possibly break the two-by-four stud beyond. But he could just as easily direct that power at a moving target—a temple, a knee, a throat. He stepped into the doorway and stared up into the pitch-black stairwell. His mind screamed at him to close the door, slam the latch back into place, run down the hallway, out the front door. Just keep on running.

Instead he controlled his fear the way he had been trained to since childhood and placed his foot on the first step.

It was a long way up those stairs. And once to the top, he had to come back down.

Shadows gripped his leg as though he had stepped into a pool of black liquid. There was a deep chill to it, something beyond the temperature of the darkness alone. He kept climbing, his left arm protecting his head, *jodan uke.* His hands stayed open, *shuto,* so he could attack with the knife-edge or grapple with an opponent.

As he raised his head slowly above the level of the ceiling joists, he prayed that whatever had happened to the light in the bathroom hadn't affected the wiring in the pitch-black attic. The house was ancient. Maybe it was just one blown fuse. Somewhere above him hung the pull chain for the single attic fixture. He circled his arm around but felt nothing. He would have to go up another step or two in order to reach it. His hand was shaking, and he breathed deeply, forcing it to stop. Finally, his fingers found the cord and he tugged. The light flashed on, and for just an instant the darkness seemed unwilling to die, slinking away like a wounded animal.

As he turned slowly on the top step, cold sweat tickling the notch between his buttocks, he eyed every corner, every nook.

Gradually the sense of presence receded, and the emptiness mocked him. He stepped carefully across the bare joists, searching for anything that might have awakened him, that might have caused the smell that was still thick around him. There were rat droppings on the insulation, and he made a note to buy poison, but there was nowhere for anyone to hide. Still, he backed down the stairs, and he left the light on.

In the hallway he slammed the door, ramming the bolt into place with a finality he didn't feel. His fingers couldn't seem to free themselves from the latch, as though there were some clue embedded in its ancient, paint-encrusted steel that, given time, he could decipher. Finally, he stumbled exhausted back to bed.

Just sleepwalking. That was normal enough.

Only it wasn't.

Normal people didn't go to bed in one room and wake up in another. Normal people didn't imagine spooks in their houses all the time, and *he* had been imagining them for over two years. When he awakened he was never surprised to find himself somewhere other than his bed. In fact he usually had a misty *almost* idea of where he was and an equally murky memory of getting there, but a memory so crazy he always tried to put it immediately out of his mind. Sometimes he wondered how in the world he'd made it through the past months without being locked up. But he knew in his heart that it was karate that had saved him. After Ronnie's death he'd concentrated completely on his small dojo in Needland, working out there for as many as fourteen hours a day, training students, instructing his assistant, Amy, in the finer points of the art for her Nidan test, her second-degree black belt.

But it wasn't just the presence that kept him awake nights. It was the nightmares as well. And between the sleepwalking and the dreams, and the dark thing that haunted his nights, he was coming terribly close to losing his mind.

By the time Dylan reached the dojo the next morning and climbed the stairs to the second-floor space that he had rented, the three Clairedon girls, a middle-aged woman named Reba, and a new student with a crew cut and a black eye stood in the ready stance, performing blocks and punches. Dylan nodded to Amy through the window between the waiting room and the practice floor. He slipped into his office and tossed his clothes on the chair behind his desk, reaching for his *gi*. The weight of the heavy, brushed cotton on his shoulders was reassuring, reminding him of his training, of who he was. As he entered the dojo everyone turned toward him, crossed hands, and bowed. He bowed in return and waved them back to their lessons, blocking out the shouted commands and the stomping of bare feet on the hardwood floor.

He faced one of the banks of mirrors and dropped slowly into a full Belgian split, legs out 180 degrees, toes pointing toward the ceiling. Although he had trained his body to accept the exercise, it was still painful after all these years. While he waited the mandatory thirty seconds in the stretch, he performed *Ibuki* breathing exercises. He knew that to the newest of the students the rasping sound would be disconcerting—as though he were about to hawk up something gross and spit it on the floor—but to a neophyte everything a black belt did was strange and exotic. To Dylan, it was merely relaxing.

Finally, he rolled one of the heavy kicking bags out into the middle of the floor. Flowing naturally into a fighting stance, he lashed out with his left fist, purposely missing the bag. As his body slid forward he rose on the ball of his left foot and—spinning backward—snapped out with his right hand, pounding the bag hard with the back of that fist, causing a loud popping noise. Instantly he spun counterclockwise and did the same with his left fist.

Amy gave Dylan an odd look but continued with her class.

Dylan lashed out with a front snap kick, tipping the bag. Before it had a chance to right itself he spun, driving his right heel into it. He whirled again, and repeated the maneuver, aiming all his energy at the center of the bag, focusing on it as though it were a real opponent, throwing vicious roundhouse kicks with the top of his foot, calculated to strike the target where his opponent's temple would be. He blocked two imaginary punches, then ripped out two of his own in reply. From the corner of his eye he noticed that everyone was watching him in the mirrors, but he couldn't stop.

Thump. His right shin bent the bag to his left.

Spin. Thump. His left shin buried itself in the vinyl.

Jab. Roundhouse. Uppercut.

His brain was on fire. Screaming at him. Strike! Strike! Strike! Before . . .

Before what?

He grabbed the bag and drove his knee into it, again and again. A hand landed on his shoulder and he spun, trapping the hand, cocking his hip and drawing back for a palm heel strike. Suddenly the feel of skin under his fingers clicked in his brain, and he switched off like an old piece of farm equipment. Amy wiped his forehead with the sleeve of her own *gi*.

"What was that all about?" she asked.

Dylan's breath came out in short gasps as he glanced around the empty dojo. "Where's the class?"

Amy shrugged. "I told them Sensei Barnes was in training, and not to be disturbed. You are, right? I mean you sure as hell look like you're training for something. You want to tell me what it is?"

Dylan sighed. "I don't know what came over me."

Amy nodded. "Does it have anything to do with what's been keeping you awake nights?"

Dylan's mouth dropped open. "How do you know about that?"

"For months you've come in looking like something the cat dragged through the door. You look worse than you did right after Ronnie's . . . It isn't drugs. I know it isn't money trouble. What's the matter with you?"

Dylan slumped to the floor against the bag. The exhaustion of the past minutes combined with the stress and lack of sleep was another unseen opponent, one that he could not beat but only try to hold at bay. At least it was an opponent that was *real*.

Amy slid down onto the floor beside him. "I can't help if you don't let me in. Are you in trouble with the law?"

Dylan laughed. "No," he said, shaking his head. "I wish it were the law."

"What could be worse than the law? It's not the Mob, is it?"

The thought of the Mob operating in Needland made

Dylan laugh again, but the humor quickly deserted him and it all came out in a rush. He told her about his recurrent nightly travels through his house, about the strange presence that haunted him. Everything but the dreams. He didn't know *why* he didn't want to talk about them, since he could never remember much about them anyway. The words just couldn't seem to reach his lips.

"Wow," said Amy. "Have you seen anyone about it? I mean, it sounds like stress or something."

"I don't do counseling," said Dylan, his face tightening. Counseling smacked of something spiritual, another person touching his innermost being in some way that to Dylan was not quite *right*.

"I didn't mean anything."

"I know."

Dylan fought hard not to frown. The trouble was that there did seem to be some presence in his house. Either that or he was imagining a lot of something evil, and either explanation would probably require someone objective to assess.

"Karate helps. That's why I'm here."

"There's deeper meaning to it, too. When I do *katas* it's almost like I'm in another world. It's metaphysical. But you must know that."

Dylan's frown won out. "Doesn't work for me. Never has."

Sosei Masoyama, the founder of Kyokushin, had promised that after ten thousand days of intense practice of Kyokushin, what he called the *mysteries* would be revealed. But from long talks with Sensei Ashiroato, Dylan had come to realize that those mysteries were not something he could believe in. They dealt with a universe beyond what he could see, and smell, and touch, and—while he was happy for Sensei for the inner peace the old man had obviously attained—Dylan lived in the here and now. The secrets of the universe were not why he loved Karate. He loved it because it made him feel strong and self-assured. At least it had until recently.

"Maybe if I came over and spent the night?" said Amy, shyly.

"No!" said Dylan, surprising himself by his abruptness. He hadn't been with a woman since Ronnie, and he knew that he'd be vulnerable, liable to do something he'd be sorry for later. But mostly he didn't want to expose Amy to whatever it was in the house. If it was his madness then he didn't want her to see it. If it was something more sinister, he didn't want to be responsible for endangering her. Whatever it was, it was something of this world, whether shadow madness, or some kind of creature that inhabited the night like a dark chameleon. It was *not* something that would dissipate with a wave of a psychiatrist's hand or an amateur exorcism by a pastor. And it certainly wasn't going to just disappear if he gave in to lust and dishonored Ronnie's memory.

"I just thought—"

"No," said Dylan again, touching her on the hand. "I don't think that would be a good idea."

She sighed. "Are you ever going to have another relationship?"

He couldn't believe she'd asked. She knew how much he loved Ronnie. How much he missed her. "I don't want to even think about it."

But he did think about it. He thought about it a lot. And every time he thought of it he felt his guilt tightening another notch around his heart.

She sighed again. "What are you going to do, then?"

"Work it out," said Dylan, standing up and lifting her with him. "I have a class coming in soon. I guess I'd better shower."

"Right, that should fix things," said Amy, faking a backhand shot at his ribs.

"Some things can't be fixed," he said, leaving her standing in the shadow of the punching bag, shaking her head.

Lucy could still feel the cop's blood on her skin as she eyed the speedometer of her rusted Caravan, keeping the needle pegged right on the limit. She'd stopped only long enough to clean out her bank account at a branch in a neighboring town and then hit the highway. Rather than following the instructions of her mysterious *benefactor* she had driven aimlessly most of the day, searching for a way out of her dilemma. Since her father's death she had been on her own, and she was accustomed to the loneliness that entailed. But the idea that there might be someone out there on her side was a revelation to her. Still, she was reluctant to place her trust in anyone, much less a voice on the phone.

She was wolfing down a burger in a rest area off Interstate 20 when she noticed two guys watching her from the line at the restrooms. They didn't look like men ogling a pretty woman. Their eyes were hard as glass, and, glaring back at them, she made a decision.

She strolled as casually as possible back to her van, trying to spot the pair when they came out. But they didn't. So she drove slowly across the wide parking lot toward the freeway, entering the flow of traffic east again, so intent on her rearview mirror that she ended up taking the high traffic route through Birmingham. She continued scrutinizing cars ahead and behind, shooting glances skyward whenever a plane or helicopter was anywhere near. She knew that if she hadn't been mistaken, and the two men *were* connected with the men who had kidnapped her, then she was leading them directly to the location she had been given.

For years she had tried to convince herself that her entire childhood had been a mistake, that she had been the victim of a couple of bizarre but nonetheless loving parents who lived the way they did because they were convinced they had no other choice. But what had kept her from screaming her name at the top of the metaphorical rafters of the Internet in her search for her real parents was the fear that she'd learn more than she wanted to.

Still, even if this was related to her strange childhood, what possible reason could someone have for wanting her dead, and how could they get the police to go along with it? Whatever the answer to that, she had already flunked Lucy Devereau's Important Rules of Self-Defense twice in twenty-four hours. The rules weren't specific. In fact there was no order to them, and rule number one was always whatever she had failed most recently. But she wasn't flunking again by making the mistake of calling any more cops. Not until she'd met the man who claimed to have saved her life and got him to answer some of her questions.

In Atlanta she pulled off the highway, driving aimlessly through the city. Occasionally she thought she spotted a tail, but then the car would disappear and not return. If she was being followed, what were they waiting for? They hadn't shown any reluctance to use extreme violence before. It was almost as though they'd received new orders. Kidnap her. No, kill her. No, follow her. Maybe *the Boss* was crazy. Or maybe she was imagining things, and she really had gotten away from them. She felt like a fly dragging itself slowly across a web, but was she headed toward safety or the spider?

By the time evening approached she was still in Atlanta, and the last drop of adrenaline had worked its way through her system. In a residential district she spotted a sign that said ROOMS FOR RENT DAY/WEEK/MONTH. Parking on the street, she trotted up to the door. A pleasant little blue-haired lady looked her over through thick, horn-rimmed glasses, and in a dripping Georgia accent invited her inside.

Lucy insisted on a room with a view of the street, and she was no sooner in it with the door locked behind her than a familiar sense of intuition caused her to glance out the window as a dark sedan slowly passed by out front. The car didn't stop, but the men inside appeared too intent on *not* looking at her van or the house. She watched them until they disappeared down the darkening street. Now she was sure she was being tailed, and she didn't know what to do. She couldn't chance leading the men right to the only people who might be trying to help her.

The old woman knocked on her door, offering magazines or books. Lucy told her she was tired and wanted to go to bed. What she really intended to do was sleep in the chair by the window, where she could keep an eye on her van and hopefully devise a way out of the predicament she was in. She was still sitting in the chair—no plan formed—when her watch announced a new day. She stumbled to the bed, grabbed a pillow and blanket, and found her way back to the chair without turning on a light. Only once in the intervening hours had she seen another suspicious-looking vehicle, and that one held only one man, not two. But the night was thick with their presence.

A shadowy movement in the big old hackberry tree on the front lawn caught her eye, but what she had at first believed to be a gust of wind fluttering the night-blackened foliage turned out to be flock of crows, not quite settled in for the evening. The sight of the birds touched a nerve, like a long-forgotten song in which only the faintest of melodies still echoes in the memory. But it was a calming sensation, and she drew in a long, deep breath, knowing in her heart that nothing bad would pass beneath the tree that night without disturbing the birds.

When her cell phone rang she slapped at it as the noise seemed to shake the old house. She lifted it to her ear, but before she could speak she was greeted by the same voice that had started her on this trek.

"Why didn't you go directly to the meeting place?"

"I was too tired, and I was being followed," she whispered.

"Of course you were followed. If you hadn't been, you wouldn't be alive."

"I don't understand."

"More than likely the only reason they haven't killed you is that they know we're in contact, and now they expect you to lead them to us. Just go to the meeting place."

"All right."

It occurred to her that the man on the phone might be one of the people after her. She had no way of knowing if he was really with the men who had been shooting at Ed and Frank. This could be some elaborate plot to get her to go exactly where they wanted her to be. But what choice did she have? If the people following her wanted her, they could have gotten to her at any time. Finally, thrusting her worry aside, she tucked her head into the pillow and, surprisingly, slept.

The little man was barely five-and-a-half feet tall, with a broad chest and narrow hips, and his limp was more than just pronounced. It was a swinging gait with a wild leg that barreled around beside him, causing him to half turn with each step, shoulders moving stiffly, his gray eyes fierce. His face beneath the snarl had the rough, weathered skin of a seaman, or a ditchdigger. He was middle-aged, but the limp made him seen even older. His knee-length coat was a new camel hair, the belt swinging loose at his waist and his hands jammed deeply into the pockets. The temperature hung well below freezing, and snow had started to fall.

He saw only three people from the time he turned the

corner off Elm until he reached the crossing at Willow. At three o'clock everyone in Manchester, New Hampshire, was either at work or safely ensconced in their warm living rooms, behind high, mullioned windows with heavy drapes.

The street he was headed for was a cul-de-sac lined with two-story duplexes built in the fifties, pine-sided with uncounted layers of white paint, brightly colored shutters, and small garages designed for a time when one-car families were the norm. As he neared the house with the bright blue door and tightly drawn shades he slowed, glancing into the empty garage. He nodded to himself as he hobbled up the drive, slipping through the gate into the backyard. Fortunately the rear walk was kept shoveled and he would leave no tracks.

He gripped the iron railing on the back stoop tightly, throwing himself up each granite step. Fumbling in his coat pocket he withdrew a brass cigarette case. When he opened it a number of sharp, wiry-looking tools bristled from it, and he inserted one into the lock. As he jiggled the pick he began to hum "The Battle Hymn of the Republic" under his breath. Finally, he twisted the knob and leaned against the door, silently coaxing it open.

Closing the door behind him, he stalked into the kitchen, shaking some of the cold out of his bones with a stiff shivering motion. He went quickly to a small bedroom that had been converted into an office. Two tall bookshelves framed a narrow window half-blocked by a monitor and keyboard, and stacks of computer manuals. He dropped into the chair and booted up the computer. Tapping his fingers absently on the table, he watched as the machine went through its setup routine. He clicked the mouse several times, switching through programs, his frown darkening as hundreds of images suddenly popped up on the monitor. One in particular caught his attention, and he stared at it, shaking his head.

He removed a mini CD from his pocket, placing it in the drive drawer. The computer chirped contentedly as it loaded the program, and he felt a pang of sympathy watching the machine conduct a lobotomy on itself. But the computer had one more service to perform.

When the installation was complete, the speakers gave a satisfied little beep, and he removed the disk from the drive. He slid down to the floor, groaning as he rolled into a more comfortable position before pulling the computer tower out from under the table to remove the cover.

When his work was completed, he passed quickly back through the house, wiping any surface he might have touched. Then—with one last glance around the kitchen—he exited the house, stopping at the gate to make certain no one was on the street or peering out of neighboring windows. Then he hobbled quickly back to Elm, where he climbed into his Ford van and waited.

At five minutes after five Gregor Oskand passed the van without giving it a second glance, turning onto his street in a mindless rage. His office manager—a man he loathed—had reprimanded him for being lazy and late, and the cocksucker had done it in front of the entire staff. Gregor couldn't storm out of the office because his current chances for other employment were nil, so he had seethed all day, until he was finally able to slip out fifteen minutes before quitting time.

By the time he pulled into his driveway his anger was slowly rechanneling itself. Instead of imagining his office manager hanging from a meathook in the cellar, he now envisioned a very young girl in a completely different, but no more comfortable position, and the heat in his belly started to drift lower. He tossed his overcoat onto a chair as he headed for his office. Across the living room he noticed a wet spot staining the salmon-colored carpet. He waddled straight to the dark area, feeling his erection wither, and his knees shook as he listened for movement inside the house.

"Is someone here?" he croaked, hating the sound of his squeaky voice.

The stain might have been snow he'd tracked in yesterday, but that wasn't likely—he was fastidious about the house. He squatted down on his enormous haunches and touched the spot. It felt wet and cool but not cold. He hurried to the fireplace and chose a heavy brass poker from the ornate tool rack, taking a couple of practice swings as though it were a tennis racket.

There was no one in the bath. Ditto for the office. So he checked the upstairs closets and bedrooms. When he lowered himself ponderously to the floor, inspected beneath his bed, and found no one there, he breathed a sigh of relief. He fought his three hundred pounds back to an erect position and caught his breath. It must have been old snow after all.

The tension washed out of him, and suddenly he remembered what he had been doing before he got sidetracked. He stroked himself as he lumbered slowly down the stairs, anticipating the photos he would select from his huge collection of pornography. He sat down at the computer, one hand on the power button, the other still on his crotch, and clicked on the machine. As the hard drive whirred, Gregor closed his eyes, counting the seconds. When he reopened his eyes he was surprised to find, not his familiar wallpaper, but text in a very large font, running the width of the screen. He read it slowly, goose bumps crawling up his arms.

"Reap the whirlwind, asshole," read the monitor. The message was signed—*Crank*—.

Gregor didn't feel the blast that separated his torso from his lower body, or the compression that shoved his skull so far into the Sheetrock wall the coroner had to pry it out with a loose board. He didn't see the left bookshelf disintegrate into toothpicks and paper snow, or his monitor launch itself across the neighbors' yard and into their bedroom window.

And he certainly didn't hear an old Ford van start up two blocks away.

Dylan stood numbly beside the woodstove in his living room, trying to remember what time of day it was. He'd returned home immediately after his late-morning class, started a fire in the stove to cut the chill, taken a quick shower and changed, then uncharacteristically poured himself a teacup full of brandy from a bottle that had been gathering dust under the sink since his wedding. The sharp taste of the liquor and the burn in his chest had nauseated him but then had begun to do its work. Now he felt unsteady on his feet, and he knew that if he turned just an inch to the right he'd be face-to-face with Ronnie's picture. He'd see her mischievous grin, her dark eyes, and her soft, soft lips.

Twenty-three months, one week, four days, and nine hours ago he could have held her. Now all he had was the picture. Amy would have him believe that somewhere Ronnie waited for him, that death was not the inexorable end of human existence, that her *life force* was greater than the sum of her whole. That there were *mysteries*. But Dylan knew better. He could sense the harsh reality in the fluttering of his own heart that threatened to stop every time he allowed Ronnie's image into his mind.

He forced himself to look at the photograph anyway. She was smiling as only Ronnie could, her eyes gleaming like beacons. But the longer he stared at the familiar old photo, the more her expression seemed to become one of her how-could-you-be-so-stupid looks.

Shit. He'd been so distracted when he left the dojo that he hadn't stopped at the cemetery. He hadn't missed a visit to Ronnie's grave since the funeral. Of course the day wasn't over, but now he'd be buzzed when he got there, adding another notch to the heavy belt of guilt.

He dropped into a chair and stared blearily at the photo, trying to see if she really was frowning. But he couldn't focus that far. The woodstove radiated a pleasant warmth against the bottoms of his slippers, his eyes drooped closed, and he felt himself drifting into that place where waking and sleeping intertwined. For an instant he felt himself gliding into the universe where the nightmares lived, the dreams that wracked him every night but which he could never quite remember in the light of day. And from out of the very depths of that murky *reality* Ronnie's voice touched him as soft as brushed suede.

I'm sorry.

He sank deeper into the chair, reveling in the sound of her voice but wondering what *she* could possibly have to do with forgotten nightmares. What was she sorry for? What remorse had ever plagued her? Having no children? Dying?

His chest felt heavy, and the air was warm cotton in his lungs, forcing him nearer to oblivion. But Ronnie's voice slipped into his mind again, and he opened his eyes a crack, shaken by the view through the living-room window. He couldn't be certain whether he'd slept until twilight or the gloom he now saw outside was a part of his drunken delusion.

It's coming, and it's my fault.

What was coming? When he turned back to the photo he noticed that she seemed to be frowning even more. Ronnie never frowned like that unless he'd *really* fucked up.

Suddenly Dylan could feel the thing that haunted the house, taste it, smell it. He could *hear* it, like another whisper inside his head. Nonsense words flowed into a chant or maybe a moan. He glanced out the window again, and saw for the first time that the encroaching darkness was something far more sinister than just nightfall. Although the grandfather clock in the corner said it was still noon, outside the sun was almost gone, sinking so fast that shadows were tearing across the lawn like the silhouetted claws of a giant raptor hovering over the house.

He climbed shakily to his feet, stumbling into the hallway, breathing in the smell of the place, testing, listening. The hair on his arms tingled as though lightning were about to strike. The gross metallic odor assailed his nostrils, and the nonsense chant separated into words in his brain.

Rantasas megana moor.

The sense of a palpable danger looming in the darkness hounded him. The tiny childlike voice of his own fear beseeched him to run away, but instead he stepped slowly down the hallway, slipped into the bedroom, flipped on the light, and froze.

Without making enough noise to disturb him as he dozed in the living room only twenty feet away, someone—or something—had ransacked the room. Every drawer had been jerked out of his dresser. A pair of briefs and a sock hung from the twisted valance. The curtains rested across the straight-backed chair that lay smashed on its side. The floor was littered with clothing. Torn shirts and twisted slacks smothered the bed, while the linens and blankets were scattered across the carpet. The bedside tables were overturned, and the lamp near his dresser looked as though it had been run over by a truck. A volatile brew of fear and anger stewed within him.

If this was his own mind betraying him, then he had to accept the fact that *he* had done this, somehow without knowing, without admitting the madness to his own conscious mind, to his own memory.

If he was not going mad, then there was *something* in the house that had the power to totally devastate a room . . . silently. And he did not for an instant believe that the choice of rooms had been random.

Either his own mind, or some preternatural monster, had decided to destroy the one room that held the last memories of Ronnie. Although Dylan had chosen to blank the final moments of her life from his mind as though it were a simple slate to be erased, this was the room in which *she* had chosen to spend her last hours. He slept in this room immersed in her spirit, or as much of it as he could believe in. Anger welled, overriding all but the most primordial of his fear.

And all the while the ominous chant continued.

Rantasas. Rantasas megana moor.

"What the fuck do you want?" he gasped, backing against the wall, slapping at his ears. The weird singsong didn't stop but did drop a few decibels, transforming itself into an incessant humming in the back of his mind.

Snatching up his duffel bag, he kicked all the shoes out of the closet into the light. There was one salvageable pair of sneakers, and he stuffed them into the bag along with all the intact clothes he could find.

Outside the bedroom window rested a wall of impenetrable darkness, and the overhead fixture seemed to be dimming, too. He had the terrible feeling that the thing in the house was growing larger, more powerful with each candlepower lost. He was afraid it would creep up on him while his back was turned, but he had one final task to perform before being evicted from the home he and Ronnie had shared for so long.

For over a year Dylan had known that the horror that was growing in his mind, taking control of his nights, might beat him in the end, and although a part of him accepted the fact that the thing had to be a delusion, another part insisted that it was not, that there *was* a deadly presence in the house. A presence that watched and waited, real and deadly. It had never before happened in the daytime. But apparently it could control day and night.

Dropping to his knees in front of the dresser, he stared up into the guts where the drawers had been and reached inside, ripping down a thick manila envelope. Slipping open the metal clasp he glanced quickly at the credit cards and cash inside. There was also a copy of his favorite picture of Ronnie, smiling from her desk.

"You didn't find this!" he shouted, waving the envelope at the empty room.

Immediately he sensed a change in the presence, a rage that was far more concrete and dangerous than anything he had felt before. He grabbed the duffel bag and ran out into the hallway.

The door to the attic was slightly ajar. The latch lay on the floor, and the chair he had placed against the door was nowhere to be seen. The light from the single overhead bulb seemed dimmer than ever. He hurried to the front door, glancing nervously over his shoulder.

Even though he twisted with all his strength, his hand slid over the doorknob without moving it a millimeter. He dropped the duffel bag and envelope and tried both hands. The knob felt as though it were welded in place, the predatory darkness outside seeping into the very pores of the old building. The hallway ceiling fixture resembled a distant candle in a cavern, and the light from the bedroom struggled to form a hazy wedge on the hallway floor. The entry was smothered in gloom as the house grew smaller. The sense of it shrinking around him seemed to be more than just the dimming of the light, as though the cottage really were being pressed from without between two giant claws. He forced himself into *Ibuki* breathing, taking comfort from the familiarity of the odd grating noise deep in his throat.

The light blinked off in the hallway, leaving only the narrow ray from the bedroom. Suddenly the old hinges on the attic door screamed a warning, and a vibration ran along the floorboards. Something had taken a step into the hall. Dylan forced his eyes to slits and waited. When the bedroom light blinked out there was only darkness and the terrible chant in his head.

Rantasas megana moor.

The tenor of the otherworldly voice took on an even more menacing tone, as though the singsong itself had become a direct threat.

Dylan dropped into a front-leaning stance, protecting his head and torso with his arms. He'd practiced fighting blind before, but that was in the dojo, in a controlled environment. Bones might be broken there, but no one was going to get killed.

Another footstep.

He concentrated on becoming a relaxed spring. An unfired bullet.

Another footstep.

Open yourself to the mysteries, Dylan-san. The world is much more than you can see and touch.

The words seemed more taunting than teaching now. Dylan was afraid the world that he couldn't see was about to touch him in a very real and deadly way, and Sensei Ashiroato's mysteries weren't going to help him one way or the other. Either there really was a monster in his house, or his own mind was going to drive him over the edge.

Faint echoes told him the thing—whether real or imagined—had reached the bedroom door. He fisted then opened his hands into knife-edge position, tightening them until they were hard, bladed weapons. Sweat trickled down the middle of his back. He was sure the monster was only five or six feet from him. The familiar rotten-metal odor was nauseating—rancid oil overlaid with the smell of burnt rubber or maybe flesh—and the entryway was a frigid crypt.

Dylan reached out slowly, testing the air, ready to strike with his other hand or the heel of either foot the instant he made contact with anything solid, but there was nothing within reach yet. He left his hand stretched, waiting for the thing to collide with it, loathing the thought of touching it.

When he began to imagine rotten breath in his face he lashed out with a front snap kick, lifting his knee to waist level before whipping his foot forward like a lead ball on the end of short chain, throwing all his momentum into the kick, but there was nothing there. He released his frustration in a blasting *kiei* shout, kicking out again into the darkness. And again, screaming at the top of his lungs, using the power of his diaphragm to force his *ki*—his inner force—outward.

The fight reminded him of his one-sided battle with the punching bag, only here it was the unseen beast that kept *him* off-balance as again and again—with ever-increasing fury and frustration—he attacked empty darkness. Although he couldn't find his opponent, Dylan could feel the weight of its presence on his shoulders, sapping his strength, until it was all he could do to stand, much less attack. The darkness was a sodden blanket clinging to his body.

Rantasas megana moor.

The words pounded in his head, and he realized that it was more than just the monstrous voice. The thing was trying to insinuate itself into his mind. He could feel terrible tendrils burrowing into his brain, and he struggled, willing the alien thing out. As he felt himself succumbing to the horrible mental onslaught everything started to get fuzzy, and he knew that there was no fight left in him and nothing left worth fighting for.

"Finish it," he whispered, staggering back against the

door so hard his shoulder popped. His fingers slipped over the knob at first, but then it turned, and he lurched forward a half step, allowing in just then the faintest ray of light, like the first glimmer of a far-off dawn. He looked into the living room and noticed sunlight once again streaming through the windows. The sense of presence had vanished, along with the mysterious gloom.

An unexpected voice from the porch behind him shocked him almost as much as the return of the light. He spun, jerking the door fully open and squinting out into the glare.

"Mr. Barnes?"

Although they had never been introduced, Dylan recognized the larger of the two uniformed men as the town's new chief of police. "Are you all right?"

Dylan hastily tucked in the tail of his shirt, glancing back down the hall where sunlight now flooded the blue-carpeted expanse.

"I . . . I'm okay," he stuttered.

"No one answered, and we thought we heard a scuffle," said the chief.

The cops looked at the duffel bag and envelope on the floor, then back at Dylan.

"No. No, that's all right," said Dylan, wiping his hand on his trousers.

"I'm Chief Mills. This is Officer Wilkes. Mind if we come in?"

Dylan hesitated, glancing down the hall again before stepping aside. Neither officer removed his coat. Both held their hats in their hands as they followed Dylan into the living room.

Finally, Dylan's courtesy kicked in. "Can I get you something to drink, a soda, coffee?"

"No, thanks," said the chief. Dylan watched his eyes slink from one place to another, taking in every nuance of the room. The teacup on the table beside his reading chair, the dusty windowsills, the magazines on the floor.

"You don't have any children, do you, Mr. Barnes?" said the chief.

"No," said Dylan.

"Are you friends with any neighborhood children?"

"There aren't any kids in this neighborhood. What is this about?"

"But you have kids in your dojo."

"Yes."

The chief nodded. "Were any of them close to your wife?"

"My wife?" said Dylan, losing his train of thought. At first he'd had the ugly idea that he was being questioned because someone had accused him of molestation. But he was always careful in the dojo to make sure no adult was ever alone with kids. He just didn't want any situation where there could be a misunderstanding. That was a basic tenet of karate. Don't put yourself where you can be hurt. That thought brought him full circle to what had just happened and he glanced toward the duffel bag on the hallway floor.

"Did she know any of your girl students well?" asked the chief.

"My wife didn't take a lot of interest in the dojo. Do you want to tell me what this is about?"

"Mr. Barnes, to tell the truth," said the chief, "I was kind of hoping you could take a little ride with us. There's something you need to see."

Dylan frowned. He could see Ronnie's picture over the cops' shoulders, but now it was just the old photo again, smiling Ronnie. "What is it?"

Chief Mills sighed. "Mr. Barnes, I don't quite know how to tell you this. . . . Your wife's grave—it's been . . ." Dylan could see the man's mind working, trying to slip around the right word, but it didn't seem to be coming.

"Been what?" said Dylan, reddening. He felt heat rising in his chest. "Been *what*?"

"Mr. Barnes, your wife's grave has been . . . opened."

"*Opened?*" That sounded like something you did to a

can of sardines, not the precious ground where Ronnie now lay entombed. "You mean someone tried to dig her up?"

A glance passed between the officer and the chief, and when the chief turned back to Dylan he *knew.* He gasped, backing against the wall. When he was finally able to breathe again his voice was more gag than speech. "Tell me what you mean. Tell me what you want me to see."

"She's gone, Mr. Barnes," said Chief Mills.

"Gone?" he whispered. Was this some kind of sick joke?

"We were hoping you might come with us to the cemetery," said the chief.

Dylan turned from the chief to the officer, wondering why the second cop was present since he seemed to be mute. Then it occurred to him that he was there in case the chief needed help, in case Dylan went ballistic. Did either of them really think they could stop him if he did?

"Mr. Barnes?"

Dylan's mind was filled with the picture of the dark hole in the ground that he'd stared into only twenty-three months ago. Only then he'd seen the top of the polished bronze casket—a box the undertaker had assured him would protect Ronnie for eternity.

"What about her coffin?" he asked.

"What?" said the chief.

"Ronnie's casket. Did they . . . you know . . . did they desecrate it or anything? Or did they just open it?"

The chief shook his head. "Gone."

"They took *that* too?" said Dylan. What kind of grave robbers stole a metal coffin that had to weigh three hundred pounds?

"Yes," said the chief, glancing at the deputy again.

"Let's go," said Dylan, slipping his jacket off the hook beside the door and snatching up the duffel bag and envelope. The chief and policeman waited while he tossed the gear into the trunk of the Saturn, then climbed into the rear of the police cruiser. As they backed out into the road, Dylan could have sworn a shadow passed across the living-room windows.

"You planning on taking a little trip, Mr. Barnes?" asked the chief.

Dylan was so distracted the question didn't register until the chief asked it again, and he realized the cops were curious about the duffel bag.

"No. I just needed to get out of the house for a few days. I'm taking a room at the Marberry."

The chief nodded, and when neither of the cops spoke again, Dylan was glad he didn't have to try to carry on a conversation with them. He couldn't get the terrible minutes before they had arrived on his doorstep out of his mind. He could still smell the rotten odor, but if he *wasn't* mad, then why didn't the cops smell it as well? Or did they think it was *him*? Were they politely ignoring it like body odor or a fart?

They'd been driving for some time before he realized he had no idea where they were. But wherever it was, it was to Hell and gone from Meekham Cemetery, where Ronnie was buried. Was it possible the cops were mistaken, that *someone else's* grave had been robbed?

"Where are we going?" he croaked.

The policeman glanced over his shoulder, but it was the chief who spoke as usual. "Meekham."

"This is the wrong way," said Dylan.

The chief shook his head as the deputy turned back to face front. "There was an accident at the intersection of your road and the highway. This way's faster."

They drove down a long lane bordered on either side by snow-covered fields. In the distance a dilapidated barn was supported by rustic flying buttresses of four-by-fours spiked into the ground. The chief turned at the next intersection, and Dylan realized they were headed for Lanks Mills, where Route 26 would take them back to Needland. Cars passed in the other direction, and the chief waved at the drivers. It all seemed so *normal*. The smell seeped slowly away like mist burning off under a summer sun. Or had it ever been there?

They turned off on County Road 12, and Dylan realized

they were approaching the cemetery from the *other* side. He'd never come this way before, and he began to search for the old gravestones. The winter had been a weird one, only about six inches of snow on the ground all year. The markers jutted out of the sterile white blanket like bristles out of a marble brush.

"You all right?" asked the police officer.

"I'm okay," said Dylan, surprised to hear the man speak.

"You looked a little shook."

"Wouldn't you be?" said Dylan, struggling to keep himself under control.

The cop shrugged, turning back toward the windshield.

The road through the cemetery was nothing more than two deep tire ruts, and the cruiser bounced like a pinball between the gravestones. Ahead, beneath an ancient elm that was one of the few proud survivors of its breed, with branches as thick as a man's waist, Dylan could see a mound of fresh dirt, just the way it had looked twenty-three months ago. The chief pulled over so close to the grave Dylan could see the long shadows of the tree limbs reaching downward into the hole, as though in supplication. When the policeman opened Dylan's door, he had to lean against the fender for a moment, steadying himself.

I'm not there. But I was never really there. You have to believe that.

Ronnie's voice warmed him, and he shook off the officer's hand as he stumbled over to peer down into the empty grave. There were no fine cloths covering the open wound in the earth this time, and the excavation wasn't as neatly done. But Dylan suddenly realized that this was no kid's prank. The giant paw of some heavy machinery had gouged downward in a sweeping arc, ripping through grass and rock-hard soil into the unfrozen earth below, depositing it there beside the grave, in that still-steaming pile. Dylan wormed his fingers through the crusty top layer of dirt. The mound was just beginning to freeze. He held a clod up to the light, crumbling it in his palm as he turned to the chief, and the chief nodded.

"Not long. Maybe around dawn we figure."

Dylan wiped his hands on his pants and stared into the hole. The outline of the coffin was visible in the undisturbed soil at the bottom. He squinted at the impression, trying to make sense of it.

"What are those scrapes?" he asked, pointing at two knifelike cuts in the side of the grave.

The chief studied the gashes, as Dylan moved around to the other side of the grave.

"There's two on this side, too," said Dylan. "They must have rigged some kind of straps to the equipment, then just lifted it out. Why would anyone go to this much trouble to rob a two-year-old grave? And they did all this, and nobody saw them?" But glancing around he remembered how secluded the spot was. That was one of the reasons he'd chosen it. Ronnie loved quiet, secluded places.

"Apparently not," said the chief. "We've spoken to the people living on both sides of the cemetery, but the houses are pretty distant."

Dylan could see wide tire tracks beside the grave and back down the way they had come. A heavy truck had been in here. A truck big enough to move large machinery. Ronnie's stone had been knocked over. A white gouge as wide as Dylan's thumb slashed across its face from top to bottom, probably caused by a tooth on the excavator bucket. It was a small thing, but it should never have been done.

"Can we go?" he asked.

Staring down into the hole reminded him of how empty his life had become. Now he wouldn't even have Ronnie's grave to visit, and against all reason he felt that he was somehow to blame for this outrage as well as everything else that had happened. Dylan had never let a simple thing like cause and effect mitigate the sorrow or the guilt that crushed him. He knew his heart would not take much more. That thought was almost comforting.

"Sure," said the chief, nodding toward the car.

Instead of driving him home the chief pulled into the

parking lot behind the town office, which also housed the small police station.

"Why are we here?" asked Dylan.

"Need you to fill out a report," said the chief, opening Dylan's door.

"But I don't know anything."

"Formality."

Once inside the chief's office Dylan took a seat in front of the desk. The chief dropped into a torn red-leather chair and started rifling through a bottom drawer. Dylan took in the cracked pane in the window out front where NEEDLAND POLICE DEPARTMENT had been painted in gold, the giant shadow box on the far wall filled with marijuana pipes, rolling papers, and other paraphernalia, and the big old clock high up near the painted metal ceiling. He noticed that the policeman who had stationed himself in the doorway behind Dylan was staring at that now. It was after lunchtime, and he was probably wondering when he'd get a break.

"Where the hell is that form?" muttered the chief.

"Do I have to do this now?" asked Dylan.

For a moment the horror in his house was all mixed up with Ronnie's empty grave. He had a vision of the thing slipping out during the night, using not an excavator but a claw the size of a refrigerator, ripping and gouging its way through the frozen soil, then lobbing Ronnie's coffin out into the graveyard like a man tossing the wrong-colored sock out of a drawer. Or had *he* somehow done that as well? But he had no experience with heavy equipment and would not even have known whom to call to rent any. Certainly the madness within and this insanity without could not be connected. Not really.

"Now's good a time as any, and you're here," said the chief. "Ah! Here it is." He flattened the wrinkles out of a deposition form and handed it across the desk to Dylan along with a pen.

Dylan leaned across the desk, reading the instructions. The most important thing was to print legibly. Print what?

"What should I say?" he asked.

The chief shrugged. "Just tell what happened in your own words."

"I don't *know* what happened. I wasn't there. Who discovered it?"

"A woman visiting her husband's grave" said the chief. "And this is just procedure. Help us out here. You can say that the officer and I arrived at your house today about . . . noon, say . . . and we informed you of the crime committed at your wife's gravesite. We drove you to the cemetery. You witnessed the . . . evidence of an exhumation, then we brought you here. Maybe you'll think of something else while you're writing."

"Why did you want to know about the kids?" asked Dylan. "Why did you want to know if Ronnie or I were close to any little girls?"

The chief frowned and crossed his arms, glancing again at the policeman. "I'm clutching at straws, Mr. Barnes. Trying to figure why anyone would do this."

"What could this possibly have to do with little girls?"

The chief looked as though he were searching madly for an answer. "I really don't want to say. It was just a thought."

The only scenario Dylan could imagine that would entail little girls was if someone thought that he *had* committed some offense against a child, and an irate parent had decided upon this bizarre way of getting revenge. Did the chief really believe that was possible? Dylan didn't even want to ask.

"It was stupid," said the chief. "Why not just fill out the form?"

Dylan wrote down verbatim what the chief had said. But nothing else came to him. There was no earthly reason for someone to steal Ronnie's body or her coffin. It was a simple act of insanity. That brought him back full circle to his original problem. The Saturn was still parked in front of the house, with his duffel bag and credit cards inside. Now, with the bright light of day shining through the front window of the station house, his panic seemed distant, the terror more dreamlike. Was he *really* going to abandon his house because of that?

But he couldn't get the picture of the ransacked bedroom out of his mind, couldn't erase the memory of that awful smell, the impossible darkness at midday, the terrible sounds creeping down the hallway, slipping around him at the front door that *would not open.*

If whatever was inside his house was merely a hallucination, it was one so powerful he knew he couldn't face it again, at least not right now. Tonight he'd stay in town, have dinner at the Marberry Tavern and take a room. He'd tell Josh, the manager, he was treating himself. No one would question a grieving widower getting out at last. He shoved the paper back across the desk. The chief glanced at it and frowned again.

"Nothing else comes to you?"

"You're starting to get on my nerves," said Dylan. "I want to go home now."

"Okay," said the chief, filing the paper back in the same bottom drawer. "But you'll have to wait until Officer Wilkes gets back."

Dylan looked around in surprise. He hadn't heard the man leave. "Where'd he go?"

"To get coffee."

Dylan noticed the Mr. Coffee on top of the low file cabinet in the corner.

"Broke," said the chief.

Dylan sighed again and leaned back in the chair.

"Your wife wasn't from around here, was she?" asked the chief.

Dylan shook his head. "I met her at college. University of New Hampshire."

"Where was she from originally?"

"Nevada."

"She live in Nevada long?"

Where the hell was this going? Did the man think that someone had traveled all the way from Nevada to ransack

Ronnie's grave? Why wasn't he out finding the men who had committed the crime instead of asking these questions?

"I don't really know how long she lived there. Her father died before Ronnie was born. Her mother passed away a few years ago."

"You see much of her mother before that?"

Dylan frowned. "Very little," he said. "Why?"

The chief shook his head. "Any information might help us find who did this."

Dylan nodded toward the door. "Where did he go for coffee?"

"Down the street. He'll be right back."

"What are you going to do now?"

The chief drummed his fingers on the worn green desk protector. "Check into heavy equipment rentals. Question all the people locally who *own* that type of machinery. I'll also call the state troopers and the sheriff's office to see if anything like this has ever happened before."

"But you don't have any real leads?"

"No."

"What do you think the chances are of finding Ronnie's . . . everything?"

"To be honest, I don't have any idea, Mr. Barnes."

A couple of cars blared their horns on the street, and the chief leaned around to look through the front windows, but there were no screeching tires or shouted insults so he went back to studying Dylan.

"Mr. Barnes, I know you must have had a hard time with your wife's passing and all. But when we got to your house you looked like you'd just seen a ghost. You want to tell me what happened?"

Dylan shook his head. "I . . . I haven't been sleeping well lately."

The chief nodded slowly, watching Dylan a little too closely. "Any particular reason? I mean, it's been two years since your wife's death."

"Just bad dreams. I have dreams every night."

"About what?"

"I can never remember them. I just know they're bad. Nightmares."

"Are you seeing anyone?"

"*Seeing* anyone?"

"I mean about the dreams."

Dylan shook his head.

When he offered no more information the conversation lagged, and he found himself staring at the floor. There was a tension in the room that didn't mesh with the dialogue. He was just about to ask again what was taking the officer so long, when the man walked in.

"No coffee?" said Dylan, staring at the deputy's empty hands.

The deputy gave him a curious look that told Dylan he had no idea what he was talking about.

"Can I go home now?" asked Dylan, rising.

Even in the confines of the chief's office, in the reflected light of day, Dylan felt as though the entire world were off-kilter, as though nothing around him were what it seemed, and madness might be hovering in the room, hanging on the dusty old metal ceiling fan ready to drop like whirling sword blades toward his throat. The image of swords seemed to resonate with an old memory he couldn't quite put his finger on, but he knew he was drifting dangerously, and he had to get a grip on himself.

"Sure," said the chief, nodding toward the police officer. "You want to give Mr. Barnes a ride?"

Officer Wilkes shrugged, opening the door for Dylan.

Dyland stood up slowly, feeling shaky. At the door he glanced over his shoulder at the chief. "You'll call me as soon as you find out anything?"

The chief nodded.

All the way home the policeman didn't say a word, and once again Dylan didn't feel like conversing. Wilkes insisted on escorting him to the house even though Dylan had no intention whatsoever of going inside. But when they reached the door it was open.

Dylan found himself staring so intently at the half-open door that at first he didn't notice the cop leaning to peek in the front window. Dylan followed the man's gaze and gasped. The furniture was scattered as though cattle had stampeded through. The woodstove was askew on its tile base, and all the photos were gone from the walls. Dylan spotted the picture of Ronnie on the back of the overturned sofa.

"Oh, Jesus," he said, hurrying inside.

"You sure your wife didn't have any friends? Any kids?"

Dylan whirled to face the man, and the officer took a step back, his hand resting lightly on his pistol butt. "Why do you keep asking me that? Who did this?"

The cop glanced around, shaking his head. "How would I know?"

Why wasn't the man more surprised by the mess? Wasn't this as much a crime scene as Ronnie's gravesite now? Dylan glanced at his recliner, which had been ripped to shreds. Bits of paper lining from the drawers of the side tables littered the floor, and suddenly he knew that *this* wreckage had not been caused by the mysterious presence that shared his house. This was no mindless destruction, no supernatural haunt out to drive him mad. Someone had been looking for something here. The edge of the carpet had been peeled away from the baseboard all around the room. The plastic covers were removed from all the electrical sockets, the tiny screws lying beside them on the bare floor.

Dylan insisted the cop at least tour the house with him, and they discovered that even the insulation in the attic was torn up and tossed aside. All the old boxes in the basement had been dumped out, used clothing, appliances that had broken or he and Ronnie had outgrown—just *junk*—littered the concrete floor from wall to wall. Even the furnace had been broken into. Twisted sheet metal hung in knifelike shapes where someone had opened every heating duct to get a look inside. But even amid the chaos, Wilkes seemed more interested in Dylan than in the mess, and

Dylan got the funny feeling that the guy somehow thought *he* was responsible even though he'd been with the cops all the time.

"Don't you think you ought to call the chief?" asked Dylan, frowning. "I mean, shouldn't you guys be taking fingerprints or something?"

The officer glared at him. "I know how to do my job."

Dylan led the man back into the living room, snatching up Ronnie's framed photo from the sofa. He slipped the picture out of the broken frame and headed for the door, oblivious of the cop, who followed him down the walk.

"Where are you headed now, Mr. Barnes?" he asked as Dylan slid behind the wheel of his Saturn.

"I told you. I'm taking a room at the Marberry," said Dylan, wondering if he needed to fill out a police report on his whereabouts from now on. "Do you expect me to stay in *there*?" He nodded back toward the house as he started the car.

"No. I suppose not."

"You're calling the chief, right?" said Dylan.

The cop nodded. "I'm on it," he said.

A tiny beeping noise caught Dylan's attention, and he noticed that the trunk warning light was on. He climbed out of the car and lifted the lid, knowing what he was going to find. The contents of the duffel bag and the envelope lay scattered around the trunk, but nothing seemed to be missing. Dylan shoved the money back into the envelope along with the photo he'd reclaimed from the living room and pocketed the credit cards. The officer just glanced at the mess and shrugged.

In the morning Lucy left a tip on the bed, slipping out while the old woman was vacuuming in a back room. The tree was devoid of birds, and a faint sadness lingered in their aftermath, as though she and the crows had been old friends who had passed on neighboring trains, able only to nod and wave.

Gotcha, she thought, watching a sleek sedan pull out of a driveway a block behind her. Instead of a husband and wife off to work, both the driver and passenger were men wearing dark glasses. Spotting her mysterious pursuers again keyed her up, but as she drove down the interstate they disappeared from view. When she crossed into South

Carolina she quickly located the exit she wanted, winding through several mountain villages before finally reaching Merly.

The town boasted a sign informing visitors that it considered itself to be the *Tourist Capital of South Carolina.* Lucy had her doubts. A one-horse Main Street led to the ubiquitous Civil War Memorial Statue on the town square, but there weren't more than seven or eight people moving on the sidewalks, and the downtown parking places held only five cars. The temperature hovered in the forties—frigid for the Carolinas—and an old man in blue denim overalls and a heavy corduroy jacket sat on a bench under a giant live oak, reading a paper. Lucy stopped in the middle of the street and stared at him. He glanced up and nodded.

"Can you tell me how to get to Webber's Bridge?" she shouted, checking her mirror. There was no car behind her, but she could feel her pursuers, hanging back just over the hill.

The old man slowly folded his paper, placing it on the bench beside him, and Lucy wondered if he'd heard. But he pushed himself to his feet and slapped his worn-out work boots across the pavement to lean on her door, looking her over with rheumy eyes.

"Why you want to know?" he asked. His voice threatened to break at any time, as though his vocal chords were made of dry parchment.

"I need to get there."

"Do you?" he said, nodding thoughtfully. "You got people following you, maybe?"

Was everyone in the world in on this except her? "Maybe."

He glanced behind the van, and his eyes appeared clearer than they had before. She noticed that his age didn't seem to affect the tight muscle and sinew beneath the weathered hide. Suddenly he looked as though he might reach out and punch a bony hand through the side of her door.

"You just keep going on this road," he said, still looking back. "When you come to the first fork, you go left. At the second fork you go right. Now, don't you pay no mind to nothin' happening there, you hear?"

She nodded.

"Good. You go like I told you. And you just keep going till you get to the bridge. And anytime you see anyone behind you, you drive as fast as you can. You got that?"

"Yes."

His face softened. He placed a hand on her shoulder, and she was surprised at how gentle it was.

"Everything gonna come right," he said.

"Can you tell me what's going on?" she pleaded.

"You got your mama's hair and eyes, girl. You know that?"

Lucy was speechless. His words rang true, but he wasn't speaking about her adoptive mother, who had blue eyes the color of lilacs, and light hair. Of course, if the men who waited and the men who were after her really were one and the same, they would probably know about her lifelong search for her birth parents. It would be no great trick for them to have the old man feed her false information. But for what? She was already following their instructions.

"You knew my mother?"

As though sensing he'd said too much, the old man frowned and shook his head. "You just drive fast if you see anyone. Now go!"

She started to argue, but he slapped the van hard and turned away, watching the road behind her.

At the four-way stop in front of the feed store there were no businesses across the street, only fields of dark brown dirt. A couple of miles farther, pastureland gave way to thick stands of live oak and pecan. The asphalt was a pothole-scarred no-man's-land, the barbed-wire fences were decrepit, power lines nonexistent. Lucy drove deeper and deeper into hillbilly country, dense with grapevines and Spanish moss, continuing to wonder if the old man was really a friend or not.

Six miles out of town she reached the first fork and veered left. The second fork was upon her before she realized it. A tractor lay on its side in the other lane. A rusted red pickup with a crushed passenger-side door and smashed front fender had skidded into the ditch. A man sprawled in the center of the crossing with blood on his head, arms, and legs, and another man in greasy overalls knelt beside him.

Lucy pulled alongside, but the injured man sat up with an angry expression and growled at her. "Keep moving!"

The Samaritan beside him waved her on without taking his eyes from the road.

She took the right fork onto a gravel lane, tires spinning. She thought she spotted a man's head peering out of the underbrush and another dropping behind a culvert in the drainage ditch as she raced past. In the mirror she saw the injured man lying still once more. She was a half mile away when the crack of gunfire sounded behind her, and she sped up, barely keeping the car under control.

The rusted beamwork of the bridge appeared suddenly around a wide bend. Beyond that lay more forest, where the narrow lane disappeared into the trees. She drove across slowly, tires clacking on the loose boards. On the far side she pulled off onto the grass. A couple of minutes passed, and her nervousness reached the breaking point. She switched off the engine and climbed out, her pistol clutched in both hands. A big man wearing a camo ski mask stepped out of the trees back by the bridge, then three more appeared, and she covered them nervously.

"Miss Devereau?" said the big man.

She nodded.

"We'd best be going," he said. "Unless you want to go ahead and shoot us."

"Who are you? Why should I trust you?"

The man's stolid stillness was as good as a shrug.

"We could have killed you from the cover of the woods," he said.

"Maybe you just want to capture me."

"Again," he said, "it would have been a simple matter to shoot out your tires and take you alive."

The gunfire in the distance seemed to be dying down.

None of the men made any move with their weapons, and finally Lucy returned the pistol to her holster. She had no other choice. She could go with these men or wait for the iron-eyed killers on her tail.

Two of the men approached her, the others fanned out. The big man in front pulled his cotton camouflage mask up onto his forehead, revealing diamond-blue eyes and a chiseled, handsome face. He appeared to be in his late forties, maybe even fifty, but he had the rugged physique of a man twenty years younger, and his rifle swung easily under his right arm. The other man climbed behind the wheel of the Caravan and started the motor.

The big man spun on his heel and was off the shoulder and into the woods before she broke through her paralysis and followed. She caught up to him twenty yards down a narrow trail that seemed to appear and disappear in the thick bracken.

"Where are we going?" she asked. The two men following spread out as the leader stopped and turned.

"Taking you to safety," he said, as though that should have been obvious.

"Who are you?"

He shook his head, nodding back toward the road, then up toward the sky, obscured by an almost solid canopy of foliage.

"Who are the men following me?" she asked.

"You'll learn everything soon enough," he said. "Right now we can't stop. Unless you'd rather stay here . . ."

She shook her head. He smiled and headed down the winding trail again.

In the distance the sound of a helicopter approached.

Dense undergrowth riddled with sharp thorns and rough bark clawed at Lucy's legs and scratched any bare skin. Overhead, oak limbs intertwined with hackberry and pecan to form an impenetrable canopy shaggy with gray beards of Spanish moss. The big man with shoulders wide enough to carry bales of cotton led the group of four through the morass with a calm assurance, pushing aside the thick bracken and occasionally managing to lead them onto animal trails that eased their journey.

All three of the men were clearly well trained, probably ex-military. The leader with the diamond-blue eyes and ready smile hardly had to glance back or wave his hand before one of the others would disappear into the woods, or stop to guard the trail, catching up later. Barely three words were spoken in the first hour the group tramped through the forest.

When the leader stopped and motioned for the three of them to follow suit Lucy knelt wearily on the trail. Adrenaline had burned away most of her stamina, and she hadn't had a bite to eat all day. The two men following spread out and the leader dropped down beside her, offering her a small water bottle from a pocket on his trousers. Lucy drank greedily, handing it back empty.

"Enjoy that," said the man, smiling again. "It'll be a while before we get where we're going, and you don't want to drink out of any of the mudholes they call creeks around here."

"Where are we going?"

He sighed loudly. "I'm afraid I can't tell you that yet."

"Why not? You're supposed to be saving me, right? Who were those men following me? If you're on my side, then why the secrecy?"

"Because those were my orders."

Lucy stared at him for a moment, nodding slowly. "I'm Lucy Devereau," she said, offering her hand.

"I know that," he said, laughing. "Is that the name you're going by now?"

She frowned. Lucy Devereau had been the name she'd worn the longest, the one she'd created a life and a career around. To tell the truth she had begun to believe that that was who she was.

"Lucy is my name," she said.

"Lucy it is, then."

"And *you* are?"

His smile turned rueful as he took her hand. "Wagner," he said.

"Wagner . . . ?"

"Just Wagner."

"And the other men's names?"

The smile spread. "You'll have to see what you can get out of them."

Lucy nodded again. "What branch of the service were you in?"

"I wasn't."

Lucy studied him, but there was no sign of guile. "And the others?"

"Again, you'll have to ask them."

"Meaning I won't get an answer."

"We have our orders."

"From whom?"

He stared at her silently, his tight-lipped smile solid as rock.

"Is the headquarters of this secret organization in Atlanta?"

The smile melted into a confused frown. "Why would you think that?"

She shrugged. "I just thought you might be working out of your hometown."

"How did you know I was from Atlanta?"

"There's no other accent like it."

This time *he* nodded. "Time to go," he said, helping her to her feet.

The bigger of the two men holding up the rear, a man with the hair, eyes, and complexion of a native Scandinavian, signaled sharply with one hand, then faded away into the brush back down the trail. His partner, a small, wiry black man with hands that always seemed to be moving, backed up the trail in their direction, and Lucy knew to be silent.

Wagner's eyes scanned the woods and Lucy tensed. Her perceptions were heightened by fear, and suddenly she had the sensation of having walked right out of her sneakers. She concentrated, struggling to keep herself from being drawn into it. That way led to madness, discovery, maybe death.

But even though she knew that her shoes and socks were still on her feet, the earth felt cool and forbidding as though it were pressed against her bare skin, and the sensation began to bore in as it never had before. Although she could see no movement behind them through the dense undergrowth, she was suddenly certain that their pursuers were close.

A rifle barked, then others answered, and Wagner grabbed her shoulder, shoving her ahead of him down the trail.

"Move!" he said, signaling to the little black man.

The rifle fire died away, and the only sounds were their own feet pounding the dirt, gasping breaths, and bracken scratching clothing. A mile up the trail, where the trees began to thin and blue sky could be seen overhead, Wagner signaled a halt and both the little black man and the huge blond caught up. In the distance Lucy thought she heard the thrump of a helicopter again, and she could tell by the way Wagner searched the canopy that he heard it, too.

"How many?" he asked Blondie in a hoarse whisper.

Blondie shook his head. "I took out two. But the woods are full of them. If we don't get moving, they're going to figure out where we're headed and be waiting for us."

Wagner nodded. "We have to get to the cars. But I wasn't counting on being herded this far south. If we keep going this way, we'll have to cross open ground."

"We don't have time to double back."

"All right. Best to do it fast, then. Let's move."

The underbrush thinned quickly, and as they negotiated a dry streambed bordered by stately pecan trees Wagner leaned against the far bank, staring out across a wide-open stretch of grassy fields. When Lucy slipped alongside he pointed across the innocent-looking meadow.

"A mile through those trees on the far side there's an old

barn. We have two Jeeps there. But we have to get across this field."

"I don't hear the chopper now."

He nodded. "Trouble with choppers is they move real fast. If we hear it when we're out there, it'll be too late."

Lucy could almost picture the men stalking them, images of stealthy movements forming like shadows across her mind. These were well-trained, cold-blooded killers.

"Do we have any choice?"

Wagner shook his head. "Not that I can see."

"Then let's get it over with."

He smiled again. "A lady after my own heart," he said, slapping her gently on the shoulder.

They climbed cautiously out of the streambed, sheltering in the thin brush at the edge of the forest. Lucy stared across the sunlit earth, and she experienced an even deeper sense of oneness with it. She could feel footsteps pounding a heartless rhythm against it, hunters on their trail. Without waiting for Wagner or the others she started running toward the distant trees.

They were halfway across the broad open expanse when the rumbling of the chopper blades drew her attention to the wall of trees in front of them. The aircraft was flying right at them and in seconds would appear overhead. She and the others would be easy targets with nowhere to hide. She picked up her pace, but she knew there was no way she could run fast enough to beat the approaching helicopter.

"Drop and freeze!" shouted Wagner.

Lucy dived hard onto the dry earth, scraping her arms and shins. Glancing over her shoulder she saw Wagner kneeling, aiming his rifle up over the trees. The little black man was ripping through Blondie's pack, and the chopper was almost on them.

The sound of the aircraft as it blasted over the last barrier trees was deafening, and the accompanying wind flattened the tall grass. Dirt and debris slapped Lucy in the face as she glanced up to see the big whirlybird rocketing past, then making a graceful loop over the forest they had just departed. Wagner's last-ditch effort to hide in plain sight had failed. The chopper was coming back, and Lucy could see a nasty-looking machine gun sticking out of the side door, being brought slowly to bear in their direction.

Wagner's rifle barked again and again, and Lucy noticed that the black man had a device over his shoulder that looked like an ugly green drainpipe. It took her a moment to realize that it was some kind of rocket launcher and that he was preparing to shoot down the chopper. But the bullets striking the ground in front of him told her that he wasn't going to fire in time. The machine gun cut him to pieces, and the launcher fell beside him as the chopper blasted past again. The engine screamed as the craft whipped into another sharp, banking turn.

She jerked the pistol from her holster, rolling onto her back and aiming over the trees. Wagner cursed behind her, and she heard his rifle blasting again. Out of the corner of her eye she saw Blondie dive for the rocket launcher. The chopper cleared the trees already firing, bullets chopping limbs and leaves into a swirling green blizzard, and Lucy began pulling the trigger slowly the way she'd been taught, holding half a breath, leading the machine as she caught glimpses of it through the canopy, knowing her little automatic was going to have no effect on the heavy aircraft.

As the chopper cleared the last of the trees the rocket made a whooshing noise, and Lucy was close enough to see the look of terror in the pilot's eyes just before the aircraft exploded. She rolled into a fetal position as Wagner dropped on top of her, sheltering her from the debris. The ground shook as the remains of the aircraft impacted the field, and as she climbed to her feet she covered her face to protect herself from flames that were dangerously close. Wagner hurried to Blondie's side, and she followed him, shaken by the sight of the small black man and the hideous wounds the machine gun had caused. But the man's face was untouched, a smile or grimace on his lips, and she realized that he had died for her just as the men had on the road. Who were these men who would do such a thing for a total stranger, and why did they feel compelled to do it? She stared at Wagner as he closed the little man's eyes, and when he turned to face her she saw his own eyes were watery.

"We need to get going," he said, forcing Blondie to his feet.

"You're going to leave him there?" said Lucy, staring at the body.

"We have no choice," said Wagner, spinning her around and shoving her toward the nearest trees. "If we make it to the cars before the men behind us figure out where we're going, we have a chance."

He stared at Lucy for a moment, squinting.

"You took off before I told you to back there," he said, shaking his head.

"It was time to go."

He frowned. "Why were you so sure?"

She glanced at the dead man, fighting back tears. "You call that sure?"

Wagner shrugged, nodding for Blondie to take the lead. They were into the woods and running before Lucy realized she could sense the men behind them again.

Gregor Oskand died on Saturday. On Monday a man who knew Gregor only as Cool Daddy met an untimely demise in the back of his hobby shop when *his* computer developed a ground fault that turned him, the machine, and the shop—filled with highly flammable glues, plastics, and resins—to a pile of ash.

Driving north through the night, Crank felt an unusual sense of unease. By the time he reached the Vermont border he should have been as relaxed as he ever allowed himself to be, ready to rest and recharge, but the odd gloom hung over him like a dark storm cloud. For the first time he'd disobeyed orders. But he was a hunter. That was what he did. Oskand and Cool Daddy were Qedem Melech, and there was no way he was going to let them live.

The moon glittered across the snow in jagged prisms of blue glass, and the wind rustled the branches of the skeletal pines along the highway. Two miles down a winding dirt road he pulled into the wooded drive leading to his house.

Once inside his little log cabin, he poured himself a large dollop from a bottle of Hennessy on the counter, swirling it in the glass between his palms. Drinking in silence, he listened to the familiar creaks and groans of the house as the night got colder, the temperature dropping below zero. A gray cat with shabby fur and a curious tilting walk ambled slowly across the pine floor toward the table, and Crank and the animal locked eyes. The cat slowed, taking each step deliberately—as though the floor might be mined—until it reached Crank's feet and waited, crouching. Crank finished the last sip of brandy and shoved his snifter away.

"Come on, then," he said.

The ancient feline leaped into his lap, a mangy, cordless vibrator, rubbing against his belly.

"How you been, Azimuth?" asked Crank, glancing into the kitchen at the bowl of dry cat food and the automatic water dispenser that was still three quarters full. "Do you really miss me or do you just act like this when I get home so I keep leaving food?"

Climbing wearily to his feet he carried the cat into the sparsely decorated bedroom and placed it gently on the king-sized waterbed resting against the far wall. A computer desk stood across the room from the bed, and the console on top clicked quietly, the monitor blank. Crank listened to the familiar noise for a moment, before sighing and dropping into the chair at the desk. A message window appeared on the screen, and he typed a reply.

"No, sir," he said, frowning as a new message appeared on the screen. "Been here all along. Computer must have been down."

Clayborn wasn't stupid. But *maybe* he'd believe that.

The next message was longer, and as he read his eyes narrowed and his lips tightened.

"Is the girl in custody now?" he typed.

No reply appeared on the screen, and he grunted, the feeling of unease returning with a vengeance. He'd been given to know that the girl wasn't his concern, but he'd had to ask.

He got up and walked over to the closet. There weren't many clothes inside, a couple of suits, a few slacks and shirts, and a very heavy winter coat with a wolf ruff on the hood. He reached behind the parka to retrieve an automatic pistol and hideaway hip holster from the rack. Retrieving two clips of ammunition from the parka pockets, he carried them to the bedside table. He removed the pistol from his shoulder holster and checked to make certain there were rounds in the chambers of both guns, then placed them under the pillow beside Azimuth.

"Like that, you ugly old cat?"

The cat regarded him with one drooping eye. Crank nodded, sitting on the bed and starting to undress. The feeling of unease was now a nagging certainty that things were not running right, and Crank had an overweening need for things to go according to plan.

"I'm not supposed to get involved in this one, either, Azimuth. But I'm afraid if I don't handle this personally now, they're gonna screw it up."

He slipped under the covers and flipped off the light, shoving the cat out of his face.

For three days and nights Dylan had been living like a hermit in one of the nicest rooms in the inn, coming out only for meals or trips to the police station. It had been a hateful existence—as though he were exiled from his own home—but his madness had not manifested itself there, the monster had not followed him. Apparently either his insanity was tied to the house, or—even harder for him to believe—there really was something there.

Standing in the cold and depressing afternoon sunlight in front of the post office, he watched cars passing and people walking down the sidewalks without really seeing them. He opened the door of his Saturn and tossed his mail onto the passenger seat, glancing once more up and down the length of town.

Needland consisted of Center Street, which intersected on one end with Route 26—the major east–west artery across the southern half of the state—and on the other end with Route 5, a small two-lane that meandered through miles of farmland and forest and eventually ended up in New Hampshire. Old, well-established residential areas flanked both sides of downtown, along with Colton Academy, a small and very exclusive private school that catered to upper-class students who seldom interacted with the locals on anything other than a retail basis.

But unlike many other small villages in Maine, Needland did not exhibit the run-down, out-of-time appearance caused by an economy that had been sluggish since the Asians had learned how to make American shirts and shoes in the fifties. Since the town was a bedroom community for nearby Fall Mountain Ski Area, Needland could count on a heavy influx of New York, New Hampshire, and Massachusetts greenbacks every winter. Instead of dollar stores and consignment shops the downtown businesses were more like New England versions of trendy California boutiques.

Dylan had met with the chief several times since their trip to the cemetery, but the man never had any news. They had found no fingerprints in the house except Dylan's and none on the car. The more Dylan hammered at the man to do something the less seemed to get done. According to the chief the Ouachita County Sheriff's Department was on the case, too, but Dylan had seen no evidence of that, and the chief didn't seem to know exactly what they were doing. When Dylan called them he found out that the chief had indeed informed them of the grave robbery but that they were not actually involved and didn't want to step on the chief's toes. The chief seemed far more interested in having Dylan keep him updated as to his whereabouts than doing any real investigating. In fact he had begun displaying what Dylan thought was an overdeveloped concern for his well-being. More than once he had asked if Dylan was all right, if he needed anyone to stay with him, and Dylan wondered if the man had noticed symptoms of his neurosis, if perhaps the chief thought he might be suicidal.

The trouble was that Dylan didn't know himself. He had to admit that the idea had occurred to him several times since Ronnie's death, and with his growing fear of losing control he had considered the solution more often. But he had never acted upon it, never even pondered exactly *how* he might go about it. Lately, though, as he had begun to be caught up in his delusions, unable to think of anything else but the darkness and presence all around him, he knew that he could not go on like that for long.

Ever since the trip to the cemetery Dylan noticed movements in the shadows, just around the corner, people talking in low voices that he couldn't quite make out, and he couldn't get the crazy idea out of his head that the police were somehow in on the whole thing. Why had the chief taken him the long way to the cemetery, really? No one at the inn knew anything about an accident closing any roads. And why the runaround that day at the police station? It smelled a lot like they'd been trying to keep him in town while someone rifled the house. But for what? When he realized just how paranoid he was getting he took a deep breath, trying to shake it off.

A man in a dark, late-model Chevrolet parked alongside the opposite curb caught his eye but then turned too quickly away. Dylan glanced once more down the length of the street and noticed that another man—parked a block farther down—also looked away. Dylan climbed into his car, trying not to notice the pulse in his palm throbbing against the steering wheel.

Keep your shit together now. Take another deep breath and calm down.

Instead of making his customary U-turn at the top of Center Street, he took a left onto Route 5, headed for Newell. But three miles up the road he pulled over to the shoulder and waited. Several cars passed, some of the drivers slowing to give him the once-over. None looked suspicious, and none of the cars held either of the men he had seen in town. Feeling foolish, he drove on.

The car seemed content to steer itself, turning first down this old farm road, then that unknown lane, until Dylan was thoroughly lost. A couple of miles farther and the car slowed as though it *needed* to stop. Hills sloped away on either side, and the balsam firs were so thick that perpetual twilight lurked beneath their spreading branches. Remembering that *he* was driving, Dylan pulled over and climbed out of the car, listening for other motorists. But on the tiny lane at that time of day there was no traffic.

A rough logging trail intersected the road. Dylan knew that most of the leases on this side of town had been logged years before, and the crews had moved on. But there were tire tracks in the crusty snow. A jagged sliver of irrational fear caught in Dylan's throat, and he fought to master it.

There's a million old logging trails around here. Anyone could be using it. Hikers, snowmobilers, kids looking for a place to neck or smoke pot.

But the impressions were deep and wide, created by a large, dual-wheeled vehicle, perhaps even a truck hauling an excavator. He glanced up the trail and spotted the kind of chain from tree to tree that loggers used to secure lease roads. Everyone knew that was standard procedure in country where stealing valuable timber or even heavy equipment off another man's property wasn't unheard-of. A gnawing in Dylan's guts told him those innocent-looking tracks were terribly wrong. He crunched through the ankle-deep snow and inspected the heavy rusted chain that was knotted—not padlocked—around the tree. The loggers Dylan knew were always leaning back on brawny, flanneled shoulders, smoking unfiltered cigarettes, drinking their beers with broad elbows sticking out the windows of their four-wheel-drive trucks. Loggers didn't *hurry* anywhere. None of them would be in such a rush they'd slap a chain around a tree without locking it.

He glanced at the other tree across the trail. Same story.

No lock. And there was only the one set of tire tracks. Either they had driven in but not out or vice versa. Maybe they were still up there. He knelt and ran his fingers along the edge of the tracks. Sharp as a knife, and iced over more than once. The ruts had been there through at least a couple of days' thawing and refreezing.

He slipped under the chain and headed up the trail, seeking answers beyond the crest of the hill. But as he glanced back at his car and listened to the quiet soughing of the breeze through the evergreens, everything seemed so normal, and he wondered for the thousandth time if he wasn't going mad.

"I must be," he muttered, blowing warm air into his ungloved hands.

Ronnie's voice came clear as the whispering wind this time.

No, you're not.

Dylan glanced hurriedly around, but the forest was as empty as Ronnie's grave.

"How do you know?" he muttered.

There, out in these pristine woods, it was all right somehow to have a conversation with his dead wife. Not like sitting on his ass in his ten-year-old L.L. Bean pants chatting up her photo.

Crazy people kill themselves.

"Yeah. Well, I was gonna get around to it."

No, you weren't.

He was waiting for her to say that he didn't have the guts. That was how he'd know it wasn't really Ronnie, but the voice refused to elaborate.

The day was growing overcast, and he pulled the collar of his sports coat tighter around his throat. A crow taunted him with caws that echoed through the tops of the trees. He spotted the bird on the longest limb of a tall fir, perched out over the trail. The bird had its head cocked, staring directly at him. It waited until Dylan had hiked halfway to it, then flapped away into the dense foliage, and he spotted it up ahead, shifting along a branch to get a better look at him.

He followed the road over the first rise and discovered a long flat run leading to yet another hill. The exercise had warmed him, working out some of the stiffness left over from days of sitting by the phone. It felt good to be doing something, even if he couldn't quite explain what he was doing, so he hiked on.

The trees were tall and the undergrowth was so thick he couldn't see more than twenty yards into the forest, and he wondered why loggers hadn't taken the wood after all. But Maine was a shotgun pattern of timber leases, state, federal, and private land, with access roads and trails strung through like spaghetti. Around here a man could wander in circles a few hundred yards from his own house and die of exposure even if he was lucky enough to *find* a trail, so Dylan had no intention of venturing off the path and possibly forgetting what direction he was traveling. But what was *on* the path? An image of Ronnie's coffin lying open, surrounded by vermin flashed across his mind, and his fleeting sense of well-being deserted him.

What if the coffin was right up ahead somewhere? Maybe the grave robbers *had* just left it out in the open. But why would they do that? Unless they did something to it. To her. But what?

The more he tortured himself, the worse the pictures became.

Calm down. Keep your feet on the ground.

The crow perched on a limb directly overhead now, calling softly, a mournful sound. Dylan had never seen one of the black birds so close before, and the creature's unusual scrutiny made him nervous.

"Get out of here!" he shouted, waving both hands over his head.

The crow flapped its wings at the sudden movement but held its ground, cawing louder, as though it felt that it were having the best of the repartee.

Dylan found a three-foot piece of deadwood and waved it threateningly in the air, but the crow was still unimpressed. Frustrated, Dylan threw the branch, succeeding in striking the limb the crow was resting on. The bird flew off up the trail, cawing irritably, taunting Dylan with aerial somersaults. Dylan noticed that there were no answering calls. The bird was a loner, and that, too, struck him as odd.

Trying to shake off his apprehension, he started up the path again, careful to stay in one of the tire tracks and not sink into the crusty snow on either side. Tiny chips of ice had already filled the bottom of his shoes and melted to soak his socks. He reached the top of the next hill and was disappointed to see that this *still* wasn't the end. The road dropped down into a depression a hundred yards wide, then disappeared over another ridge. But the idea that Ronnie was somewhere just up ahead would not be denied.

He took a deep breath and trudged on.

The crow was circling low overhead when Dylan spotted the tail end of a tractor-trailer rig. The truck was parked in the center of a wide, grassy, clear-cut area, a big orange excavator resting atop the trailer, bucket drawn in tight like a giant chimpanzee scratching its armpit. The clearing was an anomaly since none of the rest of the forest had been logged, and clear-cutting had been outlawed for years. Either the loggers here had broken the rules, or more likely, the harvest had taken place years ago, and something had stopped the trees from taking root again.

The flatbed was lower than most, built to load the heavy excavator using two flip-down, metal ramps. He rested his hand on the cold metal, glancing fearfully forward. But the front of the trailer was empty except for the thick chains and turnbuckles securing the excavator in place. Dylan peered at the big bucket with its six-inch teeth, and he knew that the frozen bits of earth clinging there were from Ronnie's grave. He slapped the machine so hard his hand ached. Edging quietly along the trailer to the truck itself, he pulled himself up on the chrome handrail to peer inside. But thick frost lined the dash and hoarfrost rested lightly on the vinyl seats. No one had been in the cab for days.

His premonition had been wrong. He *hadn't* found any answers there. All he had were more questions. The driver of this truck had draped the chain across the trees to fool anyone passing, driven the ten miles of logging road to a deserted clearing, then disappeared with Ronnie's coffin into thin air. Surely the cops would have something to say about that. Even an idiot could see that something really weird had gone on here. *Weirder* than just grave robbing, he reminded himself. He glanced around the clearing, wondering again at its treelessness amid the wildness of the surrounding forest.

Just then he heard the bump and crash of a car beating its way up the road. His first thought was that maybe it was the assholes who had robbed Ronnie's grave. His second thought was that they might be armed, and he would be able to find no justice for her dead, but it was fifty yards in any direction to cover, and the snow would give him away.

He raced back the way he had come, careful not to step out of the hard-packed bottoms of the tire ruts. As he reached the edge of the clearing and peered nervously down the trail, he heard the car spinning its tires but getting steadily closer. Twenty yards down the slope lay a fallen pine, the top limbs almost touching the truck tracks. He ran to it and leapt from the tire rut onto the thin upper trunk, clutching the jagged branches, fighting for balance. He reached the base of the dry old pine without leaving any telltale footprints in the snow and threw himself into the bracken, still burrowing his way into the dry foliage as the car chugged by, not more than fifteen feet away. But he couldn't just hide there. As soon as the car stopped he had to get back to the clearing and see who was driving. As he pulled himself shakily to his feet and staggered back to the trail, the motor noises died and two car doors slammed.

"Mr. Barnes?"

Dylan started to answer, but then he began to wonder who in the hell would be looking for him way out here on a frigid late afternoon.

"Mr. Barnes! We know you're out here. We found your car on the road. Are you all right? We thought you might be hurt."

That was unmistakably the chief's voice, and once again Dylan was tempted to answer, but the feeling of something off-kilter that he had been getting from the man all along was amplified by the silence of the forest and the way the chief's voice echoed through it like gunshots.

He hiked slowly through the trees toward the top of the hill, trying not to make noise. The chief and Deputy Dawg had parked their cruiser right beside the trailer, obscuring most of Dylan's tracks, and their backs were to him as they stared out into the woods. When they turned back in his direction the two appeared tense, nervous. Why should they be? And why were neither of them interested in the truck or the excavator?

Instinctively he slipped deeper into the trees, working his way around the clearing, closer to the car. His footsteps crunching the snow sounded to him like an elephant stomping on bubble wrap, but he hoped that the distance and trees would muffle the noise. Finally, he dropped behind a dense but leafless alder bush, staring through its tangled web of bare branches.

"Mr. Barnes!" shouted the chief. "We just want to talk to you. Come on out."

We just want to talk to you?

What kind of thing was that to say to someone who you were worried was lost in the woods? Officer Wilkes turned suddenly and glanced back toward the trail, and Dylan heard the unmistakable sound of another car battling its way up the rugged stretch.

Who the hell would that be, more cops? Why send out two cop cars?

Suddenly Ronnie's voice sounded in his head.

They're coming.

He shook his head, trying to get his stupid subconscious to leave him alone. He was nervous enough already. He didn't need that.

But it wasn't a cop car that pulled up, at least not a marked one. As the big sedan rolled to a stop behind the police cruiser Dylan slunk back farther into the brambles. Maybe this was all routine and not part of his paranoid delusion, but he was going to wait and see.

He didn't recognize the two men who climbed out of the car. They both wore army-style parkas over dress slacks and black leather shoes. Their heads were uncovered in the icy air, revealing matching crew cuts.

"Find him?" said the tallest one, a man with gray hair and broad shoulders.

The chief shrugged. "Who are you? What are you doing here?"

"Helping."

The chief seemed jittery, unsure of himself. "You're interfering in an official police investigation. We're looking for a man lost in the woods."

"Why don't you go into the woods and look for him, then?" said the tall man's partner.

"He'll come out when he's ready," said the chief. "We got time."

"He might freeze to death in there," said the tall man.

"Just who the hell are you?" said the chief, turning to stare around the dell. "And how did you two know about this place anyway?"

"The question is," said the tall man, not intimidated at all by the chief, "how did *you* know about it?" He took in the excavator and stroked his fingers along the metal track exactly as Dylan had. "Nice machine. Do some heavy digging with this, I bet."

The chief nodded. "Bet you could."

"Dig up an old grave maybe."

"Or a new one maybe."

The tall man and his partner tensed like coiled cobras.

"Seems to me there's only one reason for you two to be here," said the chief.

Dylan was surprised that the chief didn't seem aware of the implied threat in the two men's stances. Wilkes took a step back though, placing his hand on his pistol grip. Dylan noticed that, while the officer was shaking, both the parka-wearing men were steady as deep water, and both had their hands inside their coats.

"We're not talking about Barnes now, are we?" said the chief, a bleak smile crossing his lips. "You fellas aren't just looking for Barnes today, are you? . . . *Rantasas.*"

The tall man shook his head and drew his pistol at the same time. His partner did the same. Both pistols fired in one blast. The chief and the other cop collapsed where they stood. As Dylan watched, dumbfounded, the man and his partner placed their pistols close to the cops' heads, then two more shots echoed away into the night.

"Mother of God," muttered Dylan.

The pair holstered their pistols and dragged the two dead officers toward Dylan. He slouched as low as he could get in the bracken, praying they would miss his hiding place. By the time they reached the edge of the woods they were still thirty feet from where he lay, close enough that he could hear their voices clearly but not see what they were doing, but the crash of branches told him that they were hiding the bodies. When the noise stopped he held his breath.

"That happened fast." The tall man's voice sounded at though he were standing on top of Dylan. "What now?"

"Find Barnes. Those had to be his tracks beside the truck."

"What about the cops' cruiser?"

"We'll worry about it later."

Dylan pressed himself into the snow-covered earth.

"He must have followed the tire ruts back down. If he got off into the woods without leaving a mark, he's going to be hell to find, and if we lose him, we're fucked."

The tall man stepped back out into the center of the clearing and his partner followed. The tall one cupped his hands, and shouted, "Mr. Barnes! Come on out. We need to talk to you!"

Right. Everybody wants to talk to me today.

Dylan noticed that while their pistols were holstered again their coats remained open. He had been astounded by how quickly they had drawn and fired the guns with such incredible accuracy.

"Mr. Barnes! It's getting cold as hell. You're going to die out here. We're your friends."

Jesus! This guy was a real kidder.

"Got any ideas?" asked the partner.

"If he's here, he's got to come out on the road."

"And if he doesn't?"

"One thing at a time."

Dylan watched the pair stomp back to their sedan. He ducked as the car spun around in the clearing, and the headlights passed overhead. The sun was just a dull red glow through the trees, and the temperature was dropping fast. The past few minutes of inactivity had already chilled him to the bone. He thought of the long walk in the dark, back down the logging track where the tall guy and his partner could be waiting at any turn. Then he thought of the chief and Officer Wilkes lying somewhere beside him. How could what had happened to Ronnie have anything to do with these killers? Why did they want *him*? And how in the hell was he going to survive the night?

He listened to the sedan, bumping away down the logging trail, as he shoved himself to his feet. But he couldn't use the trail. He had to make his way back through the woods and try to find the road somewhere they weren't looking for him. In the brief span of time he'd been considering his options the sun had completely disappeared behind the mountains, and he glanced up at the stars just beginning to wink on in the clearing, trying to get his bearings.

He thought he heard gunfire somewhere down the trail, and he stopped to listen until it ended. No way he was going back down that trail now. As he plodded along through the ankle-deep snow between the tall evergreens, the chief's last words echoed in his head. Had he really heard what he thought he'd heard?

Had the chief said *Rantasas*?

Crank poured a bowl of milk for Azimuth and a snifter of Hennessy for himself and carried them into the bedroom. Outside it was as frigid and dark as the North Pole, and even with the woodstove blazing and the liquor burning his throat, the interior of the cabin seemed cold. In thirty years of service he had often been out of contact with the Keep for extended periods, but always it had been a silence of his own making.

Ever since childhood Crank had been a loner. A stint in juvenile hall and a later close brush with prison had only enforced his natural instincts toward introspection.

"You got any idea what it's like in the can?" he asked the cat.

Azimuth ignored the question.

"You watch your back," said Crank. "You don't talk out of school, and you don't make enemies *or* friends. One's just as bad as the other. I'd probably still be in there if it weren't for the Boss."

The cat turned and pattered out of the room as though the conversation were over, and Crank nodded.

"Yeah," he muttered. "So what do I do now?"

Twenty-four hours ago he had e-mailed another demand to be let into the action in Needland and received no reply. Yet another e-mail brought a similar silence, and when he had finally broken down and tried the Boss's private line, it registered a constant busy signal. *That* had unnerved him. Finally he'd really gone out on a limb and called the number Baxter had given him years before—knowing full well that Clayborn would have a shitfit if he even found out that Crank knew how to contact Baxter—only to discover that Baxter and his partner were the only *good guys* in Needland, and that just didn't make sense. Crank was trained to deal with unusual situations, conditioned to handle whatever was required of him in order to fulfill his mission. His hands weren't quivering, and his heart wasn't pounding. But he felt a tingling between his shoulder blades, and he knew that the wrong move now might not only get him killed but a hell of a lot of other people, too.

He had no authority to interfere in Needland, and with no contact possible with the Keep he was not likely to get any. But he couldn't just sit here while everything fell apart. He glanced out the window at the silky whiteness of the snow that seemed to dance beneath the cloud filtered starlight. The cat wandered back in to rub against his calf.

Of all the contingencies he had planned for, losing contact had not been one of them. He hoped that whatever the reason for the lack of communication, the Keep hadn't been compromised.

It had taken the organization so damned long to track Ronnie Barnes that by the time they did find her, she was already dead. Now their only hope was that somehow her husband could fill her place. Crank's gear was already in the van. But if he simply charged off up the highway now, no telling what he'd run into when he got to Maine, and without more info he'd have a hell of a time finding Barnes and getting out alive. When his laptop finally beeped he stared in disbelief at the screen.

He's lost.

He typed furiously. "Lost where?" realizing as soon as it was sent how assinine the question sounded.

Sending assumed coordinates.

A topo map appeared and Crank printed it out, studying roads in and out, shaking his head in disgust. He had to have Baxter's help to find Barnes, and if they did manage to find him they could never come back here. The road ahead looked as bleak and danger-filled as any Crank had ever faced, and although he eschewed such beliefs, he had a sudden premonition of his own death. He feared that he might not be able to take care of himself in the days ahead, much less Barnes.

"Looks like you and I have to part company," he said, following the cat back to its bowl.

He waited until the animal was through eating, then picked it up and carried it under his coat out to the van, placing the animal gently on the snow.

"I should never have taken you in, Azimuth," he said.

The cat glanced around nervously, hunching its shoulders against the cold, deciding whether or not to make a run for the warmth of the house. But the door was closed.

"I'm sorry," said Crank. The pistol was out from under his arm in one slick motion, and he put a pinpoint shot through the cat's brain before the animal could blink. He reholstered the pistol, drove over to the shed, and hitched up his snowmobile trailer. When he climbed behind the wheel again there were tears in his eyes, but he drove away without glancing at the cat's body.

In the deepest, deadliest part of the night the silence outside the motel room Lucy shared with Wagner and the man she knew only as Blondie seemed ominous. All day she had felt a foreboding, as though the air itself pressed down on her with a great new weight, as though the sun going down had been not just a repeat of something the bright fiery orb had done millions of times in the past, but some final hurrah. Although the convenience store coffee burnt the pit of her stomach, the caffeine kept her wide-awake. She passed one of the energy bars from the coffee table to Blondie, sitting next to her on the bed. Wagner stood beside the front window, peeking out through the dirty green curtains at the neon-lit strip of highway beyond. Finally he let the drapery fall and dropped into the one chair in the room, unhooking another button on his camo tunic.

"Now?" asked Blondie.

"Very soon."

Lucy glanced at Wagner's cell phone on the bedside table, and he frowned. For three days they had been wandering in what seemed to Lucy to be an aimless manner, first west, then north, then east again. And all the while Wagner hadn't managed to contact anyone from the mysterious *group* he referred to as Rex Deus. It was clear, though, that all they were doing in the meantime was trying to stay one jump ahead of the men after them, and although Wagner and Blondie put up a brave front they were obviously worried.

Even though Wagner was sitting beside the window Blondie checked it anyway, periodically pacing to the rear of the room to inspect the window in the bath. For all his size he moved with the same silent tread and feral look of a big jungle cat.

"How did you know about the cop in front of my house?" she asked Wagner.

Wagner frowned, as he did each time she started asking questions. "We got away with one drive-by. It was the best we could come up with on short notice. If we'd tried to snatch you there the couple of men I had would have been slaughtered. The cops had people in all your neighbors' houses waiting for us. I'm surprised that detective didn't try torturing you to get you to reveal what you knew about us."

"But I don't know anything."

"They don't know that, and besides, some of them just enjoy torture."

Lucy shuddered. "Why would those people want to kill me?"

"Because of who you are."

"I'm nobody," she said, glancing away. "I don't even know who I am."

He smiled. "You're Lucy Devereau, a bright, beautiful woman who got stuck with a couple of jerks for a while. Unless *you* want to tell us why you're special."

"I'm not special," she lied.

"Okay, then you're not."

But she could tell he didn't mean a word of it.

"So what if I just get up and walk out of here?" she asked, ignoring the question again.

"I hope you don't try that," said Wagner.

"You'd stop me?"

"No."

"Why not? You're here to protect me, right?"

Blondie nodded at Wagner that all was clear out front and disappeared into the bathroom again.

"Yes," said Wagner.

"And it's dangerous out there, right?"

"Very."

"But you wouldn't stop me from walking out that door?"

"No."

"Why not?"

"Because we all have our own destinies."

"What the hell does that mean?" she asked.

"We," he said, nodding toward the bathroom to include Blondie, "are charged with your care, *if* you will have it. We can't force it on you. We tried that before and our charge escaped, placing herself in terrible danger. We realized then that the only way to fulfill our mission was to offer our services and have them fully accepted."

"You wouldn't let a woman commit suicide, would you?"

"Not if I could help it."

"But you'd let me walk out of here and get caught or killed by those . . . people."

He nodded. "That would be your fate then, I suppose, although I would attempt to dissuade and to protect you."

"Even if you got killed doing it?"

"Yes."

"That's crazy."

Wagner shrugged.

Blondie returned to the room, wiping his face with a towel.

"It's time," said Wagner, rising.

Since Merly, he'd made the same pronouncement eight times, and eight times they had left wherever they were without a backward glance. Regardless of what he said about not stopping her from leaving he had no compunctions against shoving her to the waiting pickup, as Blondie tossed a couple of rifles behind the seat.

The city lights faded almost immediately, and rolling farm country surrounded them. Moon and stars and silver-lined clouds lidded the dark coffin of the earth. The truck's engine sent a menacing growl through the floorboards, and Lucy wondered again what tick of the cosmic clock had commanded her arrival at this strange place and time riding between two secretive and dangerous men in what might very well be a stolen vehicle.

Wagner drove just under the speed limit, cruising back roads that he seemed to know by heart through a night that was darker than the moon and stars should have allowed it to be.

"What are you looking for out there?" she asked, glancing at Blondie, who kept his face pasted to his window. The fields were winter fallow and empty. Wagner watched the landscape to their left, equally intent. The two men glanced at each other. Wagner shook his head, and Blondie shrugged. But *something* had her two guardians unusually nervous, and that made her anxious as well.

As they rounded a wide bend, clouds buried the moon, and what was left of the starlight barely illuminated the funereal night. Suddenly the truck's engine died without so much as a sputter, and the headlights went out. Wagner flipped the key over a couple of times, as though he could physically crank the motor, but nothing happened, and they coasted through darkness as silent and still as some ancient battlefield.

"There!" said Blondie, pointing ahead and to the right.

Lucy followed his finger, but saw nothing but the dim black outline of the rolling horizon. Nevertheless, she had the feeling that there was something both abhorrent and invisible hovering in the air.

Wagner nodded, slamming the truck over onto the shoulder. He opened the door and climbed out, extending his hand to Lucy, and Blondie reached behind the seat for the two rifles, handing one to Wagner. The three of them slipped across the road, dropped down over the shoulder and into the drainage ditch. Wagner lifted Lucy across the fence, and Blondie leapt over it as though it were a root in his path.

"What's happening?" whispered Lucy.

Wagner slapped his hand over her mouth, making a yapping motion with his fingers and a slashing movement across his throat. She hoped he was telling her that if she talked she'd get herself killed rather than that *he* was going to do it. He took off across the furrows, and she followed, Blondie bringing up the rear.

They ran for perhaps two hundred yards before Wagner spun and dropped onto his belly, pulling her down beside him breathing hard. The dank odor of damp earth filled her lungs as she stared back toward the distant silhouette of the truck. Slowly, a misty darkness enveloped the vehicle, as though the surrounding gloom were gathering in one place and devouring it, and several figures slipped through the shadows, moving stealthily back and forth like hounds on a scent.

"How did they follow us here?" she whispered.

Wagner slapped his hand over her mouth again. The two men lay tensed against her as the dark figures dropped down into the ditch and approached the fence.

But Lucy could feel them all around. She sensed their presence through her fingertips—buried in the cool, damp soil—through her body—pressed tightly against the earth. It was a terrifying feeling, one that Lucy knew deep down had haunted her since childhood. The same sense of the earth around her that had overwhelmed her in the forest outside Merly.

But there was something new as well.

Before, she had sensed danger in the footsteps that dogged their path through the forest outside of Merly. Here she sensed something far worse. A foulness, a desecration. A wrongness that she had never experienced before.

She glanced at Wagner and saw something new in his eyes.

Fear.

Harry Waldrip's house sat in the nicest section of Chevy Chase surrounded by a high privacy fence. He didn't like strangers coming around, and as far as Harry was concerned *everyone* was a stranger. Having been employed by the CIA for twenty-two years, paranoia was an integral part of his life. Harry worked in Middle Eastern Intel. He spoke Arabic, Hebrew, and five regional dialects, and although he had never once been overseas, he knew the geography and the demography better than any Oxford-educated native. Unbeknownst to his friends and coworkers, he also worked for a much older and more far-reaching organization known only as Qedem Melech, and that was where Harry's true loyalties lay—if *true* or *loyalty* had been words in any way applicable to Harry.

He had joined the organization while he was still a fat, pimply college geek. Qedem Melech appreciated Harry's talents and his proclivities. It was they who got him his first interview at the Agency and assured his rise in the infrastructure. It was they who periodically made installment payments to his numbered account in Zurich, and although Harry never asked, he suspected Qedem Melech had a great many people like him working in Washington and other world capitals. And finally, it was Qedem Melech who supplied the not-so-willing subjects for his periodic dabblings in Satanic worship. Harry didn't really believe in Satan, but he did enjoy the trappings of the ritual and his power over his victims.

Unlike Aldrich Ames—and except for his infrequent dabblings in demonology—Harry lived simply, well within the means of a government employee of his pay level. Neither his bitch of a wife nor his faggot son—who now stayed mostly in the apartment over the garage so that Harry hardly ever had to lay eyes on him—knew anything about his extracurricular activities. One day soon, though, he was going to withdraw that hefty lump sum, then have an accident on his boat. His body was never going to be found. But his spirit was going to be partying in a lovely villa in Brazil. Rio had the raunchiest bars and the hottest whores on earth, and he was going to be able to afford all he wanted of both. And one or two prostitutes a year going missing wouldn't be anything new in Rio.

Unfortunately, upon awakening that morning Harry had discovered a problem with his vision. The light in the bedroom was so bright it pierced his eyes like laser fire. In desperation he'd stumbled into the den and draped a blanket over the one window there. That helped, but still too much light filtered in, so he'd stapled the edges of the damned thing to the wall, then stuffed magazines against the bottom of the door to shut out the glare from the hall. Then he'd called in sick and poured himself a stiff drink.

But the bourbon tasted like french-fried crap, and he'd tossed it into the sink in disgust. He'd lain for hours on the sofa after that, covering his eyes with a pillow, feeling as though worms were eating his flesh and wondering if he was suffering from some unknown disease or whether perhaps the shitheads in the Agency had decided to use him as a guinea pig for some new kind of chemical weapon. When Marie had arrived home from work at the hospital and pounded on the door to ask what he wanted for supper he'd screamed at her.

"I don't give a shit! Just cook something."

"Nice talking to you, too," she said, stomping off down the hall. At two hundred pounds Marie stomped pretty good, but he could still take her in a free-for-all.

After a while he sensed the sun going down outside and began to feel even funnier all over, crawly like, as though his bones had turned into snakes feeding on the worms. Rolling over on the sofa, he started to shout for Marie, but couldn't seem to get his voice to work. He stared at a half-empty can of beer he didn't remember opening, and lifted it, sniffing. It smelled incredibly strong, as though every hop were exploding right inside the can.

He'd heard of the Agency drugging people or poisoning them to eliminate problems. Maybe they *knew* about his extracurricular activity. Maybe they'd given him some new drug to drive him crazy so they could put him away rather than eliminating him. Or maybe it would just be easier to do him once they had him in custody in some Agency-sponsored nuthouse.

When the sun was just a bad memory, Harry ripped the blanket from the window, tossed it onto the floor, and stared out into a night that still seemed so unusually bright he could barely stand to look at the stars. Leaving the solitude of the den at last, he paced down the hall like a caged coyote. Marie was nowhere to be seen. If he'd pissed her off enough, she'd probably gone to her whore sister's and wouldn't be home until the next day. The whole place was silent, empty.

Even with the crawliness inside, he felt a lot better now that the fucking sun had finally disappeared, better than he ever had in his life, in fact, and he noticed that although all the lights in the house were off, he could see just fine, and his sense of smell seemed to be heightened as well, although *what* he was smelling he couldn't tell.

He also discovered that he was ravenously hungry. But as soon as he stepped into the kitchen and sniffed the indefinable odors wafting through it he knew he would not be able to eat anything that came out of there. He glanced into a pot Marie had left on the stove and saw that it held pork and beans, usually his favorite meal. But for some reason the beans—which looked all right and could only have been out for a few hours at most—smelled rotten and disgusting. He was going to have to go elsewhere to satisfy the gnawing in his guts.

Finally, he slipped out into the night, breathing in deeply of scents he had never experienced before, wild smells laden with the promise of food. He began to run, his head tipped back, sniffing loudly.

The exotic odors that drifted in the air excited him in ways that he had never realized he could be excited, and the sense of being a hunting creature was almost as lustful as sex. He loped through Chevy Chase only vaguely aware that there were no lights on in any of the houses, that no cars drove along the streets, that no one but he was on the sidewalks or lawns. Twice he followed the tantalizing aroma into houses, breaking in the doors or crashing through windows, unmindful of broken glass. But in each case he found that the odor was residual and whatever it was he lusted after was gone.

On the outskirts of town he came to a small, two-story brick colonial with a wide stone walk and the odor there drove him into a frenzy akin to the final moments before orgasm. He raced to the door, striking it with his shoulder so hard the frame shattered, and he stood in the foyer, breathing in deeply of the aroma that propelled him into madness. Once again he noticed that the darkness held no shadows for him. He could see down the length of the hall-way as though all the lights were on.

"Bill? Is that you? What happened?"

The woman's terrified voice intensified Harry's lust. He clenched and unclenched his fists, discovering that his nails daggered into his palms. But he enjoyed the feeling. He strode down the hall just as the woman appeared in a door-way. The gun in her hand quickened Harry's heart, but he was compelled forward by the hunger, by the smell, by his lust.

"Who are you?" she screamed. "Stay back!"

The gun fired, and for an instant the flash blinded Harry, scorching his corneas. But the shot went wild, and he slapped at her with an open hand, intending to force her back into the bedroom. Instead the nails that had pinched his palms slashed through her throat like hot wires through soft cheese, and a gush of blood exploded in his face. As she started to collapse to the floor he caught her in his arms, reveling in the heat of her against him, realizing immedi-ately what the smell was that had been driving him mad.

Blood. Human blood.

He buried his face in her throat, drinking in great draughts, gorging as the last of life drained from her.

He left her lying there and stood for a moment on the front porch, newfound strength surging through him. Fi-nally, he leaned his head back and howled, and the cry elicited an answer somewhere in the distance.

After hours of stumbling blindly through the woods, the very real possibility of dying of exposure finally overshadowed Dylan's fear of the two killers, and he decided he had to chance the trail again. But the longer he searched for the logging road, the less certain he became of its location. The night was deadly dark, the trees and lowering clouds draining the life from the stars. The cold had taken its toll, and his face was cut from numerous run-ins with unseen branches. He remembered reading somewhere that freezing was a peaceful way to die. All he had to do was lie down and go to sleep and everything would be over. But he wondered how long it would take before the pain in his cheeks and hands would ease, whether he'd stop shivering first or simply fade into eternal oblivion shaking like an unbalanced blender.

As he crunched through the snow beneath tall firs, he heard the unmistakable sound of a snowmobile, and he saw light flickering through the trees. So he'd found the trail. Unfortunately, it looked like the killers were back. But where had they come up with snowmobiles? He glanced at his watch—1:00 A.M. Who else would be out riding at *this* time of night?

He tripped, and the gritty snow pounded into his face, ice crystals barely stinging his skin. The last of his strength was draining, and he realized that even if it was the killers on the snowmobile, it didn't matter. He was going to die unless he got help in the next few minutes. He struggled weakly to his feet and half trudged, half crawled to the logging road.

By the time the one headlight illuminated the woods around him in a blinding yellow glow, his body was no longer shivering. It was convulsing. In a dream he heard his name being called and realized that it must be the killers after all.

"Mr. Barnes!"

The voice echoed around his head, buzzing with the rattle of the snowmobile motor and the crunch of the track on the hard-packed snow. He closed his eyes, praying to sleep and never wake up. Surely that was a more peaceful way to die than a bullet through the brain. Or maybe they'd just leave him here and not shoot him. Why waste a bullet? If only the damned snowmobile would go on past and let him be, he could rest. Just a little rest.

"Mr. Barnes!"

The voice was closer, but the engine noise faded as though the vehicle had left without the driver. Wasn't that funny?

"Shit," said the voice. Rough hands rolled him over onto his back, and he saw the silhouette of a man. He tried to protect himself, slashing at the man's throat, but his muscles wouldn't obey him.

The little man slapped Dylan's hands aside easily. "What are you doing? Calm down!"

It took a moment before Dylan realized that maybe the guy wasn't one of the killers after all.

"Can you stand?"

Dylan thought that was a funny thing to ask. He was standing, wasn't he?

The man shook him hard. "Help me!"

Dylan felt himself being lifted roughly to his feet. He tried to stagger along, and the two of them collapsed together across the snowmobile seat. The little man rolled out from under Dylan, wrestling him into a seated position against a bar on the rear of the machine. Dylan laughed, and the man smiled.

"Hysteria," the guy muttered, wrapping Dylan in a blanket and securing him to the bar with bungee cords. "But at least you still have a little energy left in you. I've got to get you to someplace warm and soon."

"Dylan Barnes," said Dylan, unable to raise his hand because of the bungee cords. That set off another round of laughter.

"My name's Crank," said the little man, grinning mischievously.

Dylan frowned. "Thought you said it was hysteria."

"Just a nickname," said Crank.

"Funny," said Dylan.

Crank climbed onto the machine and revved it up. Twisting on the seat, he took off the woolen cap he was wearing and pulled it over Dylan's head. Dylan felt the machine roaring to life under him and realized that Crank was fighting it around and back up the hill.

"Where . . . where you going?" he sputtered. Crank didn't hear him over the roar of the machine, so he shouted. His quavering voice came out in a telegraphic stutter.

"Back to my van," shouted Crank, nodding ahead.

"Tried to kill me," said Dylan.

"Who?"

"Men . . . killed police chief."

To Dylan's surprise Crank nodded as though he knew all about it.

Dylan was thankful for the thin blanket that blocked the wind, even though it seemed to do little to cut his inner chill. When they reached the clearing the little man stared for a long moment out across the wide-open area.

"Whatcha waiting for?" asked Dylan.

Crank made a signal for him to keep quiet.

The grinning skull of the moon nipped at the clouds, the flat snow lit haphazardly by its dismal glow.

"Whatever," muttered Crank. He lifted his chin toward the far side of the clearing, goosing the machine at the same time.

Dylan felt the bar press hard into his back. He tried to lock his legs against Crank, but they were shaking too violently, and he was grateful for the bungee cords. They were a third of the way across the clearing when he thought he saw movement off to his right. A dark tunnel had been carved through the night itself, and a hazy shape undulated inside the darkness.

"Crank," he said. But the roar of the machine, the hiss of the wind, and his own weakness diluted his voice. He managed to nudge Crank with a quivering right knee.

"Crank," he said, louder.

They were halfway across when the moon finally gnawed its way through the overcast and spotlighted them like rats in a flashlight beam. Crank glanced back, squinting into the darkness.

So it isn't a dream, thought Dylan as Crank gave the machine more gas.

Dylan's fear was a jagged icicle. As he watched, a giant creature cloaked in darkness raced across the clearing. The thing was nearly as tall as the trees and fast as a speeding automobile. In no time it was almost upon them, and they were only three-quarters of the way to the tree line. As it drew closer Dylan could see its eyes, illuminated with a flickering inner light, hear the crunch of its giant feet on the hard snow, feel its panting breath, hear the all-too-familiar word echoing in his brain.

Rantasas!

The word was more than a cry inside his head, it was the foul touch of something *willing* its way in, clawing at his mind.

"Oh, my God," he rasped.

"Hang on," said Crank, leaning forward, and punching the machine hard.

Just ahead lay a barely defined snowmobile trail, wedged between a stand of birch and a couple of bent balsam firs. The headlight made it look like an inviting hidey-hole, but the thing behind them didn't seem like it was going to be deterred by a few trees. Dylan wanted to lean forward, wanted to shove his body against Crank's back, to try to pass under the threat of the thing, to miss its giant grasping hands with their gleaming black talons the size of butcher knives. But he was strapped bolt upright like a virgin being sacrificed to a fucking dragon. He could feel the thing now, breathing down the back of his neck. He could feel it inside him as well, spreading like a virulent organism, weakening his will, stilling his heart.

"Jesus," he panted. "Jesus, Jesus, Jesus."

His body was no longer shivering. It was so tense he could barely breathe to curse. He imagined the razor-sharp claws slicing through his neck, leaving Crank blasting off through the night, not realizing that he was hauling a headless corpse. The hidey-hole was still ten yards away. Cold wet breath surrounded him. Claws slipped around his throat.

And then they were wrapped in the embrace of the surrounding trees. Overhead a skein of needle-thin branches diced the slivers of moonlight into a shower of diamonds, and they dropped away into a twisting roller-coaster ride. They were miles into the woods before Crank finally stopped, both of them staring silently down the dark trail behind them, panting like a couple of winded foxes. Nothing moved, and nothing the size of the shadow could have possibly made it down the heavily overgrown trail without tearing the forest to ribbons.

Dylan shook his head. "What the hell was that thing?"

"What thing?" said Crank, making a whistling sound through his teeth.

"Come on! You saw that thing in the clearing."

Crank gave him a strange look. "I don't know what you're talking about. I felt nervous. So I punched it out of there. I've stayed alive listening to my hunches. What did you see?"

Dylan shook his head, frowning, the cold seeping back into him. The night pressed in on him again, as though the darkness were alive.

Finally, Crank revved the machine again and slammed it on down the trail.

As Father Anton Remedios awakened, his mind returned slowly to his surroundings, and he listened intently. The complex in which he had been held for four long years was filled with sinners like himself—many of whom were awake at all hours—and even in the dead of night the warders could often be heard, going about their business. But all the other inmates along the corridor seemed to be sound asleep. Even the ancient nun who believed that extraterrestrials had ravaged her, then returned again and again to take her against her will, was oddly subdued, her incessant shouts less pronounced than usual.

Remedios lay on his back, staring up into the darkness

where his overhead light should have burned—as it did constantly in its little steel cage—imagining the white ceiling overhead, wondering what could have awakened him, and why the power had gone out. Even the battery-powered emergency lights were not working.

Eventually he noticed that the crazy priest who never stopped muttering Hail Marys must also have drifted off. The man *did* sleep occasionally, after all, having to recharge for yet another day of madness. But seldom were both the priest and the nun quiet at the same time, and tonight—as the old woman croaked slowly into silence—the ward became *truly* as still as death.

Sometimes—on those rare occasions when this floor grew peaceful enough—the wind could be heard even here in the deepest depths of the asylum, raising the pressure in the heating and cooling ducts, puffing out into the cells like a flatulent old woman. But there was no wind.

Remedios slipped to the floor in the middle of the room and sat perfectly still. The cell was so small he could reach out with either hand and touch the hard fiberglass of his bunk or the cool concrete wall. The walls now were cold indeed, for, although the building was large and stored heat like a brick pulled from a fire, the winter outside was slowly creeping in. He realized then that he had not felt warm air running through the heat ducts since he had awakened, either.

In the darkness, while he waited to discover what had caused the sudden power outage—fearing that he already knew—he tested himself against the cold, sitting in only his cotton shirt and pants on the frigid floor, his feet burning from the chill, but he would not allow himself to feel it. He could will the pain away. He breathed deeply through his nose, relaxing his body, forgetting the cold, the loneliness, and the darkness all around.

Suddenly the woman began to moan loudly, then to call out in that childlike cry she used almost constantly.

"*Qui Vient la?*" she wailed. "*Sacre bleu!* Where are

you? Who are you? Let us out. For the love of God, let us out! Oh! It's you! I knew you would return, *mon ami*."

Then the crazy priest awakened and took up the cry, but there was no sense to his words, just a guttural, animal noise.

"No!" screamed the nun. "Don't leave me! Don't leave me again!"

And then for a blessed moment there was total silence once more, the priest stopped in midcry, the nun struck dumb. Remedios leaned toward the door.

"Who are you?" the woman cried, shattering the silence again. "You aren't him! You don't belong here! *Grace à dieu!* What did you do to the moaner?"

The woman's words skittered under Remedios's door on tiny rat feet, and he wanted to shout at the crazy old Carmelite to be quiet lest she draw the thing back to her. He could feel the presence in the corridor now as he slid across the slick cement to lean against the steel door. Whatever was in the hallway was no alien come back to have its way with a deranged nun. It was a hunter prowling the night. And Remedios knew in his heart of hearts that *he* was its prey.

There was a time that he would have taken refuge in prayer. But that time was long since past and he knew there was no salvation there. Whatever lay on the other side of the door would not be held at bay by superstition.

"Where are you?" shouted the nun. "Answer me, demon!"

He could tell by the quaver in her voice that she sensed *something*, a wrongness to whatever it was she was seeing out there. It touched her madness but could not terrify her enough to still her cries.

"God damn you!" screamed the nun.

Before the dark blanket of silence dropped over the ward again, Remedios heard the ominous click of the integrated system of bolts—worked by a heavy lever down the cellblock—that locked the steel doors on the other side of the corridor. The thing had opened both the lunatic old priest's and the woman's cells. Remedios stared at the small cruciform keyhole in his own door. All the rooms on his side of the hall had been built years before the cells across from them and used the old-style locks, and that thing in the corridor would not be able to open them without finding the warder or his heavy set of keys. At least Remedios *hoped* it would not be able to if it had not already.

He pressed himself even closer to the door and—against his will and convictions—he began to pray silently, a prayer that he would pay for later by biting and clawing his flesh. For he prayed the thing would be glutted with the woman and old man and not feel the need to cross the corridor.

His fingertips stroked the smooth steel of the door like antennae. The proximity of the thing beyond the thin barrier of the icy metal repulsed him, and he quietly withdrew his hands and head from the door, suddenly certain that everyone else in the ward was dead. Outside the cell lay the sinister silence of a morgue, but he knew the thing was prowling the corridors again, not sated but made more ravenous by the kills.

He thought he saw movement at the spot on the door where the viewing window should be. But he knew that was impossible. At that time of night, with all the power out, there was pitch blackness throughout the ward, no reference by which to gauge movement. But against his will he rose shakily to his feet, lured by the merest hint of light.

Suddenly, an even more mind-numbing terror drifted over him. The movement that he had sensed before was an ink-dark eyelid, opening then closing over a gleaming red eye, and he felt as though he were already bound for perdition, only waiting for the creature on the other side of the glass to pronounce the stop. His heart threatened to explode out of his chest, and a pain struck him there like a knife. He looked one last instant into the depths of that terrible eye, then collapsed to the icy floor, gasping for breath and clutching his ribs.

Consciousness mercifully fled.

When he awakened the cell was still blindingly black.

But the red orb no longer hung in the little viewing window. He rose silently, wondering what was happening in the outside world, where his warders had gone, if any of his fellow lunatics survived. The thing might have departed in the night, leaving him alive, but he knew it would return in its own good time to claim him. Or perhaps it had merely murdered all the others and left him there to die, alone.

Still, the change was not yet complete or else he would surely be dead. That meant that there was hope, meager as it might be in the tiny chamber cut off from the world. But even that feeble promise lay in others. He didn't delude himself into believing there was any way he could burst the heavy steel door on his own. But, even though he chided himself for such superstitious foolishness, he grasped the heavy door handle and pulled, wondering if perhaps like John the Baptist he would simply walk out of his prison. But it was locked and solid as ever. No great and all-powerful God was going to release him.

In frustration Father Remedios fell to his knees and began steadily pounding his forehead against the painted concrete wall until warm blood ran into his eyes, until he tasted salt on his lips, until his mind once more went mercifully blank.

Dylan and Crank reached a side road just as the moon slipped through the clouds again, and Dylan felt naked in its glare. Instead of following the narrow lane, Crank weaseled the snowmobile back into the trees and climbed off, disappearing into the woods. A few minutes later a big blue van came roaring up the trail.

"Hang on," said Crank, as he hurried to help Dylan into the van. "We got to get something wet and warm in you before your insides just shut down."

Sleep tugged at Dylan's eyelids. He had enough of his wits about him to know that he was in the last throes of hypothermia, and he'd better snap out of it. But all he wanted was to close his eyes and drift off.

Eventually he became aware that he had been in the van for quite a while, wrapped in a blanket. There was a warm cup of coffee in his hands, and the van was meandering down another stretch of country road he didn't recognize. He stared dully into the night, listening to the reassuring hum of the motor, the fan blowing a warm breeze toward his face.

"Where did you come from?" asked Dylan, hugging the blanket tighter around him.

"Vermont."

Dylan stared at the strange little man for a long moment, taking in the hard face, the eyes that looked as though they'd seen things Dylan didn't want to ask about. "You didn't just happen on to me, did you?"

"No."

"Who are you?"

Crank chuckled. "So you've forgotten our introduction. You can call me Crank. Everyone else does."

"But what are you doing here? Why were you looking for me?"

"It's my job."

"You're some kind of cop?" said Dylan.

"Not hardly. Are you warming up?"

"Starting to. Where are we?"

"Way the Hell and gone from Kansas," said Crank, grinning. "What do you know about the people who were after you?"

"Not a damned thing. Except I'm sure they're the same people who robbed my wife's grave. That's how this all started. They took the casket and everything. That excavator in the clearing was used to steal it. But Ronnie's casket wasn't there."

"How did you know the machinery was there?"

Dylan gave him a sheepish look. "I spotted a chain across the road that didn't look right. I just had a feeling about the place."

"A feeling?" said Crank, staring at him strangely again. At least it seemed like a strange look to Dylan. But then he reminded himself that *everyone* had been looking at him strangely lately.

"I don't know," he said. "It sounds silly."

"The machinery *was* there."

Dylan nodded.

Crank chewed his lip, still studying the road again. "Do you have any oddball talents, Mr. Barnes? I mean, other than *sensing* things?"

"I'm a karate instructor."

"You any good?"

Dylan shrugged. "I'm a *san dan.* A third-degree black belt."

"I didn't come out here to get my ass shot off bringing in a karate expert."

"What did you come out here for?"

"To save your ass. If, that is, I can get us out of town alive."

Crank glanced at a map in his lap and autodialed his phone. When someone finally answered he sighed. "Glad to hear you're still around. I got the package. I'll meet you on Route 5. Know a good spot?"

The phone hummed with an unintelligible answer, and Crank nodded, listening for a second, then clicked the phone shut.

"Who are we going to meet?" asked Dylan.

"A friend. We're going to hunker down for a while and take things slow and careful."

Dylan glanced around but still couldn't find his bearings. "Seems like I've been lost for days."

"This is Route 5, headed into Needland. According to Baxter there should be a mechanic's shop ahead."

As Crank was speaking a bright red light lit the sky, followed almost immediately by the sound of a huge explosion in the distance and the pulsing glow of a large fire.

"What the heck is that?" said Dylan.

"More than likely Baxter," said Crank, grinning. "Buying us some time."

When Crank tucked the van in behind the large cedar-shingled shack that served as the local auto repair, there was a ten-year-old Chevy sedan idling at the far end of the parking lot. He pulled up behind it, humming a tune that sounded like "The Battle Hymn of the Republic."

"What are we doing?" asked Dylan, staring at the back of the man's head in the car ahead.

"Waiting," said Crank.

"For what?"

"For Baxter to decide whether he needs to kill us or not," said Crank.

"Are you serious?"

"Relax," said Crank, nodding toward Dylan's window. Dylan glanced to his right and nearly leapt out of his skin. The tall, gray-haired killer he recognized from the clearing was staring directly at him.

"Roll down your window," said Crank.

Dylan did as he was told. Very slowly. If the man made any sudden moves he was ready to reach out and clip him in the throat with the tip of his fingers. Hard enough and the guy would be dead before he hit the ground. Out of the corner of his eye he noticed that the *man* in the sedan had never moved. It was a cardboard cutout, a decoy.

"Have a little trouble?" asked Crank.

"Yeah. Reese got killed."

"Too bad," said Crank. "Get in."

Baxter slumped in the backseat, and Crank pulled around the garage and back onto the road.

"What happened?" asked Crank.

"We were waiting halfway down the hill," said Baxter. "Hoping Mr. Barnes here would make it back onto the trail."

"So you could shoot me?" said Dylan, glancing from Crank to Baxter.

"Baxter's on your side," said Crank.

"He murdered the chief of police and another cop," said Dylan.

"So you *were* in the clearing," said Baxter.

"I was there," said Dylan, his hand still on the door handle.

"Those cops were there to grab you, or probably worse, Mr. Barnes," said Baxter. "I couldn't let that happen."

"You expect me to believe the chief of police and the deputy were out there to kill me?"

"Maybe. Maybe they only wanted to take you into custody. But it wouldn't be the kind of custody you might expect."

"Where to?" said Crank.

"Take a right out of the parking lot and head toward town."

"You sure?"

"Shouldn't be a problem right now," said Baxter, and Crank nodded.

At the outskirts of Needland the tips of giant flames licked the sky.

"And that is?" said Crank.

"The gas station. I'm afraid it's a bit of a mess."

"You blew up the gas station?" said Dylan.

"Don't lose any sleep over it. The new owner was just as bad as the police."

"What the hell are you talking about?" said Dylan.

"What I'm talking about is the fact that eight out of ten people in this town seem to be working for the bad guys, Mr. Barnes. And I can assure you the kind of people we're dealing with wouldn't shed a tear about eliminating you like scrap paper once they were done with you. Haven't you noticed how many new people there were in town over the past few months?"

Dylan shook his head. "I haven't been paying attention, I guess."

"That fire's a good enough diversion for the *real* locals," said Crank. "But what about our friends?"

"We're going to slip in and out of town like bunnies," said Baxter. "And this van shouldn't attract their attention."

"What happened to Reese?"

"We got jumped by six or seven of them when we decided to drive down the hill from the clearing to wait for Mr. Barnes on the main road. If Reese hadn't spotted them, I'd be dead, too. We took out a few of them, but the car was shot to pieces. I ran it to death a couple of miles farther up the road and whipped into a guy's driveway, where I liberated that old sedan."

"We got no company so far," said Crank.

"Too bad," said Baxter, looking back over his shoulder. "I wouldn't mind meeting a few of the fuckers on my own terms."

"You'll probably get a chance," said Crank, fiddling with the radio knob. "But right now we need to hole up."

"You won't get anything on the radio," said Baxter. "Everything went to static about twenty minutes ago."

"Where to?" said Crank, frowning.

Baxter pointed down a side road. "Follow this. Five miles up there's a gravel lane marked Songo Pond. I scouted out an empty camp there. We should be able to hole up for a while."

Snow was starting to fall, and the darkness seemed too close, too immediate outside the window, as though it were not just the absence of light, but something palpable, something toxic and deep, and Dylan was sinking into it, out of control.

The stillness of the fields all around Lucy and her companions reminded her of the silence the day she had discovered her father's journal, the way the cabin had closed in on her, the air too thick to breathe. Wagner pressed her head back toward the earth, but not before she was able to glance over her shoulder and see more figures creeping through the woods behind them, sealing off their escape. If they were about to be attacked, she wanted to see what was going on. She could feel the pulse at Wagner's wrist where it rested gently now against the nape of her neck. Blondie was so still beside her he might have been a corpse.

Who were the people slipping stealthily around them? They seemed more like specters floating through the darkness than men. But more than the residual terror that she absorbed from Wagner and Blondie, she sensed something terribly *wrong* with these people. They were silent as any professional killers on the prowl, but as they drew closer she noticed they moved more like predatory beasts. And though she could see no weapons silhouetted in the feeble starlight, they radiated a cold determination. She wanted to scream at Wagner to do something. Instead she lay as still as death, like her two protectors, slowly giving in to the weight of Wagner's hand. If it was time to run, Wagner would tell her. But she dearly wanted to run right now, because she sensed stark terror in the two men who had faced death for her, who had guarded her with their lives for days. They were the bravest men she had ever met—the only men she had ever had the slightest inclination to trust—and their fear swelled her own. Her head sagged a millimeter deeper into the crusty soil, as she breathed quietly between pursed lips.

Finally, as more thick clouds rolled in and the sky above folded itself into total darkness, Wagner pulled her against him, bringing his lips so close to hers she thought at first he was going to kiss her.

"Don't move," he whispered, reaching across her to tap Blondie.

As the terrible sense of impending doom became overpowering, Lucy could feel her senses seeping into the ground again, and this time she did not even try to repress it. The earth around her became an extension of her own body, and she could feel heavy feet pressing down on the rich clay with every foul step, defiling the very soil with their touch. She knew then that these things hunting them in the night were definitely not men. And whatever they were, there were nine of them. Three in front, approaching from the fenceline. Four in the woods two on each side. Two behind, slinking up silently. With each footfall the feeling that they were not stepping on the ground but on a part of *her* grew stronger, and she shuddered.

"Relax," whispered Wagner.

The things crept ever closer, and now her urge to run was almost overwhelming, but she knew there was no escape. They were going to have to kill all of these beasts or die here in this godforsaken field, and she could not believe that Wagner and Blondie continued to lie so stoically beside her.

Lucy hesitated.

"Nine," she whispered back, giving him the location of each of the attackers. She could barely make out his eyes in the darkness, but when she nodded at him he nodded back.

"Go!" shouted Wagner suddenly, rising to his knees and snatching up his rifle just as Blondie did the same. Carbine fire rattled across the fields, and Lucy was blinded by the muzzle flashes. As she heard Wagner eject an empty clip and rack in another, she squeezed the damp earth tightly in her hands, counting the dark beasts falling to earth, feeling their blood desecrating the soil far more than their mere touch had.

Six down.

But the other three weren't running away. Two were still staggering forward. One had dropped flat, dragging itself toward them like a venomous snake. And it was close.

"Blondie!" she screamed, over the roar of the guns. "Behind you! On the ground!"

Wagner shot one of the two coming at them from the woods, but then his firing pin clicked on an empty chamber again, and the second creature was almost upon him. Lucy jerked the Beretta out of her hip holster, and the gun barked again and again, the flashes spotlighting the last falling beast as she emptied the fourteen-round clip into its chest and head. And then the night was silent except for the clack of Wagner slamming another clip into his rifle.

"Is that all of them?" he asked after a moment. She glanced at him, realizing he was speaking to her and not Blondie.

"I think so," she said, her voice shaky.

Suddenly two of the creatures began to pull themselves slowly to their knees. Wagner fired again and again, but it was not until Blondie hit both of them in the head that they dropped and stopped moving. She leaned to inspect one of the hideous creatures. It was dressed like a man. It had a head and two arms and two legs like a man. But the eyes were crimson orbs, and canine teeth as long as scalpel blades peeked out of the thing's lips, which were drawn back in a death rictus, and the body seemed to have swollen like a day-old corpse, ripping through shirt and pants. What appeared to be jellylike scales covered most of the exposed skin.

"What are they, some kind of mutants?" she whispered, glancing back around the field, no longer trusting her feeling that the things were dead.

"Something like that," said Wagner, spitting into the dirt.

"They're all dead," muttered Blondie, giving one of the things a good kick. "Why aren't they changing?"

Wagner stared at the beast and shrugged. "That might be just a myth."

"What do you mean, 'changing'?" asked Lucy, glancing from Blondie to Wagner.

"Come on," said Wagner, nudging her back toward the road.

He hurried her over to the fence, helping her across as Blondie reconnoitered. They all met at the truck, and Wagner turned to Blondie.

"Try to start her up."

Blondie leapt into the truck, but the only sound from the vehicle was the clicking of the key in the ignition. "It still won't start," he said, leaning out the door and shrugging. "And the lights and radio are dead."

"Great," said Wagner.

Lucy closed her eyes and tried to feel the ground again the way she had only moments before, but the oneness with the earth was gone now, and she felt weaker and more exhausted than she ever had in her life.

"How did they do that to the truck?" she asked.

Wagner shook his head, glancing nervously back down the road. "No telling. *If* they had anything to do with it. I guess we'd better be walking out of here."

"What are you going to tell somebody if they stop for us?" asked Lucy, glancing at their mud-covered clothing and their rifles.

Wagner shrugged. "We're hunters and our truck broke down."

"We aren't dressed for it. It's the middle of the night, and I don't think it's hunting season."

"We'll think of something."

"You're lying to me. I'm not going anywhere until you tell me what's going on."

"We can discuss this later," said Wagner, reaching for her arm.

Lucy jerked away and stared at Wagner for a long minute. Then she turned and ran up the road through the darkness.

Of course there was nowhere for her to go, no one else for her to trust. But she had to get away, to feel her legs working, her arms stroking, to feel something *real* again. Her footsteps pounded away in the awful gloom. Cresting a low rise she spotted a small foreign sedan resting in the tall grass of a ditch and she ran to it, desperate to find a way out of this situation. She wrenched open the door, but her heart sank when no overhead light appeared. She could hear Wagner and Blondie trotting up behind her, but she refused to look back, fighting down the tears of frustration, fear, and anger that welled within her. Her hands shook as she leaned against the car.

"What the hell?" said Wagner, staring at the driver's seat where a suit of men's clothes lay bunched. On the floorboards were socks and a pair of suede loafers. He glanced around the fields.

Blondie reached past him and tried the key.

"Dead," he said, shaking his head.

Wagner sighed, trying once again to take Lucy's arm, but again she shook herself free, glaring at him.

"We can't stay here," he said.

She only nodded, wiping her nose on her sleeve as she followed him back up the embankment to the road.

They walked for over an hour and more than eight miles before Wagner stopped. When he glanced at his watch for the third time in ten minutes Lucy asked him what was wrong.

"Busted," he said, glancing around.

They were approaching the outskirts of a suburb of Knoxville. The land was still rolling fields with scattered groves of trees, but there were more homes in the area. Lucy could see three houses ahead on the right-hand side of the road; the left was obscured by forest.

"Mine's dead, too," said Blondie, shaking his wrist.

Lucy frowned, staring at her own watch that showed a black, dead screen. "All the batteries went dead at once? Do you think those *things* did that when they shut the truck down?"

Wagner shrugged, glancing around again nervously. "It'll be dawn any time now. I'd expect we'd be seeing more traffic. There's a major intersection about a half mile ahead. We should be hearing trucks, seeing headlights on the horizon."

Lucy looked around again, noticing just how dark it was. The odds were that someone in one of the few homes they had passed was an early riser or that they had at least a porch fixture that stayed on all the time. But not one light shone, and she knew that with the sky overcast the way it was, the lights of cities or even towns reflected off the sky and could be seen for miles. Yet the heavens were equally flat and gray from horizon to horizon.

"We aren't going to learn anything standing on this back road, and it's a good place to get caught again," said Wagner. "Come on."

When Lucy didn't automatically fall in between him and

Blondie he stopped. She had her arms crossed and a hard look in her eyes.

"Please. Tell me what's going on. What were those things back in the field?"

"We need to get moving," said Wagner.

"Why was Blondie surprised that it hadn't *changed*? What did he mean by that?"

"I promise you you'll get answers soon."

"We've been running around in circles, Wagner. You keep saying you're taking me somewhere so someone *else* can tell me what's going on. Only I've seen the looks you two keep giving each other, and I think the plan has changed, and you don't even know it. Are you telling me that everything that's happened to us in the past few hours was part of some master design?" She noticed Blondie looking at Wagner with raised eyebrows.

"Call them up," she said, nodding toward the bulge in his jacket where he kept his cell phone. "Tell them what's happened and ask for orders."

Wagner sighed, digging out the phone. "It's dead," he said, tossing it into the ditch in disgust. "I'll try calling from the next town."

"What makes you think you'll have any better luck there?"

Blondie turned away when she glanced at him.

Wagner sighed, but before he could speak Lucy hammered on. "I saved your life back there. I saved Blondie's life, too, when I knew that thing was creeping up on him. Did you already know I could do that?"

"Not exactly," said Wagner.

"This is all some experiment," she said. "Isn't it?"

"Experiment?"

She nodded. "The military or some huge corporation trying to create superhumans, maybe. Instead they've created these monsters."

But Wagner shook his head. "No experiment, Lucy. No government agency."

"Who are you, then? What's going on? Don't you think it's time to tell me?"

"Lucy, I promise you'll get some answers. If I can't get through by the time we reach the next town, I'll tell you what I know. Only not here. Not now. We can't chance stopping, and I don't want to talk about it out here in the open."

"What better place could there be? Who's going to hear us here?"

The vaguest promise of dawn tinted the base of the sky. Lucy felt Wagner's hand on her shoulder, and when she glanced back into his eyes they were pleading with her.

"Tell me what's going on, or we go our separate ways," she said.

Wagner nodded, looking past her. "You'd go back down that road? By yourself?"

"I don't want to. But are you telling me it's any more dangerous than going *up* this road with the two of you? Maybe you're leading me into danger, not out of it."

"Do you really believe that?"

She shook her head. "No."

"So?"

"So tell me or here we stay. Unless you want to drag me out of here against my will. And I'll fight you."

He smiled at her.

"All right," she said. "It wouldn't be much of a fight. But you'd still have to take me against my will. Would you do that?"

"No," he said at last, his shoulders sagging. "Lucy, I'm not supposed to—"

"Sir," said Blondie.

Wagner waved at him without looking back. "Lucy, I've been following orders all my life—"

"Sir!" hissed Blondie.

Both Wagner and Lucy followed his fixed stare back down the road. A distant figure slunk out of the haze, moving in their direction.

"Shit," said Wagner, taking the rifle Blondie offered. "Now can we agree to carry on this conversation later?"

"It's probably just someone else who was stranded when their car died like ours did," said Lucy hesitantly. But she knew better than Wagner or Blondie that it was another of the mutant beasts. She could feel the desecration seeping up through the soles of her feet.

"Walking out here at this time of night?" said Wagner, nodding at Blondie to get moving. "Do you want to stick around and ask?"

He placed the rifle stock against his right shoulder and fired. In the distance the figure crumpled to the ground, then climbed to its feet. Wagner fired again, and this time the creature was slower getting up.

"There!" said Blondie, cocking his head toward the trees on the other side of the road. Out of the forest several more silhouettes emerged. But then they disappeared back into the darkness and were gone. It happened so quickly that Lucy wondered if she'd really seen it at all. Over the trees the first dim rays of dawn appeared.

"Coming now?" asked Wagner.

Lucy nodded.

"God help us," muttered Blondie, slinging his rifle.

"I don't believe in God," said Lucy, backing away up the road. She could see more figures slipping through the trees, closer to them.

When Wagner laughed she glanced in his direction.

"God doesn't care what you believe in," he said, turning to shove her gently along ahead of him.

Harry rambled around for hours after feeding with no idea where he was going, only the inexorable feeling that he had to get there. Something *pulled* him forward as if a cable were attached to his spine and drawn out through his belly button. It wasn't like the bloodlust that had erupted earlier, although it had the same sense of inevitability about it, the same feeling of overpowering *need*.

As he'd stumbled through the empty streets, he was sidetracked several times by the smell of more fresh blood. Even though he was sated, his lust kept driving him to kill again and again as long as there was prey. But whenever he strayed too far from the pull he ran into an invisible barrier of pain that sent agony blasting through every inch of his body, and he would fall back, recover slowly, and return to the path like a chastened puppy.

The odd changes in his body continued to pain him, like a churning cauldron of something hot and yet cold at the same time bubbling within him. His bones seemed to have melted into an amorphous mass of cartilage that felt as though it were constantly re-forming itself and growing, pressing against muscle, sinew, and organs in odd places. The talons that had appeared at first as feeble nails had already become hard as iron and razor-sharp even as the woman's blood was drying upon them. But his skin continued to evolve, no longer soft doughy flesh, but slowly molding itself into a chitinous covering resembling black thorny scales.

He knew that his mind was not nearly what it once had been, and his willpower—sadly wanting to begin with—was now all but gone. Although he had fleeting memories of the man he had only recently been, he was beginning to exist on another, more beastly, plateau, and in this strange new world an alien voice spoke to him, as though trying to break through to what was left of his reason, and it felt so *right,* as though he had heard this voice all his life, and *this* were who he had really been all along.

Rantasas!

The word thundered through his head, and he fell to his knees in the middle of the road, clutching his pounding skull as the word echoed again and again.

"*Rantasas!*" he screamed, finding that the strange sounds came easily to his scratchy new vocal cords. "*Rantasas megana moor!*"

Out in the open, against the backdrop of woods and stone fences, the words sounded tinny. But with his acute ears he was certain he had heard echoes of others, just like himself, somewhere in the distance.

Rantasas.

I serve.

Rantasas megana moor.

I serve the Old Ones.

At first Harry thought that the voice was telling him that *it* served the Old Ones. Then he realized that that was only part of the message. The voice echoing in his head was telling him that *he* served the Old Ones, too. When he understood that he felt a swelling of something akin to pride, and he knew that there was nothing better in the entire world than to be a servant of the Old Ones, and that by serving he would be fulfilling a destiny that he had never even dreamed of before. And best of all, he knew that as a servant, he would be well fed.

He was twenty-five miles from Chevy Chase before he became winded and had to rest, finding himself staring up a narrow lane between overgrown stone pillars. Ahead he could smell fresh blood, and something else. He sniffed his own arm where the scales had now hardened like steel plates, then sniffed the air. There were others of his own kind up there.

A wrought-iron sign crossed over the road, and Harry discovered that he had trouble making sense of letters that he believed he should be able to read easily. When he finally puzzled out the words he repeated them several times, unable to find any more meaning in them than he had the letters that created them.

"Sacred Light," he muttered over and over, padding on down the long, winding drive.

Periodically Dylan checked the window that had the best view of the long, winding driveway. The snow that had started after midnight had buried their tire tracks, and Crank's van was undercover in a shed beside the cabin. There was no way to trace them to this hideout that Dylan could think of, but the storm was clearing and the day lightening. He stepped out onto the porch, glancing up at the metal flue. The gravity-fed oil stove was running clean and not sending up a telltale plume of soot.

So far he had weaseled little real information out of either Crank or Baxter, but he had been able to infer that Crank was at least nominally in charge. They treated Dylan like a very important or dangerous person—one whom neither cared to have out of sight for any length of time—and Dylan began to wonder if maybe *they* were the ones who were crazy. Baxter had murdered the chief and his assistant, and now he and Crank claimed that basically the whole town of Needland had been taken over by people intent on doing Dylan bodily harm at the very least. But what evidence did they have? There were two dead cops and what was left of the gas station and for all Dylan knew someone had already tied him to the men who had done the crimes.

But there had been people watching him in Needland. He was sure of it. And the chief and the other cop had never *felt* right from the beginning. But you couldn't go on *feelings*. He needed answers and neither man was giving him any. His best bet was going to be to wait for the first chance and give himself up to the closest authorities.

But an inner voice kept urging him to take things slow, to bide his time. He felt as though he were inside a giant clock that he could almost hear ticking, and he knew that when it stopped the alarm that sounded was going to be impossibly loud and deadly. He couldn't get the image of the darkness inside his house, the same darkness he was certain had attacked them in the clearing, out of his head. The same voice said that somehow, impossible as it might sound, the darkness, and the nightmares, and these men were all connected.

But he still couldn't even remember what the nightmares were about, although he seemed to be recalling more than he ever had before, brief snippets of Ronnie's voice, a darkened room, cold sweat. What if they weren't just nightmares but some terrible memory that he had blanked out? What if the thing in his house, in the clearing, wasn't a figment of his fevered imagination? And what if he hadn't been sleepwalking all those nights? He'd awakened each time with the feeling of somehow having *shifted* from one place to another without actually walking. He could still conjure up the nauseous twisting in the bottom of his gut that each odd nocturnal sojourn had caused. He felt as though he were sliding closer and closer to the brink of an answer that he feared to discover, and reality and madness both seemed to hold their own dangers.

According to the clock over the sink, the power had gone out around two o'clock. That wasn't too surprising with the heavy snow still falling. But all their watches had stopped, cell phones were dead, and the batteries in the car and Crank's snowmobile had failed as well.

"I read somewhere that an electromagnetic pulse will cause power loss," mused Dylan.

Baxter glanced at Crank, but Crank turned away.

"A pulse big enough to shut down all the power around here would require a detonation large enough to level every tree and building for twenty miles," said Baxter. "We're right in line for the traffic pattern from Bangor International. This sky is always webbed with contrails. I haven't seen any planes this morning."

"Are you saying that the power is out *everywhere*?" asked Dylan.

Crank shoved past Baxter, heading for the door. Dylan noticed that he was humming "The Battle Hymn of the Republic" again. He'd been doing it all morning, and the unceasing tune was getting on Dylan's nerves.

"Where you going?" asked Baxter.

Crank shrugged. "Reconnoitering. I'll hike down the road and see if anything's moving."

They both watched the little man hobble slowly down the drive.

"He's an odd duck," muttered Dylan.

"Crank's okay. But you're right, he is a little hard to figure. And he's got a very short fuse in case you haven't noticed yet."

"How long have you known him?"

"Almost thirty years, but I don't think anyone really knows Crank."

Dylan gave him a long look.

"What?" said Baxter.

"I figured Crank to be in his fifties. You don't look that old. That's all."

"Thanks." Baxter laughed. "I age like fine wine."

"Why are you both here? Why am I here?"

"Because we got orders to come find you."

"Find me for what? You expect me trust you two without knowing what's going on?"

"You should."

"Why?"

"Because you're alive."

"I saw you kill the chief."

"He deserved it, believe me."

"You really expect me to believe that the chief of police and the other cop were bad guys?"

"You met them. Did they seem *right* to you?"

Dylan frowned. Every meeting he'd had with the two cops had been *off*. Why had they kept asking about kids and little girls specifically? And why hadn't they cared about his house being ransacked? In fact, he'd gotten the distinct feeling that they knew all about what had happened in the house. Did that mean they knew who had robbed Ronnie's grave as well?

"Why did someone steal my wife's coffin? Why did they tear my house apart? Why are they after me? Why were the cops so curious about little girls? And who are you, and who do you work for?"

"Anything I tell you will just make you more confused," said Baxter, holding up both hands. "We work for an organization called Rex Deus. But that won't mean anything to you. All you need to know is that the bad guys want you bad, and that's enough of a reason for us to want you, too."

"Who are the bad guys?"

Baxter frowned. "They're a group of nuts. But they're more dangerous than you can imagine."

Dylan smirked. "How do I know that you two aren't the nuts who are the most dangerous?"

Baxter shrugged. "I guess if you don't, you don't."

"What's going on with the power? You know more than you're saying about that, too."

"It could be just a temporary glitch."

"You say that like you don't really believe it."

"We'll know more when Crank gets back. Now, where are you going?"

Dylan slipped on the heavy coat that Baxter had found in one of the closets and opened the door. "To the outhouse. Do you mind?"

Baxter waved him out.

Dylan stood for a moment on the small stoop, half-hoping that he was still at home, sitting in his chair, hallucinating. But the cold air stung his cheeks, and he could smell clean pine in the air.

He circled around to the outhouse entrance, the tiny structure shielding him from the windows of the cabin. Stepping inside, he relieved himself without bothering to close the rickety door. The acrid smell of fresh piss steamed upward, and he zipped hurriedly and backed outside again. Turning slowly, he realized he was staring through the trees at a narrow trail, and curiosity tugged at him. Glancing only once over his shoulder to assure that the privy would disguise his movement, he trudged through the calf-deep snow toward the trees.

Once he reached the trail, the forest was so thick overhead that most of the night's snowfall remained in the branches. He followed the narrow, winding path for two hundred yards, always downhill, until through a clearing ahead he spotted a pond. He stepped out of the trees onto a small pier, now frozen into the lake ice. Off to the side an old fiberglass canoe lay bottom up, stored for the winter. Far out across the flat white surface of the lake twenty or more ice-fishing shacks huddled up like wagons circled against attack, and he wondered if he shouldn't step back into the shelter of the woods before anyone noticed him. One of the fishermen might very well know whose dock this was and wonder that someone was visiting the camp this time of year.

A man appeared from the back of one of the shacks, but even at that distance Dylan could tell that the guy wasn't going to spot him. He was pounding on one of the huts and screaming. Then he raced to another of the small sheds and did the same thing, and again, stumbling so fast through the snow that he fell down three times while Dylan watched, then popped up again like a bug with a live wire up its butt. It was hard to tell what he was shouting, but it sounded like he was screaming someone's name. Maybe he'd lost one of his kids or something. But no one was coming out of any of the other shacks, and Dylan watched as the guy ripped a door open, stared inside, then raced to another shack leaving the first door swinging.

It looked as though the guy'd gone crazy.

But where the hell was everybody?

Dylan's first thought was to race out onto the ice and help. But the longer he watched—the man falling again, crying and pounding his fists on the ice—the more he became certain that there was nothing to be done. The silence all around was far more ominous than he had wanted to believe.

He stared at the chimneys along the lake, noticing for the first time that they were all devoid of smoke in the freezing weather, and a shudder that had nothing to do with the cold raced up his spine.

Crank peered up and down the length of the lane, the morning sun peeking through the still-blustering flakes, light glittering on the snow in angular patterns like broken glass. It looked as though no plow had been that way all night. He didn't know the area well enough to be certain, but he was relatively sure that one should have come along. Six inches of snow would hardly be enough to shut down road service in rural Maine.

He stared at the glistening sheet of fresh snow, troubled by the lack of tracks. There should be *something* to break the flawless white surface. Footprints from someone who had gone out to find help. Maybe hoofprints or sleigh tracks. He didn't see so much as the feeble trail of a squirrel marring the perfect cottony surface.

The wind had slackened, and the road was well protected by tall firs, but occasionally a gust dropped down between the trees like a bowling ball following the gutter. When he reached the intersection he wasn't all that surprised to find the main road as buried as the one down which he'd just trekked, and just as devoid of life. A half mile up he could see a large farmhouse, but no one was moving, and no smoke rose from the chimney. He stood quietly in the middle of the intersection and closed his eyes, but there was no sound except the whistle of the breeze through the branches. No far-off auto noise. No equipment in the woods. No airplanes overhead. No buzzing power lines.

He clutched his gloved hands under his arms, taking in a deep breath of cold air, wondering how things could have gotten so screwed up. He had to get Barnes to the Keep and hope that things would work out when he did. Without word from Clayborn there was no telling what had happened back there. And now it didn't look as though there was any way to *get* word. It was a thousand miles from here to there, and it appeared they were going to have to hike it.

Damn.

He knew what Baxter would make of all this. Already was making of it. And he had to admit that he had no reasonable explanation for things off the top of his head. But that didn't mean he was about to start believing in fairies and hobgoblins, either.

Crank didn't buy the reasons Baxter had for taking Barnes to the Keep. The only thing that mattered to Crank was that Clayborn would want Barnes at the Keep so Barnes was going to the Keep, come hell or high water. This new situation was just another problem to be dealt with.

He glanced around at the silent woods, shook his head, and trudged back up the road.

"Anybody moving on the highway?" asked Baxter.

"Not a soul," said Crank, taking a bite of crusty corned beef hash right out of the pan on the oil stove. "It hasn't been cleared."

"They haven't plowed the county road, either?"

"Maybe they've had some major breakdowns."

Dylan told Crank about the man on the lake.

Crank shrugged. "The guy probably lost his kid."

"And where's everyone else?" asked Dylan.

"Who the fuck knows? Maybe they're all out looking."

"Maybe we ought to tell him," said Baxter.

"There's nothing to tell," said Crank irritably. "Sitting here isn't doing us any good."

"What's going on?" said Dylan irritably. "Tell me what?"

Crank shook his head. "We'll know more when we get to town," he said with a finality that let Dylan know he'd say no more on the subject.

"Then let's get moving," said Baxter, throwing on his jacket as Dylan followed suit. The three of them tromped out of the house and down the meandering drive without a glance back. When they reached the county road there were no new footprints added to Crank's.

"Which way?" asked Crank, glancing at Baxter.

"Going back to Needland is a bad idea," said Baxter.

"I agree," said Crank.

"It's twelve miles in the other direction to Arcos."

"So, let's go," said Crank.

"Why should I go with you?" asked Dylan, standing his ground.

Crank frowned, and for an instant Dylan was certain he was about to reach beneath his coat. Dylan tensed. But Baxter stepped between them.

"You don't want to go back to Needland," he said.

"Why not? I didn't kill anybody."

"People sure got killed because of you," muttered Crank.

Baxter sighed. "It's not that far to Arcos. Trust us that

far. We'll know better what's going on by then and we can talk. Fair enough?"

Dylan didn't think it was fair enough by half, but the look in Crank's eyes told him that was as far as the little man was going to stretch. Dylan nodded and fell in step in between the pair.

As they trudged through the snow, Dylan happened to glance into the treetops and caught sight of a single crow. He and the bird exchanged curious glances, and Dylan was suddenly certain he'd seen the bird before. As the threesome approached its tree the crow took to the air, landing again a hundred yards ahead of their path in the branches of a tall pine. The bird continued the ritual for a couple of miles.

"You think he likes us?" asked Baxter, nodding toward the bird, perched now on a dead branch fifty yards ahead.

Crank shrugged. "Been following us for a while. Probably hopes we'll drop something interesting."

"I think that's the bird that guided me to the clearing," said Dylan.

"What do you mean, 'guided' you?" said Baxter, glancing sideways at Crank.

Dylan told them the story of the crow and his hike up to the clearing.

"Not likely," said Baxter. "Unless he's a tame bird that got away from somebody. It is funny him being alone though. Crows like to hang together."

"He picked a bad bunch to latch on to," said Crank, drawing one of his pistols.

"Don't!" said Dylan, catching his hand. "What the hell are you doing?"

Crank shrugged, leaning around Dylan to keep an eye on the bird. "Target practice."

"Crank," said Baxter. "Leave the bird alone."

"Okay, okay," said Crank, hunching his shoulders, reholstering the pistol, and starting off again. But Baxter and Dylan stood watching the crow, and finally Crank stopped and turned toward them with a questioning expression.

"Where's the flock?" said Baxter, glancing at the snow at their feet, then back down the long length of road behind them. "Where is everybody? There must be a couple of hundred homes along this road, and twice that number on all the side roads."

Crank frowned, glancing back past Baxter. "Probably just waiting for the power to come back on."

"And the people around the lake?" said Dylan.

Baxter nodded. "If all the batteries are dead, then a lot of them must be just as worried and curious as us. How come nobody else is on the road?"

Dylan thought the look that Baxter gave him then seemed sad, the kind of look he got from people at Ronnie's funeral. But Baxter turned quickly away, and Dylan nudged the feeling aside.

"Come on," said Crank, starting off again. "We aren't going to get any answers here. We'll check the next house."

The first driveway they came to had a car buried in snow in front of the closed garage doors. But again, there was no smoke from the chimney.

"Wouldn't be," said Crank, shaking his head. "The house has an oil furnace." He pointed toward the black tank leaning against the garage. "Takes power."

The three of them stomped up onto the front porch, and Baxter knocked on the door. When no one answered he shook the knob, but the door was locked. They trudged around the little ranch house, peering in the windows, but no one was home, although the beds looked slept in.

"Maybe they walked out during the storm," said Crank as he and Baxter glanced in the window. "The snow covered their tracks. They probably hiked to a neighbor's who has a woodstove."

"Mmm," said Baxter, nodding toward the woodstove standing in the corner of the living room.

Crank just shrugged.

Dylan stared at snow marred only by their own footprints. When he glanced up at the crow again it flew on up the road.

At the third house Baxter kicked the door in.

A big Persian cat spit at them, then raced out of the living room and disappeared down the hall. Crank followed it.

"Here, kitty. Here, kitty kitty kitty."

Baxter shook his head. "Leave the cat, Crank. We got bigger problems."

"It'll starve to death if we leave it here," muttered Crank, under his breath.

"We'll leave the door open."

"It'll freeze. I can't stand to see a cat suffer."

"Forget the cat," said Dylan quietly from one of the bedrooms.

"We could at least leave it some food," said Crank.

"I said forget the fucking cat!"

Crank and Baxter followed his voice down the hall.

Dylan stood with his back to them, staring down at the big brass bed. A heavy beige comforter lay across the mattress. There were indentations in the pillows where people's heads had lain, but that wasn't what Dylan was pointing at. The collar of a plaid pajama top lay just brushing the nearest pillow.

"People put their pjs under the covers all the time. Keeps 'em warm," said Crank.

Dylan jerked the blankets to the foot of the bed.

"Do they tuck in their lace teddy and panties too?" asked Dylan. "'Cause this lady laid hers out as though she were lying on her side. That's kind of funny, don't you think? They're all wrinkled."

"What are you saying?" said Crank. "That something sucked these people right out of their underwear?"

But Dylan was already out the door and down the hall.

"The whole damned family lays out their pjs!" he said, jerking back the sheets on a couple of bunk beds that had flannel pajamas intact beneath the covers.

"Don't jump to conclusions," said Crank.

"Come on," said Baxter.

"Where are you going?" asked Dylan.

"To kick in some more doors," said Baxter.

Three more houses revealed the same results. Only apparently some people slept nude, and in the last house someone was either up early or very late. A small heap of clothes lay draped across a pair of slippers in front of the open refrigerator door. Pants over socks, shirt over pants, with white boxer shorts neatly inserted right where they belonged. Dylan and Baxter stood staring at the pile as Crank stirred it with the toe of his boot.

"Think someone put them here so he could get an early start this morning?" Baxter asked him.

Crank didn't answer.

Dylan was staring at the dog dish in the corner.

"What?" said Baxter.

"Where's the dog?"

Dylan found a half-full bag of dog food in the cupboard.

"We've seen a cat and a crow already," said Dylan. "You heard any dogs barking?"

Baxter shook his head.

Crank grunted and kicked over the pile of clothes. "Let's go," he said, heading for the door. "We're just wasting time."

It looked to Dylan like Crank wanted to be out of the house more than he wanted to get anywhere, and Dylan couldn't have agreed more. The same lone crow sneered at them from the peak of a tall spruce as they reached the center of the road again.

"Where the hell *is* everybody?" asked Dylan. The silence was nerve-wracking. He wanted to hear a car honking, a door creaking, a radio—if only for the static. Instead, even the weather conspired against him. The wind had died, and the day was still as death.

"Let's go," said Crank, breaking trail for them again.

Baxter glanced at Dylan and shrugged. "We'll find out for sure in town."

But to Dylan, Baxter's assurance sounded hollow, and his eyes darting up and down the empty road seemed able to see things Dylan could not. As Dylan glanced back at the house the weirdness of the day came crashing down on him, and he wasn't certain he wanted answers anymore. He was really afraid now that somehow the disappearance of Ronnie's coffin, the thing in his house, the thing that he'd sensed in the clearing, and these disappearances were all tied together.

Arcos was far too quiet for a county seat, even one with no electricity. Most of the town backed up against the snow-covered body of ice everyone in the area simply called the Lake, and the old brick buildings reached above its flat white expanse like the stubby fingers of an obese pianist looming over a keyboard. Dylan was happy to see a couple of people out, but they scurried along the snow-covered walks, hurrying inside. No cars moved. No neon sign was lit.

"Whatever happened," said Dylan, "it wasn't limited to the back roads."

The crow flew ahead to perch atop a brick facade at the foot of Main Street. As they drew alongside the front doors of the building, they saw that it was the town office. A short man with a wide spare tire rushed out and pulled them inside.

"Man alive, are we glad to see you fellows!" said the man, introducing himself as Carl Smith and slapping Dylan on the back as though they had known each other all their lives. Hanging jowls jiggled whenever he spoke. "Thank God you people are all right! So many are missing! Where'd you come from?"

An older woman with a torn red jacket and eyes crossed so badly Dylan could barely focus on her face introduced herself as Agatha, the postmistress. She and a couple of men in overalls and logging boots gathered round solicitously. Dylan noticed that Crank gave fake names for each of them, and informed Carl that they had been passing through in their car during the night when their vehicle suddenly died.

"Do you have any idea what's happened?" asked Dylan.

"Not a notion," said Carl. "People are just *missing*. My

wife, God bless her, is gone. Agatha here has lost her two brothers. Went into their bedrooms this morning and both of them had just flat disappeared. We can't find the sheriff or any of his deputies. A few folks have been filtering in, then leaving. They all tell pretty much the same story. And with the power not working we can't get any word out or in. If it runs on electrical power, it's gone. No cars work. No generators. No batteries."

Carl waved his hand out toward Main Street. "Mike Tapley came by earlier, and he's hiking down to West Paris to see if he can find out anything. The assistant fire chief is going from house to house checking on people. I told him any folks he finds that have no heat, send them over to the high school, and if they're all right, tell them to sit tight at home for now. But pretty soon if people don't see something happening, they're going to get antsy."

"How many people have you found so far?" asked Dylan.

"Maybe fifteen."

"Fifteen? In the whole town?"

Carl nodded. "Out of maybe eight thousand all told. It looks like people climbed right out of bed, and went out buck naked." Here he started to whisper. "But there's no tracks in the snow."

"Must have left before the storm hit," said Crank, glancing from Dylan to Baxter.

Carl nodded. "But where did they go, then?"

"What's your theory?" said Baxter.

Carl frowned. "I don't have one." He glanced quickly at Agatha, who was nodding to herself, and wrapped his arm comfortingly over her shoulder.

There were tears in her eyes, but a smile gleamed on her face. "You ought to know what it was. You all ought to know. It was the Rapture. And we missed it."

Carl just nodded.

"The Rapture?" said Dylan.

"The chosen of God," said Agatha. "He took my whole family and all those others unto his bosom."

Carl helped her into a chair and motioned for one of the men to stay with her, then shepherded Dylan, Baxter, and Crank back to the front windows.

"Got to be another explanation," muttered Dylan.

"I hope so," said Carl. "People are getting real jumpy. I mean, do you *know* the story of the Rapture?"

Dylan shook his head.

"Well, it isn't pretty for the people like us who get left behind, I can tell you that."

"How long will it take Tapley to get to West Paris and back?" said Crank, frowning.

Carl studied the sun glinting on the ice-rimmed surface of the window. "Four, maybe five hours over. I told him not to stop at any houses along the way unless he saw people. Get over there, see if he could find out what's going on, rest for a couple of hours. That's a long hike for a man on snowshoes. Then four or five hours back."

"When did he leave?"

"Around noon," said Carl.

"So he's afoot, and he won't be back until tonight at the earliest," said Baxter, and Carl nodded.

"That's another thing," said Carl. "The horses."

"What about them?" asked Dylan.

"There aren't any. Mike had twelve. All his were gone right out of the barn without the door being open or one single print in the snow." He glanced at Agatha before whispering to Dylan. "All the cows and pigs and sheep have disappeared. Seems like all the dogs are gone, too, and I don't think livestock and pets are supposed to be taken up to heaven."

They thanked Carl for his hospitality, slipping out with the excuse that they were going to hike to Lovell to check on friends. They could see him and Agatha through the front window of the post office all the way to the end of the street.

"What now?" asked Dylan, wrapping his coat tighter around his throat against the wind.

"South," said Crank.

"Hike, you mean?"

Baxter nodded. "We don't have any choice."

"But where are we going? South where?"

"Just south," said Crank.

"Why?" asked Dylan, crossing his arms argumentatively. "What do I have to run from now?"

He glanced meaningfully around the empty town.

"Do you want to know who the men were that were after you and why they stole your wife's body?" asked Crank.

"Yes," said Dylan.

Crank nodded. "The answers are south."

"I'll have some here," said Dylan, staring at Baxter instead of Crank.

"It's called the Darkening," said Baxter.

"Don't get him all wound up in that superstitious tripe," said Crank, shaking his head. "Getting to the Keep will be hard enough now as it is."

Baxter shrugged. "Crank doesn't believe in superstitious tripe," he said, glancing around meaningfully.

"What's the Darkening?" asked Dylan, as Crank turned irritably away.

"It's when the Old Ones return to claim this world," said Baxter, his eyes darting like a cat in a dog kennel.

"Old Ones?" said Dylan, wondering again who was crazy and who wasn't.

"This isn't the place for it," said Crank, glancing back down the street where Carl had stepped back out to watch them. "And it's way too early to start believing in fairy tales. You'll get answers at the Keep. If you want them."

"He's right about this not being the place," muttered Baxter, waving one last time at Carl.

"You two act as though it's dangerous just to talk about this Darkening," said Dylan, feeling a strange tickling between his shoulder blades.

"There are some things better discussed in closed rooms, behind locked doors."

Dylan glanced once more around the empty town, wondering who in the world Baxter was worried might hear. But against all common sense, the tickling along his spine became more intense, and he shivered.

"I'll go with you two, for now," he agreed. "But I want answers."

"Me too," said Baxter, following Crank, who had already taken off up the street.

"Bill," said Lucy, watching Wagner shake his head and grin. "Earl, Stan, Frank."

Blondie pretended not to hear, marching ahead of them with his broad back blocking her view of the street ahead. The world was devoid of people, and the small Virginia town they were passing through was as empty as every other place they'd been. The homes on either side of them appeared to have been built by families with *Gone With the Wind* wannabeitis. Brick fronts with tall columns and stone steps on houses that wouldn't have been large enough to provide slave quarters at Tara. But the lawns all bore giant live oaks with the requisite dangling moss.

"You'll tell me if I guess it?" said Lucy.

When Wagner glanced in his direction Blondie shrugged, and Wagner nodded at Lucy.

"Okay," said Lucy. "It's got to be bad, then. Or something with a stupid nickname. Cuthbert? Maximillian?"

Wagner laughed out loud. "Why not just stick with Blondie? I think he likes it."

"It's not in my makeup to give up that easy," said Lucy.

When she didn't return his smile, Wagner shook his head.

"Tell her your name," he commanded Blondie.

"No!" said Lucy as Blondie glanced over his shoulder again. "I'll get it."

Wagner shrugged, and Blondie went back to scanning the road ahead.

"Do you take everything so seriously?" asked Wagner.

She frowned. "Most things, I guess. I just don't like to get beat."

"We weren't trying to *beat* you. It's just that we've been trained to be secretive. I don't suppose it matters now. Who's going to hear?"

He glanced around at the empty houses, and Blondie chuckled and nodded.

"So tell me where we're going then," said Lucy. "You have a destination in mind now, don't you?"

Wagner took a moment before answering, but once the disappearances had come to light along with the appearance of the creatures, it had been apparent even to Lucy that his priorities had changed. "Just outside of DC. It's a place we call the Keep."

"And what happens when we get there?"

This time he frowned.

"You really don't know what's going on, do you?"

"No. I mean, I have some ideas, but this . . ." He waved his hand around. "I never expected anything like this."

"So what are your ideas?"

Once again there was a subtle pause before he answered,

and Lucy noticed that Blondie had cocked his head. "It could be what we call the Darkening starting. But that's just a guess, Lucy. I'm way over my head, here."

"What's the Darkening?"

He hesitated. "The Darkening . . . is supposed to be when the Old Ones return. It's what happens to our world when they do."

"The Old Ones? Who are they?"

"Not *who*. More like what. The Old Ones are a race of beings that ruled the earth eons ago. They were driven out, and they've wanted back ever since."

A tingle of fear shot up Lucy's back, but she wasn't certain whether it was because of the image Wagner had just created or because he appeared to *believe* every bit of it. "You're joking, right?"

"Afraid not."

"Those things, those creatures back in the field, they're Old Ones?"

Wagner shook his head. "The Old Ones have minions on this side, followers, a group called Qedem Melech. But they're men, just like you and me. Those things you saw in the field . . . I've heard of them. They were called Rhothag."

"What do you mean *were* called?"

"No one has seen a Rhothag since the last Darkening."

"Are you telling me something like this has happened before?"

He nodded. "Many times, if you believe the old tales. And each time the Darkening begins, Rhothag appear to bedevil the survivors. They're soldiers of the Old Ones. The lead infantry, you might say, before the Old Ones cross over onto this side."

"This side of what?"

"This dimension, I guess."

"You don't seem all that knowledgeable for a man who claims to work for an organization that's fighting these Old Ones."

He laughed. "I'm just a foot soldier."

She nodded thoughtfully. "So the Old Ones live in another dimension."

Wagner shrugged. "I don't know if that's a good explanation or not. They don't exist in our reality, or they haven't for thousands of years."

"And you really do believe this."

"With all my heart."

"And you expect me to believe it, too."

"I hope so. For all our sakes."

"Why?"

"Because you're our only hope," he said simply.

She stared at him as though he'd just placed a pinless grenade in her open hands.

"Okay," she said, trying to shrug off the weirdness of the conversation. "What have *I* got to do with anything?"

Clearly events had taken another strange turn, even wilder than the loss of all power, the missing population and animals, the overcast that seemed more somehow than just a lingering weather pattern. Lucy knew in her heart that there was a logical explanation for everything that had happened, regardless of what Wagner and Blondie believed. But her own ability to theorize was running out of steam. If this was all some government experiment gone badly awry, she couldn't understand what it could have been.

"You are the reason Blondie, and I, and all the others like us, exist," said Wagner, without the slightest trace of hedge in his eyes or voice.

"I'm just a private investigator," she said, feebly.

The echo of a gunshot brought them all up short. Wagner stepped in front of Lucy.

"Could you tell where it came from?" he asked Blondie.

Blondie pointed up the street.

"Well, let's find out who fired it," said Lucy.

"Wait," said Wagner, catching up. "You don't know who's up there."

She shrugged. "I don't think it was one of those Rhothag firing the shot. Seems more likely to be someone in the same situation as us."

Wagner signaled for Blondie to run on ahead, then he paced Lucy, eyeing every house as they passed. She shook her head when Wagner glanced at her.

"Whatever the guy was firing at," she said, "I don't think it was one of those creatures."

"That's good."

"But there's something wrong. Something's off."

Blondie had stopped at the intersection ahead, and he waited there in the center of the street until they caught up.

"What?" said Wagner.

Blondie pointed toward the front lawn of the old brick house on the corner, where a weathered gazebo stood. Lucy could see a woman sitting on the floor inside with her back to them. A long black ponytail hung midway down her back. Lucy's sense of unease increased the longer she stared at the unmoving woman.

"She might have shot herself," whispered Wagner.

That thought had occurred to Lucy. But as they watched, the woman shook, and the ponytail swung lazily from side to side before settling into place once more. Lucy stepped past Wagner, heading for the gazebo, and once again he ran to catch up.

As she started to place her foot on the bottom step of the gazebo the woman held up one empty hand without glancing back at them.

"That's far enough."

Lucy froze in place. Wagner and Blondie ignored the order, each easing around different sides of the gazebo. A pistol shot fired at the ceiling stopped them cold.

"I know what you are," said the woman. Her voice was so calm it made Lucy think of the sound of someone's last words. "Now stay back until I'm done."

"Done doing what?" asked Lucy, gently rising onto the first step.

She could see the woman sighing, either from exhaustion or resignation. What was happening here? *What* did the woman think they were, Rhothag?

"We can't live without Peter," said the woman, barely louder than a whisper. "We looked all over for him."

Lucy took a terribly slow step up onto the next tread, praying it didn't give her away with a telltale creak. "Peter was your husband?" she asked.

The woman nodded. "You knew that."

"How would we know that?" asked Lucy, watching both Blondie and Wagner take furtive steps forward.

"You did this. You took them. But you didn't take us. You just left us to die here alone. Was that some kind of joke?"

Lucy was dumbfounded. A thin veneer of calm seemed to cover a deep well of madness inside the woman.

"We didn't do this," she said, taking the last step before the top. "We're as lost and alone as you are."

The woman seemed not to hear. For the first time Lucy noticed that Blondie had his rifle aimed toward the woman. A sickly breeze scattered bits of paper along the street, and a flock of ravens dipped low overhead but then whirled away as though not only this small green were dangerous but the very air above it fouled by some presence Lucy could barely sense. The moment seemed frozen in time, and Lucy felt suddenly disassociated from it, as though she were viewing a television program, not participating in the event at all.

The woman glanced over her shoulder, and Lucy froze with her foot already on the landing, but the woman seemed not to have noticed that none of them were obeying her orders. Instead her red-rimmed eyes locked on to Lucy.

"You're not angels, then?" she whispered.

"Angels?" said Lucy, shaking her head.

The woman seemed to accept that at last, turning away again. "I thought you were the angels who took Peter and the others. I thought maybe I'd made a mistake. That you had come back for us. But I was right to do it."

"To do what?"

Blondie was staring at the ground on the other side of the gazebo, and as the woman spoke Lucy saw his face harden as though he'd been slapped. She glanced at Wagner. Whatever was over there, he'd seen it, too. He turned to stare at the woman with a look of astonishment and disgust. As Lucy finally rose up onto the floor she could see that the woman held a large revolver in her hand. On the ground on the far side of the gazebo lay three bodies, all children, about four to six years old. Each had been shot near the heart. The grass was scuffed around them, and Lucy could easily guess why. The woman might have surprised the first child, but the other two would have probably run or at least struggled. She'd dragged them back here to lie in state together.

"Are those your children?" Lucy managed to whisper.

The woman shook her head. "My Beckie died two years ago. It was just Peter and me."

"You said *we* looked all over for him," said Lucy, easing closer even as Wagner waved her back.

The woman frowned. "Did I say that?"

"Yes, you did. You're not alone anymore, though. What's your name?"

"Terry."

"You aren't alone, Terry. Not anymore."

"Peter's gone."

"Yes . . . I know that."

"You don't know what it's like to be alone."

"Yes, I do," said Lucy, feeling a rise of anger toward the woman. "I've been alone all my life. More alone than you can imagine."

The woman shook her head. "Everyone went away. Everyone. Then I found the children, and I knew that God had sent them to me so I wouldn't be alone. But without Peter I was still alone and so confused. Now they're with Peter. I want to be with Peter, too."

"You will be," said Lucy, sliding one more step closer, wondering if she could slap the gun away or if she'd simply succeed in getting shot herself. Wagner waved one hand through the air warning her to back off, but she ignored him. "You just need to be patient."

"Were you patient?"

Lucy sighed. Patient? An entire lifetime with no friends, no one to trust, hiding like an animal, was that patient?

"Yes," she said. "I was."

"I want to be—"

"Good," said Lucy. She took another step forward so that she was only three steps away, but then the woman's frown spread, she shook her head and raised the pistol. Lucy saw Blondie's finger tightening on his trigger.

"—with Peter," said the woman, raising the pistol to her temple.

"You're not alone anymore," said Lucy, desperately trying to break through.

"Peter's gone," said the woman. "We can't live without Peter."

"Sure you can—"

The gunshot blasted Lucy with blood and detritus. In a daze she watched the revolver clatter to the floor, the woman slowly sag forward as though praying. Lucy dropped to her knees, tears streaking her cheeks, unable to remove her eyes from the woman whose ponytail had managed somehow to remain clean and unspattered.

Wagner rushed to Lucy's side, and he and Blondie dragged her down the steps onto the grass.

"Why?" she gasped. "They were all alive. There was plenty of food, water. Everything they needed to survive. She murdered those children, then killed herself. Why?"

Wagner shook his head. "Those kids had the misfortune to survive in a town where the only adult was crazy already. The disappearances just drove her over the edge, I guess."

It took the rest of the day to bury the woman and children, and Wagner insisted that Blondie fashion four crosses from scraps of wood. They had no names to put on them, but Lucy wrote *Peter's Wife* on one and *Innocent Child* and the date on each of the others. As they stood with bowed heads over the humps of soil marking the new graves Lucy heard Wagner mumbling under his breath and realized it was a prayer.

"It was a waste," she said, shaking her head.

He nodded. "They're together now."

Her frown came so sudden and hard it hurt her lips. "You *believe* that?"

"I want to believe it. I need to believe it. There has to be more than this—"

He waved a hand around the common, and she noticed his eyes glistening.

"When we die we're dead, absorbed back into the ground," she said with a finality that rung hollow in the still air.

"That's a hard way to live," said Wagner, studying her face.

She turned quickly away from the compassion she saw there. "Living *is* hard. No one ever said any different."

"You don't believe that there's more to the universe than—?"

She shook her head. "I believe what I can see and feel."

"But you feel a lot more than anyone I've ever met."

She turned back to him.

"I think you *know* what I only want to believe," he said, quietly.

Anger rose like a rough steel rod screwing its way up her already constricted throat. "You don't know what you're talking about," she gasped, letting the tears flow, telling herself they were for the unknown woman, the motherless children who now would never grow up.

He reached for her, but she stumbled back a step, warding him off with both hands.

"You *want* to believe there's a logical explanation for everything," he said, letting her go. "But there isn't."

"There's nothing beyond logic but superstition and madness."

He frowned, waving Blondie ahead of him back to the street.

"Beyond logic lies faith," he said, without looking back to see if she was following.

As they walked away from the impromptu cemetery, Wagner's words pounded like her own heart, and Lucy couldn't rid herself of a terrible guilt even though she told herself there was nothing more she could have done to save the woman. She found herself edging closer to Wagner. And against all *logic* she discovered herself drawing strength from his silent stoicism. With the light waning they reached the edge of town and realized they'd taken a wrong turn. Instead of the highway, they found themselves in a small subdivision where the road ended abruptly, and Lucy began to sense the terrible feeling of desecration once again.

"What?" said Wagner, noticing her unease.

Lucy stared past him, shaking her head. Finally she raised her hand and pointed across the wide drainage ditch that ended the lane, into a dark line of forest ahead. Wagner peered expectantly into the trees, where the ever-present overcast glowed red in the last rays of the feeble sun.

"They're coming," she whispered.

"In there," he said, pointing to a small cottage across the street.

Lucy and Blondie raced behind him, around the corner of the house to the back door that fortuitously was unlocked. Wagner waited to shove both of them inside before him, then he bolted the door. Lucy followed Blondie into the front room, where the three of them crouched at the window, peeking through the thin curtain.

"You're sure you felt them?" whispered Wagner.

Lucy nodded, leaning to peer across the drainage ditch at the darkening trees. "They're there," she said, shivering.

Wagner dropped an arm around her shoulder and squeezed. "I'm sure they don't know we're here."

"What if they saw us?" she said.

He frowned, shaking his head. "The sun was still up pretty high, and their eyes seem to be sensitive. Even if they did see movement, at that distance I doubt if they could tell what it was."

"Do you think this is a good hiding place?"

Wagner glanced quickly around, shrugging. "There's too many windows in any house to make a good hiding place from those things. But at least in here we can put a wall to our backs if they do get in."

"What about the basement?" asked Lucy.

Blondie frowned, and Wagner shook his head. "Only one way in, maybe, but only one way out, too. We'd be trapped. We'll just have to lie low, and with any luck they'll miss us."

"And if they don't?"

"We'll hope there aren't that many of them." He glanced at Blondie. "Check the rest of the house."

As Blondie slipped out of the room Lucy turned to face Wagner. "I watched them in the field. I don't think they hunt just by sight," she said.

He nodded.

"They're going to smell us in here," she said.

"There's nothing we can do but keep our heads down."

Blondie slipped back in, nodding that all was secure. He took up a position in the corner by the only other window in the room. The last rays of the sun drifted across the room as dust motes stirred up by their passing floated like snow in a glass globe. As darkness engulfed them Lucy noticed movement at the ditch. Something the size of a rabbit. Then rabbits, shifting back and forth as though tethered on short ropes.

"What the—" she whispered.

"Quiet!" whispered Wagner, as she realized what she was seeing.

Not rabbits. Heads.

The Rhothag had crept into the ditch and were surveying their surroundings. As Lucy's vision adjusted she could see their eyes, glowing red in the night. A faint click told her Wagner had the safety off on his rifle. She eased her pistol out of its holster and clutched it tightly, willing her hands not to shake.

The Rhothag stood up slowly, and she counted seven of

them. They all looked huge, and it was difficult to credit Wagner's assertion that they had once been men. They moved with a peculiar stoop-shouldered walk, twisting their heads back and forth, searching for a scent, and as they neared the house she thought she heard them conversing, or at least mumbling to themselves in some kind of guttural chant.

They stopped suddenly in the center of the street, and Lucy held her breath. The big alpha male at the head of the group glanced slowly around until he was staring directly at the window, and Lucy would have sworn he was looking right at her. Wagner squeezed her shoulder again, and she held her breath.

The leader started in her direction, and the group followed as one, their crimson eyes taking in everything, heads constantly moving, their clawed fists almost dragging the ground as they stepped from the lane onto the grass out front. Lucy sensed Blondie edging toward her. From the corner of her eye she saw him press against the wall, ready to spin and fire out the window at a moment's notice. She breathed slowly through pinched lips, as she fingered the trigger of the pistol.

Finally, the big male stopped—not five feet from the window that she hoped was mirroring the street outside—staring directly at her, and Lucy felt sweat trickling down her back. The Rhothag twisted its head to the right, then the left, its gleaming red eyes never leaving her, as though it were deciding whether it really saw what it thought it saw. It reached out slowly, pointing toward her face with one thin, black talon, and she started to raise the pistol.

A raucous scream slashed the air, and the eye contact was broken as the male turned back to see which of its companions had made the noise. A twisted Rhothag with one leg bent almost backward had slunk back out into the center of the lane and was shrieking, stumbling around, and pointing down the street. The noise sent the others into a bedlam of echoing cries until the house was filled with the sound. Finally, the other Rhothag joined the shrieker in the center of the road, then followed as it hobbled away.

Lucy released a breath that seemed days old and sagged against the window frame. Wagner patted her back, and she heard him breathe out slowly himself.

"Find out what set them off," he said, signaling to Blondie, who disappeared again.

Lucy lowered herself to a sitting position against the wall. Every muscle in her body ached with exhaustion as the adrenaline burned away. Wagner dug a bottle of water from his pack, sipped from it, then handed it to her. The darkness outside was a thick, murky jelly that turned the silhouettes of the surrounding house and trees into flowing caricatures.

"Why did you send Blondie after them?" she said. "He could get killed."

He smiled. "It's not that easy to kill Blondie, and if they double back, he'll take a couple of them out before he returns, even up the odds a little. Besides I want to know what attracted them, what they're doing here."

"You say that as if you already know what they were doing."

He frowned. "I think *you* know, too. Are you sure you're okay?"

"I'm all right. When that thing was staring into my eyes like that . . . for a moment I thought I was going to lose control and just start shooting."

"No one would have blamed you. We were lucky."

They sat for a while in silence, shoulder to shoulder, staring out into the gloom. A tiny creak from the back of the house caused Wagner to raise his rifle and nudge Lucy, but it was only Blondie returning. He leaned his rifle against the wall and leaned back in a worn recliner, staring at the floor.

"Where'd they go?" asked Wagner.

Blondie sighed. "A couple of blocks over."

"Why'd they leave?"

Blondie didn't answer. He glanced at Lucy, then out the window.

"Oh, my God," she whispered, seeing that the realization had struck Wagner at the same time. "They smelled the bodies."

Blondie nodded. "They're digging up the graves with their bare hands."

Lucy pictured the innocent children, the mother lying now in peaceful repose, and she felt her gorge rising. Wagner pulled her to him, and she didn't resist, resting her head against his chest, sucking in deep long breaths.

"Are you sure we're okay here?" he asked.

Blondie shrugged, hesitating. "From the looks of it they're going to be busy all night. Better to stay here and wait for sunrise than to be hiking and chance them getting wind of us again or running into another group of them."

Wagner nodded. "Bunk down," he said, easing his arm out from under Lucy. "I'll take the first watch."

"Why do you do this?" asked Lucy, hoping at last to get an answer even if it was one she couldn't believe.

Wagner shrugged. "My line—and Blondie's—have been members of Rex Deus for more generations than we can count. In our families the eldest son is always brought in. Sometimes others. But always the eldest."

"And you just followed tradition?"

"It isn't just *tradition*," he said, and his voice told her that she was by no means the first person to have been so informed. "Do you think the Rhothag are tradition? Do you think the disappearances are some kind of tradition?"

After a moment his glare softened, and he took a long deep breath. "Sorry," he said, shaking his head. "You have to understand that it hasn't been easy, living the life that I have. That Blondie has. Knowing that we were the last line of defense against something few living human beings even knew about much less believed in. Men have been killed. I've killed men. Men who deserved to die so badly . . . And yet had I been caught, I would have been imprisoned for life or even executed for their killings."

She stared at him, seeing yet another facet to this man. A facet that she did not quite understand or trust. "You murdered them?"

"I killed known members of Qedem Melech. As they would have killed me had the situation been reversed. This is a war that has been going on for longer than you can possibly imagine."

"You're like two religious cults."

He shrugged. "Some people think so. Simply put, Rex Deus follows the light. Qedem Melech follows the darkness. In the past, though, we have both been relegated to the shadows. And we were both easily dismissed as crackpots if any of our actions ever did surface. Things have changed, as you can see. It's time to choose sides."

"Who are the Old Ones? What do they want here?"

"They are evil personified. Creatures that devour life and even life force until there is nothing left. We believe that where they come from it's devoid of life, empty and dark, and that is why they hunger for our world."

She shook her head. "*Where they come from*. You're talking about Hell."

He shrugged. "The shoe would fit, I guess."

"I don't believe in Heaven or Hell."

"One does not require the other. But I would argue that balance would warrant both."

"Heaven implies God just as Hell implies the Devil. I told you before I don't believe in God."

Wagner's chuckle wasn't quite humorless. "And I told you that he didn't necessarily care. I believe in God and I believe in the Old Ones. But I suppose you would not have to accept God to believe in the existence of evil. The Old Ones do exist, just as the Rhothag exist. The Darkening is coming."

"And I'm supposed to stop it."

She saw an impossible faith in both Wagner's and Blondie's eyes, and she wanted to slap it away.

"Just how am I supposed to do that?" she asked. "By *sensing* the Dark Ones when they come?"

Wagner shrugged. "I accept who I am. You have to accept who you are."

"I'm a woman with a strange talent. And it's a passive talent at best. I think you have the wrong person."

"Qedem Melech found you just before we did. They didn't think they had the wrong person. Nor do I. There is more to you than you know, than you accept."

She shook her head. "You've made a mistake. There might have been more to me. Maybe there was *supposed* to be more to me. But it's missing. Something has been missing from me since I was born. I've felt it all my life. Maybe it's the thing you should be searching for."

Wagner gave Blondie a quick look, as though Blondie had uncharacteristically been about to blurt something out. She glanced at Blondie, but he was poker-faced.

"Our journey is not yet complete," said Wagner, and she heard a sadness in his voice that had not been there before. "Rex Deus has not been what it once was for a great length of time, and I'm afraid that those of us who remain will owe a penance someday for our failings toward you and your family."

"I've been paying a penance all my life," muttered Lucy.

He nodded. "Our lives were consecrated to yours, and we failed you. I'm sorry."

She shook her head, trying to understand. "You saved my life. More than once. How can you say you failed me?"

"We should have found you earlier. We should have tried harder. You should have never had to hide yourself or suppress your talent. Had you been with us, you would have been nurtured for what you are instead of never knowing. Never understanding."

She stared at him, torn between the moment and the memory.

She remembered lying in bed in the summer of her twelfth year. Low-lying clouds brushed the stars outside her window, and crickets chirruped loudly. It was almost Halloween, but the Texas panhandle was still hot at midnight, and she lay atop the sheets letting the wisp of a breeze cool her bare legs and arms.

Something was wrong.

She'd known it as soon as she stepped off the school bus that day. There was a tension in the air that raised the hair on the back of her neck. Her mother greeted her at the front door like always, but her smile was forced, and her eyes shot up and down the street before she closed the front door behind them. Lucy watched silently as her mother baked cookies and chattered continuously, talking about the neighbor's dog that barked all the time, about the girl she'd seen in the grocery who had a tattoo, for God's sake. When she asked how Lucy's day was Lucy just shrugged.

"What's wrong?" she'd asked.

"Nothing," said her mother, trying to smile.

"Where's Dad?"

The smile disappeared. "Working. You know that."

Lucy nodded. Picking up her books, she went to her room without further comment.

But once *in* her room, the feeling of something about to happen had only grown stronger. She couldn't put her finger on what it was exactly . . . a tickling along her arms, a nervous feeling that someone was watching her . . .

When her father did finally arrive home later than usual their dinner conversation was strained. Lucy could tell there were things he wanted to say, but to her mother, not her, and she wanted to scream at him to tell her what was going on. But she had been taught from birth to respect her parents and not to make waves. People who made waves came to bad ends, although she had no idea what those ends might be. So she excused herself from the table and went to watch television, trying to catch any conversation coming from the kitchen. But none did. When she looked in on them her mother and father were simply staring at each other across the table, and Lucy's feeling of impending doom became a pulse that echoed the throbbing of her heart. She kissed each of them good night, but they felt cold and unmoving, like statues, or corpses.

She lay awake in the darkness of her bedroom, listening to the crickets, wishing they'd lull her into sleep so she could awaken to a nice new dawn, and the whole weirdness would be just a bad memory, something she'd imagined.

Suddenly she felt as though something touched her. Something nasty and dangerous maybe. She shivered, jerking into a fetal position, and for a moment the feeling disappeared.

But then it returned, like awful things touching her all over, like teeny tiny drops of something she didn't want to think about. She rubbed at her body with the sheet, but whatever it was didn't come off and she couldn't see anything on her skin in the starlight. She climbed from bed, but before she'd taken three steps across the bedroom carpet she wished she hadn't.

The feeling assaulted her through the bottom of her feet, and suddenly she felt as though she were standing on a giant drum. A deep-rooted vibration ran up through the floor and into the soles of her bare feet and she knew instantly what it was. The feeling of footsteps. Someone else's footsteps. Someone bad.

She raced down the dark hallway to her parents' room and shook her father awake. He stared at her with bleary eyes, holding her shoulders, but he didn't seem angry to be awakened. What she saw in his eyes was more like fear. She told him about the terror she felt, and he gave her mother a strange look.

Just then the crickets stopped chirruping.

"Get in the car," he whispered, as her mother started toward the closet.

"I'll just get dressed."

But he shoved her and her mother down the hallway toward the door to the garage. "There's suitcases in the car. Go!"

That was the only time Lucy ever heard her father squeal the tires of his car.

As they raced away down the street Lucy wondered what could be so terrible that she could feel it before it ever got close. What could frighten her father and mother so much they'd run away from home and leave everything they owned? Because she knew without being told that they weren't coming back and that she must never mention this night to anyone.

"I felt them," she whispered from the backseat, where the night wind was at last cool.

"Forget it!" said her father over his shoulder. "Never speak of it again."

She'd known before that she was different, had *felt* things. But never as strongly or as definitely as that night. That was the night that she realized her parents might not be crazy. Maybe they were sane, and everyone else was crazy. It was the night she understood that her father was right. There was no one she could trust. Ever. And she also knew that the emptiness that inhabited a part of her soul wasn't something she'd dreamed up after all. It wasn't an adolescent problem that she would outgrow. It was as real as the sense of awful presence she'd experienced in the moments before her family had had to run for their lives.

"I've paid plenty," she whispered, and Wagner nodded that he understood.

It took several hard days on the road to reach southern New Hampshire. The trek revealed that Crank and Baxter weren't in near the shape Dylan was, but they were game enough. That morning they'd been trudging through the snow already for over an hour, and the sight of dawn breaking above the mountains seemed bleak as a distant candle. As they stumbled into the tiny town of Edly Pond, a man surprised them by hurrying out of the gas station and flagging them down.

"Where you folks coming from?" said the man.

"Maine," said Dylan, mentally slapping himself when Crank frowned.

The man appeared on the verge of tears. "That's quite a piece. Anybody but you left up that way?"

Baxter nodded. "A few. Everybody gone around here, too?"

"There's no one left in town 'cept for me and my old ma, and she's got the Alzheimer's so I can't leave her alone for long." He nodded in the direction they were traveling. "I hiked for five miles yesterday and checked every house. Had to lock up my ma in the bedroom. I can't do that again. 'Fraid she'll hurt herself. My Amy's gone, too. Do you know what's happening?"

Dylan shook his head, glancing meaningfully at Crank and Baxter. "No more than you do."

"It's God's will," said the man, staring at his feet. "It's like the Bible said. All the good Christians were taken straight up into heaven. Now we have to wait for the *Coming*."

"Is that what you think?" asked Dylan, remembering Agatha's words in the post office.

The man's eyes slowly rose to meet his, and the man nodded. "Don't you? Doesn't it make sense?"

"I suppose," said Dylan. But if this was the Rapture, then a hell of a lot of people were gone, and he had trouble believing there were that many good Christians in the population.

"It ain't just the people, either," mumbled the man. "Have you noticed the water?"

"What do you mean?" asked Dylan.

"You fellas drinking bottled water?"

"Yes," said Dylan. The bottles were easy to come by and to carry.

"Don't taste funny to you?"

In fact Dylan had noticed a slight acrid flavor to the last bottle he'd opened, but he'd written it off to nerves. He glanced at Baxter, who shrugged.

"And the food," said the man. "All the canned foods are starting to taste a little off. Canned goods shouldn't go bad."

"Maybe you just got a couple of old cans," said Crank.

"Maybe so. I sure would like to hear some news," said the man, sidestepping to counter Crank's attempts to edge around him. "Are you going to be coming back from wherever it is that you're going?"

Crank shook his head, and the man's expression grew even sadder.

"Well, if you do happen to, how about stopping in and letting me know what's going on?"

"Sure," said Crank, gently nudging the man out of their way. When they rounded the first turn, a half mile up, the man was still standing in the road, watching.

They hiked until the twilight was cold and gray, their own breath surrounding them with mist.

"I can't go much farther," said Baxter, wobbling.

"I don't think I can, either," said Crank, staring dully at the tracks behind them.

The next driveway led them to a summer cabin. They kicked the door in and tossed their packs on the floor, falling together onto the wide sofa along the back.

Baxter smiled. "At least the snow hasn't returned. It's warming up, and farther south the hiking should get a lot easier."

"We need to eat something before we pass out," said Crank. "And let's see if we can't get some heat in this dump."

He lit a candle from his pack, then rummaged through the canned goods in the cupboard. Baxter worked on getting the hand pump over the sink flowing, while Dylan found enough kindling to start a fire in the tiny woodstove. Finally, Baxter lay back on his sleeping bag, staring at the candle glow dancing on the ceiling and sniffing at the smell of canned stew rising from the pot Dylan was stirring over the little camp stove.

"Ever get this much snow in New York?" asked Baxter.

"How did you know I was from New York?" asked Dylan. "What else do you know about me?"

Baxter closed his eyes, reciting as though reading from the back of his eyelids. "You were born twenty-nine years ago in New York City, where you stayed for your first two years of school. You didn't like it much." When he opened his eyes Dylan was staring at him.

"No," said Dylan.

"When you were in the third grade your family moved upstate to Newton, where your father went to work for an electrical supply company. You didn't like school all that much there, either."

"Okay," said Dylan. "So you dug up my sordid childhood. Why?"

"Actually it sounds pretty much like the childhood a *lot* of kids have to go through," said Crank.

"Really?" said Dylan, jerking one pant leg up to reveal a tight mass of scar tissue the size of a fist in the middle of his calf. The scar was bumpy and twisted, as though the area had been healed, then scarred over numerous times.

"What is that?" asked Baxter.

"Cigarette burns. So you don't know *everything*."

Baxter frowned. "Why'd they do that?"

Dylan shrugged. "I had learning disabilities when I was a kid. I was dyslexic. I was short for my age, and I used to stutter. Kids don't need any more reason than that."

"So you decided to take karate lessons."

"Not right off," said Dylan. "When you're as beat down as I was it's hard to convince yourself you can ever change things. Fear does that to you."

His father had taken him to Sensei Ashiroato's dojo because he was ashamed of a son who was a coward. To Dylan's father there was no excuse for not standing up to bullies, no matter what size you were or how many there were of them. Fear was something a man dealt with.

Dylan remembered sitting in the small waiting room, watching his father and the little Japanese man talking and nodding. Sensei Ashiroato wore his unbleached *gi*, with the traditional black belt adorned with four golden stripes. Dylan had no idea what the stripes meant although he was aware that a black belt was someone to be either respected, feared, or both. But the little man didn't look fearsome. He was a head shorter than Dylan's dad, and couldn't have weighed 150 pounds.

After a while Dylan was waved onto the training floor. He glanced at the large mirrors, the punching bags, and assortment of strange weapons near the far wall. His father disappeared into the waiting room, and Dylan knew he was supposed to remain, but he was filled with fear. He was *always* filled with fear.

"So, Dylan-san," said Sensei Ashiroato, "do you think that you would like to study karate?"

Dylan stared at the floor, shaking his head.

"Why not?" asked Sensei.

Dylan shrugged.

"Do you know the worst thing about fear?" Sensei Ashiroato asked, causing Dylan to look up. What had his dad told this man?

Sensei laughed. "We all fear," he said.

Dylan couldn't believe that everyone was afraid like *him*.

"You think that your fear is greater than all other fears," said Sensei. "But a little fear is just as bad as a big fear. There is only more of the big fear. *Karateka* have no fear. Do you believe that?"

Dylan shook his head, and Sensei laughed again.

"You are right," he said. "But *karateka should* have no fear. Not the kind of fear that you have, Dylan-san. Would you like to end your fear?"

Dylan nodded. But he knew his fear would always be with him. Because he was weak.

Sensei squatted down in front of Dylan until Dylan was forced to look into the old man's eyes, then he balled his hand into a fist and lifted it over his head. "Watch."

With lightning speed he brought his fist down, knuckles first, onto the hardwood floor. A sharp crack echoed across the large room, but Sensei's eyes registered nothing but the same mirth Dylan had seen in them upon entering.

"Do you think that hurt?" asked Sensei.

Dylan nodded, but Sensei shook his head, showing the

back of his hand. The knuckles were swollen, but Dylan guessed that they had been swollen before.

"Why not?" asked Dylan, at last unable to contain himself.

Sensei smiled. "Because I know how to control my pain. And I control my fears in the same way, Dylan-san. Would you like to learn how to do that?"

Dylan nodded, but then Sensei's smile turned to a frown, and Dylan was afraid that it wasn't possible, that this was just another of those weird tests like the counselors were always giving him, asking meaningless questions and never giving answers.

"It doesn't happen like that," said Sensei, snapping his fingers. "It takes training, and discipline, and hours of hard practice."

Dylan nodded again. He could do that. He could do whatever it took to rid himself of the terror that was always with him.

"Months," said Sensei. "Perhaps years."

Dylan swallowed hard, and Sensei's smile returned. He stared deeply into Dylan's face and Dylan thought he could see just a little pain behind the old man's eyes.

"I will make you a promise, Dylan-san," said Sensei. "If you will dedicate yourself to this training, I will promise you it will work. I will dedicate myself to making it work for you. Is that fair?"

Dylan nodded again. Sensei made an odd crossing motion with both fists and shook Dylan's hand.

"*Osu,*" said Sensei, pronouncing the word *oos*. "We will train together."

And they had trained together for eight years, until Dylan had attained his *san-dan,* his third-degree black belt, and become a sensei, an instructor. Long before that he had convinced the bullies that he was no one to be trifled with, and most of the fear had faded.

But he had never managed to acquire the one thing he had really wanted during that period, his father's love and respect. When Dylan was thirteen, his mother died, and his father grew even more distant. He provided shelter and food and little else, and when *he* died—during Dylan's third year in college—Dylan didn't attend the funeral. It was at college that Dylan, a reclusive senior, met Ronnie. He was shocked that a beautiful girl would speak to him, much less ask him out. Later, when she told him she wanted to get married, he was floored.

He discovered an inner peace with Ronnie that even karate had never brought him, and he had been surprised to learn that she knew a lot about fear herself, although she would never tell him exactly what it was that frightened her. Some darkness from her past inhabited a space in her heart that she would not or could not share with him. But Dylan dedicated himself to making certain that no one would ever hurt her again.

On numerous occasions after they were married, Dylan made the long drive back to Newton, just to practice with Sensei Ashiroato. But there was always a spiritual level of karate that Sensei promised him was there, waiting for him, but which Dylan could never quite see, never believe.

"It is not just a mystery, Dylan-san," Sensei told him the last time he had seen the old man, when the setting sun outside sent bright yellow squares of warmth across the wooden floor of the little dojo. "It is a wonder. And one day you will reach it. I promise you. Do not give up."

But Dylan had shaken his head and smiled. "I don't need it, Sensei," he'd said, seeing the disappointment in the old man's eyes. "I'm happy that you have it. But I don't need the mysteries now. Karate has given me peace. I'm free, and I thank you for that."

"But you are not a true *karateka* until you attain the final level," said Sensei sadly. "And you are the best student I have ever trained. I want this for you."

"I know you do, Sensei," said Dylan, bowing and crossing his fists. "But I have enough. A man should not search for more than enough, *osu*?"

"*Osu*, Dylan-san," said Sensei, taking both Dylan's

hands in his own, and shaking them. "If that is the way of it, then I will be happy for you."

Although he sensed that Sensei was right, that there was a deep level of karate that he had not yet attained, he tried to write it off to mysticism and oriental superstition. And, although his life with Ronnie was more than he had ever hoped for, he knew that for her there was still something missing, some hurt deep inside even she didn't seem to understand herself.

When the doctors informed them that Ronnie was infertile Dylan suspected that she had known all along, that her barrenness was the empty spot within that he could never fill. They discussed adoption, but for Ronnie that would never be the answer. She wanted her own child more than anything else in life, and so he had wanted one with her. And when she died, a vast part of himself died with her and he had quit wanting anything at all.

"You fought in Japan in 1996," said Baxter, snapping Dylan back into the present.

"I did okay."

"Better than okay," said Baxter, glancing at Crank. "Number two in your weight class."

"Now you know all about me. Tell me why I'm here."

Baxter frowned. "Ronnie was a very special lady, Dylan. We've been looking for her mother since before Ronnie was born."

"Why?"

"Because they were the last of their line. The followers of the Old Ones, Qedem Melech, dug up Ronnie's coffin—we assume to make sure she was dead."

"Sure she was dead?" said Dylan, stunned.

Baxter nodded. "We believe they thought she must have passed something special on to a female child, but when they finally accepted that that hadn't happened, they had to make absolutely certain that she hadn't somehow escaped them again. When they were sure, they came after you. That was why the chief and the other cop were in the clearing that day."

"What do you mean, something special?"

Baxter shook his head. "Ronnie's line *was* special. We lost track of her mother, Veronica, in the early seventies. Crank almost found her, but then he lost her again."

"Why did you want her so badly? Why does this Qedem Melech want something that Ronnie had?"

"Because what she had is the key to everything," said Baxter. "To all that's happened."

"That's impossible. How could all this be connected to a single person?"

But the idea that the strange dislocations, the dark presence in his house and in the clearing, were all related resonated deeply. He felt like a tiny piece of bait, sinking on a hook into a deep ocean.

"What about that thing in my house? What was it, and what did it want?"

"I don't know what it was," said Baxter. "But it probably wanted the same thing Qedem Melech wanted. You."

"Why in the world should I believe all this?"

"Because I think you already believe it," said Baxter, evenly. "Were you and Ronnie very close?"

Dylan glared at him, knowing the words he could not bite off would damn him into Baxter's reality. "Ronnie and I were like one person. We completed each other's sentences."

Baxter nodded. "She must have passed her talent to you, Dylan. Whatever it is. Don't you know?"

"You guys are nuts," said Dylan, shaking his head. But he knew in his heart that Baxter was right. Shadow monsters didn't chase normal people. And normal people didn't hear voices in unknown languages and *almost* understand them, didn't feel the claws of alien beasts worming their way into their minds. Either he was a normal guy going normally insane. Or Ronnie had passed *something* to him.

"When was the last time either of you had contact with Ronnie's mother?"

"She was killed in a car wreck a few years ago."

"You didn't attend the funeral."

"We didn't even know about the accident until Ronnie

called Nevada, and the new tenants of the house told her. I never understood how Veronica could have been killed and not left any record of her next of kin. I guess she didn't have many friends, either."

"Qedem Melech killed Ronnie's mother trying to capture her. She left no trace so that Ronnie would not be found."

"Killed her? Veronica was a quiet woman who kept to herself and never bothered anyone. You're saying some wacko group killed her to gain her *power*?"

"I take it Ronnie made no further attempts to contact anyone in Nevada?"

Dylan shook his head. "What does Qedem Melech mean?"

"It's Hebrew for 'Servants of the Old Gods.' The organization has been in existence a *very* long time. So if Ronnie distanced herself from any contact with Nevada, you couldn't have known her mother's coffin was stolen, too?"

Dylan felt as though Baxter had slugged him in the gut. He couldn't think of anything to say.

"We followed Qedem Melech agents to your wife's mother, but we got there too late," said Baxter. "Then we were too slow tying Veronica to Ronnie and you. There's no record of Ronnie's mother ever having a child."

"But there must have been something. A birth certificate, school records, photographs?"

"Nothing."

"If you knew all this, then why didn't you warn me?"

"We didn't know any more than Qedem Melech did that Ronnie had passed her talent to you. As far as we knew it had never been passed to any but a direct female descendant. Anyway, would you have believed us?"

"Believed what?" said Dylan. "You haven't told me anything except some story about a crazy cult and some line about my wife having a weird past."

"Would you have believed the chief of police was working for an organization that was willing to steal your wife's body and kidnap or murder you?" asked Baxter.

"No," admitted Dylan.

"When we discovered that Ronnie was dead we waited and watched," said Baxter. "We needed to see if they would give away their intentions, show us what they were looking for and why," said Baxter. "Did Ronnie never tell you anything at all of her past, never intimate in any way that she knew she was special?"

The question dredged up memories of dreams unremembered in the harsh light of day, half-recalled comments on the edge of sleep. Dylan shook his head more in frustration than answer.

"What does this Qedem Melech want?" he asked.

"They're dedicated to the destruction of mankind," said Baxter. "They worship the 'Old Ones,' or they're sometimes called the 'Old Gods.' They believe it's their mission to bring them back to rule the earth."

"And you're telling me that you really believe in these Old Ones?"

"I believe, though I don't expect you to believe me just yet. Just give me the benefit of the doubt, the same as you would any madman, okay? Your wife knew enough about Qedem Melech to make herself scarce around Nevada after her mother died, and I have to assume that Veronica told Ronnie about her 'inheritance' if she hadn't already realized it herself. It's in the nature of their family that Ronnie would want to pass the birthright on to her progeny. She would probably have been driven to bear children. Since you didn't, we have to assume that one or both of you were unable."

Dylan nodded.

"So, as I said, we *assume*," continued Baxter, "that rather than taking her legacy to the grave with her, she passed it to the one survivor closest to her."

Dylan was stunned at how closely Baxter's speech mirrored his own musings about Ronnie's desire for children. Was it really possible that Ronnie had been involved in something so far-out as all this, and he had never known?

"You believe in these Old Ones, too?" Crank had turned his back to the conversation.

Crank shook his head, smirking. "I believe in what I see, touch, smell, taste, and hear. But Qedem Melech is real enough and crazy enough and powerful enough."

"And you're saying my wife was the only thing that stood between Qedem Melech and world domination? And that now the torch has passed to *me*?" said Dylan, turning back to Baxter.

"There's one other," said Baxter. "But we don't know where."

Snow began to fall just as they left the cabin the next morning, and it snowed off and on for three days, the noontimes nearly as dreary as the silent, swirling nights. Other than the man in the gas station parking lot, they had not met another human being since leaving Arcos. No smoke rose in the still air. There were no footprints other than their own in the snow, and no house they entered had occupants, although most had *remnants*—empty clothes, beds slept in. At the foot of one frozen toilet Dylan discovered a pair of briefs over a couple of slippers. The toilet needed to be flushed. The world itself had a curious fading quality to it that Dylan could not quite define. The old man in the village hadn't been exactly right. The water and food didn't taste *off*. It tasted *less*, as though the flavor were slowly dissipating. And even the constant overcast could not completely account for the way everything in the distance seemed to fade—not into mist—but *away*, as though the entire world around them were receding faster than they could reach it.

Baxter insisted they forge on mindless of the weather, informing Dylan that regardless of everything that had happened this was only the beginning and it was imperative that they reach the Keep. He believed that the men there would have the answers he lacked, would be able to help Dylan in ways he could not. Even Crank—who professed not to believe any of the superstitious claptrap Baxter extolled—assured Dylan that the only place any of them would be safe would be the Keep. But Dylan feared that they were all on a fool's errand because he knew in his heart that he was not the answer Baxter was looking for, and he feared that upon reaching the mystical Keep, Crank's boss would inform him that he, too, had made a mistake.

For days they trekked from village to village along roads that were little more than lines of drifts between the surrounding forest and fields. Where the landscape broadened into open fields, it was impossible to tell what was highway and what was farmland. More than once they found they had wandered off the highway and were forced to backtrack, adding more miles to the arduous journey. Finally, the night before, while they were enjoying the heat of a woodstove in yet another empty house, the weather had begun to break, a warm front blowing in.

Since they had crossed into Connecticut earlier that day, snow had been dropping from the trees in giant noisy clumps, and it sounded as though a troop of giants were tramping through the woods with them. The warm wind did nothing to dissipate the heavy cloud cover that draped over every day now like a gray shroud, but strangely the overcast seemed to clear with each nightfall, leaving the lackluster stars and faded moon alone in a field of vast inky emptiness.

They had been hiking since sunup, and by late afternoon they wandered onto a long stretch of interstate with no farmsteads and they hadn't yet found a place to camp for the night.

"We should have stopped at the last farm," said Dylan.

Crank shook his head. "We have to keep pushing."

"I've never seen snow this deep from one storm before," said Dylan, staring at the four-foot-deep blanket that glittered in the low light. "It's almost like someone didn't want us to get to there."

Crank laughed. "I imagine that would be about true."

"But you don't really believe Qedem Melech could cause a snowstorm, do you?" asked Dylan.

"More than likely it inconvenienced some of *them* just as bad as it did us," said Baxter.

"Well, it's warm enough now," said Crank. "Must be up to near fifty."

"That'll make traveling harder, not easier," said Baxter, glancing at his snowshoes, which threatened to sink deeper into the melting snow with each tread.

"For more reasons than one," said Dylan as they reached a small bridge over a nameless creek.

"The thaw's liable to cause a flood. It happens every time Needland gets a heavy snowfall followed by a warm spell. The rivers can't handle the runoff."

"Great," said Crank, as they hiked across the bridge.

They hadn't run into a lot of stalled cars so far, since the Darkening seemed to have started late at night. But for some reason this stretch of highway appeared to have been handling a fair-sized group of travelers at the time. Three semis were overturned, twisted together in an odd mating ritual, and behind them stretched a long line of wrecked cars, vans, and pickups. They plodded down into the ditch, then back out to get around the big trucks.

"People," said Dylan, pointing to an exit ahead where a

group of men waited in the late-afternoon shadows of the trees.

"I don't like the look of that bunch," said Baxter. Crank already had a pair of binoculars out, perusing the group, which appeared to consist of eight adults.

He passed Baxter the glasses without comment.

"What's wrong with them?" asked Dylan, squinting. "They aren't moving or waving. What are they doing out here?"

Baxter lowered the glasses, but kept staring at the group of men thoughtfully.

"Let me see," said Dylan, jerking the glasses out of Baxter's hands.

The mob was hard to make out in the twilight, especially the way they were standing in the deep shadows of the trees, but some wore heavy coats, others almost nothing at all. And yet none seemed to be affected by the breeze that—although warm enough to melt snow—was hardly suitable for bare skin. The strangest thing about the group was the way they stood, just waiting. None of them seemed to be talking among themselves like Dylan, Crank, and Baxter. Dylan twisted the focus knob on the binoculars until he had one face locked into view. In the dim light the skin looked leathery, wrinkled, and oddly distorted, as though the head were a bag filled with broken bones, but it was the bright, bloodred eyes that held his attention.

"What's wrong with them?" asked Dylan.

"They're Rhothag," said Baxter. "Creatures of the Old Ones. They're dangerous as hell."

"Bullshit," said Crank, shaking his head. But Dylan thought there was confusion in his face. "They look like mutants, all right—"

Baxter aimed his rifle at the group and eased his finger onto the trigger.

"What are you doing?" said Dylan, shoving the rifle barrel down into the snow.

Baxter jerked the gun out of Dylan's grip. "You don't

know what those things are," he said. "We'll be damned lucky if we can kill them all."

"And you don't know what they are, either," said Crank, holding out his hand to stop Baxter from firing.

"So what do you suggest?" said Baxter, glancing around at the forest, which was thick with brush between the tall spruce and pines, ample place for a thousand attackers to lie in wait.

Crank shook his head. "I thought Rhothag only came out at night. Look at them. They're out in the sun."

"It's almost down, and with the trees and the damned overcast they probably aren't even feeling it. They may be drawn here by Dylan. If that's so, even the sun might not stop them."

"Still, it's not like the stories. Come on. Just be ready."

"This is crazy," said Baxter.

But he and Dylan followed.

Crank kept his rifle slung but removed both pistols from his holsters. Baxter carried his own rifle at the ready, and Dylan clicked the safety off on his shotgun. The closer they got to the group the more Dylan knew for certain that Baxter was right, the things weren't men at all. They looked more like giant hunchbacked trolls.

"Just ease around them," muttered Baxter while they were still out of voice range. "Don't show fear."

Dylan started to say that was easier said than done but bit his lip. Even with all his training, after all the years he had devoted to learning to control his fear, the things engendered a deep-rooted terror that would not be denied.

But easing between the Rhothag and the press of stalled and wrecked vehicles became problematic when the things strode out into the snow to block their path, and as Dylan drew closer still, he could see that there were nine, not eight. Their movements were slothlike, and yet there was a crouching sense about them, as though they might be able to strike with incredible speed if they needed to. Among the mob there were eyes that were way too close together, teeth that stuck out of closed lips like tusks, and arms that dragged the ground like those of apes.

Dylan could see that Crank was right about their aversion to the sun. Once out of the shadows the things shielded their eyes even from the feeble twilight, and the low rays seemed to affect their scaly skin as well. Several of the beasts shifted and scratched, trying to cover themselves with what remained of their clothing.

"Jesus," said Baxter, grimacing as though he'd just swallowed something toxic. "Check out that big bastard."

The tallest one looked as though it might have been involved in a major automobile accident. Its nose was so flat Dylan wondered that it could breathe through gill-like slits, and the ears were just flaps of pale white skin against the sides of a very bumpy skull.

The snow only reached the giant's knees, although it came to midthigh on most of the others. Still, it wasn't deep enough to give Dylan or his companions an advantage on their snowshoes. The muscular-looking beasts could probably plow through the drifts as fast as the three of them could maneuver on the ungainly devices.

Twenty feet from the mob they halted. Eighteen lizard-lidded eyes locked on Dylan, who shifted nervously, his shotgun not *quite* aimed at the Rhothag.

"Hello," said Dylan, and Baxter looked at him as though he'd lost his mind.

The tall beast turned its monster face on Baxter, and Dylan noticed Baxter's hands tightening on his rifle. But the giant simply took in Baxter's form as though studying a new specimen.

"*Rantasas*," said the giant at last. The nonsense word, spoken in a voice as harsh as sand being ground between two stones, shocked Dylan to the core. The other Rhothag took up the word and repeated it several times in equally raspy voices. When they fell silent again the world held its breath.

"Yeah," said Baxter at last. "Well, you're kind of in our

way." He nodded toward the road behind the group, but none of the creatures paid any attention to him.

"*Rantasas*," said the giant again.

This time it reached beneath the rags that remained of its shirt. Baxter aimed his rifle at the Rhothag's forehead. His finger tightened on the trigger, but still the giant appeared unconcerned. When the beast opened its fist Dylan noticed that the incredibly long fingers ended in knifelike ebony talons. Baxter frowned, glancing from the claw to Dylan, then back to the giant. But in that instant something had happened. When Baxter turned back, *all* the Rhothag had opened their fists. Ninety talons gleamed with their own light.

"Shit," said Crank, raising both pistols.

Dylan felt the world around him slowing down, as though he were on some plane that none of the others could sense, his thoughts moving at lightning speed. The night seemed to stop dropping over the trees, the feeble breeze stilled in the branches. Why did the beast know the same nonsense word that had rattled around in Dylan's head when he'd fought the thing in his house, the same word the chief had used in the clearing just before he died?

"Wait!" he shouted, the echo of his voice booming back across the highway. "*Rantasas! Rantasas!*"

The giant lurched as though struck from behind, its eyes glazing. "*Rantasas Mella Duun*," it answered, its voice a low rumble.

Dylan nodded, stepping forward, shoving Crank toward the Rhothag.

"What the fuck?" muttered Crank, stumbling through the snow.

"Keep going!" said Dylan, watching the Rhothag part in front of them. "*Rantasas! Rantasas!*"

Crank straightened, trudging across the drifts and into the area of snow tramped flat by the Rhothag's bare feet, then quickly through to the other side. The beasts studied them with fierce red eyes beneath furrowed brows, their talons hanging limp at their sides, murmuring in their unintelligible tongue. Dylan sensed their hunger, and he knew that Baxter was right. These things fed on human flesh. He shoved Crank harder as the mob slowly began to close in behind them, and glancing over his shoulder he realized that while they were letting him and Crank through without so much as touching them, Baxter was not going to be so lucky.

The giant slapped a paw the size of a baseball mitt around Baxter, jerking him backward so suddenly he dropped his rifle, and Dylan aimed the shotgun directly into the thing's face. But once again the Rhothag took no notice of the weapon, instead peering deeply into Dylan's eyes. Baxter struggled but could not break free of the thing's embrace.

"*Rantasas Mella Duun!*" said the Rhothag, in a voice that sounded like a drumbeat in hell.

"*Rantasas Mella Duun!*" Dylan echoed, having no idea what he was saying.

The Rhothag nodded, as though satisfied, then jerked Baxter back even harder against its chest, its other claw drawn back for a killing blow.

"Come on!" said Crank, jerking Dylan backward. "We can't fight them all."

Dylan pulled the trigger of the shotgun. The giant's head exploded in a burst of blood and gore, and Baxter dropped out of the thing's clutches, snatching up his rifle as the monster fell.

Dylan pumped another round into the shotgun, but the rest of the Rhothag drew back a pace, confusion set deep on their craggy faces. One of them knelt beside their dead leader, examining what was left of his head with the tip of one needle claw. The other creatures watched them until they managed to make it beyond the next ridge, where the three of them collapsed, resting their guns on the snow, peering back, wondering if they were going to be pursued.

"What's happening to me?" murmured Dylan, the echo of the alien voice still hanging in the back of his mind. Insanity was no longer some dark shadow that haunted his house or attacked out of the night woods. Now it was hideous mutant creatures out of some fifties horror flick. And he was *talking* to them. He glanced from Baxter to Crank, but there were no answers in either face.

"What's happening to me?" he screamed.

"I don't know," said Baxter, too quietly. "But I think maybe you're changing because of the Darkening."

"Changing how?" asked Dylan, wondering if he really wanted an answer.

"You're becoming whatever you're supposed to become."

"Or else he's going crazy," muttered Crank, helpfully.

Dylan glared at him, but Crank just shrugged.

"And if I don't *want* to change?"

This time Baxter's face held the answer.

"Right," said Dylan, shaking his head.

"Thanks for the help, by the way," said Baxter, nodding at Dylan, frowning at Crank.

"I didn't think we could take all of them without getting killed," said Crank.

"You were going to sacrifice me, you fuck!"

"You're alive, aren't you?"

"No thanks to you."

"Barnes is going to the Keep no matter what it takes. You know my loyalties."

"I do now. You still think those things are just some mutants caused by . . . what, a secret military virus or something?"

"This fucking snow's starting to melt," said Crank, ignoring him. "If we stay on the freeway we can make better time to DC. If we don't run into another storm."

"Or more of those things," said Dylan, glancing down the road.

"Screw you, Crank," said Baxter. "We'll have this out here. Now."

"Suits me fine," said Crank, thumbing the safety on his pistol.

"You could have given a shit about Reese getting killed. Or me, you little son of a bitch."

"What the hell is that supposed to mean?" said Crank,

his eyes flashing. "You and Reese were the renegades. You and your buddies."

"What's going on?" asked Dylan, struggling to shove the two men apart. "I thought you guys were on the same side."

"Crank thinks we're a bunch of traitors," said Baxter. "A group of us that broke from Rex Deus a couple of years ago. Now we're the real Rex Deus."

"You lying sack of shit!" said Crank.

"Am I? You said it yourself: Reese and I were the only good guys in town. So why were the other Rex Deus members there reporting to the chief of police?"

"Are you saying that some of Clayborn's people were working for Qedem Melech?" asked Crank, his voice so low Dylan had to lean to hear.

"It sure as hell looked like it," said Baxter. "So tell Dylan what you believe is going on now. Tell him everything Clayborn believes."

"We're wasting time," said Crank, still glaring knives at Baxter.

"What's the hurry?" said Baxter. "Why rush back to the Keep? According to you, this is all just some technical glitch. Rex Deus can't fix that. There is no Darkening. No Old Ones. Why do you bother?"

"There's still Qedem Melech," said Crank.

"So what's Dylan got to do with that?"

Crank's frown took up his whole face. "Qedem Melech wants him. That makes him important to us."

Baxter nodded, waving one hand behind him. "But important how? Look around you. Are you still going to try to explain all this away? Do you still think those of us who broke away were wrong?"

Crank spat onto the snow. "We'll find out when we get to the Keep. Clayborn will know what to do."

Baxter shook his head. "By now even Clayborn has figured out he was wrong. Why can't you?"

"What do *you* believe?" asked Crank, looking at Dylan.

Dylan hadn't expected the question from that quarter, and he wasn't sure of his answer.

"I believe everything has a rational explanation," he said, slowly.

Crank nodded, turning up the road again.

"So do I," he said.

But Dylan thought his voice sounded more hopeful than assured.

The foothills of the Catskills glistened beneath sheets of cascading water, the streams burst from their banks, and the rivers surged across the low ground, turning the valleys and fields into seething brown seas that matched the brown tufts of grass appearing as the snow vanished. The air was heavy with the smell of decay and Dylan noticed that even the moss on the trees seemed to be fading and dying.

They found shelter to wait out the flood in a large block building that had been an industrial pump house and bottling plant for spring water. Thousands of plastic bottles sat on a spaghetti array of stainless-steel conveyors now frozen in time, awaiting the flip of a switch by a morning shift that would never arrive. Bins of blue caps rested beside a chute that fed into the guts of the machinery, and puddles of water on the concrete floor attested to burst pipes now empty and unlikely to be repaired or refilled. Huge stacks of pallets laden with bottles held enough drinking water to last the three of them for the rest of their lives. But every bottle would taste flat and acrid, each one opened a little worse than the last. Every meal they ate, every jar of peanut butter or can of salmon seemed a little more like biting into paper than food. But there was nothing else to eat.

The manager's office offered a view of the flood outside through wide metal-framed windows and was outfitted with an oil, wick-type heater that Dylan thought might be as old as the Second World War. After a day spent mostly in the confines of that little room the place reeked of old soup, sweat, and damp clothing, but at least it was warm and dry.

Three or four times a day Crank stomped outside and hiked down the steep drive to check out the water level, often going out for an hour or more, searching for a way around what had become a deluge. He was gone again now.

"He isn't going to find anything," said Dylan, staring out the window into the thick overcast sky. "Maybe tomorrow. The water's going down pretty fast now that the snow's mostly gone. But I'm not going to try hiking around a flood, I'll tell you that."

"I don't blame you," said Baxter.

"Why are you so sure you're right and he's wrong?" asked Dylan, sipping coffee—brewed from the bottled water—that tasted like . . . *nothing*.

Baxter shrugged. "Because unlike Crank I believe more than my own senses. I don't know what you are, Dylan. I only know that we have to stop what's coming, and your wife was one of the people who could do that, or that's what I've always been taught. We've been looking for her a hell of a long time." He sighed loudly. "I can't believe we lost her mother."

"Why did you ever *have* her mother? You talk as though Veronica was in captivity or something."

"I guess maybe she got to feeling that way, and you can't really blame her. I think she just didn't want to accept who she was, and she didn't want her kids to have to suffer the cloistered life she had. But she wasn't actually in captivity. Or if it was it was more like protective custody. She knew better than anyone that the Old Ones were coming back, and I think maybe she didn't want to be any part of the fight. I'm sure she was scared. Who the hell wouldn't be?"

"What was her talent?" asked Dylan.

"She was clairvoyant. She could foretell the future."

"You're serious." If Ronnie had passed anything to him, it hadn't been clairvoyance. Up to now everything that had happened to him had been so far out in left field he couldn't have prophesied it in a million years.

"Very. Veronica was an amazing woman."

"The couple of times I met her I got the feeling she didn't like me. Clairvoyance would explain why."

"What do you mean?"

"If she could really see the future, she must have foreseen the mess I made of it."

"How did *you* make a mess of it?"

"Ronnie's dead."

"Did you kill her?"

"I didn't save her."

"I don't understand. I thought she died of some incurable illness."

"She did."

"Then that's the stupidest thing I've ever heard."

Dylan glared. No one had called him stupid in a very long time.

"Well, it is," said Baxter. "Get real. People die. Most times there's not a damned thing you can do about it."

"That's what the doctors said."

"But you didn't believe them?"

"I should have found someone else. There are always alternatives."

"Did you try?"

"I didn't try enough."

"Sounds to me like you need to stop beating yourself up."

He stared directly into Baxter's eyes before speaking. "You have no idea how it feels. It hurts so damned bad sometimes . . ."

"Hurting and guilt are two different things."

Dylan sighed, sensing Ronnie's own sort of down-home wisdom in Baxter's words. He knew what the man said was true. He'd known it long ago. He just didn't want to accept it, didn't want to give up the guilt that kept him tied to Ronnie so easily.

"We've all lost someone we cared about, Dylan. I know you want to think that you loved your wife more than anyone in the world ever loved before, but I'm sorry. It just ain't so."

"In other words, suck it up."

Baxter shrugged. "She's been gone two years."

"I'm well aware of how long she's been gone," said Dylan, discovering for the first time that he'd lost track of the exact number of days.

"Veronica told me one time, years ago, that she foresaw a very eventful life for me, but that I would lose people I cared about along the way. I have."

"Doesn't sound like anything your neighborhood Gypsy couldn't have told you."

"She offered to name names. She'd done that for us before, but we learned the hard way that knowing too much of your future is not a good thing."

"Why not? I'd think it would help you plan."

Baxter shook his head. "She could foresee *some* things, others were more general, like danger coming. We used what we could. But how'd you like to know the exact moment of your death? What would you do?"

Dylan shook his head. "You could react *to* it."

"Try to change it, you mean?"

He nodded.

"Doesn't work. You might not be there to walk in front of the oncoming car, but about that time your bedroom ceiling would probably choose to fall in. Fate has a way of trying to prove itself right."

"And that was the power Veronica was supposed to have passed on to Ronnie?"

Baxter shook his head. "Everyone in Veronica's line has something different. Some are telepaths, some telekinetics, some clairvoyants. I heard that one of them a couple of hundred years ago was a shape-shifter, but I don't know if that's true or not."

Dylan shook his head in disbelief, but there was no guile in Baxter's face.

"Why her line?"

"If anyone ever knew that, it's something else lost to history. I just know it's a fact, whether Crank chooses to believe it or not. How he rationalizes Qedem Melech's need for you—his own need for you—I don't quite understand. I think all that's happened has brought Crank right to the brink of something he doesn't like."

"Maybe insanity," said Dylan, thinking that he and Crank weren't that far apart.

"Maybe," said Baxter, smiling. "But I don't think so. Crank is too hardheaded to go crazy."

"You really believe that these Old Ones are coming to take over the earth?"

"Yes."

"And they're like those things on the road, those Rhothag?"

"No."

"Then what are they?"

Baxter shrugged. "Well, no one alive has ever seen one. They haven't crossed over to our side yet, or I'm pretty sure we'd know it. But they're real enough. There wouldn't be Rhothag walking around if the Old Ones weren't gaining in strength."

"I still don't believe any of it. Except the Rhothag. You're right. They're real enough."

"Look around you. What do you think is happening?"

Since leaving Arcos they had found no power on anywhere, and they had seen only the one other survivor—the man at the store. All the domesticated animals, other than a few cats, seemed to be gone as well. But the cats they had spotted after Arcos had seemed far more feral than they had a right to be after such a short period, disappearing as soon as they were spotted.

"Even so," said Dylan, "my first thought still has to be some kind of man-made disaster."

"How? What kind of disaster? Where did everyone go?"

"You tell me. Where *did* they go?"

Baxter frowned. "I don't know. So much of past battles with the Old Ones has been lost. After all, the last battle was supposed to have happened before the Egyptians ever came to power."

"So it could be just a myth. A fable."

"And the Rhothag?" said Baxter, hammering home.

Dylan shrugged. "You knew what they were when you first saw them," he said. "How?"

"We've all heard stories about great heroes in the past battling the Rhothag. Supposedly they can only be killed by cutting their heads off or stabbing them in the eyes, mouth, or throat."

"My shotgun seemed to work well enough."

Baxter let out what could have been a long-awaited sigh of relief. "You blew its head off. I guess that would suffice. Myth says that the Rhothag who have been killed turn back to men after they're dead."

"Live men?"

"I don't know. I don't suspect so."

"That thing didn't look like it was going to change into anything."

"Even true stories have a way of being embellished over the millennia."

"That's what I'm worried about."

Baxter sighed again, but Dylan read more frustration than relief in this one. "I don't know what else I can do to convince you to believe in something you can't see or touch. There really is no way to understand what I know. I just know it."

Like Sensei and his *mysteries*.

"I almost thought I could understand what the Rhothag's words meant," said Dylan quietly.

Baxter's eyebrows peaked. "Most of us with Rex Deus have been walking on the wild side so long that we've developed *feelings*. I heard one time that just accepting the reality of another world makes you sensitive to its presence. You learn to trust your hunches. When you see shadows flickering in a dark room you don't automatically assume it's your imagination or just a curtain blowing in the breeze. Back there on the road, when those things started muttering in their foul language, it was like I was slipping down a long dark tunnel."

"*Rantasas?* You understood the word?"

"Yeah. Some of us know a little of the Old Speech. *Rantasas* means *I serve*. Only I think it can mean *You serve*, too, or something like you *will* serve, 'cause I could feel it pressing in on me, trying to force me to my knees, and I knew that once I got down there I wasn't going to get up and still be me."

Dylan was stunned that someone else had experienced the exact same feeling he had.

"You'd turn into one of the Rhothag," he whispered.

"Maybe not then and there. But if I knelt down, I was going to be giving up my soul to that voice, and I would sooner or later be one of those things, or maybe something even worse."

"I've had that same voice inside my head way too often," he admitted at last. "There was a darkness in my house. A presence I can't explain. When it came after me it shut off every light, and it even made it seem like the day outside was night."

"I never heard of the day-to-night thing. If there's something that can really do that, then that's really scary."

"So, Ronnie was the last of the bloodline," mused

Dylan, struggling to understand. "But I'm only a relation by marriage."

Baxter nodded. "You sure you've never felt any weird talents surfacing?"

Dylan sighed. "I used to have these nightmares that I couldn't remember," he admitted. "Then I started waking up in different places in my house at night without knowing how I got there but certain there was something in the house with me. Sometimes I've been certain I didn't actually *move* myself at all."

"What do you mean?"

"It seemed as though I just popped into another room. Only I was half-awake. I always thought it was part of my hallucinations."

"Only now you're not so sure you were hallucinating?"

"Maybe," he said, staring at Baxter. "What caused the breakup in Rex Deus?"

"A group of us split from the main group a few years ago. More joined over time as they started to read the handwriting on the wall. Now there's two *branches*, as you say, but neither accepts the other. Those like me who believe in the Old Ones and the Darkening and all the *hooey*, as Crank would say, are on the outside. Clayborn and Crank and the others, who believe Qedem Melech is basically just a terrorist organization, are on the other."

"But Crank's side is in control."

"They kept the Keep," said Baxter, nodding. "But I think now they're gonna have to come around to our way of thinking. Don't you?"

"Crank doesn't seem to be," said Dylan, frowning.

"I've known Crank a long time. He's about as dedicated to Clayborn as a man could be. But everything's different now."

"He would have left you, back on the road."

"Yeah . . . But I think in Crank's mind that was a logical decision. His duty is to get you to the Keep. Mine is, too."

"So you're okay with that now?"

"Not okay. But I can understand why he made the decision."

"He doesn't trust you. Do you trust him?"

"I trust him to do his job. You'll reach the Keep as long as one of us is alive. I guess I'll just have to watch out for my own ass from now on."

"That must be comforting for you."

Baxter chuckled just as Crank stomped into the room, his boots thick with mud.

"The bridge is above water," said Crank. "By morning we move out."

Lucy, Wagner, and Blondie stared numbly at the remains of Marivelle, once a pretty little town backed up against the eastern slopes of Virginia's Blue Ridge Mountains. Now, limned by stars that lit the sky in tiny shell bursts, the town reminded Lucy of photographs she'd seen of bombed-out cities in Germany during the Second World War. A conflagration had taken whole blocks, leaving nothing but ragged brick jigsaws upright. They trudged through the rubble-lined streets, glancing nervously behind them.

"What happened here?" asked Lucy.

Wagner shrugged. "Could have been a fight between

survivors and some of the Rhothag. Or it might have been an accident. The fire departments are all on strike."

Blondie chuckled, and Lucy slapped him on the shoulder, shaking her head.

"Very funny," she said. "But the map said we'd find a city here, not a pile of ash. I don't feel like hiking any farther down the highway tonight. Do either of you?"

"No," said Wagner. "I was worried we wouldn't make it this far."

The Rhothag were becoming more numerous and harder to evade. A couple of hours before dusk they'd just about decided to bed down in the small village of Evansville when Lucy sensed some of the creatures in the area and pointed to a pair of shining red eyes peeking out of the basement window of a house across the street. The curtain had snapped closed, and the three of them had voted with their feet, moving on.

"Well, we did, and we have to make the best of it," said Lucy. "The whole town couldn't have burned. There must be something left. We just have to find it."

But in the moonlight the downtown was nothing but a maze of collapsed concrete blocks, bricks, and melted and broken glass. Even though the fire seemed to have burned itself out weeks ago, the acrid air still reeked of smoke. They climbed over pile after pile of debris only to find themselves surrounded by rubble again with no ready exit. Finally, Lucy discovered an open alleyway where two walls had fallen against one another to create a giant but precarious lean-to. They passed cautiously through the towering tunnel of brick and into a street bordering a small park. Lucy fell onto one of the iron benches, and her guardian angels sat beside her, all of them staring at the macabre scene of destruction silhouetted against the night sky. Movement caught Lucy's eye and she spun, squinting at one of the massive piles of rubble blocking the street. A pair of eyes twinkled in the starlight.

Wagner and Blondie raised their rifles, but Lucy signaled for them to wait. She climbed slowly to her feet, took three steps in the direction of the debris pile, and stopped, kneeling in the street, calling softly.

"Come here, boy. It's all right. Come on. Don't be afraid."

As tentatively as a small child entering a darkened room a shaggy black-and-white dog edged out of the collapsed masonry and approached Lucy. It kept its head lowered, but its eyes never left her face. When the pooch was near enough Lucy held out her hand.

"Not too close," said Wagner. "That mutt could be rabid."

"He isn't rabid," said Lucy, slipping her hand from the dog's cold nose to pat it gently on the head. It leaned forward to let her scratch behind its ears.

"Border collie," said Blondie, easing up to kneel beside Lucy and inspect its collar. "And it's had its shots. But there's no name."

"*It's* a she," said Lucy. "I wonder where she came from? We haven't seen a dog since the Darkening started."

Wagner shook his head. "Looks like maybe there's a few doggie survivors after all."

Blondie found some jerky in his pack and fed it to the dog.

"If she could talk," said Wagner, resting his rifle on the street, "I imagine she'd have quite a tale to tell. What're you going to name her?"

Lucy stared at the destruction all around.

"Phoenix," she said.

"That fits."

The dog followed them back to the bench, placing her head in Lucy's lap, delightedly gobbling more jerky. Lucy stretched her legs and leaned back on the bench, taking in the devastation, the musty odor of burnt wood and something sickly sweet that might have been toasted flesh.

"Is this Hell?" she whispered.

"I don't think so," said Blondie, surprising her.

"Oh, no?" she said. "Why not?"

"We aren't dead, for one. And I didn't do anything wrong, for another."

Lucy had to laugh. "You're right. You didn't. Maybe I just dragged you along."

"What did you do so wrong?" asked Wagner.

Lucy hesitated. "Lots of things."

"Like what?"

"I let a little girl die once," she said, quietly. "I never admitted it before. Not even to myself, I guess."

Both men looked at her, and she knew that they would ask her no more unless she wanted to talk.

"I didn't do it, really," she said, feeling the old emotions creeping up into her chest. "I don't think . . . I wanted to help her. But I didn't."

"How old were you?" asked Wagner.

"Ten. She and her sister were my next-door neighbors. I never played with them. I wasn't allowed to associate with anyone outside of school. But I used to watch them from my bedroom window when they went to the park across the street. Annette and Debbie would take their dolls and baby carriages and play house under the trees. People would stop and talk to them, probably asking how their *children* were, things like that. I'd line up my dolls beneath the window and imagine that I was with them. I'd even make up answers to people who stopped to talk. Isn't that stupid?"

Wagner shook his head.

"One day they had all their dolls resting on the bench and Annette was lecturing them about something. She was the bossy one. Debbie was a year younger and would always follow Annette's lead. The day was hot. I remember there was almost no breeze through my window, but I could hear the trucks honking, people chattering on the sidewalk. I could smell the apple pie my mother was baking in the kitchen. I saw Annette point back toward their house, and I could see that Debbie was arguing with her. Annette got that stern look on her face and put her little fists on her hips, and Debbie gave in. Something had been forgotten at home, and Debbie had to go get it."

She could see the little girl's face as though seventeen

years and her entire adulthood had not intervened. She pictured the afternoon sun glistening on Debbie's hair and shimmering on the tops of her patent leather shoes.

"The little sister was hit by a car?" asked Blondie, when Lucy didn't continue. His voice sounded unusually gruff.

"No," she said, shaken roughly out of the past. "While she was in the house a man on a bicycle stopped to speak to Annette. She was talking to him, adjusting her dolls, placing a blanket over their legs to protect them from the sun. I think the man was just a stranger, and she seemed to be trying to politely ignore him. It's funny, but looking back, it seems like the whole world, everyone on the street, everyone in the park, was focused just on Annette and that man. But of course that can't be." Her voice had a quaver to it now.

She glanced at Wagner, and he shook his head.

"No," she said, clearing her throat. "That's just my imagination. If anything, everyone would have been watching Debbie when she came back down the stoop carrying the pots and pans."

"Pots and pans?"

"Annette had decided to have a cookout for the dolls. She'd sent Debbie back to fetch the equipment they needed. But Debbie was the smallest, and it looked as though she'd tried to carry out every pot her mother owned. She barely made it down the steps with the armload of pans and lids, and when she stepped off the curb she dropped them all. The racket caught everyone's attention. It's all frozen there. Just like a photograph."

"What happened?" asked Wagner, gently placing one of his powerful hands over hers. His hard blue eyes were suddenly soft.

"Screeching brakes. Screams. Pots and pans rolling down the street. Blood."

"You said she wasn't hit."

"Not Debbie. Annette. I had turned back to her just as Debbie stepped off the curb. When the first pot hit the pavement Annette glanced back. She saw the truck first.

She screamed, shoved past the man on the bike, knocking him right on his butt, and raced out into the street. Then the truck blocked my view, and it was all over so fast . . ."

"She saved her sister."

"Yes."

"But she was hit."

Lucy nodded, the images still clearer to her than the destruction around her now. "My mother caught me at the front door. I fought her. But I was only ten, and she had strong arms for such a small woman. I screamed and cried, but she wouldn't let me go."

"What could you have done?"

She stared into his eyes, wanting to let go, to release the horrible icy brew that had filled her for too many years to remember. "Nothing. It was too late."

He squeezed her hands between his.

"You did nothing wrong, Lucy."

"I did nothing at all. It was the first time I ever sensed a wrongness like that . . . the truck coming . . . Even if I couldn't stop it, I could have shouted a warning. I didn't even call an ambulance."

"Surely your mother did that?"

"No. Someone else must have. My mother was afraid someone would ask her name. We couldn't be involved. When I told her I knew the truck was coming she told my father, and they both sat me down that night for a long lecture on why I must never say anything like that again. Why I must tell no one."

"That was the way you had to live, Lucy. Otherwise, they'd have found you and killed you or worse. You know that. And if it was the first time your talent manifested itself, you had no way of knowing what was happening."

She nodded. "But for years I tried to forget. I convinced myself the whole thing hadn't happened at all, that it was a stupid childhood false memory. Then, when I felt it again, I always tried to deny it, except for the night the danger came so close and I warned my father . . . Even then I wanted to believe I was just like everyone else. But I knew in my heart I wasn't."

"You couldn't have understood what you were feeling. You were just a kid. This talent of yours wasn't developed enough for you to even know what it was. Some people would say you just weren't meant to save that little girl."

"What would you say?"

"I'd say that was probably the truth. When your time's up, it's up."

"So you believe in fate?"

"Don't you?"

"If I did, I'd have to say that fate sucks."

He laughed. "I didn't say any different. But it can be a good thing, too."

"How so?"

He shrugged. "Your talent has saved us more than once. And we found you, didn't we? You're alive now, right? We found Phoenix, here. Isn't that fate, too?"

Suddenly tears streamed down her cheeks and she clutched her arms tightly about her, shaking her head back and forth over and over. He reached for her, but she stopped him with a hand on his arm.

"I don't want your *fate*. I don't want to be the person you want me to be," she sobbed. "I just want to be normal."

"I know," he said softly.

"But you're not going to let me," she said. "Are you?"

His eyes were so sad they made her want to comfort *him*. "It isn't me, Lucy. If it were up to me, I'd let you be whatever you wanted."

"Then let me go."

"Go where?"

She followed his eyes across the shattered remains of the town, and she knew in her heart that there was no longer any place for her to run, if there ever had been. Finally, a heavy sigh seemed to empty all her tears, and she wiped the last of them on the back of her sleeve.

"I'm just a human being with one little talent," she whispered.

"Maybe that's all we need," he said softly.

"I told you I don't believe in providence, or God, or whatever you want to call it."

But her argument was sounding more and more like whistling in a graveyard even to her. There were creatures all around them, out of some dark fable beyond any imagining. And for the life of her she didn't believe Stephen Hawking—had he miraculously survived—would have been able to explain them. This was no experiment gone awry. It was something that *fit* no equation. Still, she battled against accepting anything on such a weak thread as something like *faith*.

Wagner leaned back on the bench and rubbed the bridge of his nose, and Lucy noticed the exhaustion in his face. She started to thank him for everything he and Blondie had done for her, for being the friends she had never allowed herself to have. But suddenly she sensed Rhothag nearby.

The dog growled low in its throat, and she glanced in the direction Blondie had taken. After a moment he appeared, trotting back toward them with his shoulders hunched. When he held up three fingers and thumbed back over his shoulder she and Wagner jumped to their feet. Phoenix's hackles rose, and the dog stiffened.

"Just over that pile of rubble," whispered Blondie, when he reached them. "They're sniffing around like hunting dogs."

"Lucy, come with me," muttered Wagner, signaling for Blondie to cover their backs.

Blondie disappeared into the debris as Wagner led Lucy and the dog into the trees. When they reached a small cinder-block restroom beside the swings, Phoenix trotted ahead to smell the door before turning back to her new masters and signifying the all clear with a wag of her tail. They slipped inside, Wagner peering back out the half-open door, while the dog sniffed delightedly once more at the thick urine odor, then began inspecting each of the three toilet stalls.

When Blondie came racing back through the park, Wagner leaned outside and waved him in.

"Well?" said Wagner.

Blondie pointed. "They're making their way through the rubble." He jerked his thumb toward the other end of the street. "There're more of them that way."

"Shit," said Wagner.

"We can't stay here," said Blondie. "I saw one of them down on his hands and knees sniffing the sidewalk. And he was looking in this direction."

"All right," said Wagner, holding the door for Lucy. "Let's move out, then."

Phoenix trotted out of the confines of the restroom, sneezing. She glanced over her shoulder at Lucy, then padded off toward the far end of the park.

Wagner glanced at the dog, and Lucy shrugged. "I don't think she likes the Rhothags any more than we do. And she's survived here all this time."

"Come on, then," said Wagner, hurrying after the dog.

The park ended in a debris pile where another large brick building had burned. A brass plaque dangling from a section of wall read COUNTY REGISTRAR OF DEEDS. For a moment Lucy feared that Phoenix had deserted them. When the dog's head bobbed up above a jumble of bricks they followed her down a set of cellar stairs into deep darkness.

"I don't like this," muttered Wagner, edging ahead of Lucy, aiming his rifle into the basement.

Lucy shook her head. "This place feels all right to me."

"It's still a dead end."

"You got any better ideas?"

Wagner shook his head, flicking a butane lighter. They were standing in a burnt-out office. Blackened file cabinets stood against the walls. Crumpled bits of burnt carpet curled beneath metal desks. This time, when the dog woofed, the sound echoed from somewhere farther back in the scorched confines of the basement. Lucy headed in the direction of the bark.

"This building probably isn't structurally sound," said Wagner, trying to keep up.

Lucy laughed, and when she did both Wagner and Blondie had to laugh with her.

When she stumbled into ankle-deep water she realized that a section of the basement floor had subsided from the heat or the shifting of the building above. A water main must have burst, or the automatic sprinkler system had enough water in it to flood part of the floor. She could hear the dog pattering lightly not too far ahead. A section of the floor above had collapsed, narrowing the path, and she could barely see by the flickering light of Wagner's lighter. The smell of ash and old mildew was so thick it saturated her lungs, and the water rose to her knees. If it got any deeper, Phoenix was going to be swimming.

Lucy knew that county records were often stored in locations like this. The cellar had probably been a lousy place to work *before* Hell actually arrived here. But because she'd spent plenty of research time in places just like it searching for lost parents, she also knew that there was often more than one exit. More than likely Phoenix had discovered it already.

"Give me the lighter," she said, taking it from Wagner.

When she turned back, Phoenix had returned, wagging her tail and dancing from foot to foot in water that was up to her chest. The dog woofed under her breath, determined to hurry her newfound family along.

"We're coming," said Lucy, waving the dog on.

Phoenix spun and disappeared around a pile of singed beams.

When they reached the back stairs the dog waited at the top, glancing up and down the street, sniffing the air but wagging her tail. Wagner waved Blondie up, and Blondie disappeared from view. When he returned he signaled for them to follow, but it was Phoenix who was still leading the troop. They trotted down the sidewalk behind her into a section of town that had miraculously escaped the blaze. The dog wended up first one business street, then another, until she led them into a residential neighborhood, scampering up a driveway and inside the open back door of a large brick home. Lucy glanced across the moonlit backyard at a small slide and plastic pool.

The dog sat beside the kitchen table, her wet tail slapping the vinyl floor, panting, her mouth forming a perfect imitation of a human grin. Blondie caught Lucy by the arm as she started into the house.

"Let me check it out first."

"No one's been in there but the dog," she said.

"You can feel that?" asked Wagner.

"I can see it," she said, kneeling down on the back steps to bring herself to eye level with the kitchen floor and waving Wagner and Blondie down beside her.

"Look," she said, pointing out the thousands of tracks in the dust of the floor, all made by the dog who now stared at them curiously.

"I'll be damned," said Wagner. "How did you know they'd be there?"

She shrugged. "I took a course once on skip tracing and bounty hunting. We had a guest lecturer who claimed you could track a man down the halls of a building. We thought he was crazy, but he proved himself. Dust is always accumulating, and people and animals leave tracks in it. All you need is the right angle and the right light." She nodded over her shoulder at the low-slung moon.

Wagner and Blondie followed her into the house still shaking their heads as Lucy ruffled the fur on the dog's head.

"You did good, girl. You did real good," she said, dropping exhaustedly into a chair at the table. The dog trotted over to the kitchen sink and nosed the handle of the cupboard, glancing back toward them. When Blondie found a bag of dog food and some doggie treats inside, he poured a bowlful for the dog and gave her water from a bottle in his pack.

"I still don't think we should stay here. The Rhothag weren't looking for *us* before when they missed Phoenix," argued Wagner.

Lucy squeezed some of the water out of her trousers. "I

think she's smarter than you give her credit for. Is it true that hounds can't follow a scent across water?"

Wagner frowned. "Bloodhounds can."

"Let's hope those things aren't as good as bloodhounds," she said. "I can't run another foot without rest."

"Even if we lost them in the water," said Blondie, "they can cut our trail if they find it after we came out."

"Well, if she can't go on, we can't carry her far and fight, too," said Wagner. "Lock the doors, check all the windows. We'll secure this place the best we can and try to get some rest."

Lucy listened to the men tromping through the house as the dog chomped contentedly on her food. Outside, the moon had dropped through the clouds to reveal a crescent edge beneath the top of the window, like a great yellow eye, peering into the room. Lucy shuddered. The dog sensed her discomfort and left her meal to place her muzzle once more in Lucy's lap. Instead of the horrible orb in the window, Lucy glanced into the dog's faithful face.

"They aren't coming tonight, are they?" she whispered, kissing the dog softly on its rough forehead. "We'd know, wouldn't we?"

The dog sat down between her legs to let Lucy hug her. The feel of a warm body and a beating heart so close to her own touched the old vacant spot in Lucy's soul. She stroked the dog's head, feeling its wet breath against her breast, wondering if it wouldn't be better just to give up, to stay there and let the Rhothag do with her as they would.

She heard Wagner slip into the doorway behind her. She could tell the two men apart now simply by the sound of their footsteps. Was that some other heightened awareness enhanced by the Darkening, or simply a reaction to a very dangerous environment?

When she turned to face him he looked so solid, filling the doorway, and she knew he was as stout inside as out. What drove these men to face hardship and danger that she could hardly have imagined only weeks before, for a woman they didn't even know?

"Men died on the road trying to save me the night I was kidnapped," she said. "How well did you know them?"

"Well."

"Another man died in the forest by the bridge, and I'll bet some died on the road that day slowing down our pursuit. You and Blondie could have been killed more than once."

"We believe in you," he said, answering her unasked question.

Once again she wondered if she were supposed to be able to read a lot more into his brief epithets than she did.

"Why?" she asked. "What am I supposed to do?"

He smiled and his eyes gleamed. "It'll come to you."

The man was just so damned exasperating.

"Well, Blondie didn't have to walk off, just because I choked up back in the park. But it was a nice thing to do."

"His name is Roy," said Wagner quietly.

In the feeble light through the window it looked as though he were about to weep, but the idea seemed ludicrous.

"He didn't walk off because you were crying," he said.

"You think he'd already spotted the Rhothag?"

"No," he said, shaking his head.

"Why, then?"

"His little sister was killed by a car right in front of his eyes," he said, letting out a long breath. "He couldn't save her, either."

She rose from the chair and stood studying his face.

"You're all like brothers," she said, envying him.

He nodded. "I've known Roy since he was a kid."

"All my life I wanted friends," she said, quietly. "To be part of something. When I was little my parents discouraged any relationships with other kids, and as I grew older I realized that I was missing something, that I'd never learned how to *make* friends. But it was more than that. There's something gone from inside me. Something I can't explain, like a hole. Sometimes I feel as though I don't have all the organs other people have."

"That's silly—"

"It's not. I wish you could feel it so you'd know. I used to have a make-believe friend when I was small. My mother said it was good that I had such a fertile imagination, but really I was just a pitiful, lonely little girl."

"You're not alone anymore."

"Tell me what you expect me to do," she said.

"Save us all."

She stared at him for a long moment.

"But how?"

"I wish I knew."

"You work for this mysterious organization that's guarded my hereditary *line*. You've done that all your life, and you really don't know any more about what's going on?"

"I know the Old Ones are real. Qedem Melech is real. And now Clayborn and the others will have to accept that. Somewhere at the Keep is the answer to all this. It has to be."

"I hope you're right."

"Me too," he said, smiling.

"Friendship has to be earned, I think."

"You think you're not holding up your end?"

She laughed. "You don't even know what my end is."

His smile faltered a little. "All the ages of man ended with the Old Ones," he said. "But a savior arose, and man made it through."

Her own smile dulled, too.

"My family."

"Your line," said Wagner, nodding. "And Rex Deus, the people of my line, protected yours. That's who you are. That's who I am."

He reached out and gently ran his fingers down her cheeks. "It will come."

"How can you be so sure?"

His smile swept away some of the weight from her shoulders.

"Because I believe," he said. "Remember?"

"I want to believe, too," she said, her throat tightening. "I really want to. But I still feel this emptiness inside."

"Maybe they'll find a way to fix that at the Keep, too."

"You're putting a lot of faith into the people there."

"Not really. My faith isn't in people. It never has been. All you have to do is believe."

"Like Dorothy."

He nodded. "That's right. Look what she did to the wicked witch."

"I think this might take more than a bucket of water."

"I think you're right," he said, slipping by her to check the lock on the door.

His final words, meant to reassure, only worsened her inner turmoil. While outside a sly wind stroked the worn clapboard siding, as though a thousand cats rubbed against the house, marking it and the occupants as theirs.

For the millionth time Father Anton Remedios wondered what fickle twist of fate had placed a man of his abilities in this solitary cell, what strange and unknowable plan had left him here, had willed his continued survival, to test his *lack* of faith. If the Holy Father had not willed that he should be allowed to study the arcane and ancient texts and artifacts in the Vatican vaults, then he would never have questioned, would never have begun the voyage of discovery that would eventually lead to heresy and finally excommunication. But being separated from the Church hurt less than separation from his studies, because he knew that for all the beauty and solace that the rituals of Roman

Catholicism represented, the basic tenets of the Church were founded on half-truths and misconceptions.

Time was running out. The portents had begun to appear long before he ended up here. Instances of strange animal behavior were being reported all over the world. Two new comets had been discovered. Earthquakes were increasing worldwide. The list went on. But the Church chose to see them all as coincidence. Anyone who saw signs in them was a kook. Certainly not someone Mother Church wanted on the rolls of the Vatican.

Cardinal Bernaldi wouldn't listen, and then the Vatican Investigator of Arcane Events, Cardinal Delancy, wouldn't listen—although they all thought that they were being more than fair bumping the *problem* of Father Remedios up one more level each time his name came up—until the Holy Father had ruled that if Remedios would not renounce his beliefs, then he would be defrocked and then finally—horror of horrors—excommunicated.

Then, on a brief stay in Milan, Remedios had been approached by an agent of Rex Deus. At first he had been overjoyed that someone else believed as he did. He had readily accompanied the man to the United States, and for a few months he had reveled in the attention the men of Rex Deus lavished on him. He had been allowed to see artifacts and texts, asked to translate esoteric and ancient stelae. He felt at last that he was accomplishing something.

But slowly he began to realize that not all the men of Rex Deus believed as he did. The men who held the real power saw no warnings in the ancient texts, only *evidence* that might be useful to them in their battle with Qedem Melech. To them the Darkening was no more than allegory or fable; the Rhothag and their ilk, mythological beasts akin to gryphons and dragons. The more Remedios attempted to show them the error of their ways the more they distanced themselves from him. Until he became as much of a nuisance to them as he had been to Mother Church, and his newfound *friends* locked him away where he could embarrass none of them ever again. Even in that final debacle, though, he suspected the hand of Roman Catholicism.

Cardinal Delancy had suddenly appeared as Remedios was dining at a small Italian restaurant on the outskirts of DC that supplied a remarkable Minestre Odorose d'erbe that reminded him of home. The old cleric looked completely out of place in a business suit that must have cost more money than Remedios had ever seen at one time but which fit poorly to Remedios's untrained eye. He stood but the cardinal waved him back to his chair, glancing quickly around before seating himself.

"I'm am very pleased to see you, Your Eminence," said Remedios, wondering what more the Church could possibly do to him.

"The feeling is not mutual," said Delancy quietly.

Remedios frowned. "Why have you come, Your Grace? I am no longer a member of Mother Church, as surely you must be aware."

That was an understatement, since Delancy had been instrumental in convincing the Holy Father to go through with Remedios's excommunication.

"That does not stop you from being an embarrassment, it appears," said Delancy, slapping a folded newspaper onto the tabletop, and once more glancing around to ascertain that no eyes other than Remedios's would see the hateful thing.

Remedios glanced at the picture on the front, trying to read the English script upside down. But he knew what the headline said even though the photo of himself was three months old and grainy.

Defrocked Priest Claims End of the World Is Near.

"So you've seen this?" hissed Delancy.

Remedios nodded.

"And you think Holy Mother Church will simply stand by and allow it?"

Remedios shrugged. "As the headline states, I have been removed from the rolls of Mother Church. It no longer shepherds me or aligns itself with my beliefs as I do not align myself with those of the Church. How can I be an embarrassment?"

Delancy read aloud from a paragraph that had been heavily underlined. "Father Anton Remedios claims that the Vatican stores uncounted texts and other pertinent artifacts and data relating to past battles with the Old Ones, godlike beings that return to earth periodically to conquer and pillage. According to Remedios the Catholic Church has known since its outset that these beings existed and that previous ages of man, now lost to our knowledge, also existed but were destroyed by the Old Ones, and that the Church has chosen to cover up the data."

"You cannot continue to make public statements such as this," said Delancy, glaring at Remedios.

Remedios noticed that the roots of the old cardinal's dark moustache were gray, and he smiled. "I am free to make whatever statements I please. If the Vatican chooses to deny them, then simply allow the reporters into the vaults beneath St. Peter's."

"You know we can't do that!"

"Because the truth would be too hard to face?"

"There's nothing in those vaults but indecipherable shards, scraps of text that you *claim* to have read, and old weapons! *You* are the one convinced that they all *mean* something."

"Then open them to the public."

Delancy shook his head, waving away a waiter at the same time. "The artifacts are too open to interpretation. You know there are thousands of manuscript pages down there that many would claim agree with you."

"Exactly."

Delancy's frown split his face. "Written by superstitious

monks, and priests from ages in which they believed that devils walked the earth, that witches flew on broomsticks!"

"I do not know about witches," said Remedios, leaning closer to the table. "But there are certainly times when devils do walk the earth."

Delancy sighed loudly. "This is your last warning," he said, rising and tucking the paper back into his jacket. "Mother Church will not suffer your insolence much longer."

"What is it you propose to do to me? Surely Rome would not murder even an excommunicate priest?"

"Don't be absurd."

"Then what?"

Delancy shook his head. "I can only say that this is your last warning." And with that he exited the restaurant, leaving Remedios frowning in his wake.

Of all the punishments Remedios had contemplated, none had matched the actuality. No one in Rex Deus had informed him that his statements were making *them* nervous. Even though Clayborn gave it to be known early on that he didn't believe in the reality of the Old Ones, he never warned the old priest that he might be treading on dangerous ground. And a conspiracy between Rex Deus and Mother Church was beyond Remedios's comprehension. But that was how it had happened.

Now he counted off thirty twisted bits of cloth in the torn mattress in which he sheltered from the ever present chill. Thirty days since the power had gone out, since he had heard another human voice. Since he had tasted a bite of bread or sipped enough water to more than wet his tongue. Only he knew that he had been so weak and parched for most of that time—in and out of a terrible, vision-filled dementia—that it was just as likely that it had been fewer days . . . or even possibly many more. Still, he should have been dead. But he was not.

I do not believe.

Ever since he had begun to study the ancient texts he had begun to question Judeo/Christian doctrine. Too much *fact* was left out for either religion to be the one true faith. And after breaking with the Church his rage against what he felt was a holy coverup caused him to disavow even his belief in God. There was no superior being. There were human beings and the Old Ones, and they had been battling one another since the beginning of time. God was simply an illusion that fouled the equation.

Still, thirty days without food, with only the tiny drops of condensation on the concrete walls for water—a man should not survive thus. And yet he lived. He was weak, and perhaps hallucinating—more than once he thought he'd seen an angel peering in at him through the glass during the day, replacing the demons that hounded him at night—but he was not dead.

Miracles do not require a higher being.

But then what *did* they require, miraculous coincidence? Why should *he* survive in this cell, when everyone else in the building appeared to have disappeared or died? Would he have survived what he was certain was the beginning of the Darkening, he who was one of the few people alive who would know it for what it was if he had not been imprisoned for that very knowledge?

"Speak to me, then!" he croaked, waving a fist in the air. "Where are you? What do you want of me, here, locked away like an animal?"

He struggled to his feet, balancing against the wall, his feet barely able to carry him. When he reached the door he tugged with all his might as he had once every day since the night the Darkening began, but it was locked still, solid as it had always been, and he barely managed to fumble back across the tiny cell to wrap himself in the mattress again, cursing his naïveté.

There was barely enough light through the tiny window to reveal to him that somewhere far away the sun still shone. But it would be down soon. And his constant companions would return to scratch a requiem over and over on the outside of his cell door.

Whether through fate or Phoenix's canine intervention, the Rhothag did not find them that night, and Lucy was able to catch up on much needed sleep. She awakened only twice, once when the dog climbed onto the bed to curl up beside her, the second time when she sensed another presence in the room and opened her eyes to watch Wagner's silhouette as he stood guard at her window.

She rose just before dawn, and Blondie greeted her and Phoenix in the kitchen with a cup of coffee for Lucy and a full bowl of food for the dog.

"I hate eating out of people's cupboards," she said, sipping the bitter coffee anyway.

Blondie shrugged. "All the food in the world is just gonna go bad. Someone ought to eat it."

"I guess. It's just that breaking into houses, sleeping in people's beds, eating their food . . . still seems wrong."

"We could just steal from stores," said Blondie, smiling. "Like Robin Hood."

She smiled back, shaking her head and pointing over the trees at the clouds. "Have you noticed a glimmering once in a while? I thought at first it was the light or my eyes. But every now and then I see a spot ahead that looks as though I'm looking at it through running water."

Blondie nodded. "I mentioned it to Wagner the first time I spotted one. He doesn't know what it is, either."

"It's like the funny-tasting water and the bad food, like everything around us is changing. It frightens me more than the Rhothag."

"It's gonna be okay."

She stared at his soft eyes and wondered how he of all people could be so certain of that.

"I'm nobody's savior, Blondie," she said, softly. But staring into his face, knowing that he would die for her without thinking, she discovered that she *wanted* to be. She truly did.

When Wagner showed up, they retired to a breakfast prepared on the charcoal grill on the broad front porch, and Lucy mentioned the glimmerings to Wagner.

He shrugged. "They'll know more at the Keep."

"Every time you mention the Keep you get this look in your eye," she said. "What is it you aren't telling me?"

Wagner frowned. "In recent years there have been two factions in our organization. But we have nowhere else to go now. We could stand on our own as long as we were just fighting Qedem Melech agents and a few Rhothag here and there. Fighting the Old Ones is something else altogether."

"You trust the people at the Keep?" she asked.

"It wasn't that we didn't trust them," said Wagner. "Clayborn and his faction just distorted things when they took over. They believed that the Old Ones were a lot of hokum, that Qedem Melech was just a bunch of terrorists disguised as devil worshipers."

"You think now they'll come around?"

"I think now they'll have to. You feeling ready to travel?"

"Ready as I'll ever be," she said, shouldering her pack.

This time Blondie took the lead instead of Phoenix, although the dog seemed to look askance at his choice of route. When they'd hiked about three blocks from the dog's home she began to whimper and appeared undecided as to whether to continue her association with the group.

"Come on, girl," said Lucy, slapping her leg.

"She'll make up her own mind," said Wagner. "We can't drag her with us."

"She's just confused," said Lucy. "I don't understand what's happening. How do you expect a dog to? She probably thinks her family will come back, then she'll have deserted them."

"I think you're giving her credit for a little more brains than she really has."

"Oh, yeah? Who saved our butts last night?"

Wagner frowned, resting his rifle on the ground. The dog ran in nervous circles, first back toward home, then to Lucy, and it was clear Phoenix wanted them to stay with her.

Lucy knelt on one knee until the dog ran into her arms. "We can't stay here, girl. We gotta go. And I really don't want to leave you behind. Do I need to find a leash?" She gave Wagner a look to let him know that she damned well would drag the dog along before leaving her to starvation or worse. The dog sighed, and Lucy could have sworn she was making a decision. When Lucy stood, Phoenix bowed her head, but then she followed along beside them, done with her dance.

"I think she has more brains than *you* give her credit for," said Lucy, smiling.

"Some dogs are pretty smart," agreed Blondie, smiling, too.

"Has it ever occurred to you that she just decided to take us on faith?" said Wagner, taking the lead.

Lucy followed, shaking her head. But the remark, obviously meant in jest, hit home. What did the dog know that she didn't? Phoenix trotted beside her now, no longer glancing back. She *had* made a decision based on something, whether it was the kind of reasoning a human being might use or not. What force told her that these were the right people to go with now? And why did she trust that force?

They foraged for supplies in a village that centered around a feed store, finally raiding the cupboards of a small bed-and-breakfast. While the three of them made a lunch of peanut butter sandwiches on bread as hard as plywood but miraculously free of mold, Phoenix explored all the neat-smelling stuff inside, returning sneezing again, her nose covered with grain dust. Lucy wiped the dog's face absentmindedly while she studied one of the road maps Blondie had procured from a convenience store along the way.

"I'll pick the routes for now if you don't mind," said Wagner, glancing askance at the dog

"Be my guest," said Lucy. "But has it occurred to you that the Rhothag have been getting closer and closer to catching us?"

"I'm aware of that. We have to keep moving. Tonight I want to find a really secure place to bunk down."

"Me too. But I was wondering if there wasn't something in the water trick that Phoenix taught us."

"What do you mean?"

"There's a creek just up ahead," said Lucy, pointing at the map. "If we walked in the shallows for a mile or two, we might throw the ones behind us off our scent."

"I don't think it was the water that confused them before," said Wagner. "Scent will float on water."

"It didn't in the basement."

"You have no way of knowing that."

"They didn't find us."

"They didn't *attack* us."

"Flowing water will throw off any hound," said Blondie. "But you have to be walking *with* the flow. If you hike upstream, your scent just flows behind you like a long ribbon. For a dog that's like a streak of fireworks, and all they have to do is turn upstream to catch you. If you walk with the current, your scent stays with you, and when you get out it's carried away downstream."

"How do you know so much about it?" asked Lucy.

Blondie smiled. "I'm an old coon hunter. Them coons are smart animals. They know about streams and rivers. If the hounds lose the scent, you wait a little while to see if it drifts on down from upstream. If it doesn't, you run downstream and try to catch it again. A lot of times the coon wins."

"All right," said Wagner, glancing at the map. "I guess hillbilly logic is worth a try."

Phoenix found the stream before they did, running through the high grass to leap splashing into the shallow water, frolicking like a pup. Wagner took in the high, brush-lined banks with a sharp eye, and he and Blondie exchanged nervous glances.

"What's the matter?" said Lucy, kicking water at the dog.

Wagner shook his head. "It's not a good position. High ground on both sides, plenty of place for concealment. If I was going to set up an ambush, this would be it."

Lucy had to admit he was right. She could imagine the tall grass full of Rhothag lying in wait. But they weren't going to be there in broad daylight even if the sunlight was as thin as rock soup.

"We'll get out well before dark," she said. "But we're here. We have to at least try this."

Wagner nodded uneasily, taking the lead again, Blondie falling behind to guard their rear. Whenever Phoenix threatened to leap out of the stream after a frog or simply to dry herself off, Lucy scolded her, and eventually she accepted the rules of this new game, trotting alongside Lucy in the shallows.

Every mile or so they stopped to check the map.

"There should be a bridge just ahead," said Wagner, frowning as Blondie tossed a stick downstream for Phoenix, careful to land it in the water. "We can take that road into this town, here. That's another ten miles, but we should be there well before dark."

Everyone agreed the experiment was completed. Whether it had worked or not they might never know. But it hadn't cost them much time, and they'd learned something new about Phoenix. She was a *very* intelligent dog. When Lucy noticed her glancing up between them at the map she jokingly held the paper in front of the dog's eyes. Instead of peering questioningly at the three of them, or begging for a treat, the dog seemed to try to understand the strange markings, studying the map until Wagner took it from Lucy and refolded it.

"That was odd," said Lucy.

Wagner shook his head. "It figures, if you were going to pick up a stray, she'd be a real doozie."

"You don't think she was really trying to figure out the map?"

"No. But she's smarter than I thought. I'll give you that."

"She's a good girl," said Lucy, making sure the dog was listening. "And she deserves a bone."

Phoenix bounced around on her rear paws, until Lucy dug one of the doggie treats out of Blondie's pack and tossed it to her. As they climbed the overgrown embankment to the bridge the dog ran ahead, stopping at the guardrail to scan the road. Then she woofed at them to hurry up.

The narrow, shoulderless highway ran between high stone fences, hemming in acres of rambling fields rampant with brown winter grass. In the distance a large brick farmhouse glared down at them as though *they* had had something to do with all the missing livestock. A flock of crows took wing as they started up the road, circling overhead for a moment, then away, and Lucy watched them until they disappeared beyond the trees.

"Awful quiet," she whispered.

Blondie nodded, glancing quickly around.

"They should have cawed," she said. "Crows always cry out when they're startled."

"Maybe we didn't startle them," said Blondie. "Maybe it was just a coincidence, them taking off like that when we came up."

"Maybe," said Lucy, not convinced. She peered into the distance where the road and horizon wove and bobbed as though viewed through a shimmering sheet of water.

"There it is again. It's like our reality is getting sucked right out from under us," she said, staring around them at the grass that browned a little more every day, at the sheet of gray clouds that was surreally flat and smooth. She kicked absently at the asphalt with the toe of her boot and wasn't too surprised when a small section crumbled like dry cake

"Move it," said Wagner, already well ahead again and not slowing. "It looks like the sun's going to be down sooner than we thought, and I want to be in a *building* by the time it does."

It wasn't so much that the sun was rushing through its cycle. Rather the heavy overcast that always blew in before dawn seemed thicker every day, wanting to put the light to bed before its time. With the veil between them and the sun it would *seem* like night by late afternoon. Maybe dark enough for the Rhothag to begin venturing out.

By the time they straggled into the village of Dooley, Lucy's legs were ready to buckle, and Phoenix's tongue lolled between her teeth. Wagner pointed his rifle at a brick bank building pressed between a real estate office and a donut shop, and they rushed to it.

"What do you feel?" he asked, watching Lucy closely.

She shook her head. "I haven't sensed any Rhothag for miles. I think we're all right."

The lock on the door was no match for three heavy

kicks from Blondie's boot, the jamb peeling apart like string cheese. But Phoenix seemed taken aback by this new way of entering a human building, and she gave Blondie a little extra room as they searched the premises.

There were no windows in the rear, and the back door was thick and heavily bolted. The windows on the front of the building supported thick iron bars, and Blondie shoved a chair under the knobs of both doors, securing them. Wagner pulled a small camp lantern out of his pack, lit it, and inspected the locked vault.

"I was hoping we could use it as a last stand if we needed to," he said, frowning. "But I suppose it's on a time lock, and now it won't open until hell freezes over."

Lucy shook her head. "I don't want to hide in any vault. Are you crazy? We'd suffocate. Lucy Devereau's Important Rules of Self-Defense Number One. Never put yourself in a position where you might asphyxiate."

"You're joking, right?" said Wagner.

She explained how the rules worked, and he smiled.

"I wasn't going to close it all the way," he said. "But that door must be a foot thick. We could rope it nearly shut and hold off an army until dawn."

"Look in the president's office, then. In one of his files somewhere you'll find the combination. With some time locks, if the power doesn't come back on by the time the backup batteries go dead, they have a safety switch that unlocks them. Then you just have to use the combination."

"How do you know that?"

"I had a client who was a banker."

Wagner did find the combination inside a folder, not in the president's file cabinet, but stashed in the bottom of his secretary's top drawer. He spun the large wheel that controlled the ankle-sized dead bolts and tugged open the heavy steel door. Stacks of bills rested atop rows of metal shelves, and the rear of the vault was lined with safety-deposit boxes of different sizes.

"We're all wealthy people now," said Lucy.

Wagner smiled. "Got anywhere in particular you want to spend it?"

"I was thinking Tiffany's. There must be a branch in DC."

"Just let me know your tastes," said Wagner. "I'll buy you anything you like when we get there."

"Very kind of you," said Lucy, making a half curtsy, noticing for the first time how close he stood to her, how his arms seemed ready to reach for her. She took an involuntary step back, flustered.

When she glanced at Blondie she noticed that he was staring into the vault, and his face was ashen.

"What's the matter?" she asked.

"It won't work," he said, shaking his head. "It's a trap."

"What do you mean a trap?" said Wagner, frowning.

Blondie pointed slowly around the interior of the small bank. "There's only three windows. If they get in and we hide in the safe, they'll gather in here like rats in a barn and just put blankets or something over the windows. We'll never be able to fight our way out then."

"Jesus," whispered Lucy, picturing exactly the scene that Blondie had just painted.

"And I don't like small spaces," said Blondie. "I never have."

"Well, I think this is about the securest place we've found yet," said Wagner, checking the front door again. "And we're not going anywhere now."

Blondie accepted the decision stoically as always, resting his rifle on the floor beside his pistol, stacking clips for both alongside. But Lucy noticed the big fellow kept throwing nervous glances toward the vault.

"I don't think there's any way they can take us here, tonight," he said, obviously trying to reassure himself more than anyone else.

What really frightened Lucy wasn't the idea of a horde of the Rhothag inside the building with them, it was the realization that Blondie had been just as afraid as she all along. And the thought that a big, strong man like him was so claustrophobic that he'd rather fight a mob of the beasts outside in the open than spend a night in the cramped vault touched her, opening just one more window into Blondie's soul. She could picture herself and Wagner having to force him into taking shelter with them in just such a place, and she tried to imagine how they might go about it. She'd thought before that he would go anywhere and do anything in order to protect her, but on the other hand, he might just choose to slam that imaginary door from the outside and sacrifice himself rather than taking shelter with them.

"Well," said Wagner, stacking his ammo beside Blondie's, "you and I can finally catch a full night's sleep."

"I'll keep first watch," said Blondie quickly.

Wagner smiled. "I know you'll be up anyway. But try to get at least a little shut-eye." He glanced at Phoenix. "I think she'll probably do as good a job of being on watch as any of us."

The dog noticed the attention and wagged her tail.

Lucy curled up beneath a long stand-up desk against the far wall. Phoenix pressed up against her, and she draped her arm across the dog, once again reveling in the strange sensation of another heart so close to her own. She stared at Blondie as he sat on the floor, leaning against a small column, his rifle across his knees. He was like the dog in his unwavering and unconditional guardianship. Blondie's was not to reason why.

Her eyes drifted to Wagner then, bundled in his sleeping bag beneath the counter of the teller station. But as she turned away from him, the old empty feeling struck again, and her breath caught in her throat. Mentally shaking her head, she drifted off to sleep and immediately began to dream.

She was running across a great empty desert, knowing that ahead somewhere lay the thing that she had searched for her entire life, the one thing that could fill the emptiness and make her whole. An invisible line seemed to draw her forward, and she knew that the line was attached to the object of her desire, that it reeled her in as fervently as she raced toward it. Even as she ran stumbling ahead she sensed that not only was the fulfillment of her quest drawing nearer, so was a terrible but unseen doom. The sky was the color of the greenest sea, and the ground beneath her feet trembled as though it were not hard rock but the surface of some giant drum.

In the distance she could see a human form facing away from her, and she raced toward it, her heart pounding, fever burning through her. Instinctively she knew that the person ahead was the answer to her lifelong quest. It was no longer an amorphous *something* for which she searched but a *someone*, and she wanted desperately to put a face on the form.

But suddenly the dream changed, and she could no longer focus on the figure. Instead she raced past it, realizing only at the last instant that the other had been standing on the lip of a high chasm, and her headlong flight had carried her over to her death. She spread her arms in ineffectual mimicry of a bird, opening her mouth in a silent scream. In that instant she felt a hand take hers, and she and the unseen *other* were both carried into the void as she struggled to turn in midair to see at last the one she had sought for so long. The face was a cloud of darkness, but as she fell she could make out lips moving within the veil of gloom, and a beautiful female voice whispered in her mind.

I'm sorry.

Dylan's sleep was also dream-tossed, and he awoke from each new nightmare bathed in sweat, trying to grasp images that faded like smoke.

The first dream had pulled Dylan into their bedroom, where Ronnie had died—wasted away to withered flesh and gnarled bones—but as always, all he could recall of that night was a terrible sense of loss and some indefinable horror. It was the second nightmare that troubled him the most, and yet it had not *felt* quite so horrifying. It had simply been strange.

In that dream Ronnie was alive, and she was trying to speak, but he could not make out her words, for a vast wind shook both of them and kept them apart. He knew that she was trying to warn him of danger, but he could not read her lips, and as he reached for her, the wind sucked her away into a great, deep darkness. Falling. The horror of the thought would not leave him.

Now his hands shook as he wiped yet more sweat off his palms onto his sleeping bag. He performed silent *Ibuki* breathing techniques, slowing his heart, focusing on his center, willing himself to sleep. And this time when he did, his slumber was deep and unbroken.

In the morning they quickly hit the road again. The fighting between Baxter and Crank had not reached the point of open warfare, but Dylan noticed that Baxter kept a watchful eye on Crank all the time, and he refused to let Crank walk behind him.

Dylan knew they both believed that *he* was somehow the key to ending this madness, although how he could bring back maybe billions of people, or stop the onslaught of some terrorist group or race of superior beings, neither could say. But Dylan was drawn along with them not only because he could think of nowhere else to go, but because he had begun to sense a *rightness* in the journey. He had begun to feel a physical pull, an unseen force nudging him constantly forward.

He wondered if it didn't have something to do with the mysteries Sensei Ashiroato had wanted so badly for him to discover. Perhaps at last he was opening himself to the other senses that he had refused to accept all these years. He could see how to a Japanese steeped in mysticism the perception of something beyond what he could see and feel might seem a natural next step in their spiritual evolution, but to Dylan the attraction to an unknown destination seemed more akin to lunacy. Still, the enchantment would not be denied. He knew now that if Baxter or Crank suddenly decided that his job was done and that they would go no farther, he would continue on his own, secure in the knowledge that he would find his way.

He still could not understand why the Rhothag had not attacked him on the road. It wasn't the shotgun that swayed them, nor even just the alien word *Rantasas*. Perhaps they *knew* he was being drawn somewhere like a bee to honey, and that was exactly what they wanted.

The desolation had begun to wear on all of them. Dylan could see hope rise, then fade in the others' eyes whenever a door creaked in the wind. Dylan found it strange that although he had lived almost like a hermit for two years following Ronnie's death, now the lack of human voices, of seeing people about their daily lives, was hard to take, and it had occurred to him that even if the Old Ones were a myth, this might still be the end of mankind. He and Crank and Baxter weren't likely to procreate.

As the three of them rested on a curb beside a four-way stop, Dylan noticed a scruffy orange cat with almond eyes glaring at him from beneath the shrubs across the sidewalk. He slowly placed a piece of canned tuna on the concrete, waiting. The cat sniffed the air, licking its lips. But each time it reached out to place a tentative paw in front of it, it glanced at Dylan and withdrew.

"What are you doing?" asked Crank.

Dylan nodded toward the cat, and Crank smiled.

"Here, kitty," he said, tossing the cat the morsel.

The cat gobbled greedily, blessing Crank with what Dylan would have sworn was a nod of its own. After Arcos they had encountered several of the feral felines. This was the closest one had come, and normally Dylan would have felt sorry for the animal. But the dark glint in the cat's eyes seemed dangerous, rabid perhaps, and he offered no more of his lunch.

Crank fed the cat from his can, and eventually the animal crept out from beneath the cover of the shrub. Fur was torn from its tail and along one flank, and a thick scab ran from one eyebrow back between the ears almost to the base of the neck.

"Cat took a beating," said Baxter. "Looks like the perfect pet for you, Crank."

"Poor thing," said Crank, placing a piece of tuna next to his hand on the grass.

The cat limped across the sidewalk, never taking its eyes off Dylan, but intent on capturing the food. It snatched the bit of fish and took two mincing steps back, chewing quickly, back bent, fur stiffly upright, tail pointing skyward.

"He don't like you much," Crank said to Dylan.

"The feeling's mutual," muttered Dylan.

Crank frowned. "What've you got against a poor little kitty?"

"I think there's something wrong with that cat."

"Maybe," said Baxter. "He's sure been beat to shit. Who knows what he's gotten into out here all by his lonesome?"

"Nothing," said Crank, holding another piece of tuna between two fingers.

The cat's hackles slowly lowered, and it strained its neck to reach the fish without chancing getting closer. But after it swallowed the bite, Crank offered another and the cat seemed to reconsider, accepting another tidbit and rubbing against Crank so it could be petted.

"See. He's just had a hard time. He's fine now."

"You planning on taking him with us?" asked Baxter, frowning.

Crank frowned as well, glancing around. "There's no snow now. And we aren't running, at least not at the moment. If he wants to come along, I can't stop him."

The cat did follow, trotting across driveways, through hedges, and zigzagging across lawns rather than simply accompanying the three of them along the sidewalks. By the time they found a likely house to requisition for the night Dylan figured the cat had tramped twice as far as they had. But the little beast still wasn't taking a shine to him or Baxter. In fact Crank couldn't coax it into the kitchen, so he finally left a can of tuna on the steps.

Dylan awakened to the feeblest light of dawn to find himself staring into two deep dark eyes that squinted below hairy brows, and he jerked away, bumping into the wall.

"Jesus!" he said as the cat leapt off the bed and scurried away.

Baxter appeared in the doorway, grinning. "Satan wake you up?"

"Satan?"

Baxter shrugged. "That's what Crank decided to call the cat. I think it's apt, don't you?"

Dylan couldn't have agreed more. For an instant he'd been certain the animal had been about to attack him in his sleep, claw his eyes out or something.

"Come on," said Baxter. "Coffee's on, and I've got something to show you."

"I don't care for the sound of that."

"I think you'll like it."

Dylan followed Baxter down the hall to the bathroom, but even before they reached the door he could feel the humidity rising and smell the wonderful aroma of soap. Baxter shoved the door wide and the two of them stood regarding Crank, up to his neck in dirty, steaming water.

"A hot bath?" said Dylan, in awe of the sweet-smelling steam and warmth pressing out of the tiny room. None of them had had anything but sponge baths since the night of the Darkening. They'd been surviving each other by liberal doses of spray deodorant and new clothes every few days, and he noticed for the first time that Baxter didn't *smell*. But it wasn't even the knowledge that they'd be able to breathe easier for a while that made Dylan weak at the knees, it was the idea of soaking in that luxurious warmth.

Baxter grinned. "We lucked out on this place. There's an old wood furnace in the basement that has an auxiliary water heater, and this town has a water tower, so we're not dependent on a pump for pressure. Be my guest. Right after King Louis gets done."

Crank shooed them out with a regal wave of a dripping hand, never opening his eyes.

By the time Dylan had finished breakfast it was his turn, and he took his time, letting the hot water loosen his muscles. It felt almost like home. Funny the way the little ordinary things were the ones that seemed to be the most important, while things like telephones, TV, and e-mail were hardly missed in comparison. The basic necessities, that's what they were back to now, and something as rudimentary as a hot bath seemed like a ritual fit for royalty.

"How you doing?" asked Crank when Dylan returned feeling clean as a whistle and already hauling his pack and shotgun.

Dylan smiled. "Great." He noticed that neither Crank nor Baxter returned his smile this time. "What's the matter?"

"I have something else to show you," said Baxter. "Crank and I just found it."

"Satan found it actually," said Crank.

Dylan dropped his pack but kept the shotgun as he followed the pair outside.

The house was bordered on all four sides by landscaping of low shrubs and wood chips. Beneath every window the mulch had been disturbed by large feet. It looked as though either someone had gone from window to window peering in, or—this thought was even more disturbing—there had been someone at *every* window.

"Rhothag," said Dylan.

Baxter nodded.

"The cat found the tracks?" said Dylan, glancing around for the animal, but it was keeping its usual low profile again. "Did it tell you that?"

"It was pawing around in them, and Crank and I heard it," said Baxter. "The damned thing seemed to like the smell, like catnip or something."

The idea of the cat reveling in the odor of the Rhothags made Dylan dislike the feline all the more.

"Where do you think they got off to?" said Dylan, glancing nervously at the basement of the house next door.

Baxter nodded. "They could be anywhere dark. But I don't think they've gone far."

"Then let's get moving," said Crank. "We ought to make DC soon."

As they hiked down the center of the street with the ugly

cat paralleling their path Dylan thought he saw more than one set of eyes glancing out from behind heavy curtains and he fingered the trigger of the shotgun. But he knew there was something he was missing, either something that Baxter or Crank hadn't told him, or something they didn't quite understand themselves.

The thing in his house and in the clearing that night had been stalking him, but for some reason had not actually attacked. The Rhothag they had encountered had acted the same way. So what was holding them back? According to Baxter they were probably too stupid to be afraid of guns, and he'd seen evidence of that when he blew the thing's head off.

The damned things were waiting for something, and Dylan had the nasty feeling that it was somewhere not too far up ahead. He could no more stand against the force that pulled him than he could stop breathing, but more and more he questioned the attraction. What power could create such a force? He tramped along, wondering if each step were not leading him closer to something he could not face.

As the day grew steadily gloomier than the series of gray days in their wake, Lucy, Wagner, and Blondie hiked wearily through miles of open farmland interspersed with large groves of walnut, oak, and maple. Maryland seemed to be disintegrating around them. The road beneath their feet often crumbled, dry grass on the shoulder might disappear in their hands like ash, to blow away in the softest breeze. As they marched faster because of the lowering sun, searching for a driveway that might lead to one more night's safe haven, Lucy sensed the Rhothag yet again. Phoenix growled and Blondie nodded at Lucy, signifying that he had already spotted the first of the beasts paralleling them through the trees.

"Run," he said, shoving her toward Wagner.

The men picked off a couple of the beasts that braved the dimming light as soon as the they emerged onto the road. The three of them raced along for a half mile after that looking for a more defensible spot as the Rhothag moved stealthily through the forest, clinging to the shadows. But the sun was quickly falling far enough behind the trees to transform the entire roadway into a tunnel of gloom, with meager daylight a flickering mirage over a mile ahead. And the Rhothag were becoming more and more audacious. It wasn't that the light didn't hurt them, it seemed more as if whatever drove them to attack had grown stronger, overpowering their will to survive. As they slipped in and out of the shelter of the darker woods they looked like children playing with fire, testing it, then leaping back with singed fingers.

But as fast as the three of them ran Lucy could see that they would not beat the setting sun. The small window of light ahead was dimming with every second. Wagner and Blondie turned, shoving Lucy behind them as the mob of beasts loped toward them from both sides of the road.

The Rhothag all seemed to have grown *through* the remnants of their clothes, and their scaly skin and sinewy build made them appear reptilian. Blondie shot three of them, one a clean eye shot that dropped the beast in its tracks. The others were wounded but not stopped, and even a barrage of bullets barely slowed their assault. There had to be thirty of the beasts, and head shots on the running Rhothag were hard to make even for marksmen of Wagner's or Blondie's ability. When it became clear that they were about to be surrounded, Wagner grabbed Lucy, dragging her in the direction of a small side road, and Blondie followed, covering their rear.

Twice they were nearly overrun when the Rhothag slipped through the trees to intersect their retreat. But both times Lucy was able to give Wagner warning, and the three of them met the ambushers with a withering fire that dropped enough of the beasts to hold them off. Finally, they staggered out of the trees and up the drive of a gentleman's farm with the Rhothag falling back. Because the house and outbuildings sat in a large clearing atop a knoll, it was still shielded by the last rays of the setting sun.

"No," said Wagner, pointing at the barn when Lucy stumbled toward the front stoop of the house.

She frowned, wondering why he would choose the open old structure instead of the more secure house. But once inside the barn she immediately understood Wagner's intention. There was a second-floor hayloft accessed only by a ladder through an entry hole. Phoenix, too, understood the plan. The dog surprised them all by climbing the ladder, her jaw clenched in concentration, tail stiff, until Blondie shoved her butt through the hatch, and she stood grinning down at them. Lucy climbed up after Blondie and Wagner followed. Blondie pulled up the ladder and dropped the cover over the hatch. The last of the day's sunlight shone through the open double doors at the end of the building, where hay was evidently loaded by conveyor. She joined Wagner there, and they peered down at the Rhothag huddling in the shadows at the end of the drive.

"They aren't going to be able to get up through the trapdoor, and if they try to climb up here we can pick them off like fish in a barrel," said Wagner.

"What would Lucy Devereau's Important Rules of Self-Defense say now?" asked Blondie, smiling like a shark.

Lucy just managed a smile in return. "I think Rule Number One would be not to let down our guard tonight."

Wagner nodded. "I think we're safe for now."

"*Safe* is a relative term," she said.

"How are you holding up?" he asked.

She was wracked by exhaustion and fear, but she shook it off, stomping her feet on the straw-strewn floor. The dry smell of alfalfa and the hard reality of the time-tested old building soothed her, easing the sense of mindless terror the Rhothag engendered.

"I'm exhausted, frightened, confused, and I smell like cow manure. Other than that I'm great."

"You smell fine," said Wagner, sniffing her shoulder.

"Thank you, kind sir," she said.

"Sit down here," said Wagner, making a place for her on a pile of straw.

He dropped alongside her, and she could see his own exhaustion in the bags under his eyes and his sagging frame. She started to touch his cheek, but when Blondie knelt down on the other side of her to keep an eye out the double doors, the spell was broken.

"Lucy," said Wagner, frowning, "I never expected it to be this hard or to take us this long to reach the Keep. You know we've been heading toward DC. I've been withholding the exact location from you because that's what I was trained to do. But I don't think I can chance that any longer."

"You mean in case something happens to you guys," she said, quietly.

He nodded.

"I don't need you to tell me," she said. "I can feel it drawing me to it. Every time you tell me to take a turn, I know in advance which way to go."

He studied her for a long moment. "Anything else?"

"I'm having dreams."

"What kind of dreams?"

She shook her head. "Nightmares. I'm in a desert, and there's someone . . ."

"Someone what?"

She sighed. How could she explain that the someone represented what she'd been searching for her whole life, when she had never known before that the thing that called to her even *was* a person?

"They made no sense," she said, tossing off her pack and rolling out her sleeping bag.

Wagner shrugged, signing for Blondie to sleep beside the trapdoor.

Lucy slipped into the bag, staring out the open loft

doors into the night. She thought she could make out Rhothag weaving through the darkness, but it might have been her imagination. She felt the straw stirring and realized that Wagner had curled into his own bag close behind, but not quite touching her. She could see Blondie—his rifle across his lap—silhouetted against the open doors, and Phoenix sitting beside him, staring out into the night.

In the morning the Rhothag had vanished again. Wagner allowed them only a breakfast of peanut butter and crackers before leaving, although Blondie insisted on stopping long enough to refill their water bottles from a tank in the barn that must have been used for cattle. At the end of the long driveway they found the grass disturbed, as though dozens of the Rhothag had milled about all night, and Lucy wondered why they had come no closer. But Wagner only signaled for her and Blondie to move out and led the way at a leisurely but mile-eating trot.

Because the day was warmer than usual and the road seemed mostly uphill, Lucy strained her stamina to the breaking point sooner than expected, and Wagner had to hold her arm when she stopped to catch her breath. They were passing through a small town that looked so modern it had to have been chopped from the environs of DC and dumped out here in the boonies. Instead of the usual assortment of brick facades and wide old concrete walks with horse rings still embedded in them, they found one-story aluminum-and-glass real-estate offices and copy shops. Unlike Lucy, Phoenix was still full of vinegar, wagging her tail at the group from the far end of the street, then trotting over to inspect some excellent garbage along the curb.

Even before they'd stopped Lucy could sense the foulness of Rhothag all around them, and she knew they were huddling from the sun in basements and closets and dark attics. But she had grown accustomed to the feeling in most of the towns they passed through now, and she knew they were safe again until nightfall.

"I hope she doesn't get into something and make herself sick," she said, staring at Phoenix. The dog was neck deep in a ripped bag of garbage, shaking something furiously.

"That mutt can take care of herself," said Blondie, leaning his rifle against the window of a convenience store, glancing into the shadowy interior.

Lucy sipped from her water bottle. She spit the water rather gracelessly near Wagner's feet, and he gave her a funny look.

"Tastes like old grease," she said.

Wagner took the bottle and sniffed its contents.

"The water seemed as good as any we've been drinking," said Blondie. "But maybe that tank was tainted."

With no further ado, he kicked in the glass door of the store and stepped inside.

"See what's in there worth eating, too," said Wagner, tossing off his pack and sitting on it beside Lucy.

"How far is it to the Keep?" she asked. Although the pull was so incredibly strong now that she could hardly stop herself from climbing to her feet and struggling on, the Keep might be around the next corner or around the world for all the attraction could tell her.

"Not far at all," said Wagner, tapping her knee and pointing his chin toward Phoenix. "Up about five miles there's a crossroads. We go left maybe eight miles farther, we're there."

Lucy heaved a sigh of relief. Thirteen miles would be a walk in the park. At the rate they'd been traveling that day they could make it in a little over four hours. "We did it, then."

Wagner nodded. "We got you to the Keep. I don't think that's the end."

"I guess I knew it wouldn't be. But there's someone there waiting for me."

"Lucy," whispered Wagner, frowning.

When she turned to face him she saw a great sadness in his eyes.

"I don't want you to get your hopes up," he said.

She felt a sinking feeling in the pit of her stomach. "Why do you say that?"

He shook his head. "There's something I need to tell you," he said. "But I don't know how."

He glanced away as though searching for words. She followed his eyes toward Phoenix. The dog had deserted its gutter treasures and started back in their direction. But now she stood in the middle of the street, watching them, her ears pointing skyward, hackles raised, tail between her legs. As Lucy stared at the dog her own senses tingled. Suddenly she knew that Blondie was in terrible danger. But as quickly as the awful feeling seized her it was gone, and she knew in that instant so was Blondie.

"Oh, my God!" she gasped, just as a loud crash erupted behind her in the store.

"Shit!" said Wagner, snatching up his rifle and rolling to his feet in one fluid motion.

Before Lucy could see what had caused the commotion he shoved her aside, slipping through the door. His shoulders were tensed, and the muscles in his neck bulged. The rifle balanced at his hip, barrel sweeping the shadowy, shelf-lined confines of the convenience store.

"Roy!" he shouted.

Lucy felt something rub against her leg and glanced down to see that Phoenix had already rejoined them. The dog's black lips curled back from white, dagger teeth, and under her breath a rumbling growl rolled.

"Easy girl," said Lucy, trying to get the dog's attention, afraid that she'd go charging past Wagner.

"Stay outside!" said Wagner. But Lucy ignored him, jerking her pistol out of its holster.

As soon as her foot landed on the tiled floor inside the door she was overwhelmed by a feeling of dread. The sense of desecration, of defilement was so powerful it sent a shiver up her spine. The ground was too violated for her to tell how many there were, but the Rhothag owned this place. And she knew for certain that she and Wagner were too late.

"Wagner," she whispered.

"Roy!" he shouted, his voice rattling around the metal shelves and bouncing off the glass cooler. Without warning he opened up an automatic burst that blasted the beer racks and exploded dark frothing soda all the way to the ceiling. Two Rhothag staggered through the shattered glass and metal, wounded but far from dead. There was enough light inside the gloomy store to force the beasts to shield their eyes, but they still stumbled toward Wagner and Lucy. She managed to put a bullet in one's open mouth, and Wagner pumped enough lead into the other to blow its head off. He slammed another clip home, scanning quickly for more targets.

Lucy noticed that there was blood on the floor near the checkout counter, and Wagner followed her eyes there, then to a door behind the cash register. She knew he was about to go charging through it, that Phoenix would follow unquestioningly, and she knew she couldn't let them.

"Wagner!" she screamed. There was enough fright in her voice to stop him in his tracks, and he stood there, undecided, horror and rage burning on his face. She shook her head. "There's dozens of them in there. Maybe more. It's a tiny storage room. And it's dark."

"You see that?"

"I feel it," she said, realizing that she could sense Wagner and even Phoenix in the same way she could the Rhothag beyond that normal-looking but sinister-feeling door. But Blondie was gone. "He's dead," she whispered.

Wagner seemed to have taken a hard punch in the chest. "Are you certain?"

She nodded, hating the look of realization that came over him. She'd come to understand Wagner and Blondie's relationship, the bond of two people who share the same deadly hazards day after day and night after sleepless night. The bond she had come to share with them. The thought of Blondie being dragged struggling into that terrible dark, tight little space slashed at her heart.

But he was gone, and they could not stay here any longer. The things were just behind the thin door, steeling themselves to burst out even now, into the feeble light of the store interior.

"We have to go," she whispered. "They're going to attack us if we stay, and there are too many."

She took his arm, leading him unwillingly out into the middle of the street. His face was now pinched into tight control, but as he squinted back at the building his eyes were sharp blades of rage.

"We're only a few miles from the Keep," she reminded him, but it was clear that he only heard her on some distant level. He was searching the buildings all around, and she knew that although he had no powers beyond his five senses, he now knew as well as she did now that this town was a warren of evil.

"I'm sick and tired of being hunted," he said, his knuckles white on his rifle grip.

Phoenix barked and danced. The dog's hackles were still at half-staff, but she had stopped growling and her lips were only slightly curled. Still, she made it clear by running in small circles that she was ready to get the hell out of there.

Lucy's own fear and grief began to well into rage. She had hidden and run all her life. For weeks she had been hunted, threatened, attacked. And still she had run. Suddenly she wanted revenge. Not just against the mindless Rhothag but against everyone who had conspired over the years to make her what she was, to steal her childhood, to make her a hunted animal, to take from her the indescribable something that she needed more than life itself.

"I want to burn it," she said, glancing at the gas station across the street. "I want to burn this place to the ground."

Wagner squinted. The little attendant's building was nothing but half walls and glass and barely eight feet long, so there was no risk of encountering any of the Rhothag inside. He kicked in the door, and stood guard as Lucy shoved past him to shuffle aside raincoats and boxes filled with cans of motor oil, returning with a four-foot-long iron rod with a T on one end and a smaller flat T on the other.

"Find a hose," she said, tossing the key out onto the pavement.

By the time Wagner returned with a section of garden hose Lucy had broken into the auto parts store next door and returned with several gas cans and a small hand pump. She used the heavy key to open the fill vent on the underground tanks beneath the parking lot and began to pump gas into the cans.

"You could have been killed in there," said Wagner, shaking his head and staring back at the auto store.

"Floor-to-ceiling glass," said Lucy. "It's as bright inside as it is out, and I didn't sense them in there."

"How did you know about the tank key?"

She smiled. "Private eyes have all kind of interesting trivia running around in their brains."

When he shook his head she said, "It's habit. When I see someone working on something I don't understand, I ask questions. I learned about the key from a guy servicing the tanks in my local station in Ruredaga. Small-town people will tell you anything."

Suddenly she recalled the ashes of the town in which they'd discovered Phoenix, and she understood how that fire had started. It wasn't an accident. Survivors there had finally realized that there was no fighting the Rhothag, that the only way to rid themselves of the beasts was destroy their own town. But total devastation had not saved them.

Of course salvation was not what this burning—and she suspected that one as well—was about. This was about retribution, about not allowing things as evil as the Rhothag to exist in a place where men and women had lived and died, a place created and built by their sweat and their blood. The Rhothag that had killed Blondie could not be allowed to wallow smugly in their dens. She lugged two of the heavy plastic jugs down the street behind Wagner.

He started by firing brief bursts of lead through every window of every store on both sides of the street. The harsh noise of shattered glass raining on concrete slashed the flat gray day, and Lucy discovered that the sound was somehow soothing and yet sad as a dirge. She wanted to hear the crackle and rumble of fire racing up and down the block, smell the rank odor of burning flesh. She helped Wagner pour long trails of gasoline along the facades, splashing plenty inside each building. Their boots crunched in the glass, and Lucy shouted at Phoenix to remain in the street, but the dog wrinkled her nose at the smell of gas and was easily convinced. When they'd tossed their last empty can into a small clothing store Wagner pulled out his lighter. He reached through the broken glass and jerked a man's shirt off the closest rack, ripping it in half and swabbing it in the gasoline. Lighting the rags he passed one to Lucy and signaled for her to cross the street. He nodded, and they both tossed the torches.

Fire roared greedily along the storefronts, leaping through the shattered windows, exploding inward, then back out as the buildings drew in great gasps and expelled them into the air. Lucy and Wagner quickly retrieved their packs, hurrying up the street, with Phoenix leading the way. Above the heavy gaseous breathing of the fire they could hear the animal cries of burning Rhothag.

"A lot of them will escape out the back of the buildings," she said.

Wagner shrugged, glancing at the sky. The day was already more than half-done, but the sun struggled nobly to break through the ever-present veil.

"We did the best we could," he said, shoving her along. "Most will get caught in the blaze. They like tight dark areas with as few windows and doors as possible. Those that do get out will have to run a long way to find more shelter. With any luck their asses will fry before they get there."

By the time they reached the crossroads the flames and smoke were so high behind them they looked like lightning-blasted storm clouds in the distance. The fire had assuaged none of Lucy's guilt or grief over Blondie's death. Instead, she felt even emptier inside, consumed by heartache and frustration. She couldn't get the picture of him out of her head, standing one moment on the sidewalk, smiling, so self-assured, the next being dragged into his worst nightmare. But even as she felt about to burst with rage and remorse the strange pull that had been growing stronger for days increased a hundredfold, and she staggered as though struck from behind.

"That way," said Wagner, pointing to their left.

Lucy shook her head, turning in the other direction. "It's that way."

"I know how to get to the Keep."

"And I know that's not where we need to go right now," she said, starting down the road.

Wagner caught up but did not try to stop her. He simply trotted alongside, studying her closely as she answered his questions without breaking stride.

"You're absolutely certain this is what we should do?"

She glanced at him. "You aren't going to argue?"

He stared on up the road for a moment. "Not yet."

She followed his eyes. "Do you know what's up here?"

"You show me where you're going first. Then we'll talk."

She turned back to the road. But she didn't need to look at it. She could have followed the pull with her eyes closed.

With only the barest trickle of light brightening his cell, Father Remedios licked the concrete wall beside him, lapping up the thin layer of condensation there. It was impossible for a man to live so long with no food and only the little bit of moisture he had been able to glean. Yet here he was. Forced to admit what pride had long denied, he had begun to renew his faith in God.

Though the blood continued to pulse weakly through his veins, his head rested constantly on one shoulder. The muscles of his arms and thighs had thinned to wasted cords, and his face was haggard, his eyes sunken. His hand dropped back into his lap, barely able to draw the mattress closed once more. He shivered, coughing until he choked. Faith or no faith, if thirst and hunger didn't kill him soon, pneumonia would. But then, perhaps, the wretched beasts would leave at last.

All the years he had tried to warn Mother Church—and then anyone who would listen—of what was coming, and all the years everyone had denied him, scoffing, heckling, casting him out. Where were the cardinals now? Surely some of them had to have survived. Someone had to realize what was happening and that he was right. Surely someone would come to save him.

But what if they couldn't? Perhaps *that* was the beasts' purpose. Who knew how many servants of Mother Church lay dead outside, or even inside the walls of this asylum? With each passing hour the reality of the Darkening rested heavier upon him. He could sense it in the air that carried the faintest sense of *fading*, as though the building around him were being slowly raised to some high peak where oxygen was a rarity. He could feel it in the very walls and floor, where the paint now peeled away with each scratch of his tongue, as though it were ancient and weathered, which it was not.

Surely the God who had kept him alive for so long would not allow him to die here for no purpose. And if the Lord was keeping him alive to fight the Darkening then surely someone would come.

Someone had to.

"Why are you so jumpy?" Dylan asked Crank. "You're fidgeting like a kid taking his first belt test."

"We're close to the Keep," said Crank.

"So? That's good, right?"

Crank nodded, stopping to pet the cat that had been following them ever since Crank had fed it on the sidewalk days before. "The last thing we want is to give away its location."

Dylan didn't need to be told *who* he was referring to. He glanced behind them. But there was nothing out there but the road, empty fields, and silence.

Several times now they'd discovered tracks outside the

buildings where they'd slept, and once Baxter found a wet footprint *inside* the house even though all the doors had been locked. Crank argued that they hadn't searched the place well enough before bedding down, but a search afterward didn't turn up the Rhothag, either. The thought of the beasts watching him while he slept reminded Dylan of the shadow in his house. Who knew what the Rhothag were thinking while they watched? And if there really had been one inside then why hadn't it attacked? He had the feeling that when they *did* get around to attacking nothing was going to stop them.

As they rounded a sweeping curve, Dylan suddenly experienced a wild burst of the feeling that had been drawing him constantly forward. He staggered, leaning on his shotgun for support. Crank and Baxter hurried to his side.

"What's the matter?" asked Crank.

Dylan squinted ahead toward a small crossroad. In the distance rose a churning cloud. It looked as though a whole town must be on fire. But even as Crank and Baxter stared curiously at the dark plume, Dylan found his attention drawn through a small copse of woods to their left. It was all he could do not to tear off the highway and race away through the trees toward the incredibly powerful attraction.

"There," he said, pointing, but barely able to speak. "That way."

Crank frowned, following Dylan's hand, then glanced at Baxter, who frowned as well.

"No," said Baxter, at last, pointing in the other direction. "The Keep is that way. Only eight miles."

Dylan shook his head. No way he was going in any other direction, not until he reached his destination and discovered what strange power compelled him. He could no more turn away from the attraction now than a tide could stop in midflow. An inner current propelled him, and he lurched down the road with Crank and Baxter hurrying to catch up.

"We're not going that way," argued Crank. "We're almost to the Keep now. You have to come with us."

"I don't have to do a fucking thing!" shouted Dylan, startling himself.

All the way to the intersection Baxter and Crank tried to dissuade him, but Dylan was hardly listening. When he neared the four-way stop he cut through the grass and back onto the road, whirling and instantly slipping into a fighting stance when Crank limped alongside and tried to grab his arm. His blood pressure was rising, and the anger that welled in his chest at the thought of being obstructed bulged his eyes and tightened his jaw. When he saw the anxiety in both Crank's and Baxter's faces he chilled just a little.

"I have to do this," he said, backing up the highway as he spoke. "I don't know what's up there, but I have to go."

"What if it's more Rhothag?" said Crank. "Have you thought of that?"

In fact he had. Not Rhothag specifically, but he had considered that it might be some trick by the dark thing that had been in his house and attacked him in the clearing. But he hadn't run into the thing again since hitting the road with Crank and Baxter, and anyway, if he was being drawn into a trap there was nothing he could do about it until he got there. He *had* to know.

"It isn't," he said. "Or at least it isn't them calling me."

"Then what is it?" asked Crank.

"I don't know! But it's up this road. Maybe we can be there and back here before dark."

As though he could understand every word, the scruffy cat chose that moment to give Dylan one of its hateful looks. Then it shook itself like a wet dog and trotted directly across the intersection in the direction of the tall column of smoke.

"Hey!" shouted Crank, limping after the cat when it became apparent that it wasn't merely wandering off to relieve itself. "Where you going, Satan? Here kitty, kitty!"

Baxter sighed loudly. "Forget the fucking cat, Crank."

Crank kept going until the cat tired of the game and

raced away into the field across the intersection. Dylan could follow its passage as the grass collapsed behind it like powder.

"Crank!" shouted Baxter as Dylan turned and started hiking away. "Come on, or we're leaving you here."

Crank shook his head sadly but followed along.

The pull dragged Dylan farther along the twisted, tree-lined lane than he expected. He glanced apprehensively up every shadowy drive, but still the tug drew him down the road until he finally stopped in front of a half-hidden lane bordered by twin stone pillars. Baxter stopped beside him, catching his breath, giving Dylan a strange, studious look.

"You know this place?" asked Dylan, staring at the scrolling wrought-iron sign overhead.

"I've only been here once," said Baxter, smiling ruefully at the sign. "But yeah, I know it."

"So why are you smiling?" asked Dylan.

"Sacred Light isn't your run-of-the-mill sanitarium," said Baxter, shrugging. "I was going to have to come down here pretty soon, anyway."

"Why?"

Baxter sighed. "I left someone here. I thought he must be dead or gone by now. But I had it in the back of my mind that if I survived all this, I'd make it over here and give his effects a Christian burial."

"Figures one of your friends would end up here," muttered Crank.

"Well, there's friends, then there's friends," said Baxter cryptically.

"Come on," said Dylan, trotting on down the winding brick drive. "The sun's going down early today."

The complex was faced in luminescent white marble and constructed in a sweeping arc, fronted by a portico that seemed to be a copy of the main entrance to the White House. And indeed that was what the place looked like, as though some giant had taken the executive mansion, stretched it end to end, then bent it over his knee. There were a few cars in the parking lot, but no movement at any of the tall barred windows and no steam rising from any of the building's heat stacks. Dylan walked the final hundred yards across the lawn and up the wide marble steps.

They all trudged slowly down the center of a broad, white-marbled corridor that opened suddenly into a huge lobby with a crystal chandelier the size of a city bus and a sweeping staircase along the far wall. The marble floors and heavily plastered walls seemed to soak up cold from somewhere deep in the earth and radiate it back into the giant room as though the building were a huge refrigerator. Overhead a massive circular skylight illuminated the vast room in shades of gray.

"One hell of a nuthouse," said Crank.

"Your tithe dollars at work," said Baxter.

They surveyed the immaculate whiteness of the circular room, taking in the marble stairs, the gleaming domed skylight high overhead, the huge portraits of saints in ornate gold frames, and the Chippendale chairs beneath them. On the far wall, beneath the gilt second-floor railing, hung a massive silver crucifix. Twenty yards of tiled floor lay between the corridor and what appeared to be the admissions center, a distance obviously calculated to make the persons approaching feel small. For what purpose? To teach them the humility the patients here must feel? To remind them of their place in the universe, of their position before God?

"That's a lot of tithing," said Dylan, shaking his head. He glanced at the guest register on the polished horseshoe desktop.

Crank slipped alongside, reading over his shoulder.

"Cardinal Elisias/Roma, Cardinal Pertosante/Roma, Archbishop De Gasteno/Rio de Janeiro," said Dylan, glancing slowly around again as Baxter pressed against the desk. "Who do you think *they* were visiting? This place is like a Bedlam for saints."

"Or where they lock up the sinners," said Crank.

"You could say that," said Baxter. "This is where the Church buried its mistakes."

Crank glared at him but said nothing further.

Suddenly, Dylan felt the invisible hand of the attraction tugging him toward the stairs. Baxter caught at his sleeve as he hurried across the lobby, and Crank limped to catch up behind them.

"Dylan, this could still be a trap," said Baxter. "Slow down."

"It is a trap," said Dylan, shaking his head. "The whole world is a trap. Can't you see that? I have to find out what this is about, why I'm being pulled like this."

He turned back and started up the stairs.

Suddenly a woman's voice—so familiar it froze Dylan in midstride—echoed across the giant room.

"Don't go up there! This place is filled with Rhothag."

Dylan whirled toward her as the woman stepped out of an alcove.

"Well, hello, Bax. Hi, Crank," said the gunman accompanying her.

"What are you doing here, Wagner?" said Baxter.

"She insisted," said Wagner, glancing at Dylan. "Who's this, then?"

"The other half," said Baxter, and Wagner looked confused.

The world seemed to be spinning wildly for Dylan. The middle-aged gunman named Wagner now stood with his weapon lowered . . . and was that a *dog* in the corner? But he turned back to the woman, wondering if the insanity of the past weeks had affected his vision. When she spoke again he *knew* he was going mad.

"You know these people, Wagner?"

He hadn't heard Ronnie's *real* voice in over two years, and here, now, it had a strange lilt to it, something syrupy and Southern. Hearing it again was like a bludgeon of hope and old hurt. He remembered the last cold kiss before the heavy brass lid of her coffin closed over her. This was not real. It couldn't be. And yet she stood there regarding him with almost the same look the old photograph seemed to take on whenever she was irritated, as though waiting for him to speak. But his vocal cords were paralyzed.

"Are you all right?" she asked, her honey voice warming the cold that Dylan had thought would be with him until he died.

He nodded, stepping closer, reaching instinctively for her. But her confused look turned to a shocked frown, and Dylan stumbled, wondering what he'd done wrong.

"Ronnie," he whispered. "I—"

"My name's not Ronnie," said the woman. "It's Lucy. Lucy Devereau."

There was silence in the room, and Dylan was aware that all eyes were upon him. He had awakened from a bad dream only to find himself in a living nightmare, and he glanced slowly around, trying to assure himself that these people were real after all.

"Twins?" said Crank, glancing from Dylan to Lucy.

"Steady," said Baxter, placing a hand on Dylan's shoulder.

Dylan turned on him. "You knew?"

Baxter shook his head. "We didn't learn until after Veronica's death that she'd secretly had a child, and not until we started tracking some Qedem Melech chatter did we have any idea there were *two*. I knew Wagner's group was sent to find your wife's lost sister. None of us knew they were twins or even that he had much hope of finding her."

"Your wife?" gasped Lucy.

Dylan nodded.

"Where is she?" said Lucy, her eyes searching the group.

"She died," he said reluctantly. "Over two years ago."

"I don't understand," said Lucy, sagging visibly. "That can't be. I felt her. I felt her as we were coming here. I dreamed about her." She glanced slowly up toward Dylan, and the agony in her eyes was almost more than he could bear. "I still feel her."

She turned toward Wagner, forcing him to look at her. "You knew," she said. "That's what you never got around to telling me. You knew my sister was dead."

"You'd never met . . . When I realized what you'd been feeling . . . I wanted to tell you, Lucy. But then when Roy was killed . . . And you were in such a hurry to get here—"

She shook her head, turning away.

"I was drawn here, too," said Dylan, taking in the lips and cheeks, the throat he had loved to kiss, the soft eyes and softer hair.

Lucy stared back at him, and for a moment he saw his own fascination mirrored in her eyes. Then it disappeared, replaced by a hard look of resignation. She'd been hurt before. She might not be able to hide from it, but she could hide it from others. All he represented to her now was a lost opportunity to reunite with a sibling she had never known.

"Why here?" she said, at last. "Why this place?"

Dylan shrugged, glancing at Baxter, who studied both of them.

"Something else . . . someone else drew us together here . . ." said Dylan. "Do you feel it?"

Lucy nodded. "I still feel the pull," she said, pointing

toward the stairs. "But there must not be many windows in that wing. Because I know Rhothag are there, too."

"She can sense them," said Wagner, when the others gave her questioning expressions.

"Who in this nuthouse could be that important?" said Crank, shaking his head, but still glaring at Baxter.

Dylan noticed that Baxter and Wagner exchanged a quick glance but offered nothing.

"Whoever it is we need to find them and get out of here, now," said Lucy. "Because when it turns dark I don't think we're going to find anyplace safe here."

Dylan nodded, starting up the stairs before anyone could stop him, and the others quickly followed. The second-floor landing was blocked by wire doors that looked as though they had been ripped apart by a small forklift. Instead of passing through the huge gash, Dylan twisted the key that hung in the lock and opened the gate, shrugging at Baxter, who glanced at the violent tableau and shook his head.

"Will you people wait for one second?" shouted Wagner, digging in his pack. He lit a small camp lantern and hurried to catch up.

The long hallway was dim but not totally dark, light reflecting from some distant windows off the black-and-white tile-floor and whitewashed walls. A couple of stainless-steel gurneys rested against one wall, and a meal cart full of clean trays stood watch beside a dumbwaiter. Door after door delineated cells, but Dylan stared down the long tunnel and sighed.

"Not here," agreed Lucy, staring down the darker side corridor to their left.

"This place is breaking up," said Dylan, tapping the wall beside him with his fist. Plaster crumbled to the floor, revealing a concrete wall beneath. But even the concrete was cracking.

"Like every other place," muttered Lucy, slipping around him.

But Dylan caught up and passed her in the near darkness, unwilling to allow her to place herself in greater danger out in front. Baxter fanned out to the far side of the corridor, and Wagner took the other as Crank hobbled along behind. Their footsteps sounded hollow, rattling away into the shadows, and Dylan wondered how many Rhothag were listening to them, lying in wait somewhere just ahead, around the next turn, maybe. He found his center, balancing on the balls of his feet.

As they rounded the next corner he noticed immediately that some of the cells were open, and they rushed past one door after another until Dylan came to another mesh gate that was ripped like ragged cloth. He glanced back at Lucy, and she nodded. This was the place inside this hallway was the person or thing that had drawn both of them here.

Lucy slipped quietly up directly behind Dylan. He could hear her controlled breathing, smell her natural scent exactly like Ronnie's, and the combination made him weak.

"They're here," she whispered, shivering.

"Where?" asked Baxter.

"All around us," said Lucy.

The trouble was, the pull was all around Dylan, too. He felt like a compass needle spinning wildly at the North Pole.

Suddenly—as Dylan neared an open cell door—a claw slashed the darkness, and he felt Lucy's hand in the small of his back, shoving him aside. He kicked out instinctively, his foot striking a chest hard as iron, driving the Rhothag backward as Baxter and Wagner opened up on it with their rifles. The beast collapsed in the corner, strobe-lighted in death by the rifle blasts.

"There!" shouted Lucy as two more of the creatures rushed them from another cell. This time Crank stepped into the fray with both pistols blazing. The Rhothag were blown back into the cell they'd exited and neither returned. Dylan nodded a breathless thanks at Lucy, and she nodded back.

"I think it's just ahead," whispered Dylan. "I can feel the pull even stronger now."

Crank frowned. "We're making enough noise to rouse the dead. If it's a person you're looking for, seems like they would have heard us. The Rhothag wouldn't have left anyone alive in here, anyway."

"It's a person. And alive," said Lucy. "I can feel that, too."

"What the hell?" said Dylan, stopping in his tracks.

Lucy bumped into his back, and Crank limped quietly around them to stand in the nearly total darkness, staring at the beam of light ahead that formed itself into a perfect cross on the opposite wall.

"Sacred Light," said Wagner, shaking his head, following the cruciform beam slowly back across the corridor to the keyhole where it originated.

Dylan stepped into the light, watching as it played across his shirt just above his heart, certain now that the man trapped within that cell had somehow drawn both him and Lucy to this place. He stood frozen for a moment, staring at the door and the blinding light that came from the keyhole and the tiny window. There was no door handle. Apparently the cells on that side of the corridor were opened only with the aid of a large key that fit the crosslike hole, and he felt an instant's anxiety wondering how he was supposed to open the door. The heavy green paint was crisscrossed with hundreds of deep scratches that had sliced all the way into the metal, and Dylan shivered, realizing that they had to have been made by a Rhothag who also had no way of getting in. What had it been like to be inside the cell listening to the things raking at the door?

"Spread out," said Lucy. "Look for a set of clothes with a key ring."

Now why hadn't *he* thought of that? Surely some warder would have been on-site when the Darkening happened. And that warder would have had keys. After a moment Crank called out from down the hall.

"Got 'em."

Dylan tapped lightly on the door. There was no answer, and Crank nudged around him to slip the key into the lock and push the door open. Instantly the blinding light disappeared and Dylan stared into darkness that was as soft and comforting as warm down. He wanted to walk into the cell and lie down and sleep forever. He felt a peace within that he had never experienced before. As his eyes grew accustomed to the dim light that Wagner's lantern reflected into the cell he noticed that what he had thought was simply an upturned mattress in the corner contained an old man, emaciated and shaking. For an instant Dylan imagined this was not a Christian asylum at all but a barracks in Auschwitz.

Crank shattered the illusion. "What the fuck is *he* doing here?"

Surprising Dylan, Crank shoved past him, raising his rifle in the direction of the inmate. Baxter rushed into the room and jerked the barrel of Crank's gun aside, and Wagner placed himself between the old man and Crank. Finally, Crank seemed to subside but not relax, and Dylan turned to watch Lucy kneeling beside the mattress.

A sick old man and this ragtag bunch certainly weren't what she'd been expecting to find at the end of her quest. Incredibly, she had discovered that the missing part of herself was her lost twin, only to learn that she was dead and they would never be united. What kind of higher power played jokes like that? To Lucy it seemed more likely to be the caprice of an unknowing, uncaring cosmos than fate.

The ancient inmate looked as though he might not make it through the night, and the entire group was a bedraggled-looking mess. She glanced at Wagner and wondered if this was the kind of reception he had expected to find at the Keep. If it was, they were doomed. This gang wasn't going to fight its way out of a paper bag, much less defeat something that could create mutants like the Rhothag, that could turn off all the power and remove the entire population of the planet.

In spite of all her misgivings she felt the wildest urge to be close to Dylan, to touch him. But she sensed that to do so would be to open herself to a world of hurt far greater than any she had experienced before. She wasn't his wife, and he wasn't her sister. Both of them had lost what they were really searching for. Now they might be drawn to each other by the residue of a dead woman, but she saw no future in that, only more terrible disappointment.

"Father Anton Remedios," whispered Crank, through clenched teeth.

Lucy noticed that the little man's fingers were still tight on his rifle, and he watched closely as though the man he called Remedios were the most dangerous of armed criminals.

"We don't have time for this," said Baxter, placing himself between Crank and the old man, who was just now beginning to take some notice of the commotion he was causing.

But Crank's stare cut right through Baxter to the priest. "You should have been dead four years ago."

"If you kill him, you'll have to kill me, too," said Wagner.

Crank nodded, unimpressed.

"And me," said Baxter softly.

"And me, I guess," said Lucy. She didn't quite know why she was involved in the fracas. But she wasn't going to stand by and watch an old man murdered.

"You have nothing to do with this," said Crank.

"I guess I do now," she said quietly.

To Lucy's surprise, Remedios tried to stand. But he didn't have the strength, and as he slid back down he reached out and placed his hand over hers.

"I'm not as far gone as all that, and you were right to come," he rasped. "There is no one left at the Keep, but we must go there, anyway."

"How could you possibly know that?" gasped Wagner, shaking his head.

"If all of you were drawn here to me, then either there is no one left at the Keep, or it is indeed in foul hands," said Remedios.

"You're not going near the Keep," said Crank.

"*I* brought Remedios here," said Baxter. "I was the one who faked his *death*. But I was following orders."

"Orders from another renegade, no doubt," said Crank.

"Clayborn is a fool," said Remedios, his hand sagging as he pointed at Crank.

"I should kill you just for that," said Crank, still glowering. "The Boss is ten times the man you ever were."

"What did you call him?" gasped Lucy.

"Most everyone just calls Clayborn the Boss," said Wagner.

"That's what the men who tried to kidnap me called the man they were taking me to," she whispered.

"You never told me that," said Wagner, frowning.

"I didn't think it was important."

"Lots of people are called Boss," said Crank, still glaring at Remedios.

"But not many would want this woman so badly," said the old priest.

"I would have carried out my orders," said Crank. "But before I got there you were *killed* in a fire. I even checked the dental records on the corpse. Everything matched."

Baxter smiled. "Good job, eh?"

"Very," said Crank. "But it's never too late."

Baxter shoved his pistol into Crank's ribs, and Wagner's carbine quivered to life again, aimed at Crank's belly. Crank glanced slowly around the room, taking in Dylan's and Lucy's determined faces before dropping his hands to his sides.

"Whether you believe it or not, Crank," said Baxter, "Remedios is a friend. And if there really isn't anyone left at the Keep, then I'd say he's in command right now."

"How in the hell do you figure that?" said Crank.

Baxter shrugged. "Remedios knows more about the Old Ones than anyone alive. Do *you* know what to do if he's right and there's no one home at the Keep? I don't."

The old man was so emaciated he felt feather-light to Lucy, but he gradually managed to sit up with her help. "There is no time for this."

"How did you live all this time?" she asked, stroking thin gray hair back out of his face.

His eyes gleamed with life in a face white as death. "Water was provided," he said, nodding toward the condensation that still glistened on the peeling paint beside him. "I do not know how I remained alive without sustenance."

"It's a miracle," said Dylan, shaking his head.

"I believe that may be so. I have been forced to reevaluate the reality of miracles of late."

"You didn't believe in them before?" asked Lucy.

"No."

"But you're a priest."

He shrugged. "I no longer serve in that capacity. Is there no one else alive in this wing? An old man and old woman, perhaps?"

Lucy shook her head, and Remedios's hopeful expression saddened.

"What happened to the light?" asked Dylan, glancing around the empty cell where the only illumination came from the tiny camp lantern.

"What light?" asked Remedios.

Lucy told him about the gleaming that had shone through the keyhole and the tiny window and Remedios smiled.

"I saw no such light," he said, glancing at Crank. "Do *you* think the Boss would have seen it?"

Lucy turned toward Crank, who, shaking his head in disgust, disappeared back out into the gloomy corridor. Remedios seemed to strengthen a little just having him out of the room. As she fed the old man small bits of chocolate and helped him to drink from a bottle of water, she found herself recalling Blondie, dead now for the same sort of trifle that was restoring Remedios to life. Remedios grasped her hand and stared deeply into her eyes, and she felt a curious resurgence of hope. There was something about the withered priest that engendered trust even though he looked for all the world like a man on his last legs.

Remedios glanced from Lucy to Dylan and his tired eyes flickered.

"How did you find me?" he asked. "Were you led here by a light such as the one you speak of?"

Dylan and Lucy both explained the pull that had drawn them to him and to each other.

"And do you both have some talent that is out of the ordinary?"

"I can sense the presence of the Rhothag," said Lucy. "Sometimes others . . . sometimes just a wrongness."

When Remedios glanced at Dylan, Dylan shrugged, but the old priest continued to stare at him.

"I never expected there to be two of you," he said. "Always there was only the one woman. I choose to see hope in this."

"We'll have to rig up some kind of litter for you," said Baxter.

But even as he spoke Phoenix began to growl, and Lucy knew it was too late.

"I don't think we have time," she said, the urgency in her voice turning them all toward the door.

At first Dylan thought the voice he heard drifting through the corridor was Crank, muttering to himself, but then he realized it was the bizarre alien speech, and he noticed that the dog was backed up against Lucy's legs, hackles high, teeth bared. The distant sound of boot soles slapping arrhythmically on marble echoed in the cell. He glanced into the darkened corridor and spotted Crank, limping as fast as he could toward Remedios's cell.

"They're coming," said Lucy.

The signature clop-clip-clop pattern of Crank's bootheels sounded faster. Dylan leaned farther out into the corridor. Crank was almost there. Behind him shadows wove furtively against a larger, more sinister darkness. Baxter fiddled the big old cruciform key into the lock, just as Dylan jerked a panting Crank past him into the cell.

But instead of slamming the door, Dylan peered into the approaching gloom down the long hall, a creeping sensation of déjà vu worming its way up his spine. Suddenly he felt as though he were back in his entryway that day just before the door opened and let in the light. The odor of rotting metal assailed his nostrils.

"Close it!" Baxter and Wagner shouted in unison.

But Dylan couldn't move. He had to see what it was that stirred in the nearly impenetrable shadows. The Rhothag were easy to distinguish now even though they were only silhouettes, and the amorphous thing behind them drew closer and closer to the thin cone of illumination from Wagner's lantern. This was the same thing that had threatened him in his sleep, the same thing that had swelled to impossible size and almost killed him on Crank's snowmobile. He began to notice swirling layers of deeper gloom within the darkness.

"Come on out, you son of a bitch," Dylan whispered, the palms of his hands beginning to sweat. Strong hands dropped onto his shoulders, dragging him back, but he resisted, leaning into the hallway, daring the thing.

"Close the goddamned door!" Baxter shouted in his ear, dragging him back another step.

The swirling movements of shadows were almost close enough to touch, blocking the view of everything else in the wide hall, and suddenly the familiar metallic odor was everywhere. Dylan felt more hands on his shoulders, and he was jerked forcibly into the cell, the door slamming shut, as the key clacked full circle, shoving the broad steel bolt into place.

Dylan could hear the thing's powerful voice, the strange language that *almost* made sense echoing inside his head.

Rantasas Mella Duun.

Seeka Mella Duun.

The thing wanted him. But he sensed confusion in it as well.

"The Rhothag come every night," said Remedios wearily. "Outside my cell, waiting. But I sense a new beast with them now. It still waits, or the door would not be enough to stop it."

He glanced at Lucy, and she shuddered, signaling that she sensed the thing as well.

"What is it?" asked Dylan, turning to the old man.

Remedios shook his head, frowning. "I do not know for certain. I have never experienced a feeling like this before."

"It's bewildered," said Dylan.

"Because its time is not yet come," said Remedios. "It fears to make a mistake and awaken its masters' wrath. The fury of the Old Ones is not something to be taken lightly, even by such a one as this."

"Do you know what the words mean?" asked Dylan, glancing at Baxter, then back to Remedios.

Remedios leaned forward to stare at him. "You hear words?"

Dylan nodded. "*Rantasas Mella Duun*. I've been hearing that for weeks. But it said something else just now."

Remedios frowned. "*Rantasas Mella Duun. I serve the Gatekeeper*, or merely *Serve the Gatekeeper*."

Dylan heard the words echoing in his head again.

"*Seeka Mella Duun,*" he said. "That's something new."

Remedios's eyes widened. "That means *Become the Gatekeeper*."

"What?" said Dylan, glancing from frightened face to face.

"You say you have experience with this creature?" said Remedios.

Suddenly, Dylan felt a quivering along his spine again, and he spun back to the door. Wagner, Crank, and Baxter were staring at the small viewing window, and Dylan's breath left him in a gasp. A huge dark eye filled the window.

"Put something over that!" he shouted. He could feel the thing's thoughts leaping from the horrible orb directly into his brain, delving, questing with nimble claws into the deepest regions of his soul. Baxter slapped his pack over the port, throwing his shoulder against it to hold it in place, and Dylan sucked in a rasping breath, falling back against the far wall.

"You have had experience with this *thing* before?" Remedios repeated.

"In my house," Dylan said, shaking. "In the forest when Crank saved me. I've heard its voice over and over."

In the hallway the Rhothag had picked up the chant that echoed in Dylan's head. Something heavy pounded against the door, and Baxter shook with the impact.

"The shadow wants both you and Lucy because you carry the wild talents," said Remedios. "But I believe the Rhothag are here for myself and the others. They have waited until we are all together, and now I believe we will not be able to hold both them and the shadow at bay for long with one bolted door."

As though in emphasis an even louder thump rocked the door, driving Baxter temporarily away, but he quickly recovered. Outside, however, the sounds of feet told them that more of the Rhothag were arriving by the minute. Night must have fallen outside and the place had become a hive.

Dylan frowned at the old man. "Do you have any better ideas?"

Remedios shook his head. "We need to reach the Keep. And we need to go now."

Crank shook his head. "How would you suggest we do that, or should I just rent us a bus?"

"I suspect that God will provide."

"He hasn't been doing a great job so far," said Dylan, glancing at Lucy. Her face was clenched in concentration, perspiration beading on her forehead, and her hands were fisted at her hips, but she appeared alert and unbowed by her fear, staring fixedly at the door.

"You did this," said Crank, staring at Remedios. "You

drew us all here. Now we're trapped. I should have killed you when I first laid eyes on you."

"I did not intentionally *do* anything of which you accuse me," said Remedios. "But perhaps you are right that I am the cause of your being here. The Old Ones surely know that I am their enemy, and it may well be that there is no one else left who may discover their weakness. Some hand guided you here. I choose to believe it was the hand of God."

"Does that thing have a weakness?" asked Lucy.

The old man smiled, placing a surprisingly firm hand on her shoulder.

"Every creature in God's universe has one," he said.

The thing outside the door was no longer a darkness, a poisonous shadow reaching for Dylan, calling to him, stalking him in the night. It had become an ocean of hunger rising up to drown him. It flooded the entire building, every cell, every office, every nook and cranny, and he knew that once it got inside this room he would become a part of it, dissolved inside its essence as though it were a sea of acid, and Lucy and the others would be left to the Rhothag.

Something massive struck the door this time, propelling Baxter into Wagner's arms. The eye was gone now, but before Dylan could glance through the window the door was struck yet again. This time the entire building shook, and the door bulged inward.

"There's no way out," said Dylan, glancing around the tiny room that now seemed even smaller than before.

"The only salvation now lies at the Keep," said Remedios wearily. "I do not believe we were meant to die in this place, else I should have expired long ago."

"I don't know what you expect us to do," said Dylan, glancing at Lucy who shook her head.

"Look into your souls. God will provide a way," said Remedios.

"The old bastard's nuts, Dylan," said Crank, shoving Baxter roughly away from the door, and drawing his pistols. "Open the door. We'll have to fight our way out."

"You're crazy," said Dylan, staring at the guns, wondering if Crank had finally gone over the edge.

Even if the shadow monster hadn't been out there, the corridor was full of Rhothag, and Dylan was sure there were even more beyond. He could sense night falling outside, and now that it was dark the grounds were probably alive with the ugly beasts. Even if they somehow made it miraculously past the Rhothag and the thing in the corridor—and Dylan was certain that he at least would not—there was no way they could fight their way through all of the beasts in Sacred Light. The dog yapped wildly at the vibrating door, and Lucy tried to calm her, stroking her neck.

"We don't have a choice," said Crank.

"Here or in the corridor, death will be the same," said Remedios quietly.

Dylan didn't see how the one bolt could last much longer, and Lucy grabbed him by the shoulder, drawing him back a step as the Rhothag continued to batter the door.

"You escaped the shadow before," said Remedios.

Dylan shook his head. "We outran it on a snowmobile!"

"What about in your house?" said Baxter. "You said it was there, too."

"That was all in my head. I just dreamed it," said Dylan, knowing now that that was a lie. But if he did have any wild talent, it had not protected him in his own entryway, and he had no idea how it might have saved him on the snowmobile.

Remedios shook his head. "No. It was not a dream, although you wish it to be so."

As he stared into the old man's eyes, Dylan wondered just how much Remedios really knew. Wagner claimed he had saved the old man from Crank and others in Rex Deus. But what kind of salvation entailed solitary confinement in a nuthouse?

Dylan knew that here and now if they had any hope for survival at all, it lay beyond his own physical powers, beyond their puny guns. He wished with all his might to be anywhere else. But staring into Lucy's expectant face all he could do was shake his head. They had only minutes—perhaps seconds—to live, but there was nothing he could do. In frustration he closed his eyes and turned away.

Suddenly he was jolted by a familiar, sickening sensation of falling, the same terrible vertiginous feeling he'd always experienced just before awakening in his house, and when he reopened his eyes he was standing in a huge glass-fronted room with a high, vaulted ceiling. Heavy leather furniture—sofas, chairs, and ottomans—was scattered widely throughout the large open space, resting on a light, highly polished hardwood floor. Outside the early evening was deep and dark, but he sensed no danger.

"Damn," he whispered, feeling guiltier than ever—having deserted the others.

So he really *hadn't* been sleepwalking. Somehow he'd been *shifting* through his house. Only now he had no more idea of how to get back to Sacred Light than he had of how he had gotten out in the first place. In desperation he closed his eyes again and wished himself back inside that tiny cell, picturing the place in his mind, praying that he wouldn't get the damned power to work again only to pop up inside the Rhothag-filled corridor or somewhere else equally deadly.

But the nauseating sense of falling didn't return. When he reopened his eyes he was still in the huge, silent room. He closed his eyes again and pictured Lucy.

Suddenly he experienced the weird sense of dislocation, but this time it lasted longer, and he felt as though he were physically dragging himself forward. When he finally opened his eyes, Baxter was gaping at him.

"What the hell just happened?" gasped Wagner.

One of the hinges hung on the frame now by only two of its six bolts, and the door rattled ominously with each new attack. It sounded as though the Rhothag were battering it with a telephone pole.

"How long was I gone?" asked Dylan.

Lucy shook her head. "I saw you *blink* out. Then you were back."

Remedios climbed slowly to his feet with one arm over Baxter's shoulder for support. Dylan felt as though *he* needed to lean on someone, too.

"I think maybe I can get us out, but I don't know how many I can take at one time," said Dylan. "It's like climbing a mountain with your fingertips."

"The old man first, then," said Lucy.

"You too," insisted Dylan.

Dylan recognized Ronnie's old stubborn streak in Lucy's eyes, but she wasn't winning this argument, and she knew it. The old priest transferred his arm to Dylan's shoulder, and Dylan grasped both Lucy's hands and closed his eyes, praying that first round-trip had not been a fluke.

"Don't lollygag around," said Baxter.

"I wouldn't have any idea how to do that."

The floor shook again, and the door rattled.

"Ready to take a short flight?" said Dylan, with forced confidence, feeling the dog rubbing against his leg.

He pictured the room with the giant windows, took a deep breath, and tried to reenact everything he had done before, but he didn't even have to open his eyes to know that nothing had happened. He felt the old man holding himself still with infinite patience, and deep in his memory he was certain he heard Sensei Ashiroato chuckling. He shook his head, trying to concentrate again.

Nothing.

He could hear Lucy's ragged breathing, but the singsong in his head had returned, and he knew it was that distraction that was keeping him from shifting.

He focused his center, relaxing every muscle in his body as he had been trained to do, using his karate skills to try to reach that space inside himself again where the power could be released. Suddenly he experienced the dislocation, his inner ear pounded, and he grasped Lucy's hands tightly. When he opened his eyes he was resting on a plush throw rug, surrounded by leather chairs and richly stained antique furniture. The far walls were distant enough to be cloaked in gloom. When he glanced at Remedios he saw something in the old priest's face he hadn't expected. Familiarity. The old man knew where he was.

"You did well," Remedios whispered, as Dylan and Lucy helped him lie down on one of the numerous sofas. The dog woofed reassuringly at the priest, and Remedios smiled and petted her head.

Weariness strained every joint in Dylan's body. He felt as though he had actually carried the group whatever distance they had traveled.

"Do you know this place?" he asked Remedios.

"Of course," said Remedios, closing his eyes. "This is the Keep. Bring the others here."

"I'm not sure I can," said Dylan. "I don't know if I have the strength left, and I'm not really sure how to control this thing I do. I can't guarantee I can get back to Sacred Light or back here if I do."

"You can't just leave them there," said Lucy in a voice Dylan knew he could not ignore.

"Just bring them," said Remedios, curling into a fetal position on the carpet as Lucy knelt beside him. "You will do fine."

Dylan stared at the old man for a second, irritated by his unwavering certainly, but there was nothing else to do but try.

This time it took him even longer to reach that point in his head where the shift happened. But as he thought about the three men left in that tiny room with the door ready to burst in he found the place again. This time the sense of dislocation was even worse, and he struggled not to lose focus. If he did, he was afraid he might end up lost in some place from which he would never be able to find his way back. And the shift was even harder than before, as though he had to drag himself on his hands and knees back to the cell, as though every foot of unreal territory were a mile.

But finally he opened his eyes and discovered Baxter gaping at him.

Dylan had to shout because the pounding of the battering ram and the sound of the Rhothags chanting outside the door had become a cacophonous roar that even managed to overpower the voice inside his head.

"You were gone a couple of minutes that time," shouted Baxter, glaring at Crank. "He tried to open the door again."

Crank shrugged, nodding toward the door that now looked like it had been rammed by an armored truck. It was clear that it would not survive many more blows. "I wasn't sure you'd be back. We can't stay in here much longer."

"We have to go together," said Dylan, waving the three of them over to them. "And you've got to touch me. All of you."

"Are you okay? Can you do it?" Wagner asked, studying his face.

Dylan nodded. But he really didn't believe it. He felt as though he had *swum* there through miles of sludge. Every muscle ached, and his legs quivered.

He closed his eyes, and surprisingly the tiny space in his head where the shift happened was easier to find this time. But a part of him was still focused on the cell, the giant black shadow just outside the door. The odor of the thing fouled his lungs, and he felt like a plane overburdened with too much weight.

"I don't think I can do it!" he gasped just as the door burst in, and they all stiffened against him.

Then he had them. They were out of the room, away from the Rhothag and the thing, but the shift was even harder than ever, and for the first time he sensed the shadow trying to ride along. Was he going to drag it with them into the Keep where they would all be too exhausted and powerless to defend themselves?

The pain of exertion increased until he thought he was going to black out, and a part of him wanted that to happen, wanted to sink into oblivion, so this day, this entire period in his life, would disappear, so the madness would just go away. But then he remembred the look in Lucy's eyes, begging him to bring Wagner safely through, and he knew he had to go on until they all made it or he died. He reached out with the last of his strength and *pulled*, and his sense of the shadow became less, and he pulled again, every nerve screaming.

Finally, he collapsed onto the floor, staring around the room in wonder.

"You made it!" said Lucy, wrapping her arms around Wagner. "Thank God."

Even more miraculous than the old priest's survival was the second wind he seemed to get upon arriving at the Keep. Followed closely by the entire group—including the scowling Crank—and supported by Lucy, he shambled through the maze of the main floor of the giant building.

The Keep itself took up approximately an acre of the surrounding grounds and was built on three floors like a drunken architect's idea of function defining form. The exterior *flowed* upward from the ground floor in heavy blocks of sandstone with tall arched windows. Above that the facade morphed to stucco and clapboard with shutters framing the rectangular glasswork there. Inside the building was equally schizoid, offices and computer cubicles interspersed with workout rooms, bedrooms, and even suites, and a large kitchen behind the giant study in which they had found themselves earlier. None of the contents of any of the files in the offices interested Remedios, and they discovered no one inhabiting the place, although many of the bedrooms had the usual empty pajamas.

"You're sure what you're looking for is here?" asked Lucy, staring expectantly into Remedios's weary face.

"Yes," said Remedios. "I did not have free access to the entire Keep. But although I was never allowed to visit the archives, or to know their location, I spent quite some time here studying ancient artifacts such as pottery shards, scrolls, and photographs of stelae. There is a great vault here somewhere. The answers we require would be there. I'm certain of it."

"How much room would it take up?"

Remedios shook his head. "The section of the Vatican archives holding merely the texts regarding the Old Ones required a space slightly larger than the study, but Rex Deus was known to have a much more extensive collection in this country. In the Vatican I once saw a compendium of all the known artifacts worldwide. If but half the items listed still exist and none others had ever been found, the site holding them would be massive."

"And you're sure they're hidden here?" said Dylan.

Remedios nodded. "Very late in the nineteenth century the collections were all brought together in a cave in New Mexico. That site has since been destroyed by Qedem Melech. Now the artifacts are all here."

"If the site in New Mexico was destroyed, how do you know the artifacts weren't?" asked Dylan.

"Because I helped move them before they were," said Baxter.

Wagner nodded.

"Then where are they?" asked Lucy.

"Beats me," said Baxter. "We picked up sealed metal

crates at a site outside Taos, drove them here in trucks disguised as refrigerated trailers for a large grocery chain, then helped off-load them out front. Clayborn had plenty of muscle here, and I for one wasn't interested in hauling those things around."

"Did you realize what the crates had in them?"

"I kind of suspected," said Wagner. "But Clayborn let us know it was none of our business. That was thirty years ago. He'd just built the Keep as our new headquarters, and Baxter and I were pretty low on the totem pole."

"How many truckloads were there?" asked Dylan.

Wagner shrugged. "I made four runs, full to the gills, and there were four other drivers besides Baxter and me. The others may have made more runs. I don't know."

Dylan whistled. "At least twenty-four tractor-trailer loads?"

"This is a hell of a big house," said Lucy, shaking her head. "But I can't see where you'd hide all that. It should be easy enough to locate. What kind of cases?"

"Big metal-sheathed crates, all different sizes and shapes," said Wagner. "Never saw anything like it."

"Sounds like museum-quality shipping containers," said Lucy.

"Exactly," said Remedios. "It is all here. We simply have to find it."

"Why bring it all together in the first place?" said Dylan. "Seems like Rex Deus would want to keep their valuables at separate secret locations. Especially since Qedem Melech attacked and destroyed the original site."

"Several factors were instrumental in the decision," said Remedios, entering a large bedroom only long enough to ascertain that there was nothing resembling artifacts inside before returning to the corridor. "Two were shortages of money and people. Rex Deus has always been a dwindling army. It is very difficult to recruit the right kind of people and convince them that what they are doing is worthwhile and *real,* and over the millennia Rex Deus's finances have waxed and waned. During the nineteenth century the organization lost money worldwide due to bad financial decisions, and again early in the twentieth century they suffered a major loss with the discovery of Tutankhamen's tomb."

"What?" said Lucy, stumbling. "Why?"

Remedios smiled. "You must keep in mind how ancient Rex Deus is. At the time of the child king's death, the organization was already many thousands of years old. Rex Deus's leaders knew, of course, of the fabulous wealth being buried with the pharaohs. They realized that over the coming centuries the dynasty was certain to falter, and the site would be looted. You will note that of fifty-seven known tombs in the Valley of the Kings, Tutankhamen's was not discovered until the 1920s. This was no accident. Over the centuries artifacts and bullion were removed from the tombs of Tutankhamen and others to bankroll Rex Deus. Lord Carnarvon and his pet archaeologist, Howard Carter, died very soon after the discovery. I have my suspicions that this was because it was feared they suspected the whereabouts of other still-buried tombs. If this is so, it does not reflect credit on Rex Deus."

"One does what one must," said Crank, mimicking the old man's stiff speech.

Remedios shot a withering glance at him. "For all we know, Carter or Carnarvon may have been Qedem Melech."

"Unbelievable," said Dylan.

"The secret of the Old Ones, their ultimate weakness, is here, somewhere," said Remedios. "Although they tried to bury it by destroying all the artifacts, many must survive."

"How can you not know how to fight them if Rex Deus has existed all along to protect Ronnie and Lucy's line?" asked Dylan. "Aren't *they* the answer?"

"They are indeed the answer," mused Remedios. "We simply don't understand the question, yet. Do *you* understand how to defeat the Old Ones using your talents?"

"No," said Dylan irritably. "I don't even understand what they are or what they want."

"They want everything," said Remedios. "Eventually

the cycle of the Darkening will complete itself and our world will be hospitable to them once again. And it will be inhospitable to us, if any of us survive that long. The Old Ones exist to devour and destroy. They create nothing—save the Rhothag, which are mindless and cruel, less than what they were created from. I suspect that we will discover that the Old Ones themselves may not be defeated by man. We must find a way to stop them from crossing into our world."

"Through a wormhole," muttered Lucy.

"What's that you say, my dear?" asked Remedios.

"Wormholes," repeated Lucy. "Gateways between dimensions. If what you say is true, then they must really exist. Too bad Stephen Hawking isn't around for me to tell him."

"A wormhole," said Remedios quietly. "I find that fitting. Did you know that there have been periods in which Lucifer was referred to as a worm?"

"You believe the Old Ones represent the Devil?" asked Lucy. "That their world really is Hell?"

Remedios shrugged. "I believe that they represent true evil. Surely if good is creation, then evil is mindless destruction for its own sake. If Hell is where only destruction lurks, then the Old Ones do indeed inhabit Hell."

"Why here?" asked Dylan, wiping his brow with his sleeve. "Why bring everything to this one place instead of any other?"

Remedios smiled, turning to Lucy. "Do you feel it?"

"Feel what?" she asked.

"You said that sometimes you could sense a *wrongness*. Can you not sense the rightness of this place?"

She frowned, concentrating. Then slowly a gentle smile slipped across her face.

"What is that?" she asked.

"*That,*" said Remedios, "is hallowed ground. This may well be the last ground of its kind on earth. I once tried to speak with Clayborn about it, but he had no feeling for it. There was nothing beyond the here and now for the Boss. I always found it a great irony that of all the places on earth he should choose this one spot to locate the Keep, the last bastion of Rex Deus against the Old Ones. The hand of God may use many tools. And *tools* do not necessarily know their own purpose. Clayborn may have been one of them."

"You knew all along that this ground was *hallowed*?" asked Lucy.

Remedios shrugged. "In those days I simply sensed a difference. Something that I knew the Old Ones would not like. I was far from believing in anything mythical such as ground that might be sacred. Sacred ground by its nature required a higher being to hallow it."

"But you believe it now."

"Yes."

"So why is this ground hallowed?" said Dylan.

Remedios shrugged. "Because God says it is so. Because in ages past when the Darkening was nearly complete this was one area the foul beasts did not touch. That is why we may be safe here for the moment. But the respite will not last. When the final battle begins this ground will lose its powers over the Old Ones and their minions. Darkness will fall everywhere and forever."

His smile faltered as he turned and ambled down the long corridor again.

Miraculous recovery or no, Remedios finally succumbed to exhaustion, and Lucy covered him with a blanket in the study, insisting that Wagner remain with the old priest in case he awakened. Although they were *all* weary to the point of collapse, Remedios's insistence that the Darkening was almost upon them spurred them on, and they separated to continue searching the huge building through the night, stopping only to snack on canned goods from the kitchen or for short catnaps in one of the countless bedrooms. But still there were no clues to the whereabouts of the vault Remedios was certain was there. The attic was an empty cavern, and the basement proved to be a vast, barren maze of rooms connected by oddly placed doors rather than corridors. Baxter and Crank became lost more than once before assuring themselves that they had seen it all and that the blank walls and bare concrete floor could hide nothing of value.

By late afternoon of the next day a bleary-eyed Lucy and Phoenix followed Dylan as he walked along slump-shouldered, studying the foundation.

She'd tried to ease her consciousness into the ground both inside and outside the house, but although the earth and bedrock around the grounds seemed normal, the building itself blocked her. Some invisible, shapeless buffer within the concrete of the foundation kept her talent from questing within.

Baxter had begun searching the grounds, probing with a long iron rod, and Crank had disappeared. To Lucy, the little man was stranger than even the oddball old priest. On the surface he seemed to be just what he appeared, a hardened killer with steely eyes and no conscience, and she wondered that Remedios could maintain such composure around him. But underneath she sensed something else, a kinship of suspicion that bothered her deeply. Crank's adamant refusal to accept this new world at face value was just enough of a wedge to keep the door open on her own lingering doubts.

Dylan was another matter altogether. She watched as he knelt beside the foundation now, running questing fingers along a slight discoloration in the cement. But even from her vantage point she could see that it was just an old water stain and not evidence of any secret vault. She admired his tenacity, the way he could focus like a laser, but she wondered how one dealt with that kind of intensity. His love for her sister burned in his eyes every time he looked at her, and although she felt a deep-seated longing to melt into those same eyes and experience that kind of wild ardor, she simply could not. A man who could love so deeply attracted and frightened her at the same time.

It wasn't only Dylan's eyes that revealed his feelings for

her. She'd felt it in the shy way he acted around her, trying to be close but never too close, as though he always had something to say but couldn't quite spit it out. She felt like a schoolgirl who had no one to talk to about her boy troubles. And the sense she got every time she was near him that some unknown part of her sister survived with him confused her as well.

She caught his eyes this time and held them. "I'm sorry for your loss. For *our* loss. I know I told you that already, but I need you to know just how deeply I feel it."

Dylan frowned. "I wish she'd known you."

The pain was so deep in his eyes and his voice that she wished she hadn't brought it up. But the air felt a little clearer between them.

"Remedios may be right about you. But he's wrong about me," said Dylan. "The power I have was supposed to be Ronnie's, only she gave it to me somehow. In my mind she keeps saying she's sorry. I think her talent was as much a curse to her as anything else."

His words struck her like a body blow, and she knew in that instant that the voice she had heard in her dream had been real.

"She talks to you?"

He nodded. "Crazy, huh?"

"Not that crazy. I told you I felt her in you. I feel her even more now. What else does she say?"

"That's about it. But I get the feeling that it's really important to her that I accept this *talent*."

"I think it's important for everyone that you accept it," said Lucy.

"Were you married?" asked Dylan, after a moment's hesitation.

"No."

"Boyfriend?"

She saw that he had embarrassed himself.

"Stupid question," he said. "So you lost someone, too."

"I've never had anyone. Ever since I was a child I've had to hide from Qedem Melech, although I never knew until now that they were the ones I was hiding from. But I could never have friends."

"I'm sorry," said Dylan. He stared at his feet, nudging the soil with the toe of one boot. "I think Ronnie must have had a life pretty much like yours before we met. She would never speak about it. Her mother—your mother—was a really odd character, cold and uncommunicative. I always figured that was just her personality. But now I know she'd lost one child and spent the rest of her life terrified of losing another."

"I've known since I was little that I had something missing inside me," said Lucy. "When I was small I thought I could fill it if only I had been allowed to make friends. Later, after my parents died, I tried, but I found that the talent for making them had atrophied, and I could never open myself, could never trust anyone. Finally, I convinced myself that it must have something to do with having lost my real parents, and I spent the last ten years looking for them. But deep in my heart I think I knew that wasn't really it at all. Now I sense that something I was searching for is within you, but I don't know what to do about it. You aren't her and yet you are. You have something that I have longed for since the day I was born, and there is no way for you to share it with me even if you would."

"I would," Dylan whispered.

Lucy suddenly wanted to run away, and at the same time she couldn't help but stare into his eyes. Fighting an inner struggle more fierce than she had ever experienced, she turned away and headed back up the path around the house.

"Come on," she managed to mutter, hoping her words didn't sound like a sob. "I'm getting hungry."

By nightfall, even though every muscle in his body ached, Dylan still felt filled with nervous energy, and as everyone else wandered dejectedly off to bed, he grabbed a lantern and headed down the hall toward the workout rooms.

He bypassed the weight benches, glanced wistfully at the pool—growing murky and stagnant—before finally entering the small gymnasium. Taking long, slow breaths, he centered himself, then raced through the *katas*—the *Teikiyokos*, the *Pinans*, then *Sanchin*, and *Soki-no*—amazed at how much he now had to concentrate on the dancelike movements he had done so many thousand times in the past. His joints creaked, and he was already breathing hard before reaching the first black belt form.

Kanku-dei had one hundred steps—eighty more than the lower *katas*—and required five times as much concentration to perform correctly. To bring all the stances into alignment, to strike at the precise point with the exact amount of power and speed so that the *kata* ended within millimeters of where it had begun, required years of training and intense mental and physical effort. As he whirled to complete the final defense and attack, throwing an imaginary opponent over his shoulder, then striking him with a downward driven fist, he relaxed, taking a deep breath and drawing back upright in the *fudo* stance with heels together, toes apart, bowing slowly to the room.

"That was amazing."

Lucy's voice shocked him, and he sidestepped to regain his balance.

"I didn't mean to intrude," she said, rising quickly from the workout bench. As always Phoenix was right beside her.

"No, please stay," said Dylan, hurrying across the floor.

She faced him with a sheepish expression. "I couldn't sleep. I thought you might be down here. You were so caught up in what you were doing, I just took a seat and watched."

"I love the *katas*."

"*Katas?*"

Dylan gave her a brief history of the intricate forms that had been conceived because hundreds of years ago the warriors had banned the martial arts for the peasant classes but not dancing.

"And the Samurai really thought that was just a dance?" said Lucy, frowning.

Dylan shrugged. "Martial artists like to *believe* that everything they do is the authentic art exactly as it was performed a hundred or two hundred years ago, but all the martial arts have evolved to meet the needs of the times. I doubt if the people who performed *katas* for the Samurai would recognize any of these, but they'd know what they were."

"They look terribly difficult to learn."

"Not at all," said Dylan. "The *katas* are ranked so that you begin easy and work your way up. By the time you reach the level of *Kanku-dei* you know all the moves involved. Then it's just a matter of putting them together and remembering them in the right order. Come on, I'll show you."

Lucy shook her head, but Dylan dragged her out onto the floor, showing her how to step out into the front-leaning stance and then down-block. She turned out to be an excellent pupil. Within minutes he had her understanding the basics of *Teikiyoko-sono-ichi,* the first beginner *kata.*

"You're a natural," he said.

She smiled. "That's amazing. It's so intense. You really have to think about what you're doing all the time. I see how you could lose yourself in it."

He nodded. "Some people really do. My sensei tried to tell me there were mysteries to be discovered there, something beyond what we could see and touch. But it never worked for me."

"Because you never believed it," she said quietly.

"What do you believe?" he asked.

She nibbled her lip thoughtfully. "I didn't use to believe anything. I thought everything could be explained rationally. I thought I took comfort from that, but really I was just hiding."

"Hiding from what?"

"From myself."

"I don't understand."

"I've known in here," she said, touching her breast over her heart, "that I was different since I was a child. But I didn't want to believe that I was different. I ignored it so strongly that I started to forget why I felt that way. Because if I allowed myself to believe that I was simply *born* different, with a talent that no one else in the world had, then I had to accept that there was some power that made me so, and that that power might have a purpose for me that maybe I didn't want to accept."

"Like saving the world."

"Like dying," she said, nodding.

Instead of answering, he showed her the longer extension of his rear leg in the front-leaning stance, the way he completed a turn with down-block and stance completed at the same time, the way his punches were aimed exactly at his imaginary opponent's solar plexus, and the peculiar way he held his fist so that only the first two knuckles would strike home. "This is what takes the *kata* up another level. But all that is just refinement."

He sensed she had reached a turning point, and he waited patiently, hopefully . . .

"Please tell me about Ronnie," she said quietly.

She followed him to the workout bench, where they sat down, her leg barely brushing his.

"What would you like to know?" he asked.

"Everything."

His smile broadened as he shook his head. "There's no way I could tell you everything about Ronnie in a million years. She was the most beautiful woman I've ever met. I never knew what she saw in me. There were better-looking guys at school, smarter ones, a lot with money. I didn't have the nerve to talk to her, much less to ask her out."

"So she approached you," said Lucy, nodding to herself.

"She asked me out, and later she asked me to marry her."

"She knew what she wanted."

"By the time I met her I thought I'd mastered my fears. But in her presence I was like a four-year-old in a dark room. I babbled, I sweated like a pig. I became a complete loser. She told me once there was something in me that only she and God could see. She said it shone like a star. I didn't believe her, but I thanked *my* stars she saw it."

"There is something in you," said Lucy quietly. "I sensed it the first time I saw you, and it's not just Ronnie's presence. It's a warm feeling. I don't know how I knew, but

I knew in Remedios's cell that you'd get us out of there. I was still scared because I didn't trust my intuition. But I felt it."

"Intuitions like that can get you killed."

"Maybe. But it didn't. What were Ronnie's likes and dislikes?"

"She was a runner. She'd get up at six every day to do her five miles, rain or shine. She loved to read. She was a writer. She'd gotten quite a few of her stories published in national magazines. She loved to ride horses. She was addicted to sweets." He noticed she was frowning, and he stopped.

"I used to run, and I love to read," she said. "I don't write much other than an old journal. But I boarded a horse in Ruredaga. I'm sure poor Newton disappeared with the rest. I hope so. I'd hate to think of him starving in his stall. Or worse."

"What else do you like?" asked Dylan, quickly.

"I love sweets, too," she said, brightening a little. "I guess that was Ronnie's and my downfall. One day I'll be fat."

"Ronnie told me more than once that there was something missing in her life. That hurt a lot because I just couldn't find a way to fix it. I used to think it was something I couldn't give her, something I was doing wrong."

Lucy shook her head. "It wasn't anything anyone could give her. It was a part of us that fought the separation even though we didn't understand what we'd been separated from. I hate whoever it was that tore us apart. I hate that we were born so different from everyone else that someone felt they had to perform an act so heinous for the greater good. But whenever I'm close to you it's as though the empty spot fills up a little, and I can breathe again."

The vast room was suddenly silent, and time seemed to have stopped. Dylan reached for her, but she drew away, not far, just enough to let him know she wasn't ready.

"I'm sorry," she said, stroking her arm where his hand had almost rested. "I just have some things to work out, that's all."

He smiled. "Work out? I'd say that was putting it mildly. We all have things to work out. In fact, I'd say our group has more than enough issues to keep a team of psychologists busy for years."

"I can't stop thinking about the Old Ones. The Rhothag are bad enough, and that thing you saw in Sacred Light, I sensed it too. It scared the crap out of me. If the Old Ones are worse than that, I'm not sure I can face them."

"Well, if Remedios is right, maybe we won't actually have to face them. But so far no one's even told me what the Old Ones are supposed to look like," said Dylan, "or how many there may be. We managed to kill a few of the Rhothag, and that was hard enough. That shadow . . . I don't know if it can be killed. And if it can't, what does that say about the Old Ones? Like Crank, I've been trying to convince myself since day one that there is a logical explanation for all this, but every day things just keep getting harder to explain. Then we run into Remedios, and he does have an explanation, only I don't want to believe it."

"Because if you do believe it, then you'll have to accept your part in it?"

He nodded. "I'm not like you. The only way I was ever special was when I won a championship. But that's not much like having some kind of supernatural power. What's it like when you sense things around you?"

"It's almost as though I *become* the earth. Like I'm living within it, feeling every inch of it, as though the soil and grass above is my skin and the rocks and ground beneath are my flesh and internal organs. Right now I can sense the world outside the grounds, and it's as if the entire planet is one vast living organism, and I can feel it breathing. Only now it's breathing slower, not so steady. I think the whole world is becoming aware of the change that's happening."

"And it's waking up?"

She shook her head sadly. "It's dying."

She gave him one last longing look, and he knew she was close to reaching out to him again, but then she picked up her lamp, and she and the dog disappeared in a patter of footsteps.

Phoenix trotted along beside her as Lucy glanced over her shoulder to be sure Dylan wasn't following. But the dancing shadows on the corridor wall told her he had gone back to practicing his *katas*.

He was so self-assured and at the same time so vulnerable. And of course he carried the essence of her lost sister within him. Sometimes she could almost see someone else that had to be Ronnie, staring out at her through Dylan's dark eyes. It was such an unsettling sensation that she wanted to pull him into her arms and draw her sister out of him like a leech, but she knew that if she succumbed to the temptation, she would be lost. Once in his arms she would never break free, and she was still uncertain if that was what she wanted. She felt more and more like a lovelorn teenager, and the idea of giving herself up to such a powerful emotion, of opening herself so completely to another human being after all these years terrified her almost as much as the Old Ones.

She closed the door of her bedroom and leaned back against it, soaking up the darkness. She was certain that she'd get no sleep that night, but as soon as her head hit the pillow she drifted into deep slumber, and almost immediately the dream was upon her.

The desert again.

Only this time the figure she now knew must be Dylan was not standing on the edge of a precipice but walking just ahead of her. There were only the two of them beneath a cloudless, sunless sky, and she knew that they had been hiking a great distance and still had a great distance yet to journey. At the same time she knew that there was something terrible behind them and something even more frightening ahead, and there was nothing for them to do but keep going.

She tried to speak, to warn Dylan that the thing she

sensed behind them was drawing closer, but her voice would not work, and no matter how hard she tried she could not catch up to him. A great darkness seemed to be overtaking them, and she wanted desperately to be far away from it, but the darkness was an integral part of the dream, and she had no control here, no power over the encroaching gloom. As it slipped over them she tried to scream, but her lungs were sealed, and the blackness engulfed them.

She awoke mummy-tangled in sweat-soaked sheets, gasping for breath, scratching for the matches atop her bedside table. Phoenix rustled beside her, whimpering lightly, nosing her cheek. The glow of the match dispelled the darkness, and she lit the lantern, glancing into the four corners of the bedroom, her heart still pounding.

"Check!" she said, knowing that even though she had not trained Phoenix to do so the dog would understand the command.

Phoenix slunk off the bed, sniffed around the room, then down the corridor, wagging her tail, returning to the side of the bed to stare at Lucy.

Lucy sighed, slapping the covers, and the dog leapt happily back up beside her.

"Just a dream," she whispered.

Dylan tossed and turned, deep into his own nightmare. He was standing in his bedroom at home in the middle of the night. The moon slashed the carpet into shards of gray the shade of a day-old corpse, and the cold light crept across the floor, slithering up onto the bed. He wanted desperately to reach out and close the drapes, to quench the light before it revealed what lay atop the mattress, but he could not move.

As slow as a cobra on the prowl the beam of moonlight slithered across the bone-white linen, exposing first the skeletal pattern of a pair of tiny feet, then the cadaverous outline of the calves, thin as a pair of clarinets. The knees poked against the sheet, and the tops of the thighs were raw bone, threatening to slice through the flimsy cloth.

"No." He mouthed silently.

Ronnie's hips were so gaunt the sheet sagged between them into a deep concavity, and the light seemed to race from there up to her rib cage, which was barely rising and falling in an irregular cadence as though she were wracked with sobs. He could hear her exhaling through her teeth, as though she were clenching her jaw to hold in each life-giving breath just a moment longer. The light continued its unrelenting climb up to the hem of the sheet, clutched in ratlike fingers with cracked yellow nails. Her throat—pale and green-tinted with disease—constricted, and Dylan knew her face was about to be revealed, that she was about to speak. He couldn't bear to look at her, but he couldn't close his eyes.

This was the nightmare memory that he had buried for so long, and he knew that its terrible ending was drawing near now, that he would awaken shaken and bathed in sweat. He approached the moment with a terrible uncertainty, wondering if the dream was going to be somehow different from the true past. But whatever the outcome, he wanted now to face the damned thing one final terrible time and be done with it.

The curtain fluttered with a sudden breeze, the moon leapt across Ronnie's face, and the memory drowned Dylan in horror as fresh and real as yesterday. The soft sweet face was completely gone, and for a moment he feared that what he was seeing was not the Ronnie he knew and loved but the visage of a Rhothag. But as his eyes focused, the face revealed by the centipede moon was no less horrible for all its humanity. Her eyes were sunken and dry, the bones of her cheeks protruded through parchment skin, her full lips were now emaciated black and cracked as charred corn husks, and her once beautiful hair looked more like the mangy mane of a withered corpse than a living, breathing woman. His feet moved of their own accord as one bony finger beckoned to him. His knees struck the side of the mattress, and it was all he could to do to keep from hurtling forward on top of her, his lips drawn tight in horror, as the gnarled hand reached out and wrapped like a manacle around his wrist, the bony grip so tight it cut off his circulation.

She lifted herself onto her elbows, bringing Dylan's face so close to her own that he could smell her breath, a fetid, rank odor. Her eyes roved wildly about the room as she brushed his ear with lips rough as sandpaper.

"I'm still in here," she rasped. "But not for long."

Her fingers bit into his skin, and he saw something akin to madness in her eyes.

"My gift," she rasped again. "You have to take it."

He wanted to hold her and to shove her away at the same time. But her other hand shot out from under the sheet and snatched the hair on the back of his head in a fierce grip, pulling him against her into a horrible embrace.

"I'm sorry," she whispered, and Dylan knew this was her final breath.

He had no strength to resist as she drew him down to her. And as their lips touched for the last time he felt the deep exhaling of her life into him, felt her growing cold in his arms, so fast, too fast, as though all the warmth had been sucked out of her, and finally she lay still as he lowered her tenderly back onto the pillow, brushing back a wisp of hair from her face, which had at last relaxed in death.

Then he heard a voice that was not Ronnie's.

Rantasas Mella Duun.

He shot bolt upright in bed, glancing around his room in the Keep. Outside the window the night was so dark he wondered if the stars were even shining anymore.

The Harry Rhothag stirred slowly, staring around the confines of the filthy gas station restroom where he had taken refuge with the first rays of dawn. The smell of old urine and disinfectants soaked into his very pores, and he staggered to his feet, kicking aside the wads of wet paper towels beneath the door and jerking it open, stumbling out into the cool night. The pull caught at his gut, dragging him across the parking lot still warm from the sun, out into the road.

All the others of his kind who had clustered together in the dark hallway of Sacred Light to batter on the old man's door were either dying or already gone. The sun had killed them because they had not been able to stand the pain of the pull during the day and had wandered out into it, while Harry had managed to suffer through the stabbing, gnawing agony, rather than burn alive. Harry's last meal had been one of his own, roasted to death two miles back down the highway.

He sniffed the air, but there was no scent of blood, not even that of base animals. The little town he was wandering through was barren, and he knew that if he roved too far off the path in search of prey, the tug at his gut would become a searing pain, and he'd run into a wall of agony again. It had happened several times before. Each time he ignored the pain in his belly to follow a blood spoor he ran headlong into torture that engulfed his entire body like fire. The pull leading him toward the old man—and the walls of pain on either side of him—would not allow him to stray.

He ambled past the glaring windows of an ancient stone church, glancing nervously at the stark white building in passing, though he could not understand why it made him anxious. Farther along he imagined angry eyes burning into his back, but peering over his shoulder and sniffing the breeze that blew across the front lawn, he knew the building was as deserted as all the others surrounding it, and he ambled on.

Though he understood little, even the Harry Rhothag could see that the world around him was changing. The days were ever dimmer, although never dark enough for him to venture out, and the buildings all seemed to be rotting, disintegrating, so much that he feared one day one of them would collapse around his ears. There was a constant smell in the air of decay and even the ground beneath his clawed feet seemed shifty and unsure. But to Harry there seemed a rightness to the change. He *fit* this new world better than he had the old. This was where he was born to be.

Now there was only him and the pull. And he knew that at the end of the road lay the old man, and this time there was no way his prey was going to escape.

By the time Dylan was up and dressed the next morning, the only person left in the kitchen was Wagner, who poured coffee and dropped into a chair across from him at the table.

"They're all out searching again already," said Wagner, without being asked. "Baxter is digging in the hole by the foundation out back. Lucy and Remedios are searching the cellar this time, and Crank says if the damned artifacts are here, there must be secret passages in the walls, and he's probably right. He found a hammer, and he's started busting through the plaster upstairs. You look like shit, by the way."

Dylan nodded, sipping coffee that tasted like mud. His

mind was still on the dream. The woman he loved had passed her talent to him before she died. She had known more about what was going on than anyone suspected, but she had not been able to pass the knowledge to him. What did she have to do with the dark thing that had haunted him ever since?

Wagner was staring at him, and Dylan shook his head, trying to clear it. "Nightmares."

Wagner shrugged. "Doesn't surprise me. I've had a few myself. To tell the truth the best thing for me would probably be to grab a shovel and give Baxter a hand or go help Crank bust the place up. But I wanted to talk to you, and I don't think I'm on Crank's good side right now."

Dylan chuckled. "I think maybe Crank *has* a good side, but it's very small and easily missed."

"Don't I know it. He's been that way for as long as I've known him. I was on a couple of missions with him years ago. He may never have accepted the *real* Rex Deus the way Baxter and I do, but he's a good man in a tight spot, I'll tell you that. We were almost killed together in Oregon once. Crank saved my life."

"When did you meet?"

"Nearly thirty years ago. He'd been with Rex Deus maybe three or four years, but out West somewhere. I think he had a pretty hard childhood. The story goes that Clayborn saved him from prison and reformed him, if you want to call Crank reformed."

"I just don't understand how he can be so hardheaded, why he can't even accept that maybe he's made a mistake about Remedios?"

"Because if he believes that, then he has to accept the fact that he was on the wrong side all along, that Clayborn was wrong. And I think Clayborn was about the only person that Crank ever really cared about. Don't get me wrong, I like the little shit. But he is kind of . . . edgy, if you get my drift."

"How come I haven't met any younger members of Rex Deus? Is that just coincidence?"

Wagner frowned. "I never had kids. Baxter, either, far as I know. But there are younger operatives. Or there were. I guess you just lucked out and ended up with the old fogies."

Dylan cleared his throat.

"You want something to eat?" asked Wagner.

Dylan shook his head, rising. "Later. I want to see if they've found anything."

"Just one more thing," said Wagner.

"Yeah?"

"What are your feelings for Lucy?"

The question caught Dylan so completely off guard he almost blurted out the truth—that he was so attracted to her he could hardly stand to be in the same room. But he couldn't be certain whether he wanted to be with her because she was a surrogate Ronnie or because she was a beautiful, intelligent woman in her own right, and he didn't know how to act around her.

"What do you mean?" he said, hoping Wagner didn't hear the quaver in his voice.

"Lucy and I have been through a lot over the past weeks," said Wagner, gauging his words carefully. "I don't know what her feelings are for me exactly. To tell the truth I'm kind of afraid to ask. I know it must be a strange situation for you, her being your wife's twin and all. I just wanted to know if I had any competition."

Dylan sighed loudly enough for Wagner to notice, and their eyes locked.

"It's complicated," said Dylan.

"Well, okay, then," said Wagner finally, turning back to the kitchen.

Dylan found Baxter sweating over a pick at the bottom of what was now a twelve-foot hole alongside the foundation wall.

"Find anything?" he asked.

Baxter shook his head, slamming the pick against the

concrete. "It's in there. I must be four feet below the basement floor. But this wall just keeps going right down to Hell."

"You think there's another cellar *under* the basement?"

"Got to be."

"Bust through the wall?"

Baxter took another slam at the concrete, and Dylan watched the heavy tool ring off the cement. "Must be eight, ten inches thick, steel reinforced. If I had some dynamite—"

"You'd blow anything inside there to smithereens and maybe destroy just the thing we're looking for."

Baxter hung his head. "I could do it with a controlled blast. But this is a waste of time without explosives. If there is a secret entrance, it's not here. They didn't burrow through the grass like earthworms to get in there."

"It isn't a waste," said Dylan. "We know it's here, now. All we have to do is find a way in." He smiled at Baxter. "Without blowing up the vault."

"I could control it," muttered Baxter, turning back to the shovel.

"Time *is* running out," said Remedios.

Lucy and Dylan followed the old priest into the study, where he dropped wearily into a chair. Although he had regained a lot of his strength he was still skeletally thin, and his age showed in the creases above his eyes. He pointed with a palsied hand toward the windows, where the light seemed feeble in the clearness of late morning. "The Old Ones are gaining power. I have been thinking long and hard about exactly what occurred at the time of the change. The gate between our worlds opened a bit more, that is clear. Enough for the power of the Old Ones somehow to stop any electromagnetic process from happening. But if the process had stopped completely, we'd all be dead, because in essence we are electric machines. I believe that somehow a buffer has been placed between electrical poles, but only in certain inanimate objects. Have any of you noticed any lightning or thunder since the Darkening began?"

They all shook their heads.

"Neither have I," said Remedios. "And I used to enjoy the sound since it assured me that there was still a world beyond the walls of my cell. And yet the electromagnetism that fuels the sun is still in effect, only it is dimming—"

"Like the lantern light dimmed," said Dylan. "It happened before, too. With the electrical lights in my home."

"The ancient texts tell us that the Old Ones have dominion over light of any kind, and as they grow stronger even their servants have some of their powers. But that is not what I meant when I said that time grows short. When the change occurred in the night several things appear to have happened at once. A buffer was created that stopped all electrical power here. Millions or billions of people simply disappeared, and others began their own change—"

"Started turning into Rhothag," said Lucy, taking a chair.

"The ones who mutated into the Rhothag were members of Qedem Melech all along, or else they were simply people drawn to the darkness. The Old Ones do not require their minions to *know* them, only to be susceptible to their attraction."

"But why did so many people disappear while others survived?" asked Lucy.

Remedios shrugged. "I can only surmise how the Darkening works, but I fear the people who vanished may have been shifted into the Old Ones' realm."

Lucy blinked, and Dylan knew she was picturing the same thing he was, billions of innocent people suddenly awakening in a realm of total darkness, surrounded by creatures that fed on life.

"So if we beat them, those people will be returned?" she asked, hopefully.

The old man's frown radiated a deep sadness.

"I have only discovered snippets of past battles in the artifacts and texts, but no, the lost do not return. And time is running out for any humans who survived but did not change. With each passing hour the darkness grows deeper, and the minions grow stronger—and hungrier."

"What you're saying is that while we fuck around here everyone else that survived is getting eaten," said Crank, stepping into the room, followed by Baxter.

"Crudely stated," said Remedios, frowning.

Dylan noticed that Phoenix, who had followed Lucy into the study to lie on the floor at her feet, placed herself between Lucy and Crank, and he knew that Crank noticed as well. One day, he was afraid, Crank would take an active dislike to the mutt.

"Dylan and I can get into the vault," she said. "We'll go in from outside."

"You're talking about him *shifting* you, the way he brought us here?" said Crank. "He doesn't even know for sure how he did it. What if you two end up someplace you can't find your way back from?"

"That's a crazy idea," agreed Baxter. "No way you're going to just *pop* into some sealed vault without knowing what's inside or if there even *is* an inside."

"It has to be possible to get in there. And no one else has a better idea. Dylan and I can do it together. I know we can."

"I'm not sure," said Dylan. "They're right. I really don't know how to control it."

She placed her hand over his, and their eyes met. "I'll be holding on to you, and I think I can sense the vault now, or at least I can tell where it is by what I *don't* sense. Either you believe we have a chance to win, or you don't. If you do, then you must believe that there's some way to get inside that repository without blowing it up."

"You could damn well get killed," said Wagner from the doorway. "Or worse. I didn't drag you across Hell to let that happen. It's too dangerous."

"Everything we do now is dangerous. The most dangerous thing we can do is sit around twiddling our thumbs."

"Amen," said Crank, ignoring Wagner's glare.

"Dylan?" Lucy asked, staring directly at Dylan again.

"I don't even know if I could do it. I have to find this place in my head, and I'm not even sure how I do that."

"Well," she said, "either you have to find that place again, or you have to figure out some other way to control it."

"You make it sound pretty easy."

She gave him a rueful smile. "No. I don't think it will be easy. Nothing has been so far."

Although Dylan didn't like the idea, Lucy decided the most logical place to start would be the bottom of the hole Baxter had dug. Dylan had no idea how the shifts actually worked, but Lucy said that being in contact might help him; so, ignoring her questioning stare, he took a deep breath, closed his eyes, and clambered down the ladder into the hole.

Lucy linked arms with Dylan, planting her feet solidly in the hard red clay. Dylan noticed she had her pistol in her other hand, and that shook him a little. The idea that there might be something dangerous *inside* the vault had never occurred to him. Weren't they protected here by the grounds of the Keep?

"Are you ready?" she asked.

Wagner's shout for them to wait brought Dylan up short.

Wagner slid on his butt down into the depression, wielding a lantern. "Did anyone stop to think that it's going to be pitch-black in there?"

Dylan let out a breath of relief. He'd been so centered on just getting his power to work that the almost certain darkness inside the vault had not occurred to him, either. What else had he missed?

"Thanks," he said, reaching for the lantern.

But Wagner shook his head. "Lucy's not going in there alone with you. You're taking me along."

"Then we all go," said Crank, starting down into the hole.

Dylan shook his head. "It'll be hard enough with the three of us."

There was a moment's staring match among Baxter, Crank, and Wagner. But in the end Crank shrugged and so did Baxter.

"Are you ready?" Dylan asked, glancing at Lucy.

"Yes."

"At the first sign of trouble you get us the hell out of there," said Wagner. "Right?"

Dylan nodded, trying to find that place inside himself where the shift always started, but he felt empty and powerless standing in the daylight, in comparative safety with his friends. Always in the past when the transference had occurred he'd been running *from* something, danger had been either barreling down on him or the others. There was nothing to drive him over the edge in his mind into that place that would allow him to move, to shift.

Lucy's arm tightened against the crook of his elbow, and he could tell she was reaching out, seeking the vault. She shivered, and suddenly her body convulsed, but in the same instant he felt the nauseating sense of dislocation, and it dawned on him that maybe the reason that Lucy couldn't sense the underground chamber was that it was buffered somehow from the grounds.

Two things happened simultaneously as they emerged into the subbasement.

Wagner jerked away from him, and Dylan saw not one but numerous Rhothag scattered about a giant room that was filled to bursting with display cases. He spotted one of the beasts pushing itself off the wall beside Lucy, where it had lain in wait for them. It struck directly at Lucy and, as she dodged away, the blow slapped the pistol from her grip.

He saw the lamp dropping out of Wagner's hand as he reached for his pistol, the lantern crashing to the floor and bathing them first in light so bright it blinded him, and then in total darkness filled with afterimages.

"Lucy! Get down!" Dylan screamed.

"Where is it?" gasped Wagner. "Give me a clear shot!"

Dylan heard a sneaky pattering sound and was suddenly certain the thing was somewhere off to his right. Moving.

"There's more than one!" said Dylan.

Sliding his foot an inch above the floor, Dylan took one silent step at a time, placing himself between Lucy and the first Rhothag, listening for movement anywhere around them. He tried to remember everything he'd learned about the beasts. Somehow they'd managed to survive in the total darkness, but surely they couldn't see in it.

"Lucy, wherever you are, stay there, and for God's sake keep quiet," said Dylan, speaking as much for the beasts' benefit as for Lucy's, trying to draw the things away from her. But he also wanted Wagner to know where he was so he wouldn't get shot by mistake.

This whole scenario was too much like the nights alone in his house, and fear threatened to overwhelm him. But he kept reminding himself that even though these Rhothag were killing machines, at least they weren't some supernatural *darkness*. They could die. But killing them was problematic. The best plan would be simply to vanish, to shift right back out of there. Only now Lucy and Wagner had both disappeared, and he feared that calling them to him would only draw the Rhothag down on them before he could make the shift.

For the first time he noticed that the room reeked of death and decay. The sickly-sweet odor of rotting flesh invaded his nostrils and fouled his tongue. The Rhothag had fed on something or someone here.

He had to find Lucy again and get her out.

Moving instinctively into the fighting stance, he eased silently across the floor, trying to draw a mental image of the room from the flash he had witnessed before the light went out. The space was large, at least the width of the building, and filled with chest-high display cases. So if the first Rhothag was no longer against the wall—and Dylan sensed that it wasn't—then it was making its way through that minefield of obstacles, as were its friends. But who knew how long the things had been living down here in the dark, familiarizing themselves with their surroundings? Dylan extended one hand in front of him as he slid carefully across the floor, waiting to bump into the first display case.

Lucy dropped to her knees and scrambled across the floor, wondering why her talent wasn't working, why she couldn't sense all the Rhothag Dylan had seen. She crouched between the legs of one of the wooden cases. The barest snick of a nail on a floor tile centered her attention. In the pitch blackness one of the Rhothag might well be leaning down to stick its smirking face directly in front of hers. Then she heard another faint click as the beast dragged its foot across the floor, and she scuttled away, across an open space, finding another case to hide beneath. She could smell decaying flesh somewhere near.

Another snick.

She reached to pull herself up and felt the big case tipping. She fell back to the floor, trying to catch the piece before it crushed her ribs. Glass shattered and small thuds told her the contents had showered out around her. But the case turned out to be bulkier than it was heavy. Still, the corner pressed tightly into her stomach, and she couldn't seem to get the leverage to lift it back up.

In the silence that followed the crash, Dylan slipped slowly along the front of one of the glass cases, careful not to let his pant legs rub against each other and give him away. He heard the faint click of what might have been a toenail in the general area where he thought the first creature might be, but he still had no idea where the others were.

He crept from one case to the next, then edged slowly along it. As he did so he heard another tiny clicking sound on the floor behind him. The thing was still following him. The farther he could draw it from Lucy the better. He turned and backed across another opening between two of the cases until his fingers contacted glass once more and he stopped, listening. A faint brushing noise caught his attention and he froze.

The sound seemed to hang in Dylan's ear as he turned his head slowly left and right, hoping for another noise so he could triangulate the beast's location. Why weren't the other beasts attacking? Or were they even stealthier than the first?

He sidestepped away from the case to gain maneuvering room. The thing that attacked Lucy had looked bigger than most of the Rhothag he'd seen. But he didn't want to make it a behemoth in his mind's eye. It probably wasn't much over six-foot-six, and somewhere around three hundred pounds. He'd fought guys almost that big before, and the old saying about the bigger they were had often been true. Of course his previous opponents hadn't been monsters with razor-sharp claws. He had to stay away from those talons, somehow had to sense them coming and react without thinking.

Sensei's calm voice sounded in Dylan's mind.

Your arms and legs will work for themselves. React before attack even happens. Don't think about hit or miss. Only do!

Of course, Sensei had never fought one of the Rhothag, either.

Dylan thought he could just make out Wagner's shallow, almost silent breathing, off to his right. With a bit of luck he might not have to fight the first beast at all. He hoped to allow the Rhothag to get as close as he dared, then to drop to the floor directly between it and Wagner. He was going to scream at Wagner to shoot, and hope like hell that Wagner was smart enough to shoot over him. It could work. If Wagner got in a lucky shot, if the Rhothag wasn't *that* fast.

If Lucy wasn't between them and the Rhothag.

He heard yet another snick, closer. He wished he'd gotten a better look at this side of the room, but he'd been turned toward Lucy when the light went out. There was no use moving any farther, though. Better to face the first beast there and then, on ground of his choosing, and hope that the other Rhothag would remain in their strange limbo long enough for the three of them to break out.

Another scratching noise on the floor. Was the thing senseless to the sound it was making, or was it simply playing with them all, teasing Wagner to shoot? If he did so immediately, there was a good chance he'd hit Dylan. Was the thing smart enough to know that?

When Dylan heard another noise directly in front of him he dropped to the floor, screaming at the top of his lungs. "Shoot! Wagner, right here!" Wagner's pistol blasted, glass shattered, and black daggers of shadow stabbed in all directions through the flashes. One of the beasts was right where Dylan had thought it was, illuminated in the gunfire. Dylan followed the thing through the flaring gunfire that turned the display cases into flying shards of glass and jagged splinters of wood, but never seeming to do any damage to the beast. The other Rhothag seemed strangely frozen, and Wagner didn't waste ammo on them.

"Shoot!" screamed Dylan over the din. "For God's sake shoot it!"

But the Rhothag kept disappearing like one of the shadows, so fast that the flashes of light from the pistol couldn't keep up with it. But with each shot the thing had moved again, and Dylan knew immediately where it was headed. He leapt to his feet: but even as he stumbled through the shattered cases, crunching broken glass, he knew he was going to be too late. With each pistol flash he saw the Rhothag drawing closer to Wagner. The look of fear on Wagner's face as he backed away from the thing burned itself into Dylan's brain. The sound of the firing pin falling on an empty chamber was followed immediately by an animal roar, and then the terrible guttural noise of rending flesh, and a last gasping breath, and finally what sounded like a body slumping to the floor.

Dylan staggered back a step, falling naturally into the fighting stance again. He heard the soft clicking noises of the thing's nails on the concrete, as though the Rhothag were struggling to find its balance. Dylan was certain that all the things would attack together now, and his and Lucy's only chance for survival was for him to find her and shift them out. Crunching noises told him that the Rhothag closest to him was now off to his left, an area littered with broken glass. Some of the beast's stealth had been stolen from it by the damage Wagner's gunfire had wrought.

As the Rhothag crept within fighting distance it stopped, and Dylan knew that it was warier than last time, but still poised to attack. Dylan lunged directly at where he thought the beast lurked, so suddenly he was sure the movement would throw the thing off guard. In that same motion he spun on the ball of one foot and slung his other leg wide and low, like a scythe, catching the thing's steel-hard heel with his own, jerking the beast's feet out from under it and knocking it flat on its ass. Before Dylan could stop himself he was dropping into a front-leaning stance, drawing his fist back for the killing downward blow. His body was doing just what he had trained it to do. React. And it was placing him right into the sweeping path of the giant paw.

The clawed fist struck him like a wrecking ball alongside his floating rib. He was lifted through the air, landing hard atop one of the glass cases, crashing through it. The bottom shattered as easily as the glass top, depositing him in a pile of shards and splinters. He started to roll aside from the blow he knew had to be coming, imagining a huge foot dropping down to crush his chest, but he was almost skewered by jagged shards and had to block the pounding heel with only his arms for protection. The blow drove the wind from his lungs, but he managed to grip the scaly foot and dig his thumbs in between the metatarsals and twist, shoving backward and up, straining the iron muscles of the thing's ankle and calf, throwing the giant beast off-balance again. As he released the foot he heard the Rhothag lurch away, crashing into another case, and Dylan could do nothing in that instant but lie back and pray he would be given time to at least catch his breath.

As he reached out to try shove himself up out of the jagged mess his hand fell across a leathery grip, and his fingers traced the wide, deeply engraved blade of a sword. He dragged the heavy weapon out of the rubble, barely managing to stagger to his feet before he heard the Rhothag crunching toward him again. He jerked the sword into the two-handed Samurai defensive position, wielding it like a baseball bat. The grip felt oddly familiar in his hands, and the heft of the sword balanced perfectly, as though it were growing accustomed to him as well.

The Rhothag lurched to a sudden halt, and suddenly Dylan was certain the things could see in the dark. So the sons of bitches had been toying with them all along. What kind of deadly game were they playing?

He sidestepped at a forty-five-degree angle to where he believed the Rhothag to be. As he did so he allowed the tip of the blade to drop behind his hip, beginning a large circle aimed at the point he thought the blade should intersect the

Rhothag's crotch. Hopefully the beast would leap aside to keep from being hewn in half from groin to gullet. When he heard a telltale crunch on the floor, Dylan suddenly stopped the arc, spun on his front foot and switched his grip on the sword so that he now held it with the point downward like a dagger. As he turned he lashed out behind him in a stabbing motion, just as the Rhothag moved into his path. Dylan felt something cold and sticky splash the back of his neck, and for the first time he heard one of the Rhothag cry out in pain. It sounded like metal being rent asunder.

But before Dylan's other foot had a chance to land, a fist hard as brick clipped his jaw, driving him back into another case, knocking it over behind him. Again the sounds of crashing glass filled the air, but this time Dylan managed to stay on his feet, clutching the sword in one hand and the edge of yet another case in the other. He knew if he surrendered to the spinning sensation and went down for the count, he wasn't going to wake up later at ringside, and then the beasts would certainly murder Lucy.

The Rhothag swirled through the broken glass like a mist. One instant it was directly in front of him, the next it was off to his left. Instinctively, Dylan dropped to one knee, swinging the sword in another wide horizontal arc at the level of the thing's thighs. He felt the wind as the beast leapt over the sweeping blade. Ignoring the glass biting into his knee, Dylan allowed the sword's momentum to spin him around full circle before regaining his feet once more.

Do not think, Dylan-san. Do.

Sensei's imaginary voice was more distracting than helpful. If this was one of the mysteries, Dylan thought he could do without it. The heavy sword was an unusual exertion, and his arms ached. He knew he'd soon be shaking from exhaustion, and the Rhothag was bound to notice. He swung wildly, and heard the beast fall backward. The crash of yet another case echoed though the room, and the crunch of giant feet padding through broken glass sounded again. Dylan hoped the slivers were biting deep.

But just as the footsteps died away and the thing melded back into the darkness, Dylan lost it. His sense of the target was just a heavy gloom hanging over his head.

"Come on out, you son of a bitch," he muttered. "Show yourself, and I'll kill you."

He spoke as much for Lucy's benefit as for his own. He was glad she had enough sense to keep silent, and he wanted her to know that he was all right. But what if *she* wasn't all right? What if one of the other Rhothag had already gotten to her? But he knew in his heart that he would *know* that. He was sure he felt her living presence in the darkness although he could not pinpoint it.

"I have a sword, and I've wounded one of the bastards!" he shouted.

At that instant there was a rush of air, and Dylan instinctively dropped to one knee, ignoring the glass, bracing the handle of the sword against his chest, point upward like a pike. The thing sidestepped just in time, but Dylan managed to swing backward with the blade as it passed, and he felt the tip slice deep through hard flesh. Again the thing screamed in agony, and Dylan scurried to his feet. But as he did so he slipped, and he realized that he must be standing in the Rhothag's blood. Maybe not enough to signal the death of the thing, but enough to make footing treacherous.

Something whizzed past his face, and he dodged reflexively as another claw zinged past his head.

"Stay down!" he shouted at Lucy. "This thing can see us!"

Dylan's shout only confirmed Lucy's fears. And Dylan was drawing them away, where they would kill him first. But then they would come for her. She'd be just as blind and trapped as she already was, only then she'd be alone. Something snicked again, closer to her head, and adrenaline gave her the strength she needed. She finally managed to worm her way out from under the first case feeling her way under another one. As soon as she reached it, she crashed it hard to the floor.

"Lucy?" called Dylan.

"Looking for a weapon!" she shouted, squatting and running trembling fingers through the shattered case. She felt books, something that might be goblets, a couple of old sticks or even possibly bones, and a lot of velvet. She stood, and strode purposefully out across the darkness until her hands struck another case, and she shoved it over as well.

"Come to me!" Dylan shouted. "We can shift out of here."

But she knew she'd never be allowed to close the distance. She continued rummaging through the jagged glass and broken wood, feeling paper and cloth but nothing like a weapon, and the noise of her search was obscuring any sounds the beasts might be making.

"Lucy, stop!" said Dylan. "It's coming for you!"

Dylan slashed at the sound of breaking glass that was all he could make out of the thing as it passed him again. This time he felt the blade strike so deep into flesh that it sliced clear through, and something plopped onto the floor. He assumed he had just cut off an arm since the beast whirled on him, and he didn't think it could do that without a head. There was another horrible cry, and now the Rhothag advanced on him in earnest, slashing, pummeling, and kicking. Dylan could only back away, swinging wildly with the sword that now seemed to weigh two tons. Finally, the foundation wall struck him hard on the back, and he had nowhere to go. The dark beast swept down on him like a giant thunderhead.

Lucy delved through the remnants of the fallen case, heedless of the cuts on her hands. There had to be *something* she could use. But all she felt here were more books, a small wooden box with some kind of ornate clasp, then . . . rocks. She gripped one of them in each hand and rose to her feet.

"Dylan!" she screamed. "Where are you?"

She raised one of the rocks overhead, preparing to throw it to one side of his voice, hoping to hit the thing and at least distract it. As she squeezed the stone in preparation for the throw it burst into life with a light that illuminated the entire room, and yet strangely her eyes did not need time to adjust.

But the light struck the Rhothag like a blow, and it wailed in pain greater than anything Dylan's sword blows had caused. It clasped its one remaining hand over its face and bent low, hiding from the bright golden beams streaming between Lucy's splayed fingers. Dylan stepped quickly away from the wall and with one swift motion severed the thing's head, and the beast crashed to the floor, blood fountaining out onto the tiles. Dylan raised the sword again and glanced quickly around, searching for the others.

But there were no others. What he had taken for more beasts in that horrible first split second were huge mannequins clothed in all manner of battle dress from medieval armor to something that looked like tanned snakeskin. Leather shields protected nude warriors wielding stone axes, and one lone Samurai held a raised sword in silent salute from the far corner of the room.

"Wagner?" whispered Lucy.

Dylan glanced quickly around. The room was immense and high-ceilinged. Hundreds of display cases covered the floor; twenty or more lay on their backs amid broken wood and shattered glass. He frowned toward an area where four cases seemed to have crashed together. "Let me go."

But he had to hurry to stay head of Lucy, praying that Wagner might be only unconscious. Even though it seemed to have taken forever, Dylan knew that—in reality—the fight had only lasted a few minutes. He might still be alive.

But the Rhothag had all but disemboweled him, leaving

him resting in a pool of his own blood. Lucy rushed by Dylan, sobbing as she knelt beside the body, clutching Wagner's head against her breast. She rocked back and forth, eyes welded shut, forehead creased, breathing through tight lips. The sight wounded Dylan to the core. Wagner had followed both of them into Hell and lost his life in their defense.

Finally, Dylan reached down and pried Lucy's fingers away, slowly lowering Wagner's head back to the cold floor. When Dylan looked into her eyes he saw the sadness of the world there, and he knew it was mirrored in his own.

"I'm sorry," he whispered.

"I should never have let him come down here."

"You couldn't have stopped him," he said, knowing he didn't need to tell her *why* she couldn't have. "Maybe I could have, and I didn't. I let him come."

"He saved me so many times. He called me on the phone and told me to go to Merly, and I didn't trust him. He protected me when the Rhothag came for us in the field, and I still didn't completely trust him. All he ever wanted to do was protect me."

As the tears streamed down her face, he raised her gently to her feet.

"Wagner," she cried, trying to drop down beside the body again.

But Dylan stopped her. "Lucy, he's gone."

She fell against him, and he held her tightly until her sobs were spent. Finally, he dried her eyes, and she pushed herself away, withdrawing inward again, steeling herself against her grief. As he eased her away from the body she studied the room with damp eyes, taking in the shattered cases, the strange statue-warriors, the glowstones still lying where she had dropped them beside Wagner's corpse. When she turned back to Dylan she regarded him strangely.

"Why are you looking at me like that?" he asked.

"You look like one of them," she said, nodding toward

the armored mannequins. "You look as though you've handled that sword all your life."

"There's something about it," he mused, holding it up in the light. "It feels right in my hands. I don't know how else to explain it."

She leaned to inspect the blade. "There's writing on it."

If it was writing, it was in a script Dylan had never seen, all sharp slashes and polygons. He gazed once more out across the room. The place was a museum. Along with the warriors, it was filled almost to bursting with fine old walnut-and-glass display cases the size of coffins, with most aisles barely wide enough for two people to pass through abreast. "If this place is anywhere near the size of the house above, I sure hope Remedios knows how to find what he's looking for."

Lucy glanced back at the body again, and Dylan knew he had to get her mind off Wagner. Later there might be time for both of them to grieve, but for the moment they had to keep their wits about them.

"Okay," he said. "I'm going to shift you out of here, right now."

But she shook her head. "We need to find the entrance. You'll wear yourself out shifting everybody in and out of here."

He could see the sense in that, though he dearly wanted to be outside again. Although the chamber they were in was massive and high-ceilinged, it felt oppressive and the smell of death was everywhere.

"Let's check that door," he said, nodding toward a small, dark opening at the far end of the room. But he had to take her arm to convince her to accompany him.

"I don't want to leave him like that," she whispered.

"We aren't leaving him. We're trying to find the exit. When we do we'll take care of him."

The contents of the cases seemed to run the gamut from hand-to-hand weapons—daggers, cudgels, rapiers, massive two-handed claymores, bronze short swords—to books, tablets, scrolls, and even stranger collectibles like bits of dried grass or carved semiprecious stones in odd shapes, some depicting animals both real and imaginary. At least, Dylan hoped they were imaginary. If some of the beasts actually existed and were any larger than the statuettes, he certainly didn't want to meet up with any of them. Many of the items had labels describing their date and place of discovery, who the finder was, and a combination of numbers and letters that Dylan assumed matched a file somewhere.

"I think most of this stuff is supposed to be artifacts from previous battles," said Lucy, staring raptly at a case bearing what appeared to be a mummified arm, its flesh black as the velvet beneath it. Upon one finger a ring of solid gold shone brightly, and Dylan noticed that the markings on the ring matched some of those on his sword.

The next room proved to be much the same as the first except that the walls were lined with glass cases that reached to the ceiling. These were filled with more swords, spears, tridents, and strange-looking devices, some resembling metal whips, others hammers or axes, although of unusual and ornate design. Many had markings similar to the ones on Dylan's sword. Others exhibited hieroglyphs or strange, swirling ciphers.

The room after was filled to bursting with file cabinets, and Dylan noted case numbers on the drawers. "This must be the background on all that stuff."

"Something died in this room," said Lucy, wrinkling her nose.

He could tell by the way her eyes teared up again that she'd immediately regretted mentioning things dying. He urged her along with him, trying not to give her time to think.

Finally, they reached a set of wooden stairs with well-worn oak rails that seemed to run right into the concrete overhead, but they could find no hidden button or lever, and the floor above appeared seamless.

"This is ridiculous," said Dylan, dropping onto one of

the treads, resting the sword between his legs. "These stairs have to be some kind of blind."

"Why would they disguise the exit?" mused Lucy. "It must open."

"I don't see how. Do you?"

She glanced past him up the stairs. "Try pushing it."

He gaped at her. "Pushing it? It's a solid block of concrete, I don't know, maybe a hundred feet by three hundred feet. I'd guess it weighs maybe . . . a hundred tons."

"Maybe it doesn't weigh as much as you think."

He sighed but rose slowly to his feet. Climbing halfway up the stairs, he placed his chin on his chest to avoid driving his head into the cement, then reached up with his free hand and shoved. Nothing happened.

"Lucy," he said. "I'm pretty sure I can shift everyone inside now. There's no reason for this."

"Even if it didn't exhaust you, you can't move everyone at once, and personally I don't enjoy popping around like that. Use both hands."

"Jesus," he muttered, resting the sword on one of the stairs treads and placing both hands against the smooth concrete. He shoved, straining and grunting to let her know he wasn't fooling around. When a rectangular section of the concrete inched upward he almost fell flat on his face. Instead, he balanced there, watching in awe as the massive slab settled slowly back into place, the gap disappearing silently like magic.

"I'll be damned," he whispered.

He put his back into it then, but the weight was just too much, and the slab kept lowering back into place.

"You'll have to help me," he gasped, sweat burning his eyes.

She slipped alongside him in the tight space, and he was conscious of the smell of her, the heat of her so close. He turned away, focusing on the weight overhead, but he knew she'd noticed his attention.

"Push!" she said, and together they were just able to raise the heavy block of concrete to the point at which some hidden counterbalance took over and lifted it fully open into the main basement of the Keep.

"Go get the others," said Dylan exhaustedly.

"We'll both go," she said, in the Ronnie voice that Dylan knew left no room for argument. "I'm not going alone, and I'm not leaving you here."

Even Remedios was astounded by the size and scope of the repository, wandering from room to room, exclaiming over this or that wonder, scratching his chin at others. When they reached the scene of the battle his expression faltered as Baxter and Crank examined first Wagner's corpse, then the big Rhothag's.

"You killed this thing with a sword?" asked Baxter dubiously.

Dylan spread his arms to show them all the rips in his shirt where the thing's claws had barely missed his skin. He hefted the sword, and it gleamed in the stones' light.

"That may be more than just any sword," said Remedios.

"Remember, these artifacts are all from past battles. There is much to be learned here."

"Shit!" said Crank. He had the Rhothag's severed arm gripped by the biceps, and was studying the hand closely. When Baxter leaned to examine the gruesome specimen, Crank turned away.

"Goddamn," whispered Baxter, whistling through his teeth.

"What?" said Dylan, staring at the thick silver band on one finger. The ring had three rows of diamonds with a sapphire in the center. The muscles of the finger had swelled so much in the change the ring had buried itself in the skin.

Baxter stared at Crank. "The ring's Clayborn's. He used to threaten to leave its impression on anyone's face who disagreed with him. I heard that enough times."

Crank threw the arm hard against the foundation wall. As it dropped to the floor he glared at it as though he could sear it with his eyes.

"So the Rhothag's being here wasn't just an accident," said Remedios, staring at Clayborn's deformed corpse. "He must have gotten trapped down here after the change."

"Anyone could have stolen that ring," said Crank bitterly. "That thing could have murdered Clayborn."

Baxter frowned. "I haven't noticed the Rhothag take much interest in jewelry."

"How could a Rhothag even enter the Keep in the first place if what you say is true about this being hallowed ground?" asked Dylan.

Remedios shrugged. "I have the feeling that if that *was* Clayborn, he was being used by Qedem Melech. But he must have truly turned to the other side at the end. If you will examine the floor at the trapdoor opening as I did, you will discover that between layers of concrete lies another layer of something resembling earth. I surmise that substance comes from someplace that is far from our world and that there is a layer of it in the walls and floor below us also, effectively *buffering* this vault from the hallowed grounds around it. When the change took Clayborn—or whoever that is—he must already have been down here, or he hurried here in order to save himself. I imagine he was trapped here when the door closed, but he would not have been able to leave the vault in any case. Once he became like a demon, he could not venture onto ground touched by a higher being."

"Demon?" said Dylan. "Is that what you think the Rhothag are?"

"Not exactly," said Remedios. "The true demons are the Old Ones and their lesser minions on the other side. Things like that"—he gestured once more toward the corpse—"one might think of as possessed beings, wraiths or ghouls who have sold their souls through their dealings with the other side. The true demons, the Old Ones, were never human. If you examine enough of these cases, I believe you will find ample statuettes and idols that resemble these Rhothag and others far stranger than perhaps you can imagine. *Demon* is only a name given by this age to the things that inhabit the dark side of existence."

"More power to 'em," said Crank, kicking the beast's head.

"Do you think you can find what you need down here?" asked Lucy, turning away quickly. "In all this? It's like a museum. Do you even have an idea what you're looking for?"

"No."

The reply brought silence.

"Well, you must have a clue," said Dylan at last.

Remedios gave him a sad expression. "Alas, no. All I know is that the answer is here, if it is anywhere."

"Well, then, Father," said Baxter, "I suggest you get looking for it."

Remedios nodded, turning away to begin inspecting the cases. "Might I borrow one of those stones?" he asked Lucy.

"There are more over here," she said, showing him the pile still lying in the rubble of shattered glass and splintered wood.

Remedios hefted one of the palm-sized rocks, and Lucy showed him how to squeeze it to get light. Everyone took at least one.

"These things are like magic," said Baxter.

Remedios smiled. "We have lost the knowledge of so many past ages, through the vicissitudes of time or the depredations of Qedem Melech. I wonder how much wondrous technology has been misplaced forever? How much magic . . ."

"Well, we could use some magic right about now," muttered Crank. "Could someone give me a hand disposing of these bodies?"

Dylan frowned as he saw the shocked look on Lucy's face. Crank had absolutely no tact and, Dylan had come to believe, no feelings other than a deep-seated rage.

"Will you say a service for Wagner, please, Father?" asked Lucy, clearly fighting back tears.

Remedios nodded sadly. "A service for a man of Wagner's nobility would be an honor to perform."

They wrapped Wagner gently in a blanket, and Dylan and Baxter carried his body carefully. As they were passing through the last file-filled room, they had to weave to find the widest path and when Baxter stopped abruptly Dylan leaned to see around him.

When his mind registered what his eyes were seeing he had to lower Wagner gently to the ground, stumbling around Baxter to stare in shock at the object that blocked their path.

A large brass coffin, scraped and tarnished from years in the earth and a recent exhumation. So this was where Ronnie had ended up, brought here by Clayborn for what . . . to try to extract her talent by some arcane ritual? What had they done with her body? Dylan didn't even hear the others, crowding alongside, but he saw Baxter reaching slowly to open the lid. He raised a hand, but it was too late.

The coffin was empty, the white linen as pure and pristine as the day he had watched the lid closing. He knelt beside it, his knee pressed tightly against the metal base. With shaking hand he stroked the cloth, the thin odor of rose petals around him, Ronnie's favorite, and he wondered if he was imagining it or whether somehow it had miraculously lingered. He glanced over the top of the casket lid and saw Lucy staring down at him with sad eyes.

"What the hell?" said Crank, catching up.

When their eyes met Dylan saw realization dawning on Crank as well.

"Shit," said Crank.

"You still think Clayborn was killed by Rhothag?" said Dylan, glaring.

Crank shook his head in passing and muttered under his breath, "I'm sorry."

Without another word Dylan returned to the blanket and gently lifted Wagner's body. They carried him up the stairs.

Upon returning they discovered that Crank had found a lethal-looking battle-ax and was using it to dismember Clayborn's body. Incredibly the blade shone as though it had just been honed, and the leather-bound grip still gleamed. Crank hefted the weapon high overhead, taking one last gruesome hack, and for an instant Dylan could have sworn he saw not Crank, dressed in twenty-first-century pants and shirt, but some long-dead warrior in fur and skin.

"I thought it would be easier to carry," said Crank, when Dylan gave him a disgusted look.

As he and Baxter were toting the gory remains through the file room, Lucy stopped beside a tall cabinet and wrinkled her nose.

"Looks like we're going to need a few more graves," said Crank, staring at the twin doors that had swung open.

As Dylan slipped around Baxter the odor of decaying flesh hit him full in the face. There wasn't a great deal left. But he could see that the remains were fresh. Neither corpse was Ronnie's.

"That's where the smell was coming from," said Baxter, pointing at the ravaged remains. "It wasn't *magic* that kept the Boss alive all this time."

When the last clod of earth was laid atop Wagner's grave under a tall oak out front, Remedios said one final prayer. The service consisted of a list of Wagner's admirable qualities and a fervent request that the Lord take his soul unto his everlasting care. It occurred to Dylan how little he knew about the man. Lucy rested beneath his arm, sobbing quietly, tears streaking her face. He noticed that Baxter, too, was wiping his cheeks, and even Remedios seemed to find it hard to speak.

Dylan glanced at Crank and wasn't surprised to see him dry-eyed. But he did have the look of a man fighting some inner battle, and Dylan could understand why. Crank had spent his entire life working in a very dangerous profession serving under a man who had turned out to be living a lie. He had belittled Wagner, accused Remedios of treason to his own race, and done everything he could to deny the truth until it was thrust into his face along with the death of one of their own. So where did that leave him?

He squeezed Lucy's shoulder, consoling her with his eyes as she swallowed a large lump in her throat.

"He deserves better than just a hole in the ground," she said.

"If we make it out of this, we'll get him a stone."

"A big one. Big enough to say something about Blondie, too."

"I promise."

Inside the house again they all followed Remedios down into the file room, where he placed several of the glowstones atop the cabinets, then squinted to read the label on a file as thick as a man's fist.

"Something interesting?" asked Lucy.

Remedios shook his head, tapping the pile of papers with his fist. "They should have let me down here years ago. This place is a hopeless muddle. There are artifacts from the first age mixed in with texts from the last. They've got books on devil worship that are as phony as the Dead Sea Scrolls—"

"The Dead Sea Scrolls aren't phony," said Dylan, glancing from face to face. "Are they?"

Remedios just chuckled. "Begin searching these files," he said, waving his hand around at the myriad cabinets. "Look for anything pertaining to the past battles that is in textual form."

"Textual?" said Lucy.

"Everything here pertains to the battles in one way or another, but I have no hope of learning anything from most of the artifacts that has not been gleaned by researchers before me. Find me something that *talks* about the battles. Hopefully something that Clayborn never let me see."

They began flipping through the drawers, dusting off

papers on taxonomy, archaeology, paleontology, star worship, devil worship, archaic weaponry. Lucy even found a file on Teddy Roosevelt. It appeared the Rough Rider president was also a contributing member of Rex Deus. But there was nothing about previous battles with the Old Ones or anything giving the foggiest clue of how to beat them. She noticed that Dylan was more intent on the few larger cabinets without glass, and she watched him open each and every one of them with an expectant, fear-filled expression, waiting to approach him until the last door was open.

"She isn't here," Lucy whispered, leaning close as he stood up again, wiping cold sweat from his brow. She took his hand, squeezing it, placing it over his heart, forcing him to look her in the eye. "Even if you found her body. She isn't in it. She's here."

He nodded. "I had to look."

"I know."

Remedios sighed, flipping pages and tossing them onto the top of another file cabinet. "I imagined if I could just get down here, bring myself among the artifacts, the writings, something would touch me. I suppose I expected some sort of divine revelation." He sent a tentative glance upward, and then quickly back to the group.

"If no one else ever found the answer, why do you think that we can?" asked Baxter.

"Because we must! Because if we do not, we are doomed."

"Can't you give us any clue as to what to look for?" asked Lucy, glancing again around the hundreds of glass cases.

"Look for hope," said Remedios, wearily waving them away.

They opened case after case, shouting to each other whenever they discovered something interesting. When Dylan chanced upon a display filled with scrolls, plates, and bits of flat porcelain covered in more of the angular writing that matched his sword, he hurried to get the old priest. Remedios found the case number and removed the file, following Dylan back into the display room, where he lifted each item out gently, placing them atop other cases, studying each as though it were made of the most fragile glass. Indeed some of the scrolls seemed ready to fall away to dust in his hands.

"Is this it?" said Dylan, staring uncertainly at the seemingly unrelated items scattered around them.

Remedios glanced at the piece of paper in his hand, then at the items on the glass tops. "Perhaps it is here," he said. "This is one of the cases marked *undeciphered*. Over the millennia Rex Deus managed to translate most of the ancient inscriptions, but these remained untranslatable. For some reason they were never brought to me for study."

"I don't understand," said Dylan. "If this stuff is as old as you say, then how did *anyone* ever translate it? We still can't read some ancient languages from our own age, and we wouldn't know as much as we know about even Egyptian hieroglyphics if we hadn't stumbled on the Rosetta stone."

Remedios smiled. "That is because to the people researching the Egyptians, the Phoenicians, and all the other great civilizations, these were dead languages. But you forget how ancient Rex Deus is. In each age those surviving members passed down to posterity as much knowledge of the world as they could save and compiled what amounted to multilingual dictionaries. Of course they are ancient beyond belief and incomplete. But back in the file room you will find examples of them."

"That's how you learned to translate this stuff?"

"Yes. And God has endowed me with a talent for language. That is *my* gift."

Remedios fingered a pair of rune-covered gold plates as though his thumbs might be able to read them if he could rub them long enough. His eyes sank into the back of his skull, and when he spoke again it was as though someone else were talking, a voice from the ancient past.

"The Old Ones were the first of the first. They dominated this realm and every Rhothag in it was their minion.

The time of their rule was as the time of stone, and the power of their dominion was as the power of darkness. They knew no beginning and no end, and their only thought was hunger."

The words echoed across the vast room, and their cold burden weighed heavily on Dylan's shoulders.

"After a time and another time beyond knowing, the one God appeared in the realm of the Old Ones, and he saw their evil, and against them he brought forth the light. And the Old Ones were driven back into the remaining darkness, there to dwell, for they could not face the light of the Lord. And into this light the Lord brought forth man to dwell. And it was good.

"And in that first age of man great wonders abounded upon the earth. Men flew across the sky as birds, and swam beneath the sea as fish, and they took dominion over the darkness that bathed half the earth, and made it theirs also, and the Old Ones bided. And it came to pass that in their time the Old Ones brought back the darkness even unto the light where the Lord had held sway, and drove the men before them like beasts before the hunters, and the day became night once more. And in that time great sorrow fell, and lamentations filled the air, for the seed of man was devastated upon the earth, and the hunger of the Old Ones was a scythe across the land, and the Lord's people were taken into captivity, and used as cattle are used, as beasts of the field and meat of the table, until few were left upon the face of the earth. Finally, in the end of that time a great warrior arose, clad in the armor of the Lord, and battle was joined with the Old Ones upon the fields of Raziman and Elduerer. Here it was that Shirath fell."

"What the hell is that supposed to tell us?" asked Crank, gripping the ax so tightly his knuckles paled.

Remedios shook his head. "The runic script is a dialect from the last age of man. These plates recite parts of a lay called 'The Ballad of Shirath.' There are many such texts in other dialects that have been deciphered over the years."

"I don't know why, but just listening to it scared the hell out of me," said Dylan.

"Me too," said Lucy, shivering.

"It is a tale that we know in our bones, without being told, because we as a people have a deep and dark past. We sense it but do not come to terms with it, except in myth, in fairy tales. This is what you feel. The *reality* of what all your lives you had thought was legend."

"But I never heard these legends," said Lucy, shaking her head.

"You had no need to," said Remedios. "It is a collective memory, perhaps in our very cells. We know. We all know. All of the tales are basically the same. The Old Ones were here. Then the Lord came and brought forth light and created man, and then the Old Ones were driven out, but eventually they returned and defeated man. Even the Bible, which is incomplete and does not deal overly much with previous ages, mentions the fact that *there were giants in the earth in those days*. According to Rex Deus oral tradition it was always the last of your line, Lucy, who went out to fight the final battle. Shirath was of your line. It is a woman's name."

When Lucy said nothing, the old man turned toward Dylan.

"Let me examine the sword," he said.

Dylan rested the heavy weapon on top of the case, reluctant to part with it.

"This is the same very ancient script," mused Remedios, squinting at the strange markings on the blade and frowning. "I believe it gives the name of the sword, itself."

"What's the name?" asked Lucy.

"It would translate loosely as Spirit Sword. No. I think a more literal meaning would be something like . . . Soul Cleaver."

"That's a pretty ominous moniker," said Baxter, staring at the blade.

"According to the inscription," continued Remedios, "it

was created in the fires of something called Athenius as a weapon never to be used against man."

Dylan frowned at him. "Are you saying it was made solely to fight Rhothags?"

Remedios shrugged. "I tell you only what it says," he said, carefully flipping the sword over. This time when he read the inscription just below the hilt his eyes froze.

"What does it say?" asked Dylan, suddenly afraid of the answer.

"Give me peace and quiet now," said Remedios, still staring at the sword. "I must study."

"But what does it say on this side?" insisted Dylan, pointing to the one word etched beneath the hilt.

Remedios studied him for a moment before answering.

"Shirath," he said quietly. "It says Shirath."

"Are you saying that sword belonged to the woman who died in the final battle?" asked Baxter.

"I am telling you what the inscription says," said Remedios, turning away. "Shirath was probably as famous in the last age as David and Goliath are in our own. Very likely thousands of swords bear that inscription."

"You don't believe that," said Dylan, feeling the same curious sense of oneness with the blade he'd experienced during the fight.

"I do not know whether or not that weapon actually belonged to the warrior named Shirath or not. I also do not know if it matters. Apparently, however, the sword is very effective against the Rhothag. And your affinity for it may be worth more than any providential ownership it may carry," Remedios observed.

"There's something else," said Lucy, staring at the old man. "Something you're not telling us."

Remedios frowned. "Some things are better left unsaid."

"And some aren't," said Dylan. "What are you hiding?"

Suddenly the priest looked even older, his face seemed to sag and his eyes saddened. "Most of what we know about previous ages and the battles that took place then is shrouded in myth, gleaned a bit here, a sliver there. We have no idea how factual any of it is."

"But?" said Baxter.

"But," said Remedios, " 'The Ballad of Shirath' states that from the time Shirath took up her sword until the time she died spanned one sun and that *that was always the way of Shirath's line*."

"You're saying we have less than a day to find out how to beat the Old Ones?" whispered Lucy, glancing around the huge vault.

"That is how the tale goes. There is no way of knowing if it is correct or if the same will hold true in our age."

"But you believe it's true," said Baxter.

Remedios shrugged. "Give me peace now. I can do nothing while we chatter."

They searched for hours but found nothing else anyone thought was worth disturbing the priest with. Finally, weary to their bones, they left him in the basement and gathered in the study, where Baxter lit a fire.

"So all the old man can tell us is that time is running out," said Crank, frowning.

"We're an unlikely band of heroes, I'll say that," said Dylan. "If we're really supposed to go out and do battle with the forces of darkness, I have to admit I would have liked an A-bomb or something."

"Now, where did all those crows come from?" said Baxter.

Everyone turned to look at him as he stared raptly out the window.

The sky was a swirling pool of inky-feathered shapes, swooping and twirling and interweaving, until to imagine any more of the fowl seemed impossible. Millions of the birds made the trees appear to throb, and arteries of their brethren bled darkly from the spreading branches out onto the grass below.

"Baxter," said Dylan quietly, touching him on the arm to break his stupor, "maybe you ought to go get Remedios."

Baxter nodded and—with one last glance at the cloud of black birds—disappeared.

"I've never seen anything like that in my life," muttered Lucy.

As she stood so close to him their bodies touched, Dylan found her face far more fascinating than the crows, noticing the way her amused smile turned up just slightly more at one corner where Ronnie's had not, the unique way she held herself, her hip shifted as she stood at rest. Every moment that he spent with her deepened his sense of guilt. He needed her, and yet he felt that the mere thought was a betrayal of Ronnie.

"Something drew the birds here," he said, at last. "But was it this place or us?"

"Maybe both," said Lucy. "The birds must sense the end is coming, and this is the last safe place."

Phoenix had her paws up on the window, wagging her tail and woofing at the crows, when Baxter and Remedios reached the sill.

"What does this mean?" asked Dylan.

"I fear the final change really does draw near," said Remedios. "The birds of the sky, the fishes of the seas, and the beasts of the field are as chaff before the Old Ones. And the land grows barren and weeps, and becomes as a hellish place, unknown to the eyes of man."

He stopped, staring raptly at a pair of ravens that danced and darted immediately in front of the window. "That is from another of the ancient lays referring to battles with the Old Ones. Some beasts, such as these, serve God, and through him, Man. Others are natural servants of the Old Ones. The animals are now choosing sides. The earth itself is changing outside the range of the power of this place. Beyond the borders of the Keep I fear we would not recognize it."

"What do you mean 'changing'?" asked Dylan. "How could it be getting any worse than it is? It was like everything was dead or dying already."

"When the Darkenings began in past ages, the survivors cowered together in the few dwellings they had in which they were safe from the Rhothag of that era, probably places such as this. But when they went out from those havens, they discovered that the landmarks they knew were no longer there. Rivers had disappeared, mountains turned to vast flat deserts, and chasms gaped where only open grazing land had lain before."

"Bullshit," said Crank. But the way he said it didn't sound anything like his usual cocksure speech.

"But I have good news!" said Remedios, ignoring Crank and waving them all together. "I discovered this!" He held up a broken shard of porcelain that looked as though it might at one time have graced a large urn. The runes upon it were engraved deeply into the ceramic, though the pigment had long since faded.

"Is it the end of the tale?" asked Lucy.

"Alas, no," said Remedios. "But it is nonetheless good news. This is part of a story urn from the second age of man. It tells of the villages in which men survived even after the Darkening. Whole cities, in fact, where there were no disappearances at all."

"Are you saying there could be a lot more survivors than we've seen?" said Dylan.

"I think so, yes."

"But where?"

"I do not know. But if I understand this correctly, it may be that there are areas where few people have disappeared. Many may yet survive."

"For how long?" asked Lucy.

Remedios frowned, shaking his head.

"And the only thing between the people out there and the Old Ones," said Crank, "according to you, is us."

"There may be others of whom we know nothing. But they cannot help us now."

"We have to keep searching," said Dylan.

"Good luck," said Crank, heading down the hall. "I give up."

Baxter looked at Dylan and shook his head.

But they found nothing more of interest though they searched until their eyes blurred and their hands shook. Finally, even Remedios was too exhausted to continue.

"It may be that I was wrong," mused the old man as

Dylan helped him to his feet. "Perhaps this has been just a test. The answer may not lie here at all, but within you all along."

"A test?" said Dylan, fighting to keep the irritation out of his voice. "What kind of test?"

"In your martial art," said Remedios, "do you not give tests?"

"Belt tests," admitted Dylan, shocked at what a different world that conjured. Had there really been a time when his life was so simple?

"And what is their purpose?"

Dylan shrugged. "Before I promote a student I need to know that he has reached the next level of his training, both physically and mentally."

"And how do you do that?"

"Belt tests are pretty intense. The students are forced to their limits and beyond."

"Beyond their limits? Is this possible?"

"The best of them reach inside themselves and find something there—" said Dylan, realizing what had been in front of his eyes all along.

Remedios nodded, touching Dylan lightly on the arm, his old eyes gleaming. "Now perhaps you and Lucy must reach inside yourselves . . . and find something there."

When they headed for the stairs Dylan noticed that Lucy was gone, and apprehension raced through him until Baxter smiled and caught his arm.

"I saw her heading upstairs a half hour ago," he said. "I think she just needed some time alone."

Dylan nodded. He snatched a glowstone and headed after her. He was almost to her bedroom when a grunting sound stopped him. He stood in the corridor, listening to the hissing of the stone, trying to discover the location of the noise that reminded him far too much of a death struggle. He clutched the sword tightly, but he didn't sense the presence of one of the Rhothag, didn't smell the awful odor of the dark shadow. He crept forward, cocking his head left and right, following the sound to the door of the workout room.

When he spotted Lucy in the middle of the floor he rested the sword and stone on a bench, leaning back against the wall to watch. She moved with fierce determination, lurching through the simple sequence of *Teikiyoko-sono-ichi*, slinging her fists into the down-blocks, punching fiercely as though a Rhothag barred her path. Her eyes were open but focused inward. Sweat rolled down her cheeks and glistened on her arms. The grunting he had heard was her attempt at the *kiei* he had taught her, the screaming blast of air at the moment of imagined impact. If this had been one of his beginner students in the dojo, Dylan would have been amused at her resolve even though she was murdering the beauty and elegance of the *kata*. But this was not the dojo, and the determination he saw in her eyes, in her jerky attacks, reminded him more of the desperate conviction of an untrained kamikaze.

When she returned to the starting position, catching her breath, ready to lunge out into yet another rendition of the *kata,* he hurried to her, not totally surprised that she did not acknowledge his approach. He knew from experience what it was like to reach that point in a training session where the opponent you imagined was more real than the world around you. But he sensed a hopelessness in her now that was never intended to be a part of any martial art. When she plunged to her left in the next attack, he caught her from behind, his arms wrapped tightly around hers, letting her struggle against him until she returned slowly to the here and now.

"It's all right, Lucy. It's me, Dylan."

Finally, she sagged, resting her head back on his shoulder, gasping for breath. He turned her in his arms and kissed her lightly on the forehead, tasting salty sweat. She began to shiver, and he knew it was not from cold.

"I'm afraid," she whispered, wrapping her arms as tightly around him as he held her.

"Me too," he admitted.

"I couldn't stand to lose you now the way I lost Wagner."

"You won't."

"How can you say that?"

It was terrible and wonderful, holding her, feeling her warmth against him, looking into her eyes that pleaded for an answer. She was Ronnie, and she wasn't, and he knew that just holding her like this was yet another betrayal of Ronnie. But he knew that there was no longer any way he could ever give her up.

"Because I'm falling in love with you," he said, kissing her gently on the lips this time.

"I can feel her inside you, now," she whispered, both hands sliding around to press against his chest. "She's so close."

Dylan nodded. "I missed Ronnie so much. I thought sometimes that all I had to do was wait long enough, and the hole inside me would swell to the point that there was no room for life in there any longer, and I'd just die of grief. But now I don't feel that way anymore. It's like the hole is gone and Ronnie's in there again, only I don't know if it's Ronnie or you."

When she finally worked her way gently out of his arms she stopped to kiss him before stroking his cheek and turning to leave. Remedios's words about there only being one day echoed in both their minds.

Dylan absently stroked the sword that leaned against the wall beside him and wondered if fate was really so heartless that it could bring him this second chance only to smash it in his face.

The house was silent as Crank tiptoed down the hallway toward the front door. The faintest starlight shone through the front windows, but he could pick out every fiber in the thick carpet. He opened the door quietly, chilled by a cool breeze. He considered going back for a jacket, but his pullover was thick, and he didn't intend to be out that long.

As he stepped out onto the wide veranda, he discovered that even it was covered with crows and ravens. The birds milled around his feet, making low noises under their breath, like disgruntled chickens. He squatted until he was almost eye level with a couple of the larger birds, and when they glanced at him with their inky orbs he nodded. He was shocked when both birds nodded back.

"Well," he said, "ask a stupid question."

He stood, shuffling his feet to reach the edge of the porch, the crows shifting aside but not scattering. Before he placed his foot on the first step the door opened behind him, and he spun.

Dylan and Baxter stood framed there, glancing from Crank to the crows.

"Where you going?" asked Dylan.

"Taking a look around. Go back inside."

Baxter shook his head, closing the door softly behind them. "Nice night for a walk. We'll go with you."

Crank sighed loudly, but they ignored him, and the three of them made their way carefully down the wide steps and out into the mass of fowl on the lawn.

"I would never have believed there were this many crows and ravens in the whole damned world," said Baxter, staring in all directions at birds that were packed as tight as sardines in a can, from the front of the house to the edge of the property. The trees were filled, and there were still hundreds of thousands more hovering high overhead.

"Good thing the cat didn't follow us here, I guess," said Crank.

"Has it occurred to you that that's because cats are not on our side?" asked Baxter.

"Yeah," growled Crank, finally. "It occurred to me."

"And that you're a cat person," needled Baxter.

"There's millions of cat people," said Crank.

"Not anymore. But there is good news."

"What the hell would that be?"

"You haven't turned into a Rhothag yet."

"You're a funny guy."

The birds continued to squawk as the three of them slowly shuffled their way the couple of hundred yards to the trees. When they got there they peered silently up at the giant oaks. Every branch, every twig strong enough to bear the weight of a crow or raven was covered, the boughs filled with huddled birds, their big black breasts rising and falling gently.

Crank had figured that once they reached the tree line they would discover the end of the giant flock. But there were more still coming. Birds landed from a new swarm overhead and wormed their way into places on the ground, while in the distant heavens another black mass of birds poured in to fill the void above.

When at last they stood on uncluttered ground—having reached the road beyond the front gate—Crank knelt, placing both hands on the asphalt. It felt good, as solid and real as anything had of late. After Remedios's speech he'd had the sudden urge to run out to the horizon and make sure everything was still there. Standing there in the feather-filtered starlight, facing off down that long empty stretch of road, he could almost imagine that nothing at all had happened.

Almost.

"What the hell is that?" he muttered, glancing toward a distant mailbox that marked a neighboring driveway. Something low to the ground and long as a semi began winding out upon the road.

"Foxes," said Dylan, squinting.

"Shit," said Baxter, as more and more of the meandering lines of animals threaded their way out of the woods toward them. "This ought to be good. We'll put two gazillion crows together with about a hundred thousand foxes, and then let's stand in the middle."

"They won't hurt each other," said Dylan.

"How do you know that?"

"I just know."

They watched in silence as several lines became an intertwined web, swept into a giant skulk, until the road had disappeared and the woods around them came alive with a million tiny feet pattering on old dead leaves, and a picture that would not quite form kept *almost* creating itself in the back of Crank's mind.

"They're friends," he muttered, leaning to pet them as

the first of the foxes passed beneath his hands and came to a halt a couple of feet away from the crows, who eyed them cautiously but not with any great fear.

"What's next?" Baxter whispered. "Elephants?"

"Maybe," said Dylan wonderingly. "Maybe this is where the original myth of Noah's Ark came from. Maybe God didn't destroy the world with a flood. Maybe he let the Old Ones do it for him."

"There's a hell of a lot more than two by two here," said Crank, shaking his head as even more foxes materialized on the far horizon. "Come on. I came out here to see if Remedios was right."

He led the way through the foxes just as they had made their way carefully through the crows. While the birds had regarded him with haughty ebony eyes that seemed to judge and somehow find him wanting, the foxes had a trusting look, as though they had come to wait out some badness that had driven their species here under the protection of Man, and he was a man so they expected *him* to do something about it.

Suddenly the woods across the road erupted with rabbits, possums, squirrels, and deer, surging forward in waves with a swirling furry current. A noise like heavy cloth ripping seemed to come from everywhere at once, and the ground shook beneath their feet.

In the distance the fabric of the world began to shred.

Where their field of view had previously ended with the vanishing road on two sides and trees across the highway in front of them, the image began to swirl, as though they were viewing it through a liquid kaleidoscope. Reality seemed to melt, and the animals pressed against one another in a slow stampede, frantic to reach the safety of the Keep. Crank could *feel* the world around him transforming into an alien, dark, and cruel reality. His legs trembled as the earth beneath his feet heaved up, then sank down as though he were standing not on solid asphalt but on the rolling deck of a ship at sea. There was a clear delineation point now between the grounds of the Keep and the madness that lay beyond. The grass on their side of the road was tall, if still winter-brown. On the other side the ground was barren and the trees faded to an amorphous filmy nothingness, then disappeared, leaving the world there devoid of the works of Man or God. Movement in the distance caught his eye, and he struggled to focus on it. The earth there seemed molten, flowing toward them.

"What the hell is that?" he said, pointing toward the lavalike movement.

"Snakes," whispered Dylan. "Billions of snakes."

"Let's get the hell out of here," said Baxter, shoving Dylan back toward the Keep, heedless of the animals scattering around their feet.

When they came crashing back into the house matches flickered and lanterns lit down the corridor. As Lucy and Remedios stumbled wearily into the study Crank stood by the windows, with his back to the room.

"I never expected anything like that," said Baxter. "It looked to me like everything just melted."

Dylan nodded, wrapping his arm around Lucy when she came to him. "There's about a billion foxes out beyond the crows. And beyond that there's a mixture. Deer, and rabbits, and possums, and more birds, all kinds of birds. And not one of them seems to want to hurt the others, or to be afraid of the others."

"There were snakes farther out beyond the change," said Baxter. "And they weren't attacking each other, either. They all just seemed intent on getting here."

"The serpents do not belong here, and they cannot yet cross," said Remedios. "The other animals sense their safety here."

"Till when?" asked Crank, without turning. "Dawn?"

"I will go back to work," said Remedios, a renewed sense of urgency in his voice. "I know we will find an answer. I know it in my heart. All of you should try to get at least a couple of hours' rest. There is nothing you can help me with now."

The old man disappeared down the cellar stairs, and in just a moment, Lucy followed. She turned on the top step and caught Dylan's eye, shaking her head to let him know she didn't want company.

"I hope so," muttered Crank, watching them leave. "Because I think this place is shrinking. And I sure as hell didn't like the look of those snakes."

Lucy stared at Remedios's back as the old man bent over a small metal desk in the corner of the file room using a large magnifying glass to study some small remnant that from a distance appeared to be a scrap of parchment.

She had been working up her courage to speak to the old priest, trying to figure out what it was exactly she was going to say, and she still wasn't exactly sure. She just knew that the time was drawing near for her to make a fateful decision and that she didn't want to discuss it in front of the group. This wasn't about some millennia-old organization that had protected her bloodline, nor was it about another ancient brotherhood that had tried to destroy it. It wasn't even about how a mere mortal like her could ever hope to win against a race of demons who wanted to annihilate her race. It was about her own inner turmoil and what she was supposed to do about it.

At last she had to admit that there was more to life than she had ever believed before. If that was so, then what *was* true? Had she been wrong all along? Was she risking eternal damnation or a future life as a cockroach by refusing to believe, or not knowing *what* to believe?

Remedios heard her and turned, resting his magnifying glass on the desktop and leaning back in the heavy old leather executive chair. He studied her as she sat on the desk across from him, bending her legs into the lotus position and taking a deep breath.

"You look as though you are distraught," he said.

She nodded. "I want you to hear my confession," she said, startling herself. That was not at all how she had planned to begin. The words had just slipped from her mouth.

"I'm afraid I am no longer a functioning priest. I was excommunicated."

She shook her head. "I don't think that has any standing any longer since the Vatican is probably defunct, and there is no other man of God I can ask. Will you hear my confession?"

"You do not understand. I'm in no way certain that God needs or wants to hear your confession."

"Please, Father."

"Very well. What do you have to confess?"

"It's that easy? All I do is tell you?"

"Not quite. But that is how it begins."

"I don't know where to start. Should I tell you everything I've done bad since I was a child?"

"No. You must have confessed those sins before. You have already been absolved of them."

"But I haven't."

He frowned. "You've never confessed before? But surely . . . You are a grown woman."

"I'm not a Catholic, Father."

"Then, I don't understand. Other faiths do not require confession to a priest."

"I don't have another faith. That's why I'm here."

"I see. You have felt a need."

"Yes."

"You are afraid of facing the unknown alone."

"Yes. Well, I guess maybe I'm not alone any longer. Not if I don't want to be. Maybe that's something I need to confess."

Remedios smiled. "Perhaps. Perhaps not. But are you speaking of God . . . or man? You find yourself drawn to Dylan, but you feel guilt because Wagner is gone. Correct?"

"Yes," she said, shocked to be so easily read.

"And at the same time you fear losing Dylan."

"I've never had anyone since my parents died. Not anyone at all. I wonder if I'm *supposed* to have someone."

"You believe that if you are too blessed, then you will have to pay in some way."

"Yes."

"That is a commonly held belief, but I think you need not worry too much about it. I have not followed the tenets of my original faith for a number of years. I reached a point in my quest for knowledge at which they simply made no sense to me any longer, and that is why you see before you an apostate priest. I could not renounce my own mind, and so the Church renounced me."

"But you still believe in God?"

"I do. I lost my faith for a number of years. I suppose being locked away was *my* test. But miraculously God seems never to have lost His faith in me. I believe we are close once more."

"I want to be close to Him, too."

"Then you are."

"That seems too easy."

He chuckled. "That idea has been the cause of more misunderstanding and suffering than perhaps any other that ever existed. It has helped to create warring religions and priestly classes, caused strife throughout the world, and perpetuated hatred and bigotry down through all the ages. There is no distance between yourself and the Almighty that you do not yourself create and that you yourself cannot break through."

"But I don't know how. Please help me confess my sins so that I feel closer to Him."

Remedios sighed. "What *sins* do you feel you have committed?"

"I've taken His name in vain. I've coveted things others had. I've lied. I've killed."

Remedios frowned. "Whom have you killed?"

"Rhothag."

"That is no sin. They are no longer men, and the killing was in self-defense or defense of others."

"I killed a detective in my house."

"Why did you do that?"

"He was trying to kill me."

"Ah, so he was Qedem Melech."

"I believe so."

"Again, self-defense."

"I'm afraid maybe I let Wagner believe that I might care about him when I didn't," she whispered.

"Did you lead him on? Did you pretend to love him?"

She shook her head.

"You say that you did not care about him—"

"I didn't mean it that way. I did care."

He waited until she met his eyes again. "You are taking a guilt upon yourself that I believe you know is not yours. If Wagner chose to believe that he might win you, there is nothing wrong in that. We all miss him, but do not bear pain that is not earned. That, I believe, is a sin."

"That's all, then, I guess," she whispered. "But I'm sure there must be other stuff. I just can't remember."

"Do you feel remorse? Are you contrite?"

"Yes."

"Then, as far as it is given me the power to do so, I grant you absolution. Go forth and sin no more."

"Do I take a sacrament or something?" asked Lucy.

"No," said Remedios, smiling again. "You are a sacrament. Believe now that there is something out there beyond anything that you and I can imagine, a power that watches over us. A power that you are now in contact with every moment of your life. We all need to believe that."

Lucy nodded. "I think in my heart I've known that all along. Thank you, Father."

"You know, I have grown so accustomed over the years to people calling me that. But I suppose I should not allow it."

"Why?"

"Because I have been defrocked. Excommunicated."

Lucy laughed.

"What's so funny?" asked Remedios.

"Father, there is no Church to be excommunicated from any longer. And what is the mission of a priest?"

"To shepherd his flock. To guide them to the good, to the light."

"I think you were just doing that to the best of your ability. I'll keep calling you Father, if you don't mind."

He seemed to mull on that for a moment before nodding his acceptance. "So you are better now?"

"Yes, thank you."

"We are all finding our way as best we can. The last thing I want to do is lead anyone astray. But I have told you exactly what I believed to be true."

"Has it occurred to you that God would not let you lie right now?"

Remedios frowned. "No. All men can lie. We are born with free wills to sin or not to sin."

Lucy shook her head. "All right, then. But God must know exactly what you believe, right?"

"Of course."

"And Dylan and I are supposed to fight the final battle with the Old Ones?"

"Yes. With all my heart I believe this. The two of you are somehow destined to fight the final battle. Or so I pray."

"Do you think He would have allowed you to teach me what you believed if it weren't the truth? Do you believe He'd send me off into battle confused?"

"You are a formidable debating partner. I have to say that I must give this much thought."

"I'll be doing a lot of thinking myself."

"And praying."

She nodded, sliding off the desk and kissing Remedios gently on the forehead. "I don't know why I was chosen, and I certainly didn't ask for this. But I'm not going to back away from it now. I'm still frightened. But you've put my mind more at ease than it's been in weeks. Thank you, again."

"You are more than welcome."

She walked slowly out of the vault, nearly oblivious to her surroundings, unaware that Remedios watched her and Phoenix until both disappeared up the stairs.

The old man turned back to the desk, then lifted the magnifying glass again but soon replaced it. He stared at the scrap of parchment, not seeing it at all, wondering if Lucy was correct. Had God chosen him to be here not to find any weapon with which to battle the Old Ones but simply to prepare her for the coming struggle? There was a certain grace to the idea. After all, that had been the mission of priests for centuries.

He rubbed the bridge of his nose between thumb and forefinger, feeling all the aches and pains of a man his age but also a curious lightness of being that he had not experienced in far too long. For years he had been tortured by his loss of faith, feeling alone and betrayed, believing that he had to face the world as a lone human being with wits and courage because there was no one and nothing standing behind him any longer. There were only birth, and life, and then death. Now he believed that once again he knew better. There was more. But how much more he had no way of knowing. There were no guidebooks he could trust any longer, no rituals, no reassuring dogma. Man was once more on a one-to-one basis with his God, and the thought was both awe inspiring and terrifying.

"So now you can send her off with a clean conscience," said Crank.

Remedios spun the chair so fast he almost fell out of it. Crank had slipped silently into Lucy's space. Now he rested the big ax quietly on the hard rubber desktop before turning back to face Remedios.

"I gave her what solace I could," said Remedios. "We all must come to terms with God in our own way, in our own time."

Crank's hand still rested on the ax handle, but where always before Remedios had seen nothing but unreasoning hatred in the man's eyes, he now witnessed something akin to anxiety, perhaps even fear.

"Why are you here?" asked Remedios.

"I came down here to kill you," said Crank.

Remedios knew the man was not one to lie about death. "So why do you hesitate?"

"Are you in a hurry to die?"

"I would be a fool if I were."

"But you believe in God. I can send you straight to Heaven."

"I don't know if there even is a Heaven."

"So you were lying to Lucy."

"I said nothing of Heaven. Nor did I mention Hell. Although I find it easier to believe in the former than the latter. I simply have no proof of either. I attempted to soothe her soul and to bring her closer to God. I did not promise her life everlasting."

"Why have a God that doesn't grant you that?"

"I have no choice as to whether to *have* a God or not. God simply is. You are free to believe in an afterlife or to disbelieve as you wish. I simply have no conclusive evidence one way or the other, although I choose to hope that there is a life everlasting awaiting me."

"Empty words," said Crank, a little of the familiar fury returning to his face.

Remedios noticed that the man's fingers were now playing with the ax handle as though they had a will of their own, and he wondered if his own work on earth was complete. But how could it be when the man in front of him was clearly in such pain?

"They are not empty because you cannot find what you wish within them," said Remedios. "You have acquired that habit of looking only for the answers you wish to discover, of seeing only that which you wish to see. Look around you. Have you not witnessed the world changing in ways that man could never have imagined? Do you not see the birds and beasts of the field gathered in this place? Have you not yourself experienced miraculous events?"

"Will your God stop me from killing you right now?" asked Crank, lifting the ax and resting it in the crook of his elbow.

Remedios prayed silently and quickly, not for his life, but for his soul. If there was an afterlife *he*, too, wanted to be right with his God. "If He is not yet done with me here, then I do not believe you will be able to murder me. If my mission here is complete, then I suspect that you may do as you will. But know that I am not, nor have I ever been your enemy, and I would that *you* would not put your soul in danger by such an act."

"In danger how? If there is no Heaven and no Hell, what do I have to lose?"

"Your mind."

"What's that supposed to mean?"

"If you destroy me and somehow aid the Old Ones, in the brief time you have left you will know that you have been instrumental in their victory, in the demise of mankind. Can you live with that?"

Crank said nothing, but his look was again less certain.

"And if my mission truly is done and you murder me and survive, it is even remotely possible that you may live a long long life, knowing every day that you killed an innocent man who bore you no ill will and who lived only for the good of Man. Perhaps you believe that you can live with that. I don't think so."

"You are really pissing me off."

"That is a normal part of the passage. I have taken that same journey myself."

"What journey?"

"From disbelief to belief. Frustration, anger, and denial come before acceptance and solace. You are a proud man, accustomed to standing alone. To admit that there is something bigger than yourself, that you *need* something more than yourself, is not only difficult, it can be dispiriting. We are all but cogs in God's great wheel. Are you going to kill me now?"

"Close your eyes and count to ten."

Remedios clasped both hands in his lap, lowering his head, offering his neck. He stiffened at the sound of Crank's footsteps, but when he looked up the little man was already disappearing through the door.

Dylan sat on the floor, his back cradled against the bed, his eyes closed, counting every breath, searching for that place Sensei had assured him was there inside himself, that place of mysteries. But his thoughts would not settle. Images of Ronnie's emaciated corpse, dead Rhothag, the dark shadow that had pursued him since her death intermingled with Lucy's face and the feel of her hand stroking his cheek. He struggled to center himself, to relax, so that he could find the inner peace to know what to do. He had a place in the battle that was imminent. But he had no idea what it was.

The sword lay on the floor beside him, and he could

sense the closeness of the razor-sharp blade only a millimeter from his thigh. The weapon belonged to him in a way that defied understanding, as though it had *always* belonged to him, as though he were born to it even though he had never touched a sword before finding it. But what possible use could a sword be in a war against beings from another dimension, against a Rhothag of mist that could invade his very mind? Instead of inner peace he sensed the cold sweat trickling across his furrowed brow, the slight quaver of his hands in his lap.

A breath of air scented with sweet-smelling soap insinuated itself into the room and he opened his eyes, shocked to see Lucy leaning silently over him.

"What's up?" he asked, hoping she didn't hear the catch in his voice.

"Still a couple of hours till dawn," she said, quietly. "Remedios found something, and now he wants to talk to us in the study."

The soft glow of candlelight freshened her cheeks, and her eyes glowed with an inner fire.

"Are Crank and Baxter there?"

She shook her head. "He wants to talk to you and me."

He climbed to his feet, automatically strapping the sword over his shoulders. Phoenix trotted down the hall with them, the patter of her nails on the marble floor sounding to Dylan like the anxious roll of a snaredrum. But Lucy was mistaken. Crank and Baxter were waiting with Remedios, who just shook his head when Lucy glanced at him.

"Hard to keep secrets around here," said Crank.

Two glowstones seemed barely able to illuminate the room. Remedios bent over the desk in front of him, the heavy magnifying glass clutched tightly in his hand.

"Has either of you felt anything different tonight?" he asked, glancing from Lucy to Dylan.

The two of them eyed each other, then shook their heads.

Remedios frowned, pointing with the magnifying glass

to the artifact on the desk. "I found some interesting text on this shard from the second age. It speaks of the birds swarming and the beasts growing restive and the last warrior going forth to the final battle. It says the warrior girded herself in God's grace. That she had to reach the gateway before the last beast arrived on hallowed ground."

"They must almost all be here," said Dylan, glancing at Baxter and Crank. "There can't be many *beasts* that are still going to be able to make it through that swarm of snakes."

"The text also speaks of Soul Cleaver," said Remedios, glancing at the handle of the sword peeking over Dylan's shoulder. "And here it says again that when the beasts blacken the sky the time of the final Darkening draws nigh."

The ground outside the window seemed to simmer as millions of crows tested their wings, others—thousands of them—had already taken flight. Even if the sun had been up Dylan doubted much light would have made its way through the mass of birds in the air. He marveled that they could stay aloft. There seemed to be not an inch of space between any of them.

"I assume we would discover the ground animals equally disturbed," said Remedios, without glancing through the window.

"But did you really learn anything new?" asked Baxter.

"Yes. The inscription also says that in the final battle the Old Ones must be defeated *before* they cross through the gate because they are more powerful on this side."

"But we don't even know where the damned thing is," said Dylan.

"I do," said Lucy, quietly.

"What?" said Dylan. "You found the gate?"

"I didn't *find* it," she said. "But I know where it is. Where it has to be."

"So you have deciphered the riddle of the Keep as well," said Remedios, nodding.

"Where is it?" asked Baxter.

"Follow me," said Remedios.

He took one of the glowstones and led them to the subcellar.

"I discovered this when I came up here moments ago," said Remedios.

"Discovered what?" said Baxter.

Instead of progressing down the stairs into the vaults the old man stopped where he was. When Baxter stepped impatiently past he encountered an invisible barrier that he could stand upon like bulletproof glass.

"What the hell?" he said, trying to kick through the barricade.

"You may not pass," said Remedios. "*You* are not the chosen."

"You think this is the gate?" said Dylan, stepping tentatively past Baxter to discover that *his* foot would slip through the opening as though there were nothing there.

"I believe it is the path to it," said Remedios.

"You knew this would be here?" Dylan asked Lucy.

She shook her head. "I didn't know how it would manifest itself, but I was pretty certain it would happen here. The vault is surrounded by something that buffers it from our own reality, so this is really the only place on the grounds the gate *could* appear. It just made sense."

She stared down into the dark cellar like a baby bird peering into the eyes of a snake.

"And what will you do now?" Remedios asked her.

She glanced back at Dylan sadly. "I have to do this," she said, finally. "There's no other choice for me. But you aren't of my blood."

"You're not going anywhere without me," said Dylan. "And besides, I'm the one who found the sword. You wouldn't know how to use it."

Dylan could tell that Lucy was relieved and saddened at the same time. Clearly she had hoped that he would not have to be part of this, but she was afraid to go alone. She seemed about to say something when Crank shoved his way to the stairs.

"Like hell I'm letting these two go by themselves. I've

got a lot of time invested in keeping him alive," he said, pointing at Dylan and thumping the end of the heavy ax hard on the floor.

"They aren't alone," said Remedios. "And you may not pass."

The old man was right. Even when Crank swung the battle-ax at the barrier it bounced off dangerously. He cursed, tossing the weapon onto the floor, running his fingers along the concrete, trying to find the border of the obstruction and peel it away.

"I guess we should go," said Lucy, straightening her shoulders, as Crank finally turned away in disgust.

"Are you two sure about this?" asked Baxter, frowning as he stared down into the vault.

"I'm not sure about anything anymore," said Dylan. "Except Lucy. If she's going, then I'm going."

"Be careful," said Crank, squeezing Dylan's shoulder. "That sounds pretty stupid, huh?"

Dylan managed a smile, surprised by the gesture.

"Here," said Baxter, tossing one of the glowstones. Dylan caught it in one hand. Then he and Lucy stepped through the opening in the floor and passed together down the stairs.

Phoenix barked wildly and scratched at the invisible barrier, struggling futilely to claw her way through it. Lucy turned at the bottom of the steps and chided the dog, and finally she stopped barking and merely whined mournfully as Baxter stroked her head. One last yip and Lucy and Dylan disappeared into the confines of the vault.

Nothing appeared different there. The files Remedios had been researching still lay scattered atop metal desks and filing cabinets, and the stench of death still lingered. That struck Dylan as fitting for a place that harbored the gateway to a race of beings intent upon the destruction of mankind.

"It's not in here," said Lucy. "It's up ahead somewhere. In one of the rooms of artifacts."

"You can feel it?"

"Can't you?"

In fact, ever since passing through the invisible barrier he had been experiencing a feeling much like the pull that had drawn him to Lucy, only with a heavy underlying current of fear attached to it.

"There," whispered Lucy, pointing into the next room.

A gentle radiance shone through the door, and when they entered the chamber that had only recently been filled to bursting with cases full of artifacts they were surprised to find it empty. In the center of the vault the light formed a pulsating green ring from floor to ceiling. In the center of the circle of light a shimmering plate of diamonds revolved in a whirlpool pattern toward a point that seemed to disappear into the distance.

At that moment Dylan wanted more than anything to throw Lucy over his shoulder and race back up the stairs. But he knew that if he did, she'd only come back down by herself, and the bond of trust they had forged would be broken. He could hear Sensei Ashiroato chuckling.

You would not look for the mysteries, Dylan-san. Now mysteries come to you!

He now accepted the fact that there *were* mysteries. But that didn't mean he understood them. And the biggest mystery of all was how the two of them were supposed to stop the Darkening.

You'll know what to do when the time comes. You weren't brought here to fail.

Ronnie's voice sounded more distant than Sensei's, and he wondered if that was because it was real and not just a memory. Did she *really* know what she was talking about or was her memory just running on faith?

And that was what it all came down to—faith in something he couldn't see or touch or smell or taste. Faith in a power that was outside him. He was afraid that ultimately *that* would be the final test, whether or not he believed. And at that moment, he would have been hard put to answer.

Lucy approached the gate, and Dylan was careful to stay close beside her. The swirling circle of diamonds looked more like glittering teeth in the maw of some great serpent, and Dylan wondered if there really was a way for either of them to survive.

Pain blasted the Harry Rhothaq from every square inch of his body. His skin was cracked and dry as old desert clay. Although it had really been only one day that he had been forced by the overpowering pull to travel in the light, it seemed a million years since he had baked and twisted like a frog on a griddle, and the thousand rifts along his back were just beginning to scab over in the cool night air. It had taken the hateful sun forever to go down and already he sensed its imminent return.

All of the day before he had sensed the old man so close he could almost reach out and touch him with one of his razor claws. He had stumbled along, blinded by the blasting rays of the sun, hungering for blood. Sometime earlier he'd staggered into a sea of squirming snakes. When he had tried to slake his hunger on the wriggling beasts, he found that they tasted too foul to eat.

Then he had struck another barrier of pain. Only this one didn't force him to hide, like the sun, or pull him agonizingly along a path to an unknown destination. This one held him out. He could see millions of birds and beasts huddling within the barrier, and the smell of their blood and the old man's fired his madness. He paced relentlessly around the perimeter of the invisible wall, the rock-hard muscles in his gnarled fingers twitching across the barrier, searching, questing for an opening, a weakness.

But as the night rolled slowly toward another burning day, Harry began to despair that there was no way in after all, that he would spend another span in Hell, slowly shriveling into a withered bit of blackened flesh as he had seen so many others do.

He delved farther and farther, questing for any opening, any way in. It was maddening, being so close to prey he had hunted for so long, only to be denied. He scratched at the invisible barrier until his cuticles bled, pacing along its length, panting and drooling in a mindless rage. Finally, his talons found a crack in the wall, and he sensed that something dark and powerful had passed that way before him. His feeble mind tried to recall where he had felt the thing before, but his thoughts were like rich blood, thick and impenetrable. Finally, though, he remembered. He had met this same presence in the hallway the night the old man escaped. It was not a Rhothag of flesh and blood but a demon of shadow and darkness, as much a part of the night as the night was of it, and even the Harry Rhothag—which had little mind left for things other than prey or the commands of the inner voice—knew terror in its presence.

Finally, the overwhelming need to track the prey overrode the terror of the thing's residue, and his long nails sank into the crevice, and he pried at it the way a dog pries at a bone trapped beneath a chair, but it would not give. He slid his talons along the fissure, following its shape across the side of the barrier where the gap seemed to expand just a little. It wasn't a way in. Not yet.

But the barrier was weakening.

"I think this is only the gate on our side," argued Lucy as Dylan slashed ineffectually at the hypnotic, swirling display, the sword slicing through the thing as though it were nothing more than a holographic image. "And it isn't something you can chop up with that blade."

"I can see that," said Dylan, resting the sword point on the floor.

"There should be a matching gate in the Old Ones' dimension."

"Why?"

"Because I think there's something like a wormhole in between."

"You said that before. I don't understand."

"It's like folding a piece of paper. Imagine the paper is everything there is and contains all the dimensions and other places and maybe even other times all on one side. If you travel across the paper it might be almost infinitely far in time or space from one point to another. But fold the paper in half so that the only thing between the two points in time and space is the thickness of the paper and you have a spot for a wormhole to form. That's a hell of an oversimplification. But I'm betting that's what this is."

"What's in the wormhole? How far is it to the other gate?"

"I think theoretically there is no time and no distance inside a wormhole."

Dylan shook his head. "If there is no time and distance, then the other side of this gate is right inside the Old Ones' dimension. So this *is* the only gate."

Lucy frowned. "I can't explain it. But that's not the way it is. There's something in between. I've seen a great empty plain in my dreams and I think that's what's in between."

"Like a wide desert?" asked Dylan quietly.

Lucy nodded. "You've seen it, too?"

"What if we're wrong, though?" asked Dylan, staring at the spinning gateway. "What if the other side of this thing is right in the middle of Old One territory?"

"We have to believe we have at least a chance," said Lucy, at last. "We wouldn't have one if that were true. I think we'll find that emptiness, just as I saw it."

Dylan stared into the spinning orb, trying to make sense of it, to spot some pattern; but it was simply a whirlpool, drawing him in, and he felt for an instant as though he had *already* stepped toward it, although he hadn't felt his feet move. He staggered, and Lucy caught him.

"I think we're gonna be drawn into it whether we like it or not," he said, reaching to take her hand.

He started toward the gate, but before he reached it the feeling of being *drawn* into it as though his body were a dense liquid overcame him. In its intensity and feeling of dislocation, the sense of motion was nauseatingly similar to a shift, but there was no effort required. Instead, they seemed to blast through a long black tunnel toward a dim green light that began as a pinpoint and swiftly grew to encompass everything around them. When the feeling of motion abruptly ended they found themselves standing beneath an empty gray-green sky, on blanched ground that resembled stone but felt like sponge. The horizon fell away from them in all directions as though they stood atop a giant ball with no landmarks. The air smelled of ozone and seemed thin, rarefied.

"Which way?" asked Dylan, glancing around at the vast wasteland that lay beneath an eerie green sky. The plain disappeared in a wide arc in all directions.

"I don't think it matters," said Lucy.

Dylan frowned. "How can it not matter?"

"This is just the passage between our world and the world of the Old Ones. It appears to be a sphere from our vantage point, but that's only because we're looking at it from the perspective of people accustomed to three dimensions. Stephen Hawking would say that a wormhole is a place where the laws of physics as we know them don't really apply. But I believe he'd be interested to know two people could actually *survive* inside one of these things, granting that this even *is* a wormhole. I think we're going to reach the other gate no matter which way we go."

There was a vastness to the flat nothingness and the ever-distant horizon that made the word *empty* seem pathetically inadequate. This was not a *place;* it was some kind of construct, there merely for them to pass through, and Dylan wished to hell they could do that and be done with the journey, even if that meant finally facing the Old Ones head-on.

"I think maybe I could shift us to the other gate," he said, staring into the barren distance.

"I don't think we ought to use our talents in this place until we really need them," said Lucy, frowning uneasily. "Let's walk a little farther."

Dylan shrugged, pacing her, the strangeness of the world around them eating away at any shreds of self-assurance he clung to. This was a totally alien place. For all he knew the gravity that held them to the ball could turn off at any instant, flipping them away into the green void overhead. Or the air they were breathing might turn toxic. He felt like a small child in the depths of a deep, uncontrollable nightmare. But Lucy was bearing up, and he had to be strong for her.

The ground echoed like a giant bass drum with every footstep and he felt the faintest pressure—like an unseen hand in the small of his back—shoving him onward.

"I saw you in my dreams," said Lucy sadly. "But I didn't know it was you at first."

"Why didn't you tell me about them?"

"I wanted to believe they were just dreams."

"And now you don't?"

"I'm afraid they foretold the future."

He took her hand again. "We decide our own future."

"How can you say that with all *this*? What do *we* control here?"

"Ourselves. We can stop. We can turn back."

"And do what?"

He shrugged.

"You sound like you want to believe that but you really don't," she said.

"So, what do you think happens, stipulating that we succeed in beating them?" asked Dylan.

"You mean beyond saving mankind from extinction?" asked Lucy, making a face.

"Well, yeah. I mean, if we close the gate, shut out the Old Ones forever, then we've rid the world of evil, right?"

"I see what you're getting at," she said, musing, "but I don't think we'll really have gotten rid of evil. Probably the most we can hope for is that we'll have rid it of *pure* evil. I don't think even Remedios believes the Old Ones caused all the bad in the world. They just preyed on it. Made it worse.

I don't believe a human being can be either purely evil or purely good."

Dylan gave that some thought. "But there'll be no more pure evil pulling us toward the bad side, only pure good pulling us toward the light."

"I'm not sure that's right. But I guess it would be what I hope happens."

Dylan nodded. "That would be worth dying for, I guess."

"I hope you don't have to," she said.

But he noticed that she turned away, and that she had said *you*, not we.

They hiked on across the vast plain until it abruptly ended when the line of the horizon turned out not to be the distant edge of a vast sphere but a high escarpment. As they approached the base of the massif, they could see that it was formed of convoluted walls as high as a skyscraper, reaching in both directions as far as the eye could see. They stood beneath it, glancing behind them across the endless plain.

"What now?" asked Dylan, leaning back to stare up the sheer sides of the wall.

"We have to go around it," said Lucy, staring at the vanishing point on the horizon where the structure met the distance.

But they hadn't gone far—paralleling the cliff—before they both spotted a misty darkness moving toward them across the plain.

"What is that?" whispered Lucy.

"I think it's the thing that's been after me all along," said Dylan.

"What's that smell?"

"You notice it, too? You're the first person who's admitted smelling it."

She wrinkled her nose, frowning. "It's what I'd expect the end of the world to smell like."

As there was no choice but to keep following the wall, they raced along with renewed vigor. Dylan watched the darkness eating up the distance behind them, wondering if this was where he died and she was forced to keep running toward the second gate alone and unprotected. The darkness was almost upon them, and although he knew there was no way to fight it, his training would not allow him simply to surrender. Suddenly he could feel the thing reaching deep inside his mind, gnawing at his resistance. It wanted to own him, wanted to *be* him, and it was all he could do to keep it out. He could hear the terrible voice hammering inside his head, and without knowing how he understood them, he began to chant nonsense words that were no longer nonsense.

"*Ectara. Meana Serra!*" he screamed at the darkness. Stay back. Do not move!

The darkness approached more cautiously, but spread like mist rising from the center of a lake. Lucy grasped at Dylan's shirt, staying behind him to avoid the sword as he raised it.

Always there was only the one. Now there are two.

Ronnie's voice was soft as rain even as the darkness gathered around them. Lucy jerked the glowstone out of her pocket and squeezed it, holding it toward the direction of the gloom, but when no light came from the stone, she tossed it aside.

You both are who you are and what you are for a reason. And neither of you are alone.

"We can't fight it here," said Lucy, echoing his thoughts, while she tugged at his shirt. "We have to keep going, to get to the second gate!"

"It's trying to get inside me," he gasped. "To change me. To use me . . ."

"Come on," she said, dragging him along with her.

The darkness followed, but Dylan's words seemed to have confused it. He sensed a heaviness in the air ahead, a promise of doom.

When Lucy grew winded and Dylan slowed to help her along with one arm around her shoulders, she stared into his eyes.

"You're doing something to me," he gasped. "I can feel myself drawing strength from you."

She nodded. "I think the change can only happen to you when you're on ground that belongs to the Old Ones. This place isn't *ground* as we know it. But even here I still feel a connection to the Keep. I'm drawing strength from it. And maybe that's how I can help you fight that thing."

But Dylan shook his head. "I can't get the voice out of my head. Remedios said that *Rantasas* meant Gatekeeper. A part of the darkness is already inside me now, and I think it's trying to turn me *into* the Gatekeeper. That's what it's wanted all along. Why it came for me to begin with. Can you tell how much farther it is to the gate itself?"

"I feel it even more now. It's close."

When Baxter spotted the Rhothag lumbering through the ravens in the starlight, he stepped out onto the porch, dropped to one knee, and—aiming his pistol with both hands—slowly squeezed the trigger. Even in that light he didn't expect to miss, and he certainly never expected the firing pin to click on an empty chamber. He jerked the slide back and was shocked when he ejected a bullet. He tried to fire again. The same thing happened.

"It won't work," said Remedios, behind him, as Baxter repeated the process again and again.

"What the hell?" said Baxter as the Rhothag drew close enough for him to see its gleaming eyes and teeth.

"The change," said Remedios. "It's almost upon us. Your weapon will not function."

"Shit!" said Baxter, throwing the gun ineffectually in the beast's direction. "Get back inside! Hide!"

He shoved Remedios back through the door, slamming it shut and bolting it behind them. He could hear the priest's footsteps echoing away down the hall, but his mind was all on the Rhothag. How was he going to stop something that size, that powerful, without a gun? There were weapons in the vault, but he couldn't get down there now, and the mere possibility of being trapped down below in the darkness the way Wagner had been nauseated him.

"Crank!" he shouted as he dragged a heavy side table over to the door and flipped it on end, bracing it under the knob. That might stop the beast for a couple of minutes. He ran to the kitchen, tearing through the drawers and racks, finally selecting a heavy old carbon steel butcher knife with a wide brass hilt, testing the edge against his thumb and drawing blood.

He shouted Crank's name again, but there was no answer. Where the hell was he? With that damned ax of his the little shit might be a real help. He'd chosen a hell of a time to wander out of earshot.

He padded stealthily back into the foyer, glancing out the sidelights by the door, but he couldn't spot the beast. So he raced around the giant house, calling quietly for Crank and checking all the windows on the ground floor, but every one of them was bolted. For some reason the exit door at the far end of the hall was open, but there was no way the shambling Rhothag could have made it that far. Baxter slammed it shut and shoved a hutch in front of it. The Rhothag could easily crash through a window now, but at least then he'd know where the son of a bitch was.

Only the faintest starlight was able to make its way through the tumult of birds overhead. Each time he passed by one of the windowless rooms on the dark side of the hall, he slowed, the knife in front of him. There was no way the Rhothag could have found a way in yet, but he wasn't taking any chances.

He had no idea where the dog had gotten off to or where Remedios had hidden, but at least the old man was obeying orders and keeping quiet. Then it occurred to him that maybe the thing *was* inside the house, and it had found Remedios first. The Rhothag might have slipped in an open window and locked it behind itself. Were they intelligent enough to do something like that?

No, that was ridiculous. There hadn't been time, and he would have heard something, a scream, falling furniture. But the longer he stood there in the dark, silent corridor, the more certain he became that somehow the thing had outsmarted him. The fact that it *hadn't* already shattered a window or tried to burst through one of the doors gave it away as far as he was concerned. He took a deep breath, slowing his stride.

He pressed his back to the corridor wall closest to the exterior of the building. He'd be harder to spot there against the almost nonexistent glow of starlight from the doorways, and he'd be farther away from the darkened rooms across the hall if the thing was in the house.

A tinkling sound behind him was so light that at first he thought he was imagining it, but there was a nerve-wracking stillness to the house afterward, and he *knew* the fucker was inside. He glanced over his shoulder, wishing the sound had been louder, lasted longer, so that he could pinpoint it. He turned and headed back.

The Rhothag was acting stealthy, and that was bad. And Baxter didn't know if Remedios was behind him or somewhere ahead, between him and the Rhothag. That meant he couldn't just pick a good spot here to lie in ambush, he had to go find the beast.

He checked each of the bedrooms first, searching in near-total darkness by touch and sound alone, trying to think if he had any leverage he could use against one of the things. He hadn't trained in hand-to-hand combat in thirty years. Still, the Rhothags were mortal. If he could stab it in the eyes or mouth or even the throat, he might have a chance to kill it. But to do that he had to get close, extremely close, and the thought of the thing's rapier claws sent a chill through him.

But he continued searching, wondering for the millionth time where Crank and the damned dog had gotten off to.

Crank sat with his back pressed against the trunk of a tall oak at the rear of the grounds, staring at the outline of the Keep against the swirling black flock. Ravens grumbled darkly under their breaths as they scratched their way up his pants to rest on his feet, legs, and lap. Others dropped onto his shoulders and cawed quietly in his ear, whispering secrets to which only they were privy. He was oblivious to the beasts. His mind was a twisted mess of what-ifs and how-comes.

For over thirty years he had followed the Boss blindly. The man had rescued him from incarceration for the murder of his whoremongering stepfather and his abusive mother, channeled his natural proclivity for violence, aiming it at what Crank came to believe were acceptable outlets, and made him a part of something bigger than himself for the first time in his life. The Boss had seen to his training, not only in the professional aspects of a violent life but in the social graces as well. Taught him how to dress, how to eat in civilized surroundings, and how to interact with others, although the latter had never been one of Crank's strong points. Whenever Crank had rebelled, the Boss had come down with an iron hand. But afterward he had explained why, and Crank had learned. For over a quarter of a century Crank had been the man's right hand, and he had done things that he had accepted as necessary because the Boss *said* they were necessary.

Crank had never believed all the superstitious mumbo jumbo about Old Ones that motivated other Rex Deus operatives, and in private, the Boss had scoffed at their belief as well, explaining that it was a part of the organization that he hoped one day to weed out with Crank's help. Rex Deus *really* existed to fight Qedem Melech, a breed of terrorists who had no other end in mind than the final destruction of their own race. If believing in demons from another dimension aided that goal, then the Boss would use the belief. If it got in the way, he would squelch it.

And part of squelching was getting rid of the meddlesome priest who had begun to delve into the artifacts kept at the Keep. The Boss explained that at first he had offered the old man free access to many of the finds, figuring that he was harmless and his expertise with dead languages would allow him to translate many of the documents and texts for posterity. But later Clayborn came to see Remedios as a threat, informing Crank that the old man was fomenting trouble within the ranks, convincing many of the young Turks that Clayborn wasn't taking the Old Ones seriously enough. In Crank's mind it was Remedios who was the root cause of the schism that split Rex Deus into rival factions, and that meant that Remedios had to go.

And Crank had almost killed him.

Baxter had no idea how close a thing that had been. The fire that had supposedly killed Remedios had taken place only minutes before Crank showed up ready to end the man's life.

Minutes.

And now he had to accept the fact that he had been used. That he had come within scant seconds of murdering a man who might have been trying to lead Rex Deus in the right direction for the first time in a very long while. The Boss was dead, lying in a burnt heap not ten feet in front of Crank that even the crows eschewed. He could still smell the sweet rotten odor of the charred corpse, although it was now nothing more than a pile of ash.

He had done everything that he could to deny the truth, but even if the world had not changed so drastically around him, he would have been forced to add things up eventually. The ring on the severed arm, Dylan's wife's coffin in the basement, were only icing on an already heavily burdened cake. There was no one else that could have been organizing the show for Qedem Melech as well as the Boss.

Crank had known that the Boss had operatives out after Dylan in Needland. What he hadn't realized at the time was that they weren't Rex Deus but Qedem Melech.

Crank knew he'd been played, and in the playing he had become as bad as any of the Rhothag or the Qedem Melech agents he loathed.

He thought back to that day on the road when he and Dylan had passed so easily through the throng of Rhothag, and yet the beasts had tried to kill Baxter. Then there was the cat that only he could touch. He glanced around at the ravens intermixed with foxes. Back in the trees he saw deer and squirrels.

No cats.

That was probably why Lucy's dog had never liked him. He was the worst of traitors. A Judas. Even a mutt could smell that stink on a man.

The thought stirred the old embers of rage that never fully cooled within, making him wish that he could dig through the moldering pile of ash and find the Boss's throat and rip it out with his bare fingers.

He had been willing to do anything to assure that Dylan got to the Keep for the Boss, even to the point of abandoning Baxter to the Rhothag on the road. Since then he'd stood by and watched as Dylan and Lucy disappeared into God knew where to face God knew what, and there wasn't a damned thing he could do to help them. He was nothing more than a crippled, hate-filled turncoat, and the best thing he could do would be to put one of his pistols to his head and scatter his worthless brains to Hell and gone. The only thing that frightened him was that now that might be just where he was going.

He'd never believed in Heaven or Hell before. Never believed in much of anything but the Boss. But finally he had to admit that there was more to the world than just what he could see and hear and kill. Still, he felt he owed the world one more death.

He removed one of his pistols and studied it in the starlight. Three men and more than one Rhothag had died with shots from this very gun, and he knew that a clean shot would be painless and quick. He slipped the cold barrel into his mouth, wincing at the taste of metal, and slid his thumb onto the trigger, hesitating for only a moment.

Best to do it quick. Or are you a coward as well as a traitor?

He closed his eyes and squeezed the trigger, jumping when the firing pin clicked.

He slowly withdrew the gun from his mouth, cursing himself for not jacking a cartridge into the chamber. But he *always* kept one in. With his hands shaking and his heart pounding he wondered whether he'd have the nerve to pull the damned trigger again. He jerked the slide back and was surprised to see a cartridge drop out. He made certain another took its place, then aimed the gun skyward and pulled the trigger. Once again the gun misfired. He tossed it aside and tried his other pistol.

Same thing.

What the hell was going on?

The crows seemed more agitated than they had before, and as he glanced toward the Keep he could see that the closer to the building the animals were, the more stirred up they seemed. A premonition of doom forced him to his feet. Suddenly he was certain that thc grounds were no longer secure. If neither of his pistols was working, then something drastic had happened. Clouds of black birds swooped and swirled around the high eaves and across the face of the building as though trying to drive something off with the beating of their wings.

And he'd left the side door open.

"Shit," he said, tossing aside the second pistol and reaching to retrieve his ax from beneath the carpet of ravens.

After searching every inch of Lucy's room, Baxter slipped slowly back out into the gloomy corridor. He heard something padding down the hall and knew immediately that the sound was not the footfall of anyone who belonged in the building. It was too slow, too stealthy, and it was coming from the direction of the study. He prayed that the Rhothag hadn't found Remedios yet. Maybe the old man had gone upstairs to hide. Hell, maybe both of them could find a place to hide and survive. But Baxter didn't really believe that. The damned Rhothags had noses like bassets and could see in the dark. Where could any human hide until daylight? Would there even *be* another daylight?

And where the hell was Crank?

Maybe he'd been wrong about Crank all along. Maybe Crank *wasn't* a fool in Clayborn's pocket. Maybe he had been running the show. Maybe he'd *let* this thing onto the grounds or even into the Keep. That thought added a new dimension to Baxter's paranoia, and he clasped the knife even tighter. Fighting a giant Rhothag with a blade was bad enough; facing Crank and that razor-sharp ax as well would be impossible. If he spotted Crank first, he didn't think he could chance giving the little shit the benefit of the doubt.

He crept along the corridor, listening intently for another footfall.

Breaking glass tinkled behind him, and he whirled, damning the darkness. He could see the vague outlines of the open doors on his left because there were windows in those rooms and the faintest of starlight flickered through. But the corridor was a tunnel of gloom and the doors on the other side were black as pitch. Another shattering sound came from the same direction. Was there another Rhothag outside now, breaking in? Was he going to be caught between two of the beasts?

The first Rhothag wasn't after *him* so it had to be stalking Remedios. That made it the more dangerous of the two at the moment. He headed toward the study, slipping once more against the wall nearest to the exterior of the building so as not to be spotlighted by the thin light that filtered across the hall. He ached to move fast, to run after the first Rhothag and distract it from the old man; but his only hope of defeating the thing lay in surprise, so he inched along by feel, his fingers tickling the smooth plaster. Suddenly he felt not paint but air, and he knew he had stepped into the middle of a doorway without realizing it.

A hand dropped onto his shoulders from behind, jerking him back down the hallway, slamming him so hard against the wall that the wind was driven from his lungs. His fingers tightened on the handle of the knife, and when a face appeared directly in front of his own he brought the blade up under the throat.

Crank's eyes widened, and Baxter froze. After a moment Crank smiled and shrugged, waiting.

Baxter took a deep breath, noticing that Crank's ax had never been raised, and his other hand still rested on Baxter's shoulder. If Crank had meant to kill him, he could simply have buried the ax in his back.

"Where the hell have you been?" Baxter whispered.

"Thinking," Crank whispered back. "Where is it?"

Baxter shook his head, nodding down the hall. "Somewhere down there. I lost it when I heard the window break. I thought it was another one getting in."

Crank shook his head, frowning. "That was me. You locked me out."

"*You* left the door open?"

Crank ignored the question, slipping past him, and Baxter followed, glad to have the little son of a bitch with him. Dynamite came in small packages, and in a fight Crank could be explosive. But the damned Rhothag was still being incredibly stealthy. He had no idea where it was, and they hadn't run into Phoenix. Where the hell had the dog gone? Everyone was disappearing at the worst time.

Phoenix was lying on the bed she shared with her master, waiting patiently for her to return, when she heard Crank passing by and glanced in his direction; but he had paid no attention to her so she followed him down the hall, surprised when he left the door open. Humans almost never did that. If they did, she'd have gotten a lot more exercise. But tonight she had no time to be running around through the stupid crows, sniffing the foxes, or marking the grounds. She was waiting for her master to return. So she gave the crows on the side porch one baleful look to let them know that they were not to enter the house, then trotted back to the bedroom.

Almost immediately she detected the odor of one of the

creatures, and her hackles rose, but she was smart enough not to growl, although she wanted to desperately. She trotted to the door, peeking out into the hall. The man-that-was-not-a-man closed the door behind it and glanced slowly around while Phoenix stood frozen. The thing's eyes swept over her but did not pause, and she breathed again. Then it disappeared through the doorway into the old man's room and was gone for a moment before returning, sniffing the air. She sniffed also, studying the smell of the thing, something like rotten meat and feces. It didn't smell bad. But she knew it was. It was up to no good here, and it did not belong inside any more than one of the crows. She sniffed again and caught hints of the last human dinner, canned dog food, and canned milk. She also smelled the fireplace in the study, the residual odors of her new master, and down the hall, the smell of the man called Baxter and the old man. The man-that-was-not-a-man sniffed again and headed down the hall and she knew instinctively that its prey was the old man. He was the weakest, the slowest. He would be the easiest to kill, and it was her job to protect him and to protect this house.

But she also knew that she had no hope of doing that by attacking the monster here. It was far too big for her, and she was alone. She had to find the old man and try to get him out of danger. She slipped out of the bedroom and walked as stealthily as a cat behind the giant beast, weaving into and out of doorways to conceal herself as it padded quietly along. Halfway down the long corridor she spotted Baxter slipping into one of the bedrooms, and she wondered if he even knew the thing was in the house. But she dared not bark to warn him, nor cross over to him. When the Rhothag passed him by she knew she was right, its target was the old man. She followed it on down the hall.

As they approached the big room near the front doors the creature slowed, and Phoenix immediately knew why. The air was full of the mixed aromas of her people because they passed through there all the time. The smells of the old man and Baxter were stronger, but they were everywhere. Phoenix knew that even though the creature had a good nose it wasn't as good as hers. The man-that-was-not-a-man would have to search by sight *and* by smell. But Phoenix already knew where the old man was. The scent of him wafted from beneath the closet door across the room, and the dog waited to see if the odor would strike the beast the same way it did her. In that case she would have no choice but to attack and hope that Baxter would hear in time and come to her rescue.

But as the creature turned and slunk away toward the kitchen, Phoenix allowed herself a silent sigh of relief, padding quickly across the foyer to the closet door, where she scratched as lightly as she knew how, whimpering softly. At first nothing happened, and she knew the old man was afraid to come out. But did he really think this thin piece of wood was going to protect him from the creature when it found him? She scratched a little harder, and finally the door opened. But before she could greet him with a wag of her tail, or dance circles to convince him to follow her out of this dangerous place, the old man grabbed her by the scruff of the neck and dragged her scuffling back into the dark closet with him.

One moment Dylan and Lucy were rushing across the great empty plain, following the high cliff that girdled the giant ball. The next instant they were sinking through the surface they had been running across. When their feet finally contacted something solid again they glanced around in awe. Overhead now, instead of the *ground* they had just passed through was *sky* that was a deep shade of azure, the most beautiful blue either of them had ever seen. In the distance the bright golden orb of the sun was just beginning to slash its rays through crimson-and-purple clouds. But beneath the dawn the deepest darkness Dylan had ever seen defied the sun, and he and Lucy hurried in that direction, both knowing the darkness had to herald the gate.

But both drew up short when Dylan almost stepped over the edge of a precipice. Lucy caught him just in time, and they stood teetering there, staring down to where a sparkling light glimmered within a vast darkness, alternately appearing and disappearing. Finally, she pulled him back from the edge.

"Now what?" he said, catching his breath, his heart pounding against his ribs. Although the misty darkness following them had disappeared when they slipped through the ground overhead, Dylan couldn't get the shadowy *thing* out of his mind. It kept hammering at him in the alien speech that he was beginning to fully understand. And he was afraid that understanding meant that more and more of the darkness had insinuated itself into his mind.

Dylan forced himself to peer down into the depths again, fighting the vertigo that spun inside him. The gate was down there. He could feel it calling to him, feel all the voices within him—those of Sensei and Ronnie *and* the horrible deep scratching voice of the darkness—willing him to jump. A heavy rumbling shook the ground so badly that he could barely stay on his feet, and Lucy fell to her knees. The tremor lasted for several minutes, and Dylan was afraid that the walls of the cliff might collapse beneath them, but finally the ground settled, and silence slowly returned. Lucy's hand felt clammy but steady in his own.

"The change is becoming more violent," he said, taking a step back.

"The sun," said Lucy, glancing past him.

The gleaming yellow disk was racing toward its zenith, the day rushing past with blinding speed.

"When it goes down this time I don't think it will rise again," said Dylan.

"No."

"Did you dream what comes next?" asked Dylan.

Lucy nodded. "But I don't understand it."

"Like there's anything we can understand here," said Dylan.

"I understand *that*," said Lucy, staring into the pit. "We have to go quickly. Or I don't think I'll be able to get myself to do it."

"Go? You mean jump?" said Dylan, shaking his head.

"It's what I saw," she said. "It's that or go back."

"No," he whispered. "How about I shift us down there."

"You don't know that you can do that," she said, pointing toward the sun, which was now already past its peak and falling like a stone. "And there isn't time to experiment."

She was right, of course. And it was her dream, but there was no way he could bring himself to step to the lip of that chasm again, much less leap off it.

You have to look outside yourselves and believe.

Ronnie's voice was as insistent as he'd ever heard it.

Believe what, that they could make that jump and survive? That was insane.

There's more than you can see and feel, Dylan. Either you believe in the mysteries or you don't.

For a moment he wondered if Ronnie had been talking to Sensei. He watched the sun dropping toward the horizon, darkness descending across the unnatural world of the wormhole, and he knew that there was no other way. Nothing this unreal could have just *been*. Someone, some power, had to have created it. And to have created him for this purpose. But even accepting all that, just thinking about that long fall was more terrifying than the darkness had ever been.

The mysteries had truly come to him. And one of those mysteries was Lucy. He peered into her eyes and saw his own fear there. But he saw his love mirrored as well.

Slowly he nodded to her.

"All right. How do you want to—" he started to say.

But she was already in midair, and there was nothing he could do but hold on to her hand.

Remedios huddled in the closet beside the study, clutching the scruff of Phoenix's neck. The dog was smart enough not to give away their hiding place with a growl, but he could feel her tensing as though to leap through the door and attack the Rhothag that had invaded the Keep. The old man's senses were not nearly as acute as the dog's, and he knew that the closet was not a safe haven for either of them, even though Baxter had told him to hide.

When Phoenix continued to tug and to paw lightly at the door Remedios knew that the dog was, after all, probably a better judge of the situation than he. He hadn't paid any attention when he raced into the closet or when he'd opened the door for the dog; but as he turned the knob slowly, he murmured a prayer for silence, happy when he was answered with well-oiled hinges.

Phoenix trotted quietly across the hall toward the study, waiting there until Remedios tiptoed to her. She ran to one of the front windows, nosing at the jamb as though trying to raise it. Indoors they were trapped. Outside at least there'd be room to run, even if that was more solace to the dog than to Remedios. He unlocked the sash, raising it as quietly as possible and trying to slide out silently. But his old legs were not meant to bend that far, and he froze, half-in, half-out, as the Rhothag sauntered into the room.

Phoenix growled and stiffened.

"No!" hissed Remedios, gripping Phoenix's fur tightly.

The dog was no match for the beast, and he did not wish to see the noble animal die for him. Enough blood had been shed already. If it was his time, then it was his time. But the dog broke free and edged out into the room, placing herself between the Rhothag and Remedios, her hackies raised tautly, so intent on the big beast that she seemed to be resting only on the points of her toenails.

The Rhothag gave her one sideward glance, then its eyes rushed to Remedios again, and the old man realized that this was the same beast that had watched and waited night after night as he lay alone in his cell. A wide grin spread across its thin lips, and he sensed that it was preparing to lunge, and that the dog would attack at the same time.

"Our Father, Who art in Heaven," he whispered.

The Rhothag lurched forward, and Remedios fell back against the window. But suddenly the beast staggered, then whirled, facing back out into the foyer, and Remedios noticed that there was a great gash between its shoulder blades and dark blood oozing from it. A wound of that nature would have felled the most powerful man, but the Rhothag seemed merely stunned. As it stepped backward into the room, though, Remedios saw something flash through the air, and the Rhothag swatted at it the way it might have had it been a bee.

Baxter slipped past the Rhothag into the room, and as it slapped at him Crank's ax swung low this time, catching the beast at midthigh, staggering it again. Phoenix chose that moment to attack, swooping in to nip at the thing's Achilles tendon, then dash away, barking savagely. Remedios knew that Crank and Baxter would do well to defeat the thing, and he wished that he were not ancient and decrepit. He searched for a weapon, but there was none in sight.

"The glowstones!" shouted Baxter, and Remedios hobbled quickly to the desk, snatching one up. He squeezed it tightly, but nothing happened, and he knew why. The gate was still opening. The powers of this world continued to falter. He shook his head sadly at Baxter, but Baxter had already turned back to the fight.

The Rhothag backed into the center of the room, trying to watch both Crank and Baxter, who edged to either side, searching for an opening. When Baxter lunged with the knife the beast slashed at him, and Crank took that moment to swing the heavy ax at the thing's head. But the Rhothag dodged the ax and snatched the blade of Baxter's knife as though it had no fear whatsoever of being cut. Its other hand caught Baxter behind the neck, jerking him off his feet and tossing him through the air like a discarded wad of paper. He struck the wall hard and did not get up.

"Get out!" Crank screamed, waving at Remedios. "Through the window, now!"

Remedios obeyed, struggling through the opening, arthritis and age defying him at every move. He was afraid he'd waste the other's efforts by simply falling two feet and breaking his neck; but he managed to slump to the ground outside and finally to struggle to his feet again. Behind him he could hear Phoenix growling fiercely, but the death battle between Crank and the Rhothag was orchestrated only with grunts and gasps.

•

The freefall into the darkness was belly-clenching, breath-catching, and heart-stopping. The edge of the cliff and the light above receded almost instantly, and Dylan couldn't help but anticipate the gruesome impact they were going to make somewhere not nearly far enough below. He clung to Lucy's hand so tightly he was afraid he might break her bones.

After what seemed an incredibly long time, he began to make out more of their surroundings, tentatively at first, then clearer, until he could see Lucy plainly and then the walls of a vast canyon, proving that they *were* still falling and at an incredible rate. He drew Lucy into his arms, and she pressed tightly against him, her heart pounding.

Beneath them the darkness shimmered like black foil, as though the air had been transformed into metallic ink.

"We're getting close," he said, placing his chin onto the top of Lucy's head and trying to twist his body to absorb the impact.

Suddenly he felt the darkness reaching for him, smothering his mind, and either the presence was speaking to him in English, or he had begun to think in its language.

Let it happen. Fulfill your destiny. Become.

The words carried powerful emotions along with them, a heady brew of malice and rage and overpowering lust. And inside his head a picture of the final Darkening began to take shape. Suddenly familiar beings—Old Ones—were transported from gate to gate by himself—the Gatekeeper—until they could take form again on the Earth side of the wormhole and once more rule the planet.

That was why the darkness had been searching for him, following him, for so long. *He* carried the only wild talent that could finally open the gateway to the Old Ones. Only once in every few millennia did a descendant of Shirath's line exhibit the talent that gave the Old Ones hope that it was their time to rule again. He wanted desperately to *Become*.

But he fought back with every ounce of discipline Sensei Ashiroato had trained him in. He struggled to block off a portion of his mind, shutting out the voice, listening instead to the steady sound of his own breathing, of the pulse throbbing through his veins, relaxing his body, centering himself the way he had practiced a million times before.

Finally, their descent slowed, and he knew that they were not going to die in the fall. He bent his knees to force himself upright, striking hard but managing to remain on his feet, still clutching Lucy tightly against him, until she pushed away.

Just past Lucy, through the darkness, he could see the glowing green ring of another gate. The whirling diamonds bulged outward as though pressed by myriad powerful hands. The gate seemed ready to burst. The mental effort required to speak lessened Dylan's control over the thing in his mind and allowed it to advance a little farther, and his vocal cords felt tight and twisted.

"The Old Ones need me," said Dylan. "They have no physical bodies and can't move across the wormhole like you and I. In order to reach our world, they need me to shift them from one gate to the other. If the shadow turns me into the Gatekeeper, I'll do their bidding. The Keep will vanish like everything else, and the Old Ones will destroy our world."

"If you're the key, then we should never have come."

Dylan shook his head. "We had to come."

"Why? Why couldn't we just stay at the Keep if they can't open the gates without you?"

"Because the Old Ones are patient. We could go back to the Keep, but that dark presence, that thing that's been after me from the beginning, would follow us there. It would never give me a moment's peace, and I don't know how long I could stand this incessant *will* inside my mind forcing me to submit. We have to finish it now."

"We have to kill the shadow," said Lucy. "That must be what Soul Cleaver was made for."

Rantasas. Become the Gatekeeper. Destroy the woman.

Dylan shook his head. The voice was a whip, but there was another voice inside as well, a soft sweet sound that seemed strange in this hellish place.

Trust each other. There are two of you this time . . . and neither of you is alone. None of us are.

Dylan wanted to drown in the warm, familiar voice. But the voice of the shadow was powerful and insistent, willing him toward Lucy. He was barely able to shake his head again, answering silently.

You can't have her. I won't let you.

There was a moment when both voices in his head went still. But when the beast's voice returned, it returned with a vengeance.

You are the Gatekeeper.

Dylan could only watch in horror as his own body staggered forward, raising the sword even higher, preparing for the kill, and Lucy seemed to be paralyzed, waiting for the blow to fall. Dylan struggled to regain any control at all, anything to hold the heavy, razor-sharp sword at bay.

The beast's cry echoed within and without. *Do as I command.*

Dylan felt himself preparing to swing the sword, saw disbelief in Lucy's eyes.

"*That's* Soul Cleaver, Dylan," she cried, staring at the sword, backing away a step. "It was not created to be used against human beings. You have to battle that thing inside you!"

"You don't understand!" Dylan gasped. "I can't control it. It controls me!"

Suddenly she swept against him faster than he could swing the blade, wrapping her arms tightly around him.

"No!" he screamed, staggering back, struggling to shake her off. But she clung to him. Her warmth blasted through him. He felt the change easing wherever she touched him, and when the presence screamed with rage inside his mind, he knew what was happening. Lucy was using all her talent to draw the power of the hallowed earth at the Keep *there* with them to keep them both in touch with their own world, their own reality. As the thing's voice within weakened, Dylan managed to shove Lucy to arm's length, turning at last to face the dark thing that had emerged from within him.

Finally, the shadowy beast had form. In this nothing place between the two gates and standing on the ground that Lucy had somehow hallowed it looked like one of the Rhothag, although it was still a thing of empty darkness and not scaly flesh. Even so, Dylan knew its talons and teeth would be deadly and that it was infinitely more powerful than the most fearsome of the Rhothag.

"Kill her!" screamed the thing, its dark chest heaving, black veins rising in its throat and face.

Dylan shook his head, as much to clear it as to deny the command. But with each second he felt the pressure lifting from his mind. He took two steps forward to meet the enemy and to distance the battle from Lucy.

The thing plunged forward, striking at Lucy, but Dylan slid inside, swinging the sword. Where the giant beast had stood emptiness and mocking laughter hung in the air, and a heavy blow to the back of Dylan's head sent him reeling. But he spun, arcing the sword low to catch his opponent on the legs. Again there was emptiness. He glanced at Lucy and saw that her eyes were closed in deep concentration. The ground beneath his feet felt familiar and safe. He glanced to his right, and the thing stood there glaring at him, arms spread as though inviting Dylan's next attack.

I can't win this, thought Dylan. There was only one way to win the battle. The same way Shirath and all the rest of Lucy's line had.

Shirath had died.

The sword was not meant to be used against man. It was meant to be used against the Gatekeeper and *he* was becoming the Gatekeeper. That was the only way to defeat the beast that had haunted him since Ronnie's death. And Lucy had seen it. Or at least she'd foreseen his death. He could see it in her eyes.

But he raced forward anyway, swinging low first, then slinging the blade up to catch the demon between the legs and halve it like a melon. But once again there was nothing there, and once again a powerful blow struck at the nape of his neck, and he dropped and rolled. He cradled the sword, managing to stagger to his feet, but the thing was already reaching for Lucy.

"No!" screamed Dylan, and in that instant he shifted, appearing beside Lucy to slash at the thing's downsweeping arm, severing it at the wrist even as the beast disappeared again. Dylan spun, anticipating a new attack.

Suddenly it was there in front of him, slashing, and Dylan backed away a step, keeping Lucy behind him.

"Dylan!" screamed Lucy as he ducked a killing blow.

When he glanced at her she pointed to a spot on the stone floor, and he knew instantly that she was using her talent to sense where the demon was about to reappear. The gleaming blade of Soul Cleaver slashed wickedly through the air, tracing an upward arc just as the demon materialized, taking it under its upraised arm, slashing through shadow to exit at the right shoulder. The two sections of torso dropped alongside one another, as the thing's legs buckled. The beast's eyes were still open, its lips moving, but there was now no air to power its voice. But Dylan read the alien words on the thing's lips and heard them inside his mind, and they chilled him.

You think you've won?

Dylan staggered back to Lucy, and she clutched him tightly.

"Is it all over?" she asked.

"No," he said, staring at the spot where the misty shape of the thing had been only a moment before. Now there was nothing there but bare ground. Still, a shudder raced up his spine. The strange runes on Soul Cleaver gleamed dully as though from an inner fire. When Lucy gasped, he glanced toward the gate.

It was beginning to open. But rather than the savage hordes of alien Old Ones he had imagined, he saw only the shadowy image of the beast, alive again. Soul Cleaver hadn't killed it. It was only a shadow until it was within him.

The closer he drew to the gate, the more Dylan felt the power of the beast again, but he knew that backing away would be a final mistake.

"We have to finish this," he gasped.

He could feel the thing, not taunting this time but willing him away—sensing his resolve—and that more than anything convinced him that he was right. He understood at last the place and the way and the time to end this.

"Take the sword," gasped Dylan, staggering as the beast struck him with a powerful blast of will. Dylan's hands shook as he handed her the weapon. It might be weaker on the other side of its own gate, but here in the wormhole the thing's will was still powerful enough to nearly wrest control of his body from him again.

Lucy grasped the weapon, struggling to raise it in both hands. "What do you want me to do with it?"

Dylan didn't have the strength to answer and to fight the beast's dominating will. He tried to drag himself through the gate, but he could barely balance on his feet. The shadow seemed to be sucking the life out of him now. When Lucy saw what he was doing she slipped under his arm and helped him stumble toward the whirling orb, staring at the bulging center in the spinning lights where the beast's leering black face shone through.

"Soul Cleaver," he gasped. "Only works . . . other side."

"I can't use the sword," she said. "And if we cross through the gate, that thing will possess you."

"Have to." He knew he was right. The closer he got to the gate, the weaker he became, but at the same time the weaker grew the darkness's hold over his mind. The Old Ones and their minions were more vulnerable on their own side. "Have to get in. Get it done. Shirath's sword. Shirath died."

Shirath, like all the warriors of the past ages, had understood the Old Ones' weakness. They had to be defeated on their own side in order to exile them there. Shirath had been alone. She'd been forced to fall on her own sword. Though her death had closed the gate, Dylan suspected that *because* she was alone, the shadowy Gatekeeper was able to slip through to Earth in the moment before her death, keeping the portal between the two dimensions ready for the next human born with the power to shift. But if *he* died and Lucy could hold the Gatekeeper at bay as the gate closed, the Old Ones could never rise again.

Before Lucy could argue he reached into the swirling circle, and once again he was drawn in like smoke through a straw, finding himself standing in a world so black that somehow the beast's darkness seemed to glow. The *air* was barely breathable, filled with the strange rotting metal odor of the dark beast. Glancing back he saw Lucy—as though he were looking at her through a rippling sheet of water—standing on the other side of the gate, and he motioned her to stay where she was.

Dylan felt a sudden pain, like poison jolting through him, his brain thrumming once more under the psychic grasp of the powerful shadow as the darkness entered him.

"No!" he screamed, dropping to his knees. He grasped his temples between both fists, trying to crush his own skull as the thunder of the demon's voice rumbled through, commanding him to submit, to be taken, to be destroyed. The thing's will was powerful now, but not quite as strong as on the other side of the gate. Dylan felt his limbs weakening, felt himself being divorced from his body, floating, but he struggled desperately because he knew that if he did not defeat the beast then Lucy would die next. Then the Old Ones would be triumphant at last, and no men would ever rise again to defeat them.

"Kill me!" he screamed, barely able to lift a feeble finger to point at the sword in Lucy's hands.

"No!" The demon's voice rumbled.

Agony raced through Dylan's ribcage. The beast was still trying to break his will, but he drew in a long breath and willed the pain and the awful voice away until they were only a throbbing in the back of his mind.

You will still be mine.

"Lucy! It's weaker here. It can die." Dylan screamed. "You have to do it now!"

She lifted the heavy weapon in both hands, but shook her head. "I can't," she said, with tears in her eyes. "Dylan, I can't."

He ignored the terrible voice inside his head and stared deeply into her eyes. "You have to!" he shouted. "It's in here now. Use *Soul Cleaver*!"

She frowned, staring at the blade for what seemed like hours as he struggled to hold off the onslaught from within. He knew she wasn't going to be able to do it after all, and that was his own fault. She'd finally opened up to another human being, and now he was asking her to murder the only person she'd ever really loved.

"Do you love me?" he gasped.

"Yes, I love you. I—"

"Then do it now."

Suddenly he saw a new light in her eyes. Something crafty that frightened him. There was no time for tricks. Every instant he could feel the beast settling inside him.

"Take my hand," she said, reaching through the swirling gate but not being drawn in. Her connection to the Keep had to be anchoring her. But she was barely able to lift the sword in her other hand.

"No time," he gasped.

"Take it!"

It was like pressing his arm through a wall of solid steel as the thing fought to control his body, but he managed to reach her. She grasped his hand tightly, and at the same time rested the point of the heavy sword against his throat. He stared into her teary eyes and nodded.

Ronnie's voice was in his head, strong and insistent, and he could almost see her smile.

Now believe. Like you've never believed before.

And in that instant he knew that his talent—the gift Ronnie had bequeathed him on her deathbed—wasn't just his ability to shift. It was the indescribable bond that connected her to her sister. The same bond that now tied him to Lucy. A bond there was no explaining. One of the *mysteries.* He felt a jolt pass between himself and her, and he could hear Lucy's voice in his mind as well.

Shift, she said, as she leaned into the blade, driving it through his throat.

And as Lucy pressed forward Dylan shifted. Only a few inches—he needed to stay in contact with her—but enough for the point of the sword to slice not through his throat but the throat of the beast, which did not *shift* with him. This was the demon's true home. Here it could be killed, and by its dying the gate that it wanted so desperately to open could be closed. And with a little luck *he* might survive.

The beast roared in agony, then sagged, life ebbing from it.

But unexpectedly Dylan's soul and that of the demon seemed still intertwined. Even though the sword had not pierced his own throat, as the beast died, he was dying too. He fell backward, choking, the feel of cold steel burning in his throat, tasting hot blood on his lips. As his life seeped away, he sensed the unimaginable wrath of the beast at having been beaten, and he felt a glow of victory that dulled the deep sadness of his own defeat. At least Lucy might survive. He barely heard the clang as the sword struck the ground beside him. When he opened his eyes Lucy was cloaked in a rippling gray haze, and he experienced a strange vision that she was dead, too, that she was in Heaven with him. But then another knifelike pain struck him, and he felt her hand, still tight in his own.

"Dylan!" he heard her whisper. "Dylan! We've got to get out of here. The gate's closing! Follow the path! Don't leave me!"

What path?

Her face was even hazier now, and she seemed to have receded into some foggy distance. He could barely feel her hand, and how could he feel it anyway, she had to be fifty feet away? Then she was a hundred feet and still receding. How did she do that without moving her feet? He was dying, of course. It was a hallucination.

You can find the path.

Was that Lucy or Ronnie? Both voices were so weak, and it was difficult to tell them apart anyway.

You're connected to her now, through me. You can't lose her unless you give up. Believe.

He just wanted to close his eyes and rest. Suddenly, the feeling reminded him of the night he'd spent lost in the woods and that seemed funny. He'd wanted to go to sleep that night, too. But if he had, he'd have died. And if he closed his eyes now, he'd be dead, too. He blinked, and something seemed to change. Lucy was even farther away now, but there did seem to be a lighted path between them. He had taken two steps upon it before he wondered how he had done it. Hadn't he been on his back? How could he be walking?

But with each step he took the stronger he became, the clearer his vision, until he was only paces away, and he could see that the path lay in midair, he was high over some deep darkness again, and he knew that if he stepped back or to the side, he would fall away into the abyss, and this time there would be no soft landing. This time Lucy would die with him because the path was not just of her making. He was part of it too. It was a path that brought them together or forever sundered them. Sweat broke out on his brow as he took one more tottering step, then another, ever forward. At the last instant, just as he felt his strength faltering once again, as he felt himself slipping into darkness, as he could see that long long drop reaching up for him, he felt her arms around him, and he collapsed against her.

Phoenix had never trusted the man called Crank. But now he was locked in a death battle with the creature that had invaded her master's house, and that made him her ally. She tried to stay out of the little man's way and the way of the giant flashing ax that she'd seen wound the beast, as she wove around and between the creature's leg, nipping and biting, crunching her teeth on the rocklike scales, now and then drawing the nasty blood of the thing. Most of her fear was gone, replaced by a deep-seated need to see this thing dead, to feel its heart pumping its lifeblood out onto the floor, to howl like all of her kind over the corpse of her enemy.

Crank had wounded the Rhothag more than once. It stooped from a bloody gash in its back and favored one leg where more blood trickled. She chomped yet again at an exposed ankle, the ax bit deep in the creature's side, and it lurched, almost falling. As she took that opportunity to nip at its outstretched hand it lashed at her, catching one claw in the soft underside of her belly. She felt the point ripping through muscle and some of her strength deserted her as she backed away, still growling a warning at the thing. Crank rushed in with the ax and made another deep cut in the thing's side. But this time he dared too much, and the Rhothag caught him, too, grasping him by the throat and lifting him high in the air. The ax fell from his hands as the beast stared at him the way Phoenix had stared into the faces of cats when they were cornered. As it tightened its grip on Crank's throat, Phoenix swallowed her pain and leapt atop a sofa, launching herself at the monster, burying her teeth in its windpipe, tasting the blood, feeling its heart pumping just the way she had dreamed. She was going to kill this thing, feel it dying beneath her paws. She would howl in triumph over its remains, and her master would pat her head, and say, "Good dog."

She felt the creature releasing Crank, heard Crank fall to the floor but not get up. And she felt the powerful arms wrapping around her so tightly the air was squeezed from her lungs until everything around her began to grow dark. And then she was flying across the room. Flying like one of the stupid crows.

Remedios knew there was no way he could outrun the Rhothag, but he stumbled away from the house anyway. He was surprised to make it almost to the trees without the thing rampaging down upon him. With every step he expected to glance back and see it climb through the window or come crashing out the front door, and now there was nowhere else to run. He would meet the thing here and die with dignity if nothing else.

He stopped and turned to face the Keep.

At that instant the creature leaned out the window, and the crows stirred around Remedios's feet. When the beast disappeared for a moment back inside the house, Remedios felt an instant of renewed hope, but when it returned to crawl out the window all his pretensions fled.

The beast stood with its head held at an odd angle, one claw pressed to the side of its throat. Remedios was certain that Baxter, Crank, and the dog were dead. He instinctively dropped to his knees and began to pray. But as he beseeched God to shrive his soul a weight fell on his shoulders.

And then more weight.

He was overcome by the smell of dust and earth, feathers and feces, and the feeling of scratching at his skin, and finally he was forced to the ground, his face pressed into the back of his hands, as tiny feet scurried over him, wings fluttered, and fur tickled his nose and ears. He managed to lift his head barely enough to see clear of the milling throng of ravens and foxes, just as the Rhothag turned slowly in his direction. Remedios lowered his head back onto his hands, accepting with a grateful heart that he was safe in the belly of this great multitudinous beast and rejoicing in the strength of the Lord.

God sent a raven and a dove to Noah. Unto me he sent ravens and foxes.

He lay there for what seemed hours, but could only have been minutes, listening to the soft breathing of the small beasts, feeling the warmth of their bodies shielding him from the chill of the night. These small animals, for which he would not have spared a second glance in an earlier life, now sheltered him with their bodies. He would never look at them in the same way again.

He heard the snuffling of the Rhothag first, then an airy, groaning sound with each rasping breath. Apparently his friends had wounded the beast badly. Good. Remedios could conjure no sympathy for such a one.

But would the tiny animals really be able to protect him from the thing? His hands trembled, and sweat ran down his palms. The ravens reassured him with low, cawing sounds under their breaths, and the foxes stirred gently against him; but it was shallow comfort when he knew the beast might reach down at any moment and pluck him up like a plump cherry.

Movement caught his attention, and through the stick legs of the birds he saw a crimson eye peering down at him. He could tell by the way it appeared and disappeared that the beast was not yet quite sure what it had found, and once again Remedios held his breath.

Tiny claws kneaded his back as though the little beasts were preparing to lunge. Would they really attack something the size of the Rhothag? The animals had all been so docile for days that he had come to think of them as being almost asleep. But now he wondered if their quiescence hadn't been a form of silent communion.

Suddenly wings flapped hard against his face. The birds' sharp nails skittered across his back and around his legs as a giant claw latched onto Remedios's arm. He was jerked to his feet so abruptly it felt as though his shoulder had been dislocated, and he found himself standing amidst a flurry of scampering and fluttering animals, peering into the Rhothag's eyes, feeling the cold breath wet on his face. The thing grinned in a deadly rictus, its lips stretched tightly over fangs the size and shape of steak knives, its nostrils flared, and it nodded to itself in satisfaction.

Remedios noticed a heavy flow of dark blood seeping from a wound in the Rhothag's throat, and once again he thought sadly of Baxter, Crank, and the dog. He wished that he too could find some way to strike at the hideous Rhothag. The beast was an affront to God's universe. But there was nothing that he could think of to do except to throw himself once more on the mercy of the Creator, and to call to Him in prayer.

"Dear Lord," he said, in a clear bright voice, "protect this sinner in his hour of need."

The words themselves seemed to infuriate the beast. The Rhothag lifted Remedios higher, the old priest dangling like a rabbit in a snare, still praying loudly as the Rhothag drew its other arm back, the talons pointing forward like a pitchfork. Remedios stiffened in anticipation of a killing blow.

But before the Rhothag could strike, the ground beneath it trembled, and it glanced around in surprise, stepping from foot to foot as though standing on a bed of coals. For the first time, Remedios noticed that all of the animals upon the lawn were surging toward them, and now the Rhothag was struggling backward amid the torrent, carrying Remedios with it.

Foxes scratched and nipped at its bare legs. Although the thing kicked them away, they were instantly replaced by others. Crows dropped down from the sky and flapped up from the ground, landing on its broad shoulders and its head, pecking at its eyes, ears, nose, and lips. The Rhothag swatted them away like mosquitoes, but more took their places, and blood trickled from a thousand tiny wounds. Foxes leapt to reach the thing's crotch, scrabbling their way up the remains of the clothing that hung in shreds there. The animals seemed oblivious to their own safety, scrambling over one another to reach the thing, to bite and scratch and peck. Finally, Remedios felt the iron claw release its grip, and he fell heavily, watching as yet more of the small animals swarmed like ants over a rotting piece of fruit, engulfing the struggling beast, driving it first to its knees, then to the ground. Fur and feathers and blood flew, but each animal killed by the thing was instantly replaced by another until finally the mound lay still beneath the birds and beasts.

Remedios climbed wearily to his feet, waiting for his heart to slow, wondering at what he had just witnessed. As he gasped for breath, the ravens and foxes turned to look upon him, not with the blank stares associated with dumb animals but rather the look one warrior might give another after a long and deadly battle has finally drawn to a victorious close.

He offered a prayer of thanks then, to the animals as well as to God.

It soothes away the savage thirst

Defeats the dark with one fell burst.

Magic lies beneath its arms

Like light that beams from shadow charms.

Just as day defeats the night

Angels play with fire bright

And twirl aloft on silken wings

To music only nature sings.

—"Thunderstorm" by Cooder Reese
From *Dead Reckonings*

Dylan found himself back in the vault, resting on the cold concrete floor, the light from the first gate fading slowly away. He was afraid that it might still have the power to suck them back if they ventured too close to it, but it looked as though it would be gone in a moment, and he knew that the battle was finally over.

"You're alive," said Lucy softly, cradling his head in her hands.

He tried to sit up, but his entire body felt as though it had passed through a blender.

"I was on a bridge," he whispered, glancing around the room lit by glowstones on the floor beside them. It looked like the same old subbasement. But it still made him nervous being there. He wanted to be outside. Wanted to feel sunlight on his face. If only his muscles would cooperate. "You were calling to me, but I started to fall into the pit."

"When I stabbed you it was as if I were in the center of an explosion. I was blown back away from the gate. I could feel you over there, and I knew somehow you were still alive, but the gate was closing. I thought I was going to lose you. I tried to extend my earth sense across to you, but I couldn't reach you. Then suddenly you reached out."

"It was Ronnie. It was her you felt reaching out." He tried once more to struggle upward, this time succeeding in sitting. "We have to find the others."

As they finally staggered out of the cellar and into the foyer a heavy peal of thunder rattled through the Keep, and the sound of rain falling followed close on its heels. They stood for a moment, gazing out into darkness that seemed different from the gloom that had been with them for weeks. Even as they watched, the sudden shower ceased. Lucy gave him a curious look.

"It's like God was washing the earth clean," she whispered, her focus on something in some great distance. "I can feel the ground here, the *hallowedness* of it spreading like a flood."

Remedios was in the study, ministering to Crank, Baxter, and Phoenix. Baxter and the dog appeared to have suffered the worst wounds; but the priest seemed certain that with care and perhaps some antibiotics, and most certainly prayer, they would both recover. Crank had no external injuries, no bleeding, but he still seemed dazed from the battle Remedios and Baxter described.

"I came to in time to see Phoenix leap off the back of the sofa right at that thing," said Baxter, shaking his head. "It was just about to break Crank's neck when she locked on to its throat. I thought she was going to tear its head off. Then it tossed her against the wall just like it did me, turned around, crawled through the window, and was gone. I guess I blacked out again."

"She's a good dog," said Lucy, stroking Phoenix's head as the pooch lay back, soaking up the attention and slapping the sofa with her tail. "She's a very good dog."

"Is it over?" asked Crank, resting in an armchair, holding his head in his hands.

"I believe you will find that beyond the boundaries of the Keep things are returning to normal," said Remedios. "As normal as they can be, after a battle with the forces of evil."

"So what do we do now?" Crank asked, without looking up.

Remedios regarded him sadly. "You dedicated your life to someone who betrayed you. Now you feel that there is no place for you?"

"I'm not sure there ever was a place for me."

"And yet you risked your life to save mine. Why?"

Crank shook his head. "All my life I followed a man who was nothing that I believed him to be. And I turned out to be a Judas. I let the thing into the house."

When he heard Lucy gasp he glanced up.

"I didn't do it on purpose. I had to get outside and think. It was stupid, I just left the door open."

"It would have broken in anyway," said Baxter.

"You'd have heard it break in. You'd have had some warning."

"And maybe I'd have been fighting it alone."

"It was the will of God," said Remedios. "Everything happened for a reason. And we all survived for a reason. This much should be obvious."

"For what reason?" asked Crank. But this time he looked as though he really wanted to hear the answer.

"To carry on!" said Remedios, smiling. "To salvage what we may and continue the great adventure. That is what life is, and that is what Man does. Everyone has a place in God's plan, and since there are few of us left, I must surmise that we must certainly be integral cogs."

He rested a hand on Crank's shoulder, and slowly Crank placed his own over it.

"Go with God," said Remedios quietly.

Lucy was surprised to see tears in Crank's eyes. She leaned against Dylan, and he held her tightly. Outside the sun began to break over the tall oaks, and Dylan realized that what he had taken to be continued darkness was the shadow of a million ravens taking wing.

ABOUT THE AUTHOR

Chandler McGrew lives in Bethel, Maine, and has four women in his life—Rene, Keni, Mandi, and Charli—all of whom wish it to be known that he is either their husband or father. Chandler is proud to hold the rank of Shodan in Kyokushin Karate, and is now studying Aikido. He is the author of the suspense novels *Cold Heart* and *Night Terror*. Chandler can be reached at www.chandlermcgrew.com.

During the exhumation of *The Darkening*, I noticed underlying *mind* strata that contained some fascinating artifacts relating to broken family bonds, voodoo spells, demon spirits, ESP, flash floods, Grandma's jambalaya, blood feuds, and rattlesnakes. One of the interesting things for me about the story in question was that it all came to a head not in Haiti or the bayous of Louisiana but in rural Maine. A lot of weird stuff happens up here. Some of it is fiction.

Be that as it may, I'd like to now offer you, faithful reader, the first glimpse into what my research has unearthed. *Blind Spot* is the story of a family ripped apart by a legacy not one of them living understands. But it is that same legacy that must bring them together again.

Or destroy them all.

Wow. That sounds pretty ominous, doesn't it? Sometimes I scare myself. Honestly.

Chandler McGrew

Read on for a thrilling sneak peek at

Chandler McGrew's

next thrilling novel

coming in summer 2005

from Dell Books . . . .

Sometimes its countenance is death
I've smelled decay upon its breath.
Just as night defeats the day
In shadows fierce the demons play
While aloft for those who cannot see
The dragon hums a memory.

—"Thunderstorm" by Cooder Reese,
from *Dead Reckonings*

Pierce Morin—thirteen years old and deaf and blind—lived in a world of touch and taste, and strange, wonderful odors that wafted through the darkness of his days and nights. He could sit for hours, angling his head like an old hound dog, catching this or that scent so faint on the breeze it was indecipherable, cataloging it for later, when it was sure to drift past him again, and with any luck he could get someone sighted to give it a name.

He was smaller than most thirteen-year-olds, and because of his disability, exercise consisted of either exploring the house or yard or following his mother on her errands through Arcos, Maine, on those days they went to town. Still, he was wirier than people expected. His fingers were calloused from hours of braille reading and working with the maze of electronic parts and tools he kept neatly organized in plastic bins over the wide folding table that took up the far side of his bedroom. His mother had grown as weary as he had of trying to explain to people how he could fix radios and televisions that he could neither see nor hear.

So Pierce spent his days in quiet anonymity, fiddling with transistors and transducers, with solid-state circuits that no one could fix. No one but him. Pastor Ernie had asked him a couple of times how he fixed them. But Pierce had just shaken his head. The most he could say—spelling it out into Ernie's palm since it was too complicated for American Sign Language, and Ernie wasn't that good with the signs anyway—was that he could see how the things were supposed to work.

But that morning he wasn't in his seat at the worktable. Instead, he sat on the straightbacked chair beside the open window, resting his fingers on the sill, feeling the warmth of the sun on them, smelling the grass in the backyard, the rich, loamy aroma of the creek down below, phasing out the leftover house odors of cereal, coffee, and his mother's perfume. Something indefinable had drawn him to the window. For over an hour now—according to his crystalless watch—he had sat there, feeling the hairs tingling as the faintest of breezes stirred the air, wondering what the strange sense of gloom was that kept him so still. He was like a hunter in a blind, but he had no idea what his prey was, only that it was coming and he needed to be ready.

When he finally sensed it, it was as though the shadow of a cloud had passed the sun, and yet the warmth still lingered on his hands. Twisting his head to one side as though he could hear, he tried to understand what was happening.

Something was definitely wrong.

But not wrong in the way an open door in the night was wrong. This was something bigger and far worse than that. It felt to Pierce as though a part of the world itself were broken. Some part that was dangerous and deadly. And against his will he began to shiver, clutching his arms around his shoulders, and leaning far back from the open window, wishing that he had never opened it to begin with. Whatever it was, it was coming this way, and he realized that he'd felt something like it before. Only every time he tried to tell his mother—when he rattled his cane against the bed frame in the night, and she ran to his bed—she'd never believed him.

"It's just a nightmare, honey," she signed into his palms as Pierce shook his head and signed back that it wasn't, that something bad was just outside the window.

It wasn't a nightmare, and now he knew that for sure. Because nightmares came at night, and whatever was happening in the valley, it was something bad, something broken, something too big, too powerful, too evil for him to fix.

He gathered up his courage and rose to his feet, sliding his fingers up to find the top of the window sash and slam it shut, tripping the latch and wishing that his curtains were more than just for show. He couldn't see them, but he knew they were silky and thin, and if sunlight could get through them to warm him in bed, then whatever was coming could probably look right through them if he even bothered to try untying them. What good were curtains like that anyway?

With his fingers still resting on the window frame, suddenly he knew that the indefinable something was right on the other side of the glass. He could feel it peering in, searching, studying him like some kind of specimen. Scientists did that to small animals like bugs, and Pierce had always wondered if the bugs minded. Now he knew. If the bugs were anything at all like him, they felt fear, the unreasoning terror of knowing they were in the grip of something so powerful, they had no defense against it.

But Pierce felt something else as well.

Still quivering with fear, he was drawn nearer and nearer to the window, bending until he was so close that he could feel the coolness of the glass radiating toward his nose even as the refracted sunlight still heated his skin.

There was something on the other side of the pane, inches away from his face. He knew it in the same way he knew when an electronic circuit had broken. He sensed something almost akin to thought, as though he were reading the thing's mind, only it wasn't a mind that made any kind of sense to him. He felt filled to bursting with powerful emotions that he had never experienced before, and before he realized what he was doing he lashed out with his fist, shattering the window, the vibration shooting through his arm.

He stood frozen there, the jagged edge of the glass pressed against the soft underside of his wrist, as the sense of the thing on the other side of the window slowly eked away. It was as though his abrupt release of anger had driven it out of the yard, but he sensed that wasn't the cause. The thing had left for some other reason.

He felt lightly around the broken pane with the fingers of his other hand, slowly and carefully drawing his fist back out of the shards. Testing with his fingers, he discovered that miraculously he had not cut himself.

Not even a nick.

Jake Crowley was a respected investigative reporter for the *Houston Chronicle*. But he had no childhood that he would admit to—no family, and no home other than his obsessively neat one-bedroom apartment in Spring Branch. He also had no girlfriend, no social life, and only one friend.

On top of that, it seemed to Jake like the whole world was going to Hell. Crime rates were soaring. Society was on the brink of some new deluge, one not of water but of madness.

Madness was on Jake's mind as he reached into the

glove box and pulled out a crumpled envelope, squeezing it so hard his knuckles paled. Slowly he relaxed his grip, withdrawing the letter, reading the opening lines for the fourth time that day.

"I'm sending this because I don't know if you're going to answer my calls. Uncle Albert was murdered. Won't you come home to at least pay your respects?"

He folded the letter, slipped it back into the envelope, and tossed it into the glove box, slamming it shut.

Rain splattered the windshield, and Jake peered at storm-tossed Galveston Bay as he tried to organize his thoughts. He'd driven from Houston through the downpour to meet a man who refused to show his face anywhere near the city, and Jake could understand why. If the guy gave up the information Jake needed, two of the biggest crime lords in Houston might be making license plates for years to come—after Jake got the hottest scoop of the decade. If, that was, they could be prosecuted successfully through the corrupt and politicized legal system that had taken hold in recent years.

The rain hammered his Ford Taurus like sticks on a snare drum. Distant cymbals of thunder rattled the air, and Jake could barely make out the rolling gray surf through the undulating curtain of glassy droplets. His cell phone buzzed, and he snapped it open expecting to hear Cramer, who was home sick with the flu. He'd bust Jake's chops for being stupid enough to hold a meeting like this.

"Yeah," said Jake.

"'Yeah'? You don't speak to me three times in fourteen years, and 'yeah' is what I get?"

"Jan?" Her voice conjured up an image—her face tear-traced and beautiful—and the old ache filled him again. In his mind's eye his cousin stood waving at the airport window, and his mother's voice still echoed through his thoughts.

Run away, Jake. Run away.

"Glad you remembered," said Jan.

"Look, I don't have time right now. How did you get this number?"

"Your editor gave it to me."

Jake shook his head. "Honestly, Jan, this is a really bad time for me."

The wind picked up as the storm roared in straight off the water. Marble-size raindrops threatened to burst through the windshield. Why the hell did Reever insist on meeting here in this seawall parking lot? Couldn't he have picked something more secluded, for God's sake?

"Jake, Uncle Albert made you his executor."

A muscle spasmed in Jake's belly, and his fingers tightened on the phone. Albert was another old, long-buried memory.

"Jake? You there?"

"Yeah." His voice sounded shaky. Hell, it felt shaky.

"The will needs to be probated, Jake. You have to come home."

The only thing visible now was the sheet of water cascading across the glass, and Jake found himself wondering how so much fluid could be diverted down into that little cavity concealing the windshield wipers without making its way into the engine compartment.

"Jake, you're not saying anything."

"What do you want me to say, Jan?"

"Nothing, I guess. I'm sorry I called."

"Can I call you back? I'm meeting someone, and it's kind of important."

He glanced around and noticed that the windows were just as useless as the windshield. It occurred to him that if this were more than just a rainstorm—if a tornado or waterspout were heading in his direction—he would have no way of knowing it was coming, and nowhere to run.

"Sure, Jake. I'll be waiting for your call." The click of the receiver on the other end was like a slap in the face.

Jake slipped the phone into the pocket of his sport coat. He and Jan had been raised together like brother and sister. Hearing her voice after so long . . . a swirling cauldron of emotions gurgled within him. The bile of hatred, shame, and fear churned in his throat, and he knew that if he couldn't stifle it, it would remind him of Mandi.

Getting fogged up with personal drivel at a time like this was bad news. He could hear Cramer's husky voice now, his deep black drawl heavy with Cajun weirdness.

"Watch yo ass, not de bitch on the street. Man, you better keep you ducks in a row or you're gonna end up on a slab." Cramer could just as easily slip into slick white jive with an inflection tighter than a frog's behind. He was a homicide detective, and he formed his persona to fit the situation. But the Cajun was real enough. Cramer's grandmother, his Memere, was black as Cramer. But she'd been raised in the deep bayous of Louisiana.

Reever was no street tough. He was a trigger man for the Houston mob who had become disenchanted after his brother had taken a fall for one of the higher-ups and gotten stiffed. Usually the organization was smarter than that. You either took care of your own when they did you a favor or you got rid of them. Apparently they'd made a mistake this time, and Jake planned to capitalize on it.

But where was Reever? The beach-front parking lot had been empty when Jake arrived. He'd driven slowly around the area, circling a couple of blocks of old Victorian homes, now mostly upper-class bed-and-breakfasts. But no one was sitting in any of the cars parked on the street. No one stared at him from the dripping front porches. Reever was probably pulled over on the highway now, waiting out a storm this strong. Jake could have gone ahead and carried on the conversation with Jan if he'd had the nerve.

A memory of Albert flashed across Jake's mind, heavy flannel shirt across thin shoulders, gray beard flecked with sawdust. Albert was equipment- and land-poor like most small loggers, and he had already been getting too old for the business before Jake left Maine. Albert was a lifelong bachelor who always smelled of pipe tobacco, axle grease, and pine pitch. And Jake loved him like a father. The dampness was seeping into Jake's pores even though it was still in the seventies outside. He started the car and turned on the heater. Over the thrum of the engine and the pounding of the rain, he heard another car. Jake flipped on his headlights and stomped the brake pedal several times, and another set of headlights answered, the car itself invisible through the deluge.

Reever peered at Jake between bursts of rain as he parked the sedan so close to Jake's driver-side door that Jake wondered for an instant if he was being corralled. He instinctively rested his hand on the gearshift. But there was no sign of anyone else, and as he watched, Reever got out and ran around to jump into the front seat with Jake, already soaked in the seconds it took him to do so.

"Fuckin like the fuckin flood out there!" said Reever, shaking rain off his greasy black hair.

"How come you didn't park on the other side?" said Jake.

Reever shrugged, water dripping off his wide forehead. "Couldn't see! It's like a fuckin Noah flood out there, you jerk!"

"Nice to see you too, Reever."

"Yeah. Fuckin right."

"What have you got for me?" asked Jake.

"I took a big chance coming here."

"Cut the crap. Do we deal or not?"

"How you gonna protect me?"

"Come on, Reever. You know the skit. The paper will pay for your story. If what you have is heavy enough for convictions, then I'll go to bat for you with the Houston D.A., and you'll probably go into witness protection. New name, whole new identity." Jake had no way of knowing if the D.A. would go for anything of the sort, and he was pretty sure Reever was street savvy enough to know that. They were both kidding themselves and each other, Jake because he wanted the story so badly, Reever because he wanted the cash.

"And money."

"And money."

"A lot of money."

"I don't know what you mean by a lot. I'm not Bill Gates. How much?"

Reever laughed again. "We'll talk once I go into protection."

"That'll be a little late for negotiation on your end. And way too late for me to get the story I need."

Reever shook his head, and Jake noticed something in his eyes, like an errant thought tightening the laugh lines at the corners, and then it was gone.

"That'll be plenty of time," said Reever. "I got a lot to tell. You can buy it word by fuckin word. Ain't that the way they pay magazine writers?"

"Yes," said Jake suspiciously. It wasn't like Reever not to go right for the money. Jake glanced out his driver-side window as the wind blasted a microburst of pebblelike rain against it. He hated the other car blocking his view on that side. Quickly he returned his attention to Reever.

"Nervous?" said Reever, laughing. " 'Course not. Big-city reporter like you. What you got to be afraid of?"

But there was something bothersome in the way Reever held his head, in the way his finger kept sliding back and forth on his thigh just a millimeter, as though squeezing a nonexistent trigger. Jake had had a lot of hunches over the years, and Cramer had drilled it into his head to listen to them. Cramer's gravelly voice—at least as scratchy as Reever's—echoed in Jake's head, and now Jake really wished Cramer were there. *A bad hunch don't cost you much. Maybe somebody will laugh at you. Being laughed at alive is a hell of a lot better than being laughed at dead. It's bad mojo ignoring hunches.*

There it was again. Reever almost turned toward the window. What was he waiting for? Who was he waiting for? Jake gave the car some gas, listening to the engine race, resting his hand casually on the gearshift lever again. "So talk," he said, playing the game. "Give me something to prove you're not full of shit."

"Jimmy Torrio's in with the Zinos."

Jake frowned. That was news if it was true. The

Zinos were big in Vegas and L.A. What the hell would they be doing in Houston? "You mean the Zinos are here?"

"Here, there, everywhere," said Reever, laughing. "Where ain't they?"

"The Torrios wouldn't share with the Zinos. They have no reason to."

Reever shrugged. "Pot's big enough, you don't mind sharing."

"There's no pot big enough for Jimmy Torrio to share. This sounds like a crock."

"Banks," said Reever.

"Now I know you're full of shit," said Jake, relaxing a little. Maybe that's all this was, Reever bullshitting, playing him, seeing if he knew enough to deal with. "Neither of the Torrios is stupid enough to rob banks."

"I didn't say they were going to rob them," said Reever. "They're going to buy them. Then they can do what they want with the money. The Torrios have the connections in town with crooked bankers. The Zinos have the laundered money in mutual funds to do the transactions clean."

Reever wasn't a Harvard economist, but Jake got the picture. The Torrios group was muscle. The Zinos had finesse. They were used to dealing in figures where the zeros strung out right to the horizon. The Zinos had plenty of people on their payroll who had graduated from Harvard. If the Zinos and the Torrios got together and ended up owning interests in banks in Houston, infiltrating their own people inside, who knew what kind of billion-dollar mischief they could concoct?

Behind the car, Jake heard the sound of a powerful

engine and splashing water. A dark sedan skidded sideways, almost striking the rear bumper, blocking his exit. Shadowy figures leapt from the car, and Jake glanced over just as Reever was reaching under his coat.

"You son of a bitch!" spat Jake.